THE GREAT REBELLION

The Great Rebellion

BOOK ONE OF THE
AUTOBIOGRAPHY
OF WILLIAM WATSON

LENNY BERNSTEIN

KIMBERLY CREST BOOKS • ASHEVILLE, NC

Kimberly Crest Books

THE GREAT REBELLION

Book One of The Autobiography of William Watson

Copyright © 2015 by Lenny Bernstein

Copyeditor: Nicole Ayers (www.ayersedits.com)
Cover art: Elizabeth Hunt (www.elizabethahunt.com)
Interior design: Doug Gibson (www.douggibsonwriter.com)
Author photo: John Stevens

Kimberly Crest Books, Asheville, NC
Contact us at www.kimberlycrestbooks.com

ISBN: 978-0-9861932-0-0

Printed in USA

For Danny, who helped nurture this story from the first.

THE GREAT REBELLION

TRANSCRIBER'S INTRODUCTION

In 2011, I purchased an abandoned farm in Wellington County, Tennessee. I plan to build my retirement home there. During the summer of 2012, whilst removing debris from a collapsed barn, I discovered an old chest. Inside was an untitled handwritten manuscript, which on reading, I found to be the autobiography of an eighty-year-old man named William Watson, which he wrote for his children, grandchildren, and future generations. He gave no indication of seeking a wider audience.

I have transcribed Watson's writings into modern North American English. The document was so long that I divided it into three books, each of which I gave a title. The only changes I intentionally made were to break Watson's tale into chapters, and to split his page-long paragraphs and hundred-word-long sentences into more readable lengths.

Despite his limited formal schooling, Watson is a surprisingly literate author. He relates that he read whenever he had access to books, but says little more about how he educated himself. This is one of the many questions the manuscript raises. I have no reason to believe he was trying to be deceptive. It probably never occurred to him that his descendants would be interested in his self-education.

I am an engineer. My education at school contained no more than a brief discussion of the Great Rebellion, dismissing it as a regrettable incident in a record of otherwise amicable relations between Britain and her North American dominions. At university I had too many scientific and technical courses to master to delve any deeper into colonial history. I remembered 1776, the year of the Great Rebellion, because that is when James Watt installed his first commercial steam engine. Watt's engine helped make Britain the most powerful nation in the world, a position she still retains, thanks, in no small part, to the contributions of her commonwealth. However, since finding Watson's manuscript, I have immersed myself in the history of the events he wrote about, boring my wife and friends with the facts I have uncovered.

I find Watson to be a credible witness. Obviously he could not have remembered, word-for-word, conversations that took place decades before he wrote them down. However, scholars assure me that in memoir and autobiography, it is acceptable to recreate conversations, as he appears to have done. His narrative is accurate. Nothing he says contradicts historical fact. But read his story and draw your own conclusions.

Watson's original manuscript has been deposited with Prof Derek Macaulay, a historian at Queen Victoria College in Busaco, Tennessee, for further study and evaluation.

CHAPTER 1

The Psalmist says that the days of our years are three score and ten, or four score by reason of strength. He holds out no hope for a longer life, and since I've now lived the biblical four score, I fear mine is nearing its end.

It's been an eventful life. I had the good fortune to know George Washington, a great man, even if he is reviled as a traitor. I was captured at Trenton, the battle that ended the Great Rebellion, but was lucky enough to escape and avoid the suffering that befell so many of the rebels captured there. I was a prisoner of the Spanish in Texas and lived with the Cherokee in Tennessee. And I was blessed to have the love and support of my helpmate, Anne, for twenty-eight years.

I've told these stories many times. My children know them by heart and I can see their eyes roll heavenward when I start one. My grandchildren still like to hear of my adventures, but they are no more than fairy tales to them, no better than "Jack and the Beanstalk". Perhaps the true curse of old age is that the young cannot appreciate your deeds.

I am sufficiently vain to want all of my life's story preserved, even the parts that do not redound to my credit. I hope I can be as honest as Rousseau, hiding no crime and adding no virtue. I will entrust this autobiography to David, my eldest son, with instructions that he not read it until twenty years after my death. I fervently hope that he will pass it on to his children, that they, in turn, will pass it on to their children, and that future generations will not judge my shortcomings too harshly.

Let me begin my tale not with my birth, which my parents assured me was ordinary, but with the day my adventures began. At dawn on 22nd August 1776, my family and I were awakened by the distant boom of a broadside from a Royal Navy ship landing on the shores of Kings County. It was followed a few seconds later by a broadside from a second ship. For the next hour, blasts came every minute or so. Those guns crushed any hopes we had of avoiding involvement in the Great Rebellion, but I wasn't afraid. I had no idea what war was like other than the stories of Greek and Roman warriors I'd learned in school.

"Get dressed," Father ordered my older brother, Richard, and me. "We need to hide everything. The bloody British and their Hessian mercenaries could be here anytime. They'll take everything they see without so much as a by your leave."

We'd been sleeping in the loft above the two rooms that made up our home. We dressed quickly and joined Father in the kitchen. It was still dark, but I didn't need light to find my way around. The oak table and benches in the centre of the room . . . the pewter cups, wooden bowls, and trenchers stacked on the pine cupboard in the corner . . . the three Delftware plates hanging on the walls as the room's only decoration were all where they should be. Mother's Dutch upbringing wouldn't let her rest at night, nor would she let any of us rest, until we had cleaned the kitchen and stored everything in its proper place.

"Get the muskets and come to the barn," Father told us. Both Richard and I had muskets, which we used to shoot ducks and geese in the bogs around Jamaica Bay, a few miles away. Father had two, a new one, which he used regularly, and an old one, which was prone to misfire. I'd learned how to shoot with his old musket and used it for three years until I got a new one as a *Sint Nicolaas Dag* present the previous year.

We took the guns and followed Father to the barn.

"Put the guns down, then take the plough, the harrow . . . all the farm implements . . . to the garden. Come back as soon as you're finished," he said, laying sheets of shiny grey oilcloth on the ground.

When we returned after several trips to fulfil Father's instruction, he was tying the last of three oilcloth bundles full of tools and muskets. We each took one and followed him to the garden.

"We need to dig up half the crop," he said, "so we can bury everything without making too high a mound." His spade easily entered the soft loamy soil and he began to uproot the vegetables we'd expected to eat the next winter.

"Chop everything up and mix it in the compost pile so it won't be obvious," Father told us whilst he continued digging. He was a short man, but a lifetime of farm work had given him powerful arms and legs. Rich brown earth flew in every direction as the hole in what'd been three rows of maize and squash rapidly grew larger. A robin edged closer to see whether Father's excavation had uncovered any worms.

Father'd been in a foul temper for the last two months, ever since the British Army had landed on Staten Island, five miles away. But as he worked that morning, he seemed like his former self. The worst had come to pass. The British had invaded and now he had to protect his farm and family. He didn't mutter to himself, the way he'd been doing for the past few weeks. When I started to dig up the wrong row of vegetables, he simply said, "Not that one, William," rather than launching into one of the tirades I'd recently endured. Despite his better mood, I remained wary, not knowing whether it would last.

"Cover the loose earth with straw. Make it look as if we've mulched the garden. If we're lucky, it'll fool the looters," he said, after we buried our guns and tools. When we were done, we returned to the house.

"Wrap the pewter and your mother's Delftware in this," he told us as he spread a large piece of canvas over the kitchen table. "We'll throw the bundle in the privy pit. That's the last place a looter'll look."

Mother and Charlotte, my six-year-old sister, hid our food, clothes, and bed linens as best they could in the root cellar. We couldn't hide our horse and chickens, so we locked them in the barn. Under orders from General Washington, our cows had already been driven east into Queens County. The rebels hoped the cattle would be beyond the reach of the British, even though those still loyal to King George III controlled much of the county. By midmorning the house was empty except for our furniture and some wooden kitchen utensils. Having hidden as much as we could, we had a breakfast of bread and cheese.

After our meal, Charlotte played with her doll. I sat silently in the empty kitchen wondering what to do. I couldn't do any of the chores that normally would have filled my day because our tools had been buried. The bombardment had stopped hours earlier, but there'd been no news of the British Army.

"I'm going to the shore to see what's happening," Richard announced after a few minutes. "Want to come with me, William?"

"Yes," I said. Mother frowned but didn't try to dissuade Richard. At sixteen Richard was too old to be treated like a boy. I was only thirteen and, however much I might have wished otherwise, still very much a boy.

"Be careful," she said as we left the house. "And come back quickly if there's any news."

After the British landed on Staten Island, Richard suggested that we leave the farm and go to the part of Queens County where loyalists were still in control. Father wouldn't hear of it. I think he'd have sooner abandoned Mother and us children than leave our farm to be vandalized by whoever passed. A month ago Richard repeated his suggestion. Father told Richard that he'd decide whether the family left. When Richard protested that he was old enough to have a say, Father struck him, something he'd not done in several years. Richard stormed out of the house and was gone for five days, until Mr Worthington, our pastor, convinced him to return home. Mother made Father and Richard promise not to fight, a promise they'd so far been able to keep.

The morning was pleasant, warm, but not oppressively hot like so many August days. A gentle breeze from the south carried the smell of the ocean. Richard and I walked to the shore, a mile away, past fields of ripening maize and vegetables. A crow flew overhead, cawing loudly. Empty pastures, which should have been full of cows and horses, were the only reminder of the war.

We joined the crowd gathered on the small rise above the shore watching a steady stream of barges carry the British and Hessians across The Narrows from Staten Island to New Utrecht, north of us. Everyone was joking and gossiping as if they were on the town green on market day. Richard saw some of his friends and went to join them. I saw my teacher Mr Anderson standing to the right of the crowd, talking to my friend Bert Van Wyk. I headed left in an attempt to avoid them – I didn't want one of his lectures – but he spotted me.

"Watson, come here," he called. He was a tall, thin, slope-shouldered man of twenty-five, who'd started a school in our village four years earlier. The school bore the grand name of The Graves End Academy, but it consisted of a single room with benches and tables for a dozen boys. It was Mr Anderson's kingdom, where, in addition to teaching us bits of Latin, Greek, mathematics, and natural history, he lectured us on moral philosophy and Christian virtue, and thrashed us for real or imagined infractions of his rules.

Mr Anderson was one of the few people in Graves End who'd remained loyal to King George III. The rebels had threatened him, but his only concession to them was to drop the portion of our daily prayers asking God's blessing on the King. Nothing replaced it. He couldn't bring himself to ask for God's blessing on the rebels.

"Watson, this is a historic day. You are witnessing the end of the rebellion. By this time tomorrow, Washington and all those who've been foolish enough to follow him will either be dead or prisoners." Mr Anderson looked expectantly at me as if he wanted me to agree with him.

I said nothing. I didn't understand why the rebellion had started, but news of the rebel victories in Massachusetts the previous year and in South Carolina, just two months earlier, had excited me. The broadsheets the rebels posted on the side of Mr Fletcher's tavern across the village green from our school made them seem as valiant as the Spartans at Thermopylae. I hoped the rebels would defeat the British here in Kings County, but I didn't want to argue with Mr Anderson. If I disagreed with him, I was certain he would've lectured me for at least a half hour on the virtues of the King and Parliament. Bert didn't say anything either.

"Run along, you two, but remember this day," he said after a few moments, when he realized that we weren't going to respond.

We hurried off to find the best vantage point to watch the British and Hessians disembark. Everyone else had the same idea, but

Bert and I were able to wriggle through the crowd and climb to the highest point on the rise. We could see clearly, but since the British were two miles away, the scene looked like one that I could've created if I had more than seven toy soldiers in my collection.

At noon, a British infantry regiment, supported by dragoons, artillery, and Hessian riflemen, marched south along the Shore Road towards us. As they approached, their drummers, who had been beating a loud cadence, muffled, and their fifers struck up a cheerful tune. Bert and I rushed to the roadside. Richard and his friends were already there. I could see the glint of the Hessians' brass buttons and smell the dragoons' horses. Nothing this exciting had ever before happened in Graves End.

"Look at those riflemen in green jackets. Are they Hessian or British?" Bert asked.

"They're Hessian *jaegers*," I told him. "See the way they've blackened their beards. That's what Hessian soldiers do."

"They look ferocious," Bert said, staring at the jaegers.

"Of course they do. They want to scare their enemies."

"I'll wager the rebels aren't scared. They've already beaten the British Army. It's the best in the world."

After the soldiers passed, everyone followed them as they paraded along DeBruynnes Lane, then on the King's Highway for a short distance before half of them started setting up camp. The rest continued their march and were soon out of sight. Richard and I ran home to tell our parents.

"British soldiers. Hundreds of them. They're setting up camp on Mr Stillwell's farm," I shouted as soon as I saw Mother and Father.

"*God zij met ons*," Mother responded instinctively. This Dutch prayer, let God be with us, was her usual reaction to bad news. Turning to Father, she added, "You mustn't worry. We will survive this."

The good cheer Father had shown earlier, whilst we were hiding our belongings, disappeared. He said nothing as he stared down the road towards the Stillwell farm.

For the first time that day, I was afraid. Hearing the guns of the Royal Navy and seeing British and Hessian soldiers march was like an adventure story. I, of course, would be the hero. But Mother's prayer and Father's forlorn look were not the stuff of adventure stories. A chill passed through me, even though it was a warm

August afternoon. I said nothing, but stood by Father's side for a few minutes until he went back to the garden to check yet again how well we had hidden our guns and tools.

Late that afternoon a foraging party of a dozen dragoons slowly cantered down the road to our farm. We'd been sitting outside, but when he saw the dragoons, Father pushed Mother and us children into the house. He stood in front of our door. From our kitchen window, I could see the dragoons ignore him and head for the barn. After they knocked open the barn door, one of them started putting a bridle on our horse whilst the others grabbed our chickens. Father walked up to a dragoon with sergeant's stripes on his sleeve. I couldn't hear what Father said, but it angered the sergeant, who shouted, "We'll take whatever we bloody well please, you damn' rebel," and slashed Father across the cheek with his sabre. Father clutched his face and retreated to our house. Richard rushed out to help him, but Father waved him back.

After a quick *God zij met ons*, Mother bandaged Father's face. Since our bed linens were hidden in the root cellar, she tore a strip of cloth from the hem of her petticoat.

"What did you say to the dragoon?" Mother asked as she worked.

"I told him he could have the chickens, but that we needed the horse to farm."

I cowered in the kitchen, certain that the dragoons would come into the house and murder us, but a few moments later, the sergeant shouted an order to return to camp. They took our horse and all of our chickens with them.

"We'll leave as soon as it's dark," Father told Mother after the soldiers had gone. "I'll join the rebels. You take the children and go to your father's house. Surely he'll take you in."

"We should stay here," Mother said in a firm voice. She was nearly as tall as Father and didn't have to look up at him. Mother rarely disagreed with Father when any of us children were present and I was shocked that she did this time.

"It's too dangerous for you and the children," Father replied, his voice low, an anguished look on his face.

"The British've already stolen our chickens and horse. If we leave, they'll steal everything else and burn the house and barn. There'll be nothing left when we return," Mother replied, her voice rising.

"I can't stand by and watch them steal everything." Father spat out these words, then took a breath before continuing in a calmer voice. "If I try to fight them alone, I'll be killed. But if I join the rebels, and God is on our side, we'll win."

"We need the house and barn." Mother was now shouting. "Let the British have the rest."

Father stepped back, as if he'd been struck, and was silent for a moment before responding. "And what about you? You've heard what happened to the women of Staten Island. Could I, or your sons, stand by if a British soldier tried to ravish you?"

"I'm no longer a young girl. The British will respect a married woman," Mother said, looking down at the floor. She appeared ashamed of her earlier outburst, but was still unwilling to agree with Father.

"Jacoba, you will do what I say." Father's face was grim and his voice stern.

Mother raised her head, a shocked look on her face, then said quietly, "As you wish, David." Father didn't reply.

My parents' argument frightened me. I'd never heard Mother shout at Father, or Father order her around, the way other husbands did. They sometimes disagreed, but when they did Mother would say, "We'll talk about this later." Later would be after I'd gone to bed and the next morning there would no longer be a disagreement. How would our family survive if they were fighting each other?

I'd been born in our house, the only place I'd ever lived. Now Father was saying we had to leave it. And I wasn't sure that my grandfather would take us in. He didn't approve of his only living child marrying an Englishman and limited Mother's visits to once a year on my grandmother's birthday. Each year Mother brought Richard, Charlotte, and me to wish *Oma* a happy birthday. *Grootvader* said very little during those visits and often went back to work before we left. Oma welcomed us, hugging and fussing over the three of us until we squirmed away. She always baked fancy pastries for us to eat. Grootvader scared me, but I enjoyed our visits with Oma.

Father's sudden decision to join the rebels shocked me. The Great Rebellion had started sixteen months earlier with fighting at

Lexington and Concord, near Boston. As soon as word of the upris-
ing reached New York City, local rebels took control of the city and
most of the surrounding area, including our village of Graves End.
Father had tried to avoid becoming involved but that proved impossible. In August, 1775, a year before the British Army invaded, the
rebels forced Father and the other men in Graves End to sign the
Articles of Association and promise to obey their orders.

A few weeks later, three rebels carrying torches came to our farm
and threatened to burn it if Father didn't support their cause. He
promised to support the rebellion, but did as little as he could to
fulfil that promise. Rebel foraging parties bought some of our farm's
produce. Father bargained for what he thought was a fair price and
if he couldn't get it was not forced to sell. More than once the rebels
left empty-handed.

CHAPTER 2

We remained in our house until an hour past sunset, then by the light of a quarter moon, unearthed some of the belongings we'd buried that morning. Father and Richard took their muskets.

"Leave your musket and my old one, William. I want you to carry more food."

I started to protest but quickly decided not to. Father's tone of voice made it clear that he would brook no disagreement. Mother took Charlotte's hand, and we each took a blanket, a canteen of water, some food, extra clothes, and whatever else we could easily carry.

"We'll take the King's Highway to Flatbush, then the Port Road to Brooklyn. The rebels are there. I'll stay. You'll take the ferry to New York."

We walked for two hours past fields, meadows, wood lots, and darkened farmhouses. I'd walked to Flatbush during the day, but never at night. Everything looked different. I started singing to myself, as I often did when I walked, but Father bade me be silent. Until we were a few hundred yards from the crossroads, I thought Father's plan would work and that we'd be safe. Then we saw campfires.

"Soldiers," Father whispered. "We'll have to circle around them."

We left the road and crossed a large field, but the Heights of Guana, the heavily forested cliffs that lay between Flatbush and

Brooklyn, blocked our way to the Port Road. They were difficult to climb in daylight and impossible in the dark. We had no choice but to spend the night at their bottom.

It wasn't the first time I'd spent a night in the woods. Father had taken Richard and me on hunting trips in eastern Queens County. We set up our tent, cooked supper over an open fire, and had a grand time. But this was different. No friendly campfire to sit around or tent to sleep in. I was scared. There was little wind and the stillness magnified every sound. The creak of the trees, the scratch of mice, even an owl's hoot in the distance seemed threatening. Most of all, I feared that we'd be discovered by the soldiers camped only a few hundred yards away. Charlotte whimpered despite Mother's efforts to keep her quiet. Father and Richard said nothing but kept their muskets loaded and ready.

Memory is a strange thing. I've reached an age where I sometimes cannot remember my grandchildren's names or what I had for supper last night, but even though sixty-seven years have passed, the events of the Great Rebellion remain clear in my mind. The 22nd August has become a memorial day for me. Each year as it approaches I can't help but remember my parents, our farm, and the horror of being swept up in that war. Not all of my thoughts are dark. I laugh when I remember how certain Bert Van Wyk and I were that the rebels would win. If only young boys could decide the outcomes of battles. How different the world would be.

At dawn we started through the woods. We hadn't slept much and were unsure of the way. Charlotte fell so many times that Father decided to carry her. After an hour, we came to the Port Road. As soon as we saw the road, Father put Charlotte down and whispered to us to stay put and be silent. I watched through the trees as he carefully made his way to the edge of the road. After pausing for a short while, he walked out onto the road, looked in both directions, then returned.

"We're in luck," he said. "No one's on the road. We can use it."

We walked north along the road. A few minutes later, we heard hoof beats in the distance. Father shooed us into the woods. We lay down behind some bushes that were tall enough to hide us. A rock pushed into my right leg, but I wasn't going to chance moving. Three British dragoons rode past us towards Flatbush, close enough for me to smell their horses. We were safe. They weren't looking for anyone.

Seeing those soldiers pass no more than ten yards from where we were hiding was the most frightening thing that'd yet happened. I shivered. When I turned to look at Father, I was amazed to see both Richard and him pointing their muskets towards the road. They'd planned to fight if we'd been discovered. My first thought was that a farmer and his son couldn't fight British soldiers, but then I realized: who were the rebels – nothing more than an army of farmers and workmen.

We stayed hidden. My fear disappeared, replaced by pride at how brave my father and brother were. For a second I wished I had my musket. I quickly changed my mind. The idea that I could fight the British was too outlandish to be seriously considered.

"Let's try the road again," Father said, after what seemed like a long while.

"Are you sure it's safe?" Mother asked.

"We can't walk through the woods all the way. It'll take too long."

Mother sighed, picked up her bundle, and took Charlotte's hand. We saw no one else during the hour it took us to reach the earthen walls of the rebel fortifications. They stretched north and east for as far as I could see.

That past February the rebels had ordered half the white males and all the male slaves in Kings County to work on building these fortifications. Father decided that he, not Richard, who was old enough to be considered an adult, would work on the construction. Father was allowed to come home on Saturday nights, but had to return in time to start work on Monday morning. Each Tuesday and Thursday, Mother had me carry food to him. Father was a strong man, but, perhaps because he didn't believe in what he was doing, this work seemed to sap his strength. After six weeks he was sent home and told he need not return. Shortly afterwards, rebel soldiers took over the work and all our neighbours returned home.

I'd seen the wall when Father'd worked on it, but then it was only half as high.

"I heard the rebels talking about their plans, but I didn't believe they'd do this much work," Father said, shaking his head in amazement. "When I left, there was no ditch or abatis in front of the wall, only trees. Now they've cleared everything for at least a hundred yards."

A gate, defended on three sides by shoulder-high walls, had been cut in the main wall of the rebel fortification to allow travellers on the Port Road to proceed. It looked like pictures I'd seen of the entranceways to medieval castles, except it was built of wood and earth, not iron and stone. The soldiers protecting the gate levelled their muskets at us when we came out of the woods.

"Richard, raise your hands to show the rebels we aren't going to attack," Father said, raising his own hands. The Marylanders lowered their muskets and one of them signalled us forward.

"Can I join your company?" Father asked when we reached the fort.

"What do we do, Corporal?" one of the soldiers responded.

"I don't know. Take 'im to see Captain Smith," the corporal, a skinny man who looked to be about eighteen and still had acne on his face, replied.

We followed the soldier through the gate into the rebel camp. Having spent the last night in the clean air of the forest, I wasn't prepared for the powerful stink that emanated from the camp's latrines. It smelled worse than a pigsty. Many soldiers were in sight, but they all seemed to be smoking, talking, or just relaxing. It wasn't the bustle of military activity I'd expected to see.

Captain Smith sat at a table in the shade of a large chestnut tree at the edge of the sea of tents that housed the rebel army. They weren't arranged in straight lines, but scattered hither and yon. He was a tall, brown-haired man wearing a hunting shirt and breeches. Even with several days' growth of beard on his face, he looked too young to be commanding a company. He was reading some papers and we waited patiently for him to notice us.

"Sir, this man just walked up. Says he wants to enlist in our company," the private said, saluting when Captain Smith looked up.

The captain stood, returned the salute, and ordered the private back to his post. He turned to Father and looked him up and down. "What's your name?"

"David Watson, sir," Father said, snapping to attention. My

mother, brother, sister, and I stood a little to the side. I knew that we were not to say anything.

"And where are you from?

"I have a farm in Graves End, south of here."

"Mr Watson, I've never had a man come up with his family and ask to join my company."

"I didn't want to join the rebellion, but the British Army is camped near my farm. They stole my horse and chickens, and when I complained, they gave me this," Father said, touching his bandaged cheek. "I fear for the safety of my wife and children."

"You know there's a company of Kings County militia about a mile east of here. Why don't you continue on and join them?" the Captain asked.

"None of those men are from Graves End," Father replied. "They're as much strangers as you are, so I might as well join you."

"Well said. I assume you know how to use that musket."

"That I do. I've been hunting since I was younger than my son William here," Father said, pointing to me.

"We're not militia with a six-month enlistment. Colonel Smallwood's Maryland Regiment are regulars. If you enlist, it'll be for the duration of the war." Then the captain's demeanour changed. He turned to us, a concerned look on his face. "What'll your wife and children do?"

Father cast a glance at Mother. "They'll go to her father in New York."

Captain Smith turned back to Father and studied him for a moment, as if deciding whether he was worthy of the honour of being part of his company. Then, as formally as a judge handing down a sentence, he said, "David Watson, are you willing to enlist in Colonel Smallwood's Regiment for as long as it takes to win our freedom?"

Father didn't hesitate. Captain Smith had given him what he wanted. "Yes, sir," he replied in a loud voice.

"Good. See Sergeant Roidan and sign your enlistment contract. Then see the surgeon and get that wound treated. You'll find both of them in that group of tents on the right. Dismissed, Private Watson."

Father looked at us and, in the same stern voice he'd used the night before, again told us to take the ferry and go to Grandfather's house. Then he turned his back to us and walked to the tents a few yards away. He didn't say goodbye or give us a chance to say anything further. Mother started crying. Perhaps she hadn't believed until then that Father would join the rebels.

Richard, who usually lorded over my sister and me when he was put in charge, was quiet. He picked up the food Father had been carrying and started down the road to the ferry. Mother hesitated, watching to see whether Father would turn around. When he didn't, she rubbed her hand over her face to dry her tears, then walked down the road after my brother. Charlotte and I had no choice but to follow them.

I was surprised when Charlotte took my hand. Normally she wanted to be free of any restraint. I slowed my pace to hers. Mother looked back periodically and stopped to wait whenever we got more than a few yards behind. Charlotte didn't say anything. She was whimpering, but so softly that I could barely hear her.

My thoughts were a jumble. We were on our own . . . Father was no longer there to protect us . . . we were behind the rebel lines . . . the British couldn't hurt us . . . they'd never be able to break through the rebel fortifications . . . would Grootvader take us in or turn us away? But out of all this confusion, a new thought grew: I wanted to join the rebel army and stand next to Father, firing a musket when the British attacked. Father would protest that I was too young, but would soon see how determined I was and allow me to fight with him. My fears vanished, replaced with speculation as to how I might return to Father. I couldn't just drop Charlotte's hand and leave.

Chaos reigned at the ferry wharf. We weren't the only family trying to leave Kings County that morning. Each time a ferry discharged its load of rebel soldiers headed to the fortifications, it was immediately loaded to the sinking point with people headed the other way. The ferry-masters shouted out their prices, which they'd raised to a shilling per person – a dozen times the normal fare. This did nothing to reduce the crush. People cursed, pleaded, and prayed as they tried to fight their way aboard, holding out their money for the ferry-masters to collect.

We circled around the edge of the crowd, trying to figure out how we could get onto a ferry, but there seemed no way that the four of us could push closer to the boarding point. We were about to give up when the Worthingtons, our pastor from St Luke's Church and his family, arrived in a wagon pulled by two oxen.

"Mrs Watson, you and Charlotte can come with us," Mr Worthington said when his wagon got closer. "Richard and William will have to find their own way across the river. We don't have room for them."

Mother seemed uncertain about what to do, but when Richard said, "Not to worry, Mother, William and I will be fine," she handed Charlotte up to Mr Worthington and climbed onto the wagon. Richard and I gave her most of the food and clothing we'd been carrying. Mr Worthington whipped his oxen forward and they slowly pushed their way into the crowd.

"Richard, bring William to your grandfather's house as soon as you can," Mother called from atop the wagon.

"I will, Mother. Don't worry," Richard shouted back.

We didn't wait to see them get on the ferry, but backed away from the crowd.

"It's too crowded here. Let's go to Queens County and cross the river at Kips Bay," Richard said after surveying the still growing mass of people trying to get on the ferries.

This was the opportunity I was looking for. "I want to go back to the Marylanders, where we left Father."

"Father told you to come with me, and I'm going to Kips Bay," Richard said, grabbing at my arm.

"Father said to take the ferry, but we can't do that. I'm going back to him," I replied, squirming away.

Richard had his musket and a bundle of clothes and food, which he wouldn't put down on the muddy, dung-covered ground. I stood a few yards from him. His face turned red and his body tensed as if he was going to charge. He had a violent temper, but I could outrun him, which saved me from beatings more times than I cared to remember. But if he didn't strike out immediately, his temper soon cooled. After about a minute, Richard relaxed and I was no longer in danger.

"Suit yourself," he said, looking at me with disgust, then walked away.

I was now free to return to Father and the rebel fortifications, but would I be allowed to stay? Father had ordered Mother and us children to go to Grootvader's house. Since making his decision to abandon our farm, he'd tolerated no disagreement. And even if I could convince him, would the rebels allow me to join their army? I'd seen no boys in their encampment during my short time there.

My fears were overtaken by a more immediate concern as I felt my stomach rumble. It was nearly noon and I hadn't eaten that day. I stopped, had some of the bread and cheese I'd kept, and took a drink of water from a rain barrel near a fine brick house. After eating I walked back to the rebel fortifications to learn my fate.

CHAPTER 3

Where can I find Private David Watson?" I asked the first Marylander I saw.

"Never heard of him."

"Can you tell me where I can find Sergeant Roidan?"

"Last time I saw him, he was by that big oak tree over to the left."

I walked over to the tree, but the sergeant was no longer there. It took a few more enquires to find him.

"I'm looking for my father, Private David Watson. He enlisted this morning." The sergeant was a big man with coal black hair and a large, rectangular face with broad-spaced eyes, a face like a map of Ireland.

"'E's on the fortifications, about fifty yards to the right. 'E's not on duty now. Ye can talk to 'im."

With these instructions I was finally able to find Father.

"William, what are you doing here?" were his first angry words to me. "I told you to go to your grandfather's."

"I couldn't get on the ferry," I replied. "It was too crowded." I explained that Mother and Charlotte got onto the ferry on Mr Worthington's wagon and that Richard had gone to Kips Bay.

"Go back to the ferry and go to your grandfather's house," he said. He was about to slap me when Sergeant Roidan came up.

"Let the lad stay. Cap'n Smith needs a messenger."

"This is none of your affair, Sergeant," Father said, giving him a black look.

"There's other boys in camp. 'E can make 'imself useful."

Father relented. "I guess you're old enough to fight the British," he said. "But it's your brother who should be here rather than running off to Queens County." He'd accepted my being with him, but I was wary. He still could change his mind.

"Find Cap'n Smith and tell him ye want to be 'is messenger," Sergeant Roidan told me with a wink, as if to say that he knew my offer would be accepted.

Captain Smith was sitting at the same table he'd been at in the morning. He was busy writing and I waited until he looked up.

"Sir, I want to serve as your messenger." I stood at attention, as I'd seen Father do.

"What's your name?" he asked, flexing the fingers of his right hand that must have been stiff from holding his pen.

"William Watson, sir."

"You're David Watson's son, aren't you?

"Yes, sir."

"And your father approves of your being here?"

I nodded, not sure how to answer that question. That must have been enough for the captain, who continued, "You know there'll be a battle here."

I nodded again.

"How old are you?"

"Thirteen."

"You're small to be thirteen."

I looked younger than my age. I wasn't quite five feet tall, weighed less than seven stone, and had my mother's Dutch features – blond hair that hadn't yet started turning brown, blue eyes, and pale skin.

"You can ask my father."

Captain Smith looked me up and down, then, in the same formal tone he'd used when Father enlisted, said, "William Watson, you are now a member of the Sixth Company of Colonel Smallwood's Maryland Regiment, subject to my command. Stay close to my tent and await my orders."

I saluted, marched off to his tent, and stayed there all afternoon, as he'd told me to do. But he didn't give me any messages to carry or any other orders.

Evening came and the soldiers started making supper. Most of them carried a cook pot and had joined a group of messmates. I had neither food nor a cook pot and was wondering what I would do for a meal when Father found me.

"William, it's time to eat. I've been invited to join some men from the second half-company for supper. I'm sure they'll feed you too." We walked a few dozen yards to where five Marylanders were cooking their supper over a small fire.

"This is my son, William," he said proudly, introducing me to his messmates. I felt relieved. Father had forgiven my not following his orders. I could stay with the rebels.

"He's welcome to join us," was the quick response from Private Wilkinson, the group's leader. "We're going to stew up this salt pork and maize. We've got ship's biscuits to sop up the gravy. Plenty for everyone."

As we ate, the soldiers passed around a jug of ale.

"None of that for you, William," Father said. I was only allowed to drink small beer, a weak, watery brew that barely tasted like the ale I'd once had. Most of my schoolmates' parents gave them small beer to drink because it was safer than water, but my family drank pure cold water from our farm's spring. My parents thought small beer should've been a treat for me, but I longed to drink real ale, the way men did.

The Marylanders were all farmers and worried about the crops they had left in the field when they had marched off to join the rebel army. The conversation over supper was much like I would have heard at Mr Fletcher's tavern in Graves End. I was disappointed. I'd expected expressions of bravery, or even concern about the British and Hessians, not a discussion of when best to pick maize.

The night was warm and dry. I slept on a blanket on the ground near Captain Smith's tent, and was awake before a cock's crow woke the rest of the Marylanders. Shortly after dawn we heard the sounds of artillery and musketry to the south. At morning parade Captain Smith told us that a battalion of Pennsylvanians had attacked the Hessians in Flatbush, but had been repulsed. Some of the rebels were fighting and I silently prayed that I'd soon have that chance.

I spent the first part of the morning as I had the previous afternoon, waiting to be of service. At midmorning I saw three boys with shovels digging a trench around Sergeant Roidan's tent.

"Hallo, what are you doing?" I asked.

"Are you blind?" the tallest one said. "Can't you see we're digging a ditch around this tent? Major Gist told us to make ourselves useful."

"But who are you and why are you here?"

"I'm Luke, this is Mark, and that gormless oaf is John."

Mark smiled and half saluted me, but John just stood looking uncomfortable. Perhaps he was as simple as Luke had called him.

"Everyone calls us the Three Gospels," Luke continued. "Our fathers are in the Marylanders. Who are you?"

"I'm William Watson, Captain Smith's messenger. My father enlisted yesterday."

"So you're a messenger, too," Luke said with a smirk. "We all are, but nobody gives us any messages to carry. That's why Major Gist told us to start digging ditches. Find something to dig with and come help. It's better than sitting around on your arse all day."

I took a spade that was meant for shovelling earth into the nearby latrine. Nobody would miss it for an hour or two. Luke was right. Digging ditches with the Three Gospels was better than sitting around doing nothing. Luke was teased for being tall, John for being short, and Mark for being enamoured of a certain young lady, whose name I never learned. They called me a Yankee, even though everyone knew Yankees came from New England. The work went quickly and we must have dug ditches around more than a dozen tents by noon, when Luke decided that he and the other Gospels needed to go back to their fathers and get some dinner.

I found Father and his messmates. After our meal, I saw columns of smoke rising to the south. General Washington had ordered the people of Kings County to burn their crops if the British came, but I knew the Dutch farmers wouldn't have done that unless our army was there to enforce the order. Father, to my surprise, didn't seem worried about whether our farm was burning. He was a soldier now. He'd left his old life behind.

General Washington inspected our fortifications at midafternoon. He was accompanied by an entourage of officers and by a tall black man in a Moorish turban and a long riding coat.

"Who's the mulatto?" I whispered to Private Wilkinson, who happened to be standing close by.

"That's Billy Lee, Washington's manservant. He's never more than a few feet from the general. You'd think the two of them were tied together with a rope."

"I've never seen a slave dressed so fine."

"You should see the livery that some of the house slaves in Virginia wear," he said. "I'll wager they're kitted out fancier than King George's servants."

I stood at attention next to Captain Smith as Washington slowly walked by, and was able to get a good look at him. He was a big man, over six feet tall. Even though he didn't have broad shoulders and was thick around the waist, he gave the impression of great physical strength. There was nothing unusual about his face – he had blue eyes and smallpox scars.

After the inspection Washington addressed us. I stood with a few hundred soldiers and officers. We weren't in formation, and except for the uniforms that most of the men wore, we could've been a group at a fair waiting for the horse auction to begin.

"The hour is fast approaching in which the honour and success of this army and the safety of our bleeding country will depend," Washington began, speaking to us as formally as if we were the House of Lords. He turned his head slowly, surveying the assembly. His gaze was confident and every man stood straighter, if not at attention, when Washington looked at him.

"Remember, officers and soldiers, you are free men, fighting for the blessings of liberty, and slavery will be your portion if you do not acquit yourselves as men." He continued by reminding us of the victory our army had won at Boston, but he ended with a warning: "If any man attempt to skulk, lie down, or retreat without orders, he will be instantly shot down as an example."

Washington's words made me wish I had a musket and could fight rather than just sitting around waiting to carry messages.

Outdoor church services were held the next day for those who wished to attend. Many of the Marylanders were Catholics. I went with them because I'd never seen a papist Mass before. The whole service, except for the sermon, was in Latin. Although I'd had some Latin in school, trying to follow the priest was very different from translating Caesar or Cicero. Much of what happened looked the same as what happened every Sunday at St. Luke's, but since I couldn't understand the Latin, I wasn't able to figure out what I'd heard or seen. The sermon, a call to avoid temptation and live a virtuous life, sounded very much like those Mr Worthington gave. When I asked Captain Smith why the sermon didn't refer to the rebellion or the upcoming battle, he said there was no need for that, since the Marylanders were all committed to winning our country's liberty. But they were far from home and a reminder about their moral obligations was always in order.

"William, what've you been doing?" Father said angrily when he saw me walking out of the service.

"I just wanted to see what a Catholic mass was like."

"You must never do that again," he said. "The priests are wicked. They forbid people to read the Bible and they tell them how to live their lives. We are free men fighting for the liberty of the United States. We don't want to give up that liberty to Rome."

"But Father, the service was all in Latin and I didn't understand what was being said."

"Promise me that you'll stay out of the clutches of Catholic priests."

I promised.

After the service, Captain Smith gave me my first task.

"Find Major Gist. Give him this message, and await his reply," he ordered. "You'll have to look for him. If I knew where he was, I'd talk to him rather than writing this down."

I saluted him and he seemed amused. I was trying my best to be a soldier, but none of the Marylanders treated me like one.

I found Major Gist near his tent several hundred yards away. He was talking to another officer whom I didn't know.

"What is it?" he said when he noticed that I was waiting to speak to him.

"Sir, Captain Smith ordered me to give you this message and to await your reply," I said, saluting. He took the message and read it.

"Very well, young man, you shall have my answer," he said with a smile as he sat down to write. "And I have new orders for Captain Smith's company."

When I returned, Captain Smith read Major Gist's reply, then told Sergeant Roidan to assemble the company. I stood next to Father as we learned that our new orders were to form up with the rest of the regiment at 1:00 p.m., then march south along the Shore Road to the edge of the Heights of Guana, a few miles from where my family had spent the night. The Shore Road was next to the water until it reached The Narrows, but then it turned inland towards the ferry at Brooklyn.

The three-mile march to our new position took three hours, much of which was spent waiting whilst the Marylanders slowly crossed the narrow bridge over Gowanus Creek. Our new line was more than two miles from the British in New Utrecht and looked down upon the plain they would have to cross to attack us. We had no orders to build new fortifications, so we set up camp and waited.

I was still Captain Smith's messenger, but again had no messages to carry. The Three Gospels were also in camp with as little to do as me. We spent many hours talking and I learned that life on a farm in Maryland was much the same as life on a farm in Kings County. The biggest difference seemed to be that they grew tobacco. Luke and Mark told me in great detail about picking and curing that crop. John, the simple soul, said very little.

None of us boys carried muskets. Whilst I wanted a musket and a chance to actually fight the British, not having one didn't bother me since I thought that messengers didn't carry weapons.

The battle began at ten o'clock on Monday night. The Marylanders weren't involved at the beginning, but I could hear the firing of muskets and cannon on the plain below. I was too excited to sleep that night, but some of the Marylanders dozed off as if the gunfire were a lullaby.

At four o'clock on Tuesday morning, the regiment was awakened by the sound of bugles and ordered to assemble. The moon was nearly full and the sky cloudless. I had no difficulty seeing as we took our place next to Haslet's Delaware Regiment to form a brigade under the command of Lord Stirling. I stood next to Sergeant Roidan, two paces behind Captain Smith. I was about to be in a battle and should have been afraid, but I was too curious about everything I saw and heard to be fearful.

"Sergeant Roidan, why would a British Lord be in command of our troops?" I asked.

"'E's a Scottish Lord and the Scots've been fightin' the English for almost as long as we Irish've," he answered.

Lord Stirling called us to attention, then addressed us.

"In Lon-don," he started, stretching out the word to make sure that everyone was listening.

"In Lon-don," he repeated, "General Grant, the commander of the British soldiers we're going to best, boasted that with five thousand redcoats he could march from one end of North America to the other. I say he's naething but a windbag and a blowhard. Are ye willing to show him how daft he is?"

I cheered as long and loud as any of the soldiers. Then the brigade marched off.

"Stay close to me, Watson," Captain Smith told me, as we started down the cliff and south along the Shore Road towards New Utrecht. The Marylanders had been ordered to reinforce a regiment of Pennsylvania militiamen who'd been fighting the British at the Red Lion Inn for most of the night. I knew that inn. It had the finest watermelon in Kings County. Father and I had often stopped there for a refreshing slice on our way back from the trips we made to New York City to sell our farm's produce.

Dawn was breaking as we neared the Red Lion. I could just barely see a large force of British redcoats attacking the Pennsylvanians, who'd formed a rough line across the road to block the British advance. They had taken whatever cover they could find behind trees and walls. The British soldiers were in formation in the open.

The Marylanders stopped about a hundred yards behind the Pennsylvanians and waited. The smoke of the battle soon was so heavy that I could no longer see the British, but I could hear the sounds of their muskets and cannon. It was the regiment's first battle, but none of the Marylanders seemed worried. The speeches that General Washington and Lord Stirling had given buoyed their spirits. They could hardly wait for the victory that all thought was inevitable.

Major Gist was in command. Colonel Smallwood had raised the regiment. His men felt a personal bond to him, but here they were, about to go into battle, without him.

"Tisn't right," Sergeant Roidan grumbled whilst we waited. "Colonel Smallwood should be 'ere, not sittin' in New York on the court martial of some Prussian."

"He only went because General Washington ordered him to," a private said. "They say the Prussian was caught red-handed trying to sell our secrets to the British."

"Then hang 'im and be done with it."

"The major's a good man. We can fight for him as well as we'd fight for the colonel."

About seven o'clock there was a lull in the British fire. The Pennsylvanians retreated behind us and we moved up to where they had been. We were now the front line. The British renewed their fire, but didn't charge.

"Keep firing, boys. We can hold 'em," I heard Captain Smith shout over and over again to hearten his company. I could do nothing but stay close to him, and try to keep something solid between me and the British, as he moved around our company's position.

The British and Marylander lines were too far apart for accurate musket fire, but with so much shot filling the air, it was inevitable that some of it would strike human flesh. Marylanders in front of me fell, some dead, some wounded. Pennsylvania riflemen had killed or wounded most of the British artillerymen, but those who remained kept their cannon firing, adding to the Marylander losses. Private Wilkinson fell dead a few yards to my left, the top of his head blown open by a British musket ball.

"Can't do anything for him, God rest his soul," Captain Smith said quietly as he watched blood stream from Wilkinson's head. "We're doomed if the British charge." Then he resumed shouting encouragement to his men.

I'd never seen a man shot before and was amazed at how much blood poured out of Wilkinson's wound. I should've been saddened watching him die – I'd eaten meals with him and heard him joke with Father and his other messmates – but his death didn't seem real to me. It was as if I were watching a play. Time seemed to move very slowly as the noise, the smoke, the stink, the cries of the wounded, all the horrors of battle enveloped me.

I was no stranger to musket fire, but I'd only heard one or two muskets being fired at a time. The sound of hundreds, if not thousands, of muskets firing at once was deafening. Despite it being a bright, sunny day, the smoke was blinding. Fire one musket and the smoke soon blows away. Fire a thousand and you can hardly see your hand in front of your face. I couldn't get rid of the sulphurous taste the smoke left in my mouth, no matter how much water I drank. The sound of the British cannon made my bowels quake. My nostrils were assailed by the stench, a horrific combination of burnt gunpowder, scorched flesh, and excrement. Even the bravest man's bowels will release as he dies. As for the wounded, my words can't do justice to the carnage. Every lull in the gunfire filled the air with their screams and moans. Squads of stretcher-bearers carried them to the surgeons, who were stitching up wounds and hacking off limbs as fast as they could.

I'd never realized there were so many different ways to die on a battlefield. Most of the dead weren't grotesque, but when I saw one of the Marylanders with his guts hanging out, I vomited. I could've picked up a musket from one of the dead Marylanders, but the thought of touching one of their bodies made me feel even sicker. I thought about running away, but Father was nearby and I wouldn't shame him. I didn't feel very brave at that moment and wished I'd gotten on the ferry with Mother and Charlotte.

At midmorning a lieutenant came running up to Major Gist, who was now standing close to Captain Smith.

"Lord Stirling's compliments, Major. The British have captured the Old Stone House. His Lordship requests that you withdraw your regiment and recapture it from the enemy."

"If we do that, it'll leave a hole in our line."

"The New York Militia have been ordered to assume the positions you vacate."

"Very well, Lieutenant," Major Gist said. "Captain Smith, withdraw your company and form a column ready to march. The other companies will assemble behind you."

Five minutes later we were marching back along the Shore Road to carry out our new orders.

We'd passed the Old Stone House on our way to the battle. It was built of grey fieldstone, impervious to anything but the heaviest cannon fire. By the time we got back to the house, the British had both infantrymen and cannon in place to defend it. Charging them seemed like certain death, but the Marylanders showed no hesitation as they formed a line and prepared to attack. Father was in the line, about ten yards to my right.

"Stay out of the formation, Watson," Captain Smith told me as the Marylanders started their charge. I didn't have to be told twice. The first charge was beaten back with heavy losses, but Father was safe. Incredibly, he and the other survivors formed up and charged again. This time they captured the house, but a British counterattack forced them to retreat. Again Father returned unharmed.

"Watson, go back to the fortifications. It's too dangerous here for a boy," Captain Smith told me after the second charge.

I headed back as quickly as I could. Crossing Gowanus Creek was the main obstacle. It was too deep to ford and the bridge was jammed with retreating rebels. The British attacked but were driven back by fire from a battery of twelve-pounders some Connecticuters had brought up.

Being small and without a musket, I was able to sneak into the throng, and was pushed and jostled across the span. Once across the bridge it was a short walk back to our fortifications. I saw Luke when I returned and he told me that he too had been sent back when the attack on the Old Stone House began. He didn't know where Mark and John were.

Major Gist, Sergeant Roidan, and eight other men returned to our lines at one o'clock. Father wasn't one of them.

"Your father was a very brave man," Major Gist told me. "He was killed in our third attack." I felt my body go rigid and for a moment thought I would fall.

"Are you sure it was him?" I couldn't believe that Father was dead. I heard Major Gist's words, but they seemed to be coming from far away.

"Yes, he was no more than a dozen yards from me when he fell. The bullet hit him in the chest. I'm sure he felt no pain."

"Thank you for telling me that, sir."

"William, you should return to your mother."

"I'll stay here, if I may," I said, still not accepting what I'd heard.

It couldn't be true. Father would soon reappear and all would be as it had been.

"Very well. Captain Smith was taken prisoner. You may serve as my messenger. Wait by my tent."

I know I saluted, turned about, and marched away, but I have no recollection of those acts. When I got back to Major Gist's tent, I sat on a log, hoping and praying that Father would return.

The fight at the Old Stone House was the last part of the battle. The British had won, but those of us who'd escaped were safe – at least for the moment – in our fortifications. The ten men who returned from the Old Stone House were soon supplemented by scores of others, including three of my father's messmates, who straggled in as the afternoon progressed. There was much to do as our army resumed its former position. After a while I became aware of the bustle of activity around me.

"Watson, come help set up these tents," Sergeant Roidan ordered.

Then Major Gist had a message for me to carry to Colonel Smallwood. They seemed to be trying to keep me too busy to think about Father.

But that night, I could no longer deny that Father was dead, and that I could've been killed at any time during the morning. I shook all over, as if I was having an attack of ague. Visions of the dead I'd seen came back to me. I pictured Father sprawled on his back with a huge red hole in his chest. I didn't weep. I'd been taught long before that men don't weep. Luckily, this happened after sunset, when most of the army was trying to sleep. I was still a boy, but shaking as I did would have been a sign of weakness, and I didn't want the Marylanders thinking I was unmanly.

For the next two days, I stayed close to Major Gist's tent. Father's messmates made sure that I had something to eat at meal times. After their initial expressions of condolence, they talked about the battle and what might happen next, the problems in the rebel camp, the weather, anything but Father. They'd hardly gotten to know him. They asked me if I was fit and I answered yes. Other than that, I was happy to remain silent.

Whilst I had much time to think about Father's death during those two days, my thoughts were again a jumble. I suppose I should've been thinking about Father and what kind of man he'd been, but I was worried about practical things. How would our family survive? Richard and I could work hard, but we didn't know how to run our farm. Father would sometimes return from New York saying this merchant or that had tried to cheat him. Would I know when a merchant was trying to cheat me? I was angry at myself for thinking about these things instead of mourning Father, but I couldn't put the worries out of my mind.

For many years I was proud of Father's decision to join the rebel army, but eventually I came to question his actions. Should he have listened to Mother and stayed on our farm? Those who did survived, and were able to rebuild their livelihoods when the rebellion ended. Or was he right about the risk that Mother would be ravished by a British soldier? Some women were. And even if he was correct that we needed to abandon our farm, was he right in joining the rebel army, a decision that cost him his life? I no longer think so. Most leaving Kings County that day were fleeing to what they thought would be the safety of New York City. I wish I could say that I've never made similar, misguided decisions. Only luck has allowed me to survive.

Luke and John came to Major Gist's tent the morning after the battle.

"I'm going home," Luke said. "My mother will need help with the harvest."

Luke's father also had been killed at the Old Stone House. He was ashen-faced and red-eyed, and looked as if he'd not worried about weeping. John, whose father had been taken prisoner, looked solemn. If he'd wept, he showed no signs of it. He said nothing, but it was clear that he was leaving with Luke. There'd been no word of Mark, and I could only assume that he was either dead or a prisoner. I would be the only boy left in the Marylander camp.

"You boys take care and give my condolences to your mothers," Major Gist said. "Your fathers were brave men."

"Perhaps we'll meet again under happier circumstances," Luke said as he passed me on his way out of camp.

"Yes, under happier circumstances," I replied. It sounded so formal, like something my parents would say, but I had no other words to use. I hadn't met Luke's father, nor had Luke met mine.

The British started their preparations for a siege of our position late on the afternoon of the battle. Our front line was strong, but we were vulnerable from the rear. If the Royal Navy could've got into the East River, they would've been able to bombard us at their leisure and destroy our fortifications from behind. Our army had set up cannon at The Battery at the southern end of New York City and at Red Hook on the Brooklyn side of the East River to prevent this, but the Royal Navy had shown they could sail safely past our batteries whenever they wished. Washington didn't seem to recognize this danger because he moved more men from New York to Brooklyn. In addition, stragglers from the fighting kept returning. Soon there were as many men on our fortifications as there'd been before the battle.

We had the weather on our side. A cold nor'easter blew in. It soaked me and the others sleeping outdoors, but it prevented the British from sailing into the East River. Two days after the battle, Washington realized the folly of his position and ordered a retreat from Brooklyn, which started after dark and took all night.

At first, getting our soldiers aboard the ferries to New York was as chaotic as boarding had been on the day Mother and Charlotte escaped from Kings County. Many were afraid that the British would see them leaving and attack immediately, whilst they didn't have the protection of the fortifications. They scrambled to get on a ferry as quickly as possible, ignoring orders to stay in formation and board by company. Then a fog rolled in, hiding our army from the British and calming the men. Eventually the officers restored order. At about two o'clock in the morning, I was transported the half mile across the river to New York City with the remnants of Smallwood's Regiment. We were rowed over by a regiment of Massachusetts fishermen that included black sailors, who were treated the same as the white sailors. This astonished me. Whilst some slave owners treated their favourite slaves like family members, as Washington did with Billy Lee, this was the first time I'd seen a free blackamoor being treated as an equal.

When we landed in New York, my only thought was to see my mother, sister, and brother. They needed to know that Father had been killed. I went to Major Gist.

"Sir, I request leave to visit my family to tell them of my father's death," I said as formally as I could.

Major Gist looked amused.

"William, you're not a soldier," he told me. "You're free to go as you wish."

"But Captain Smith made me a member of the regiment."

"You didn't sign an enlistment contract, and even if you did, you're too young. Samuel was just making certain that you didn't cause any trouble." He smiled at me, as if trying to soften the blow. "Please give my condolences to your mother. Your father was a brave man. May God rest his soul."

I couldn't help but notice that his words were almost exactly the same as he'd used two days earlier to Luke and John. He had as much difficulty expressing the pain that death caused as I had.

CHAPTER 4

I waited until an hour after dawn. The fog that had sheltered our army as it crossed the river had begun to dissipate as I walked the short distance to my grandfather's ironmongery shop and home in Queen Street. It was an unpainted building made of rough-cut planks. The shop, which took up most of the ground floor, was already open, and by the light of a single candle, Grootvader was selling nails to a workman.

"You need a bath," was his gruff greeting.

It was only then that I realized that I was covered with the mud and filth of a week's worth of living in the fortifications and sleeping on the ground.

"Where's my mother?"

"Upstairs in the kitchen."

The kitchen was the largest room in my grandparents' home, and where we had spent most of our time during our annual visits. There were also three bedrooms. A kettle hung over the small fire in the fireplace, heating water for Grootvader's tea. The fog was now gone and sunlight streamed through the windows.

Mother and Oma were at the counter along the sidewall of the kitchen preparing breakfast. Despite my filth, Mother hugged and kissed me. I squirmed out of her embrace as soon as I could. Then it was Oma's turn, and again I had to squirm to get free.

"Where have you been?" Mother asked. "We've been so worried about you."

"I went back to Father and joined the rebels," I said, looking down at my feet.

"Is your father safe?" she asked, staring at me.

"No, Mother," I answered, still not able to look at her face. "Father was killed three days ago in a battle at the Old Stone House."

She gasped, then asked, "Did you see him fall?"

"No."

"Then he may still be alive."

"Major Gist saw him killed. He was very sure that it was Father. He said that Father was a brave man, and to offer you his condolences."

Mother sat down on a chair beside the kitchen table, tears slowly running down her face, which was even paler than usual. Oma came over and stood silently by Mother's side, her hand on Mother's shoulder. Others would have screamed and wailed, but my family remained stoic.

"Where's Charlotte?" I asked after what seemed like a very long time.

"Asleep in the bedroom," Mother answered in a soft voice.

"And Richard?"

"He sent word that he's with the Queens County Militia," she said in the same soft voice, then after few moments, continued much more strongly. "They're loyalists. The British won't attack them, but the rebels might. He should be here. He's too young to be a soldier."

"How could Richard join the loyalists? He knew that father had joined the rebels. He is my enemy from this day forward."

Mother sighed as if to say she couldn't do anything about Richard's choice, but said nothing more. I should've been comforting her instead of venting my rage at Richard. After a few moments, she headed to her bedroom. I knew from our earlier visits it was the room she had used as a girl.

Oma handed me a basin and a lump of soap. "Go wash at the rain barrel," she told me, then turned back to the counter to continue preparing breakfast.

I spent a long time washing. I knew Mother wanted to be alone. When I returned to the kitchen Mother was sitting at the table with my sister and grandfather. Charlotte was weeping quietly. I couldn't see Grootvader's face. He was looking down with his hand shading his eyes, as if he were deep in thought. After I sat down, Oma put a plate of bread and cheese on the table, then sat down herself. The sound of the plate being placed on the table roused Grootvader. He looked up, his face solemn, and in Dutch asked God's blessing on the food we were about to eat.

"Here, zegene deze spijze. Amen."

"And Lord, bless the soul of David Watson," he added in English. "He was a good man who cared for my daughter and their children. Amen."

We ate in silence. When we were done, Mother returned to the bedroom.

"William, come to the shop," Grootvader told me. "There's work to do."

First, he had me dust the ironmongery on his shelves, then he put me to work weeding the small patch of vegetables behind the house.

There had been death in my family before. My brother John had died of measles three years earlier and my sister Sarah of whooping cough two years before that, but this was different. My family had lost everything except the clothes on our backs and the few things Mother carried when she crossed from Kings County. Father was dead and we didn't know whether we would see Richard again. Even if Mother and I could return to our farm in Graves End, we wouldn't be able to keep it running without help.

We had dinner and supper without conversation. It was not a time for chatter about the weather or gossip about the neighbours. Each of us, probably even Charlotte, understood the dire straits our family was in, but none of us had a way out. Silence seemed the safest alternative.

"Jacoba, you and the children will stay here until the fighting is over, then we'll decide what's best," Grootvader announced the next morning.

"Thank you, *Vader*," Mother replied, but said nothing more.

Mother took ill three days later. Oma quickly recognized that she had smallpox and kept Charlotte and me away from her. Oma had survived the pox as a young woman, which made her immune to it.

The rebel army had brought the pox from Massachusetts to New York when it arrived after the siege of Boston. The army had been vigilant and quarantined anyone suspected of being infected, but still a few soldiers caught the disease. Those few were sufficient to spread it through the city. Mother had probably been infected on the ferry from Kings County.

Thanks to Dr Jenner's vaccine, smallpox is now so rare in British North America that my grandchildren have no knowledge of it. When I tell them about their great-grandmother's death, I have to explain how dreaded smallpox was ... how it started with aches and fever, and that in a day or two sores appeared, first in the mouth, throat, and nose, then over the entire body. Those painful sores soon developed into pustules that cracked, ran, and exuded a horrific odour. Many died during this stage, either quickly, if the sores in the mouth or nose haemorrhaged, or more slowly as their bodies seemed to rot away. If the victim survived for two weeks, the pustules scabbed over and gradually began to heal. The disease was still very painful, but recovery was likely. Those who recovered from the pox were marked for life. If they were lucky it was only with pockmarks, like Washington and my grandmother had. The unlucky lost eyes or were crippled.

The only protection against the disease was variolation. A doctor would take some pus from a pox victim and place it in a small cut on your arm to purposely give you smallpox. If you survived, you were immune for the rest of your life, but so many died from variolation that it was outlawed in the Province of New York and in many other places. None of my family had undergone the procedure, and now that Mother was ill, it was too late.

Grootvader didn't call a doctor for Mother. The camphor, ipecac, tartar emetic, and other medicines they could prescribe were useless against the pox. They didn't even relieve the pain. The next three days were worse for me than being in battle. I knew Mother was fighting for her life, but the only thing I could do was bring water from the rain barrel for Oma to wash Mother, who must have been suffering from the fever that accompanies the pox. The disease is not as painful at this stage as it is later, and Mother did not cry out. I could only imagine her suffering as I watched Oma become more red-eyed and tired.

On the fourth day, Oma emerged from Mother's bedroom carrying a bloody towel. Grootvader had just come up from the shop and received the news at the same time that Charlotte and I did. Mother was dead.

I did not weep when I learned that Father had died, but the news of Mother's death sent tears streaming down my face. Charlotte cried uncontrollably. Grootvader turned away, and he too may have been weeping for the last of his children. Oma didn't try to comfort any of us. She hadn't washed since handling Mother and her touch could have infected us. We stood there in the kitchen, like four separate statues, unable to console each other in any way.

We buried Mother the next day in the small, grass-covered cemetery behind the Dutch Reformed Church, a block from my grandparents' house. Moss-covered brick walls shielded the graves from the noise and bustle of the street. Mother's pinewood coffin, whose only decoration was a cross on its cover, was closed, so I did not see her in death. My grandparents' pastor read the funeral service in Dutch so quickly and in such a low voice that I couldn't understand what he was saying. I followed Grootvader's lead and said "Amen" several times. Charlotte held my hand and wept through the whole service. When the pastor finished, two gravediggers quickly covered Mother's coffin. For fear of contagion, Grootvader had burned her clothes and bedding earlier that morning.

After the funeral we walked slowly back to my grandparents' home. Charlotte had stopped weeping but still clung to my hand. I realized that she must have felt even more lost than I did, but I didn't know what to say to her. The only thing I could do was smile when she looked up at me, her face covered with tear streaks through the dust of the graveyard.

Charlotte was no longer a baby, but being the youngest in the family and the only surviving girl, she'd gotten special attention from my parents. She would curl up in Father's lap each night after supper. He would tell her a story before sending her to bed. My mother didn't give her kitchen chores, even though I regularly complained that she could do some of the work I was made to do. All of that would now change. I didn't think she would hear bedtime stories from Grootvader or that Oma would spare her from kitchen chores.

When we got to the kitchen, Oma warmed some milk and gave us each a slice of the apple pie that a neighbour had brought the day before. Charlotte, who hadn't eaten since Mother's death, ate her slice greedily and asked for more. I ate a bit, but it seemed to stick in my throat. I left most of my pie on my plate. Oma looked at me sadly. I couldn't meet her eyes and turned away.

Although Mother had a proper funeral and burial, her death seemed unreal to me. Five days earlier she had been cooking, cleaning, and doing all the other things I'd seen her do for as long as I could remember. Then she disappeared into a bedroom, and I didn't see her again, either alive or dead. She wasn't in the kitchen where I expected her to be, but it seemed as if she'd just gone to a shop or to visit one of the friends she still had in the city. She'd be back before supper and everything would be normal.

Grootvader didn't ask me to do any work the day after Mother's funeral. I spent most of it walking around the city, trying to cipher out what I should do. Only a fraction of the city's residents were still living there. Loyalists had left when the rebels took over the previous year, and many who supported the rebels fled when the British fleet arrived off Staten Island. About half the rebel army's regiments were now bivouacked in houses abandoned by their owners.

At midafternoon I found the Marylanders in some buildings near Trinity Church and spent a few minutes talking to Sergeant Roidan. I didn't tell him that Mother had died, not wanting him to express his sympathy or treat me differently. My deception worked and we bantered about how much better my mother's cooking was than army rations.

I hadn't thought about re-joining the rebel army until I found the Marylanders, but as I walked back to my grandparents' home, I realized that was what I wanted to do. I couldn't be a real soldier, but they seemed willing to let me help and carry an occasional message. I didn't think about what it would mean to Charlotte to be left alone with our grandparents. I didn't think about anything other than not wanting to spend any more time working in Grootvader's ironmongery shop.

CHAPTER 5

The next morning I woke up before anyone else, wrote a note explaining that I was joining the rebel army, took my blanket, clothes, some bread and cheese, and left the house. I walked to the Marylander bivouac in the growing light and had no difficulty finding Major Gist.

"Sir, may I have my old position back as your messenger?" I asked.

"Does your mother know what you are doing?"

"She died three days ago," I said, looking down at my feet. I didn't mention smallpox, knowing the army's concern about the disease. I didn't think I could've lied convincingly if he'd asked me how she died. I was lucky. He didn't ask.

"In that case, we'll have to be your family," he said.

I saluted and thanked him, then went to find the room he used as his office. I suppose Grootvader could have found me had he wished to, but no one came looking for me.

The morning after I re-joined the rebels, I heard Major Gist talking to Colonel Smallwood behind a door that was slightly ajar. Curiosity got the better of me of me, so I stopped and listened.

"Do you think the British are serious about this offer?" Major Gist asked.

"I think they are," Colonel Smallwood replied. "They paroled

General Sullivan and Lord Stirling to carry it. They were the highest ranking officers captured in Brooklyn."

"But they can't believe we'd accept their terms. Lay down our arms, revoke the Declaration of Independence, and swear allegiance to the king. Not a word about addressing our grievances. Just surrender."

"They do offer amnesty to all who accept. We wouldn't be prisoners."

"Sir, you're not suggesting we capitulate?" Major Gist said. I think he was amazed to hear Colonel Smallwood find anything good to say about the British offer.

"No, Mordechai, you mistake my intent. I was merely pointing out that what the British are offering is something better than complete surrender."

I heard a chair scrape and quickly left, fearing that either the colonel or the major would leave the room and discover me. The news that the British had offered peace terms was a shock. I thought we were in a battle to the death, with no quarter asked or given, the way it was in adventure stories.

A few days later, representatives of the Continental Congress met with the British on Staten Island, but rejected the peace offer I'd heard the colonel and major discussing. Whilst these negotiations were going on, the British established positions across from Manhattan Island, along the Kings and Queens Counties' side of the East River. This forced Washington to spread our army along the full length of the river to protect against the expected attack. Our position was dangerously exposed and our army was fading away. During the first week of September, before I returned, the enlistments of most of the Connecticut militia expired and they went home, costing Washington more men than he'd lost in the Battle of Brooklyn.

Washington soon recognized his problems. On 12th September, he ordered most of our army to withdraw from New York City. The Marylanders and several other regiments stayed as a rear guard. Half the army took positions along the East River, defending against the expected British attack. The rest set up camp at Harlem Heights, the northern tip of Manhattan Island, manned Fort Washington on the Manhattan side of the Hudson River, or Fort Lee opposite it on the

New Jersey side. These forts were supposed to prevent the British from advancing up the Hudson River.

Even a boy like me knew that keeping a route open across the Hudson was of the utmost importance for the rebels. If the British gained control of the river, they would split the colonies in two, making land communication between New England and the South impossible. Communication by sea would be slow and dangerous, since the Royal Navy was blockading our coast and capturing or sinking as many of our vessels as they could.

The British attacked late on the morning of 15th September. From New York we could hear the Royal Navy bombarding the rebel positions north of us along the East River, a sure sign that the British Army would soon be landing.

"We need to march north," Private Tims groused as the bombardment continued. "Once the British land, they'll be able to march across the island and trap us like rabbits in a snare."

"They'll be none of that," Sergeant Roidan said, loud enough for all of the Marylanders to hear him. "Our orders are to hold this position, and that's what we're going to do."

This quieted Tims for a few minutes. "Roidan, you can stay, but I don't want to end up rotting away on a British prison ship. I'm leaving. Who'll come with me?" Several of the Marylanders started collecting their kits and making ready to leave.

"You leave and you're a deserter. That gives me the right to shoot you down," Sergeant Roidan said, levelling his musket at Tims.

Tims and Roidan stared at each other, waiting for one to flinch, but before anything untoward could happen, a messenger ran up with orders to form up by company and be ready to march in ten minutes. We were to defend a position south of McGowan's Pass, on the Post Road that ran along the east side of Manhattan.

I'd been holding my breath, watching this evil scene unfold, but now I could relax. Tims and the others had gotten what they wanted. The British wouldn't trap us. Sergeant Roidan relaxed too. I've no doubt that he would have shot Tims, but I couldn't guess what would've happened if he had.

"What about our supplies?" Sergeant Roidan asked the messenger. "Ten minutes don't leave us time to load 'em on wagons."

"They'll have to be left to the British."

We were all eager to be on our way, and were on the march in less than the ten minutes we'd been allotted. Our new position was six miles away, about three miles north of the British landing. As we marched, we met groups of militia deserting the battlefield. Most weren't willing to stop long enough to tell us what'd happened. The few who did stop said that thousands of British and Hessians were boarding barges to cross the East River. Once they were ashore, they'd sweep everything before them.

A few minutes later, Washington appeared on horseback, Billy Lee, his faithful servant, riding by his side, and a handful of officers riding behind them.

"Stop, damn you. Stand and fight," he shouted at a militia captain who was running away as fast as his men. He struck at the retreating soldiers with his riding crop. He didn't hit any of them, nor did he stop their flight. The militiamen streamed around him like a river flowing around a rock. Washington was no longer the courtly gentleman I'd seen in Brooklyn, but when we marched by in good order, he returned our salute.

We reached our new position shortly before two in the afternoon, hid behind rocks on both sides of the road, and waited. Several hours later a British column marched towards us. The Marylanders fired a few volleys and the British retreated. After their experience in Massachusetts, the British were very reluctant to attack rebels they couldn't see. It was the regiment's only victory. I'd like to be able to claim that I played a role in it, but truth be told, I still didn't have a musket and stayed in the rocks, crouched as low as I could, during the few minutes of the fight.

The Marylanders defence of McGowan's Pass allowed the last of the rear guard to escape from New York City. Once they passed, we marched to the rebel encampment at Harlem Heights. Private Tims and Sergeant Roidan shook hands and agreed to forget the morning's events. I never heard them mentioned again, and this is the first time that I've told the story.

The Battle of Brooklyn and the retreat from New York City were the turning points in the Great Rebellion. Before them the rebels prevailed; after them the British prevailed. Many myths have grown up about the events of August and September 1776. One of the most persistent is that the British Army was delayed in its conquest of the City because General Howe stopped to take tea with Mrs Murray, an ardent rebel, at her farm just behind the landing area.

Howe did stop at the Murray farm. He mentions the event in his memoirs and others present have written that it was a pleasant interlude in a day of battle. And Mrs Murray may have thought she was slowing the progress of the British Army, allowing more of the rebels to escape from New York City. If she did, she unfortunately deluded herself.

Howe couldn't have known whether the rebels would stand and fight, as they had done in Massachusetts and Brooklyn, or flee, as was the case. He could have issued orders for the first wave of his soldiers to attack the rebels as soon as they landed, but this would have put them at risk of attacking a superior force. Instead he was cautious, and waited until he had all of his forces in place before moving against the rebels. His wariness allowed him to spend two hours taking tea with Mrs Murray, who all report was a perfect hostess, despite her political feelings. It also explains why the Marylanders had to wait so long at McGowan's Pass for the British to arrive.

We expected the British to march north from New York City the next day and continue their attack, but they didn't. A few days later they had to contend with a fire that consumed half the city.

"I hope the whole British Army is roasting in that fire," Sergeant Roidan said as he watched a huge pillar of smoke rise to the south of us. "And I hope it's just a wee taste of what they'll feel when they burn in hell."

I couldn't share in his pleasure at seeing the fire. I was worried about my sister and grandparents. My brother had become my enemy by joining the loyalist militia in Queens County. I wasn't going to waste any worry on him.

The next day a steady stream of smoke-stained victims of the fire passed through our camp headed north. Some of them pushed small carts or carried baskets with their belongings, but many of them had nothing.

"Did the fire burn the whole city?" I asked a man who had begged a sip of water from my canteen.

"Just the western half."

"Did Queen Street burn?"

"No, it was spared."

He thanked me for the water and continued his trek north. My fears had proven unnecessary. My grandparents' home was safe.

A few days after the fire, the British hanged Nathan Hale for burning the city. I didn't believe he was guilty. Our army burned houses and crops as it retreated to keep them from the British. Had the rebel commanders wished to destroy New York, they would've done so as we retreated, and they would've burned the whole city, not just half of it. Washington's spies reported that Hale had died bravely, and that his last words were, "I regret that I have but one life to lose for my country." This story was spread through the rebel army as an example of courage.

The Harlem Heights camp was a shambles. Many of our soldiers still slept on the ground, since there was neither wood for flooring nor straw for pallets. This had been acceptable in the warmth of summer, but now it was getting colder and men were falling ill with camp fever, which, if it didn't kill them, left them too weak to carry out their duties. There was still little discipline about building latrines or disposing of waste. Much of the camp had the look and smell of a pigpen. Food, which had been plentiful earlier in the campaign, was running short. I was never hungry, but often had less than full rations.

The nearby farms had plenty of food, but as our cause faltered, farmers were less willing to sell it for the paper dollars that our quartermasters offered in payment. Our officers couldn't use the normal approach of commandeering food; that would have alienated the farmers they claimed to be fighting for. Whilst the farmers wouldn't sell food to our army, they were happy to sell their produce to individual soldiers, provide payment was in coin or barter. Each morning farmers, traders, and less than virtuous women set up shop on the slopes beneath the camp.

"Chestnuts, tu'pence a pint," a farmer called out as I wandered through the marketplace one morning.

"Here, lad, I've got a pair of trousers that will fit like they were tailor-made for you," a merchant said in a confident voice.

"You're a fine-looking boy. For two shillings I'll make a man of you," one of the slatterns called out. She was bony and had a pinched face and stringy hair, but her offer raised unexpected surges of lust in me. I had no money, not even rebel paper dollars, and could only gawk and think about what I could do to raise two shillings.

"What's wrong? A brave lad like you can't be afraid of little ol' me. Dig into your pocket, boy."

"I've no money," was all I could mumble.

"Then get out of here and come back when you do," she shrieked.

My face turned red and I beat a hasty retreat. When I got back to camp, Sergeant Roidan pulled me aside.

"I saw ye lookin' at the hoors this morning," he said. "Didn't yeer father teach ye to stay away from them? Ye'll end up with syphilis or worse. A few moments' pleasure ain't worth it."

"We never talked about it."

"I guess ye were too young, but now that ye're in the army ye'll have to grow up fast. Ye do know about syphilis, don't ye?"

"No."

"Jesus, Joseph, and Mary! I guess I'll have to do yeer father's job, God rest his soul. Syphilis is a pox, except ye can only get it by laying with hoors. At first, the sores only grow on yeer private parts, but once ye have it, the disease stays with ye for the rest of yeer life. Even years after ye think ye're cured, it'll come back, and then ye'll have sores all over yeer body. If it doesn't kill ye, it'll rot yeer brains and make ye daft."

"Don't worry. I don't have any money."

"Aye, but some day ye will. Remember what I'm telling ye. Stay away from hoors. Find yeerself a good woman and marry her."

In late September a Hessian soldier approached our piquet line and surrendered. He was the first prisoner the Marylanders had captured, and the sentries proudly brought him to Major Gist, who tried to question him. It was soon clear that the fellow couldn't speak English. Neither the major nor any of his staff spoke German.

I was in my usual position, outside the major's tent. Listening to the prisoner, I found that I understood what he was saying – the

Dutch I'd learned along with English as I was growing up being a version of German. I told Major Gist this and was clapped into service as a translator.

He then started the questioning over again. "What is your name?"

"Jurgen Reuter," the Hessian answered, his shoulders slumping.

"What is your company?"

"I am in the Third Company of the Knyphausen Regiment."

"Why have you deserted?"

"Army life is hell." The words came tumbling out of him. "I was forced to become a soldier a year ago. Since then I have been transported across an ocean, thousands of miles from my home. I've been flogged for no reason. My sergeant hates me and gives me punishment details for the least error. I've deserted. If I return, they'll beat me to death. I can never go home. I have cousins in Pennsylvania. Help me find them. They'll hide me until this war is over. I can't go back to the army." Reuter looked close to tears by the time he'd finished.

Major Gist didn't respond to Reuter's plea. "Are the British preparing to attack us?" he continued.

"I don't know. Nothing unusual is happening in camp. The old soldiers say that we will only learn about an attack a few hours before it happens. The officers don't want to give us a chance to run away."

Major Gist asked a few more questions, but Private Reuter was exactly what he claimed to be, a scared young soldier who couldn't tolerate army life. Somehow he had screwed up the courage to desert. I knew Reuter was telling the truth and felt sorry for him. A few nights earlier, a Pennsylvania militiaman told all who'd listen about the cruel punishments he'd witnessed during his service in the Hessian Army. Being beaten lifeless with a cudgel, or forced to run the gauntlet and being pummelled to death by your company, were the normal punishments for desertion. Hanging was considered too easy a death for such a crime.

The rebel army used the lash, though the Marylanders were proud to say that none in their regiment had been flogged. And the rebels executed deserters by hanging or the firing squad, but I couldn't imagine them beating a deserter to death.

I had a few moments to talk to Reuter before Major Gist sent him to the gaol the rebels had established for enemy prisoners.

"Jurgen, Pennsylvania is a big place," I told him. "You need to know more about where your cousins live before you go looking for them."

This news greatly discouraged him, and he again looked close to tears. "Pennsylvania is not a town or a city?"

"No, it's a colony with many towns and cities. But there are many Germans in Pennsylvania, and even if they're not your relatives, I'm sure they'll help you."

This news cheered him up a little before he was led away.

"William, you've done a great service today," Major Gist said after Reuter was gone.

"I'm proud to have been able to help," I replied. I felt heat in my face and may have been blushing.

Major Gist began looking at me in a different light and soon had me working as his clerk, copying orders and keeping records of the number of soldiers available for duty, sick, or on leave. There was also a column for number of deserters, but it was a string of noughts.

The British waited three weeks before renewing their attack. General Howe didn't attempt a direct assault on the rebel army in northern Manhattan, but attacked at Throgs Neck in Westchester County, about five miles to the east, in an attempt to encircle us. A small force of Pennsylvania riflemen drove off the British. Our army claimed a great victory, even though the British had lost only a few men. To avoid being surrounded, Washington moved most of his army, including the Marylanders, north to White Plains, where the rebels had stockpiled supplies. At least we were on full rations again.

A week later, a large force of British and Hessians again landed in Westchester County, and soon were in position to attack us at White Plains. What was left of the Marylander Regiment, after its losses at the Old Stone House and to camp fever, was arrayed on top of Chatterton Hill with several regiments of militia from New York. I stayed close to Major Gist, but with so few soldiers, he had no need for a messenger.

The British and Hessians attacked, but with the help of Captain Alexander Hamilton's New York Battery, we drove off their first assault. The Marylanders suffered a few dead, but I wasn't as sickened by the sight of them as I'd been in Brooklyn. I started to take a musket, powder horn, and cartridge box from one of the dead, but Major

Gist shouted at me to leave them be. I didn't have the temerity to protest.

The British then subjected us to an artillery barrage. Many of the militiamen panicked and ran, but the Marylanders stood fast. Next, a regiment of Hessian Grenadiers charged up the hill. By this time the smoke was so heavy that our riflemen couldn't see their targets. The Grenadiers succeeded in reaching the crest. The remaining militiamen fled in panic, but the Marylanders made an orderly retreat. Both sides kept up their artillery fire, but the battle was over. In miserable rain and cold, we retreated to North Castle on the Hudson River.

CHAPTER 6

Two days after the retreat from White Plains, Major Gist told me to accompany Colonel Smallwood to a conference with General Washington. I was to stand by in case the colonel needed to send a message. Pleased at having something important to do, I cleaned my clothes as best I could and tried to look soldierly. I didn't have to worry about shaving, though my hair was a tangle, not having been cut in over two months.

Washington's headquarters was in a large stone farmhouse that had been commandeered from a loyalist. The house itself was intact, but everything around it had been ravaged. The fields were seas of mud. Only a few fence posts remained, the others having been used for campfires. No animals were in sight. The farm's horses were now hauling supplies for our army, and its cows and chickens had disappeared into cook pots.

We passed through a piquet line about two hundred yards from the house. As we got closer, we could see two sentries standing at the doorway. Much of our army was ill-clad and undisciplined, but the guards around Washington were in full uniform and models of military precision. They were from Hazlet's Delaware Regiment.

When I'd first seen the DelaExperemen in Brooklyn, their uniforms were splendid – blue coats faced and lined in red, white waistcoats, buckskin breeches, white woollen stockings, and black gaiters. They wore high-peaked leather caps with the slogan "Liberty and Independence, Delaware Regiment," and the Delaware Crest, a ship and a sheaf of wheat, embossed on a gilt badge. Their officers had red feathers stuck in their hats and gilt buttons on their uniforms. It was as if the word *macaroni* had been invented for them. Months of fighting and retreat had left the Delawaremen's uniforms frayed and shabby looking, but nothing had diminished their spirit.

Colonel Smallwood and several other officers went inside. I waited nearby and saw Washington approach.

"And who are you, my young soldier?" he asked with a tight smile. It was well-known in our army that Washington had bad teeth, which he tried to keep hidden.

"William Watson, sir," I told him as I saluted.

"Do you have a weapon, lad?"

"No sir, I don't."

"Then what is it that you do in my army?"

"I'm a clerk for Major Gist, but today I'm Colonel Smallwood's messenger."

I should've stayed silent after that, but for some reason, the words came pouring out.

"The British captured our farm at Graves End. After that my father joined the Marylanders, and even though he wanted me to go my grandfather's, I stayed with him. He was killed at the Old Stone House."

Washington had been bantering with me, but when I told him that my father had been killed in battle, he turned serious.

"William, be a good soldier, and follow Colonel Smallwood's orders," he told me before entering the house.

When Colonel Smallwood emerged, he said, "His Excellency, General Washington, needs more orderlies who understand German. Report to Colonel Samuel Webb. He's an aide-de-camp to General Washington. You'll be on his staff."

I was surprised by this turn of events, but I'd been given an order and wasn't about to question it.

"Please thank Major Gist for his kindness to me." I saluted and went into the house. I found Colonel Webb working at a desk in a small attic room and introduced myself.

"Welcome to His Excellency's military family," he said, looking me up and down. "You're not in uniform."

"I don't have one."

"In that case, we'd better see what we can do about getting you one."

"Sir, I'd like a musket and a chance to fight the British," I said.

"William, there are many men in our army who can fire a musket, but only a few who can speak both German and English. You'll help our cause more that way than by firing a musket."

"Yes, sir." I was disappointed but could say nothing more.

Colonel Webb found me a soldier's jacket and hat, but none of the pants he found were small enough to fit me. Being his orderly kept me busier than working for Major Gist had. He soon discovered that I could write in a passable hand and had me copying orders and keeping records of rations and other supplies. I used my Dutch occasionally to convey messages to the German-speaking Pennsylvanians who were in Washington's command. It wasn't what I'd expected when I left my grandparents, but I was learning that little in life turns out the way you expect.

Generals do not share their thoughts with orderlies, but rumours and what little bit of real information there was travelled fast in the rebel army. We orderlies – there were six of us – were well informed because we either copied or carried orders and messages from Washington to his generals. I was the youngest and it seemed that the older orderlies took special pleasure at showing me how much they knew. Even though I often heard the same news several times, I quickly learned that if I received each bit of information as if I'd never before heard it, my fellow orderlies would tell me all they knew.

My main source of information was Stephen Ward, an orderly for Lt Colonel Richard Cary, another of Washington's aides-de-camp. Stephen was twenty-two, tall, lean, and comported himself as if he ruled the world.

"We truly must be losing the war if the army has to recruit small boys," Stephen said to me on the day I joined the staff, as soon as all the officers were out of earshot. "What's your name, boy?"

"William Watson."

"Well, Bill, how long have you been in the army?"

"My name is William."

"Tetchy are we, Bill? I'm the senior man here. I was at Lexington when we first attacked the British. When there're no officers around, you'll take orders from me. Life'll be much more pleasant for you that way."

I said nothing and he walked away. I was wary for the next few days, but Stephen had little opportunity to harass me. There was usually at least one officer nearby and we all had much work to do. After a week he relented and started calling me William.

The other orderlies were Artimis Jones from Virginia, Joseph Singer from New York, Arthur Davis from Connecticut, and Klaus Moritz from Pennsylvania. We often saw little of each other during the day because we each had separate duties, but we met at dawn almost every morning for breakfast and exchanged what we'd learned the previous day.

After White Plains, the British didn't immediately pursue our army and we endured another period of uncertainty.

"General Washington wrote to Congress yesterday asking them to approve his plan to defend the Hudson," Artimis told us over breakfast on my second day on staff.

"And what grand strategy has His Excellency devised?" Stephen Ward asked.

"General Lee and seven thousand soldiers are to stay at North Castle to guard against attack from the north. General Greene and four thousand soldiers are to reinforce Fort Washington and Fort Lee and guard against attack from the south," Artimis replied.

"I would have sent General Lee to defend the fort named after him," Arthur Davis said.

"Lee's the best general we have," Stephen retorted. "He was an officer in the British Army and knows something about how to fight a war, not like Washington. We need him protecting our flank."

"Washington was an officer in the British Army too," Joseph Singer argued. "He fought against the French in Pennsylvania twenty years ago."

"He was a colonel in the Virginia Militia," Stephen responded, "which meant that he ranked lower than a captain in the British

Army. The one time he was in command he got himself soundly beaten by the French. Lee'd make a better commander."

I was shocked to hear Stephen speak so disrespectfully about General Washington, but I remained silent. I was still smarting from Stephen's dismissal of me as a small boy, but didn't know how to fight back.

Stephen Ward was not the only one questioning Washington's abilities. The officers on Washington's staff talked openly about the possibility of the British making another peace offer, as they had after the Battle of Brooklyn. Some hinted that we should accept such an offer, since the last two months had shown the futility of trying to stand against a British attack. Such talk was quickly silenced by other officers who said we had no choice but to continue fighting.

Washington took his staff and the remaining two thousand soldiers in his command on a roundabout route into New Jersey. We crossed the Hudson at West Point, far north of New York City, then marched south to Hackensack. As the crow flies, it was only twenty miles from our old camp to our new one, but our route was sixty-five miles long. We were well removed from the British Army. They couldn't attack us, but neither could we attack them.

I knew from the orders I copied that Washington was not being modest in taking such a small number of troops. He expected to be reinforced by five thousand militiamen as well as the thousands of soldiers who were mustered at Amboy, farther south in New Jersey. Few of these additional troops appeared. The militia was never recruited and the most of the soldiers at Amboy deserted.

Klaus Moritz was the happiest member of our little group to see me. Until I arrived he had been the only German-speaking orderly on Washington's staff. He was a broad-shouldered, light-haired man who looked to be in his mid-twenties. Klaus came from the Amish country of Pennsylvania, but he was a Lutheran. His parents had come to the colonies when he was six. Having learned English at such a young age, he didn't have a German accent. Before the war he'd been a clerk for a company in York that traded in timber. Klaus tended to look at the dark side of things. Given the travails our army faced, that wasn't hard to do.

Klaus and I didn't share the translation load equally. Washington's aides, and the German-speaking officers they communicated with, knew Klaus and went to him first. He could have used me as his dogsbody, but he was too fair-minded for that. He worked diligently on whatever task he was given and only called upon me to help when he had more work than he could handle.

Once I got to know Klaus, I often discussed the course of the war with him.

"Washington looks tired," I said one day, "and much older than when I first saw him in Brooklyn two months ago."

"Is it any wonder?" Klaus replied. "Since Brooklyn we've had one defeat after another and the future doesn't look any brighter. I don't envy him his burden."

"But aren't there other generals to help share the load?"

"Perhaps, but Washington takes it all on his shoulders. He alone must answer to Congress."

I could see that Klaus was right, but was troubled nonetheless. For a while I pondered what I could do to help Washington. It was an outlandish thought and I soon gave it up as hopeless.

Washington set up his headquarters in the house of Peter Zabriskie, a well-known rebel supporter. It was a fine, two-story house with thick stone walls. His aides found refuge in some of the nearby houses, whilst we orderlies made do in a nearby stable.

Colonel Webb thought that a musical evening might cheer Washington up. He found a fiddler and after supper as many of us as could crowded into the parlour of the Zabriskie house. The fiddler alternated popular songs like "Billy Boy" and "Black Is the Colour of My True Love's Hair" with the wild skirls of Irish jigs. I knew the popular songs, having heard them from the travelling musicians who occasionally visited Graves End, but the Irish music was new to me. It set my foot tapping.

"Gentlemen, if you'll excuse me," Washington said after listening politely for about a quarter hour. "I fear I have correspondence to attend to. Pray continue your entertainment." The music had failed to lighten his mood. We listened to a few more songs as one after another of the officers made his excuses and left. Finally, Colonel Webb thanked the fiddler and the evening was over. It was the only attempt made at entertainment during my time as an orderly.

General Howe eventually turned south to attack Fort Washington, near the north end of Manhattan Island, about ten miles from New York City. Its cannon, along with those at Fort Lee on the New Jersey side, were supposed to prevent British ships from sailing up the Hudson. They didn't. On 5th November, we watched three British ships sail past both forts, then return unharmed.

"Washington's written to General Greene suggesting that he abandon Fort Washington," Stephen Ward told us three days later. "But he's left it up to Greene to make the final decision. My God, Greene was a private when he joined the army and Washington promoted him to major general, the same rank Lee has. He isn't even fit to polish Lee's boots."

Greene ignored Washington's suggestion and reinforced the fort.

Howe moved slowly, taking two weeks to get his army in place. British and Hessian troops surrounded the fort and, after two days of artillery bombardment, attacked. I was close to Washington as he watched the battle through his telescope from Fort Lee on the New Jersey side, a mile across the Hudson River. From his comments to other officers, I knew he was horrified at how many troops the British were able to put into the fight. They outnumbered the defenders by three or four to one. Our men fought valiantly, but by midafternoon they were overwhelmed and had no choice but to surrender. Nearly three thousand men and large numbers of cannon and muskets were captured.

The Hessians were still full of the heat of battle and must have been furious at the casualties they'd suffered. They murdered several of our men after they'd surrendered. Hessian officers quickly regained control of their men and stopped this outrage. But they did nothing to stop their men from stealing whatever they could from the prisoners, some of whom were stripped nearly naked before being marched off to prison ships in New York harbour.

Washington had remained stoic during the battle and surrender, but when he saw the Hessians putting his men to the sword, he turned away from the rest of us and could be heard to weep. This embarrassed me. Washington was famous for his self-control, and I didn't want to witness his anguish. No one disturbed him, and after a few minutes he turned back, his face a picture of despair. He said nothing as he mounted his horse and slowly rode to his quarters. As always, Billy Lee was in close attendance. The rest of us followed a respectful distance behind.

Fort Washington should not have fallen as quickly or easily as it did. After the rebellion ended, the British announced that William Dermont, adjutant to Colonel Magaw, had deserted just before the battle and given them full details of the fort's defences and their weaknesses. Dermont was hailed as a hero and given a generous pension, but his actions have always seemed cowardly to me.

Our army felt secure atop the three-hundred-foot-high cliffs called The Palisades that line the New Jersey side of the Hudson, but only three days after the capture of Fort Washington, General Howe moved again. On a foggy night, a loyalist led twelve regiments of British and Hessians up an obscure path to the top of the cliff, six miles north of Fort Lee. General Greene, who now commanded Fort Lee, had been lax in not posting sentries and was caught by surprise. The fort was abandoned without a fight on 19th November. Our soldiers escaped but left most of their supplies behind. After a disorganized march south, they joined us along the Hackensack River.

"We'll probably be on half rations again before long," Artimis Jones said as we ate breakfast the next morning. "That's assuming that we survive at all." None of us disagreed with his glum assessment, and even Stephen Ward, who could be counted on to state his opinion whenever anyone else spoke, was silent.

We then began a three-week retreat across New Jersey and into Pennsylvania. Washington needed more men and sent an urgent message to General Lee, who was still guarding the Hudson at North Castle, asking him to move his seven thousand soldiers across the Hudson and into New Jersey. This would have given us a force that could have stood up to the British. Lee found one excuse after another to delay moving his troops.

"My men are shoeless," Lee complained in one letter. "I don't know a safe route for joining you," was his reason for inaction in another. "I believe it may be possible to strike a decisive blow at the British rear," he claimed in a third. There were rumours that he was inveigling to replace Washington as commander-in-chief of the rebel army. I had no way of knowing whether the rumours were true, but Lee never came to Washington's aid.

Washington left Hazlet's Delaware Regiment and Captain Alexander Hamilton's battery of five cannon as a rear guard to prevent the British from using the stone bridge at Brunswick, the easiest route across the Raritan River in central New Jersey. The river could also be crossed at a ford several miles to the west, but using the ford would've delayed the British and given our army more time to retreat. Colonel Webb told me to stay with Captain Hamilton as a messenger.

The advance guard of the British Army, a mixed force of British dragoons and Hessian jaegers, approached the bridge in the early afternoon. Delaware riflemen hidden in buildings on the south side of the river greeted them with heavy fire that caused many casualties. Hamilton's guns damaged the bridge but were unable to destroy it. By midafternoon British artillery had moved into position and started destroying the buildings that sheltered the Delawaremen. Hamilton's gunners tried unsuccessfully to silence the British guns. They were firing at such a rapid rate that they were running short of both powder and shot.

"Watson, can you carry a message to the quartermasters?" Captain Hamilton called out over the din of the battle.

"Yes, sir."

"Tell 'em we need powder and both ball and canister for our six-pounders. And tell 'em to hurry." Another officer would probably have added a curse or two, but Hamilton was a pious man who never used strong language.

The quickest way back to the quartermasters, who were about a mile south of the bridge, would have been along the Post Road, which ran through the middle of the village. But British guns were firing canister down the road, making that route too dangerous. I detoured west, through the campus of Queens College. Fewer bits of lead were flying through the air, but I still had to be careful because some of the buildings had been set afire by the British bombardment. As I made my way through the school grounds, I remembered that it was my teacher Mr Anderson's alma mater. I wondered what a loyalist like him would've thought of me risking my life for the rebel cause. It was a strange thing to think about in the midst of a battle.

It took twenty minutes to reach the quartermasters and give them Captain Hamilton's request. Once I was certain that they were loading a cart with the powder and shot he needed, I hurried back through the Queens College campus to report to him.

The Delawaremen held their positions for four hours before slipping away under cover of darkness. Since they had no wagons, they had to burn the hundred tents they'd been using for shelter to keep them from falling into British hands. The wet, heavy canvas was hard to light and sent billowing clouds of smoke into the air. The British stayed north of the river, but we could hear their sappers repairing the bridge.

With Hessian and British bullets filling the air, I was probably more at risk of being killed that afternoon than I'd been at the Battle of Brooklyn, but I felt no fear. I was too busy trying to find my way and thinking about Mr Anderson to worry. As in Brooklyn, it was only after the battle that I realized that I'd been in mortal danger. This time I didn't shake. I felt proud to have carried Hamilton's message and helped our cause.

After Washington, Hamilton was the rebel officer who most impressed me. Many of the rebel officers were young, but Captain Hamilton, with his boyish face, appeared to be the youngest.

"Hamilton's a man of mystery," Joseph Singer told me. "He arrived in New York City only two years ago and enrolled in Kings College. He won't tell anyone about his family, or even where he comes from."

"How could a newly-arrived university student become a captain in the New York militia?" I asked.

"He made his mark with fierce speeches for the rebel cause. He became the darling of the Sons of Liberty." The Sons were the rebel mob that controlled the streets of New York, intimidating anyone who didn't support the rebellion.

Hamilton was a handsome man, with reddish hair and blue eyes, and even though he was slight of stature, he exuded an air of confidence. He had strange habits. I sometimes saw him at dawn, pacing on the outskirts of the camp. From his gestures, he appeared to be practicing one of the orations that had made him famous, but in such a low voice that no one could hear him. He made an excessive show of piety at our Sunday church services, looking heavenward and almost prostrating himself when he kneeled. Hamilton was a good officer who stayed close to the six-pounders that made up his battery. Pulling these guns through the mud of New Jersey was a backbreaking task, but he jollied his men along and helped when things were difficult. Few officers, even in our democratic army, did that.

I spoke to Hamilton several times during the retreat and was amazed at the way the words and gestures seemed to flow out of him. Even in casual conversation, he sounded as if he was making a speech to the Sons of Liberty. When I asked him, "Captain Hamilton, what type of country do you think we'll make when we beat the British?" his answer was both hopeful and pessimistic.

"We shall have a country that is more grand, more opulent, and more powerful than any subject of King George could imagine. But we shall have to overcome the base instincts that rule so many of our countrymen. It is the melancholy truth that the behaviour of many amongst us might serve as the severest satire upon the human species. It has been a compound of inconsistency, falsehood, cowardice, and selfishness." He waved his hands for emphasis. Having watched Washington's army melt away before the British, it wasn't hard to see the source of such gloomy thoughts.

Hamilton had no military training, but he seemed to have an intuitive grasp of what needed to be done. Washington's other officers acted like the lawyers, apothecaries, or shopkeepers they'd been before the rebellion. They were good men, no doubt, but it was difficult to imagine them leading the colonies if the rebellion had been successful. However, I had no difficulty envisioning Alexander Hamilton making decisions about the lives and fortunes of the people of a new country.

The weather was foul, as only the late fall can be. Heavy rains chilled everyone to the bone and turned roads into sloughs of mud. Marching along them with a heavy pack was enough to wear out any man. We bivouacked each night where we could. The night after the retreat from Brunswick was especially trying. We camped in an open field near the town of Kingston with neither campfires nor rations. The tents the Delaware Regiment had been forced to burn earlier that day would have sheltered at least part of the army. Many of the men had no shoes. They'd worn them out on the long marches from Boston to New York and then through New Jersey. Everyone's clothes were in tatters and some men had only blankets to cover themselves. We were well supplied with powder and shot, and until the retreat from Hackensack, usually had adequate rations, but we never got new shoes or clothes. We were further disheartened that night when the New Jersey and Maryland Militias marched off, their enlistments over. Smallwood's Maryland Regiment remained – it had enlisted for the duration of the war – but Washington's army had been cut in half.

Being on Washington's staff didn't provide any special privileges. Washington usually was amongst the last to retreat, and we were in great danger of being captured by the Hessians, who were the vanguard of the British Army. The rebels' democratic principles required their commander to share his men's hardships. As an orderly, I ate no better than any other soldier, my clothes were turning to rags as quickly as theirs, and my thighs ached from marching through the mud, as I'm sure theirs did.

I'd replaced the jacket Colonel Webb had given me with a woollen great coat. I cut off its bottom and sleeves so it fit me. The waist was also far too big, so I tied it closed with a length of rope. The piece I cut from the coat bottom made a long scarf, which I wrapped around my ears and neck. I was far from fashionable, but I kept warm. My shoes had been mended just before I left Graves End. Miraculously they held together during the long march across New Jersey.

During the retreat I carried my orderly's tools – a portable desk, pens, and ink, and both parchment and paper. These were wrapped in oilcloth to protect against the rain, but it was so wet that writing on paper was often impossible. I also carried some of Colonel Webb's records, along with my blanket, more oilcloth to sleep on, and as much bread and dried meat or fish as I could scrounge. I'd found a pack that was too large to be comfortable, but still far better than trying to carry all of my equipment in a bundle. I think I carried about fifty pounds, far less than most men carried. Many soldiers were burdened with a hundred pounds or more as they trudged through the mud.

Most of the army was ill. Sneezing and coughing were the most common sounds I heard day and night as we marched. For the first part of the retreat, I managed to remain healthy, but two days before the skirmish at Brunswick, I took sick. At first my problems were mild, but the night without shelter after Brunswick exacerbated them. I woke up that morning with chills and fever.

"Drink this willow tea," Arthur Davis said. "You'll feel better." He waited whilst I took two sips of the scalding tea.

"I'm going home," he said. "My enlistment was up two months ago and my family needs me to help them through the winter. Come with me, William. You're ill. You need to be someplace warm and someone to care for you."

He looked around to be certain that no one could overhear us.

"The cause is lost. It's just a matter of time before the British destroy this army. If you stay you'll either be killed or end up on a prison ship."

"Thank you, Arthur, but I think I'll stay," I said after taking a few sips of the rapidly cooling tea. I'd stopped shaking. I felt weak and my stomach was queasy, but I thought I could continue.

"Good luck to you then." He shook my hand and went off to make the same offer to Joseph Singer, who also turned him down.

No one discussed Arthur's leaving. It was as if he'd never existed. We remaining orderlies split the work he'd been doing between us.

I sometimes wonder why I didn't leave when Arthur Davis offered me the chance. I wasn't a soldier – Major Gist had told me that – I wouldn't have been deserting. I think I still considered it all a great adventure. Adventures aren't supposed to be easy. They're supposed to involve hardships. If I was to be a hero, I would have to overcome these hardships. But memories of one's feelings are tricky things. The facts of the retreat can be verified, but how can I know whether what I think I felt over sixty years ago is what I actually felt? Perhaps the thought of returning to my grandparents' home over the ironmonger's shop was even less attractive than being cold, sick, and hungry with the rebel army.

Princeton was the next town on the way to Pennsylvania. Washington didn't allow the army to pause there, but had it march to Trenton. Colonel Webb took pity on my weakened condition and told me to stay with the rebel's rear guard and get some rest. I bivouacked for four nights in the College of New Jersey's Nassau Hall, a huge four-story building that was the largest in the colonies. The professors and students had vacated, and hundreds of soldiers roamed through the edifice. Some of them damaged the place, defacing its woodwork and tearing down its tapestries. It was pure vandalism. Destroying the building brought them no gain.

Discipline in the rebel army was breaking down and looting was widespread. The army was hungry, and needed shoes and clothes, but the residents of Princeton offered no assistance. Why help a lost cause? Captain Hamilton, who had also stayed with the rear guard, worried how the rebels would establish order once the rebellion was over.

"Perhaps the rebel soldiers will be like Cincinnatus, and lay down their arms and return to the plough once the fighting is over," I suggested to him. Mr Anderson had told the story of Cincinnatus as part of a lecture on Roman history.

"I doubt those looting British supply wagons will quickly lose their taste for easy spoils," was his dour reply. "We shall have bands of brigands to contend with for decades." Considering the actions of the rebel soldiers in Princeton, I had to agree.

Four days of rest was enough for me to regain my health. I still coughed every now and then, but I no longer had chills and fever. On 6th December, with the rest of the rear guard, I marched the dozen miles to Trenton and re-joined Washington's staff.

"Well if it isn't William Watson," Stephen Ward said when he saw me again. "I thought you were one of those summer soldiers who gave up at the first sign of adversity."

"Leave him alone," Joseph Singer said. "He was ill and needed a rest."

Stephen seemed to sense that the other orderlies wouldn't tolerate him taunting me and said nothing more. Still I was pained. It appeared the acceptance I'd won from Stephen was temporary and had disappeared in four days. He knew I'd turned down Arthur Davis' suggestion that I leave with him. He could see that I'd stayed with the rear guard when it would've been easy to desert. What more would I have to do to prove that I was worthy of being on Washington's staff? I couldn't change my age or size.

The Delaware is a major river, wider and deeper than the small waterways of New Jersey. It could only be crossed by boat, since there were no fords or bridges near Trenton. To be safe, our army needed to cross the river into Pennsylvania and prevent the British from doing so.

Washington sent troops to commandeer every boat on the New Jersey side for miles up and down the river. In addition he had the large flat-bottomed galleys of the Pennsylvania Navy. Each had a gun – at least an eighteen-pounder, larger than anything the British had – at its bow and was powered by twenty oars in two banks. Some of the oarsmen were captured loyalists, like the galley slaves of Greece or Rome. Collecting this armada and transporting the bulk of the rebel army across the river, had taken nearly a week. As always, Washington was amongst the last to leave, and did so only when he knew that the Hessians were on their way.

"It's as if General Washington and General Howe reached an agreement not to fight another battle," Klaus said whilst we waited our turn to cross the river.

"Why do you say that? The Hessians have been dogging us since we left Hackensack," I replied.

"Yes, but they always wait until we retreat before they advance. They've been driving us forward like pheasants at a hunt."

"But there aren't any hunters in Pennsylvania waiting to shoot us down."

"That's true. Maybe Howe's just waiting until everyone deserts or until our army is so small that we can't put up a fight."

Klaus' logic was troubling, but I couldn't find any way of refuting it. It was as if we had been in a stately minuet with the British and Hessians. We would retreat south, there would be a pause, then they would advance. That would be the signal for us to retreat again. Two days after the fall of Fort Lee, we retreated to the Passaic River. Five days later the British moved forward and we retreated again, this time to Newark. And five days after that we retreated to Brunswick, two days later to Princeton, and a week later across the Delaware River into Pennsylvania.

With the last of our army, Klaus and I boarded a boat and were rowed across the Delaware. The first Hessian jaegers appeared on the New Jersey shore just as we landed in Pennsylvania. Our artillery opened fire and a handful of Hessians fell. From our side of the river, we couldn't tell whether they were dead or merely wounded, but we cheered as if we had won a great victory. I hoped it was a good omen.

CHAPTER 7

Having reached the Delaware, General Howe tried to cross it. He sent a large force upriver to Coryell's Ferry, only to find that the ferry was no longer there. He sent smaller parties to other points along the river. For once our army had done its work well. We'd left no boats for the British to use and they didn't have the pontoons they'd need to build a bridge. Howe would have to wait until the river froze over, as it did every January, before he could cross. Our army was safe, at least for a few weeks.

Washington set up his headquarters in a large brick mansion a half mile back from the Delaware River opposite Trenton, his best lodging since Hackensack, a month earlier. The other orderlies and I also fared well. We slept on clean straw in a well-built barn behind the mansion, much better than the cold ground or bare wood floors we'd slept on during the retreat.

We took our meals in a spacious kitchen in a small building behind the mansion. All of the pots, pans, and cooking utensils had disappeared. It would've been nice to eat on proper plates, rather than using the mess kits we carried. But food was again plentiful and having a table to sit at and a fire blazing in the kitchen's fireplace

71

were great luxuries after the short rations and cold meals of the past few weeks.

Over a breakfast of bacon and porridge on our first day in Pennsylvania, Joseph Singer told us that Washington had written to Congress reporting that our army was shrinking daily due to sickness and desertions, and that without considerable help he wouldn't be able to defend Philadelphia. We pondered this gloomy forecast in silence for a few moments.

"Our only hope is to retreat farther south to Virginia and to raise a large army there," Artimis Jones, an orderly from that state, said as if it were intuitively obvious. "We can't continue the fight with so few able-bodied soldiers."

"The New England men will never march that far from home," Stephen Ward retorted.

"We need a victory now," Klaus Moritz said. "No one will support a losing army."

"Easy to say, but hard to do," Stephen replied. "Can you convince the Hessians to lose?"

"You generals can decide on grand strategy," I said. "I'm worried about more practical things, like how do I get a new pair of shoes? My soles are so thin I can feel every pebble."

The other orderlies hooted at me as we returned to our food.

The next day word spread that twelve thousand British soldiers were marching towards Philadelphia and would be there within twenty-four hours. Rioting broke out in the city, forcing Washington to declare martial law. He appointed General Israel Putnam to restore order. No British soldiers appeared, but a few days later Congress abandoned Philadelphia and moved to Baltimore. These events did nothing to help the morale of our army.

New rumours that the British were building boats and planning to cross the Delaware circulated almost daily. None of them were true. Our spies soon told us that General Howe had decided that the weather was too foul for further campaigning and had ordered his troops into winter quarters. He spread them through New Jersey to give them enough countryside to forage for their supplies, then returned to New York and the comforts of his mistress. His orders to his generals allowed them to attack if the opportunity presented itself. All of us, from Washington to his youngest orderly, worried continually about what the British and Hessians might do.

Our spies gave us detailed and accurate reports on the location of the British Army. General Grant, who commanded the British Army in New Jersey, had planned well. The fifteen hundred Hessians under Colonel Rall in Trenton, directly across the river from us, were in an exposed position. But they could call on help from a second Hessian regiment in Bordentown, seven miles south of Trenton, and from a regiment of Highland Scots in Burlington, six miles farther south. Two British regiments in Princeton, twelve miles inland from Trenton, could also provide assistance. The rest of the British Army was divided amongst more than a dozen garrisons, but none was close enough to offer immediate assistance to the regiments along the Delaware River.

Washington spread his forces along the Pennsylvania side of the river, both north and south of Trenton, to prevent the British from crossing. But as Colonel Joseph Reed, one of his aides, told him, it was impossible to defend the full length of the river. We would have to depend on our spies to tell us what the British planned to do. Washington agreed. Every order I copied from him to his officers in the field included a request to recruit still more spies and a promise to pay for them.

There was one piece of good news in all this gloom. Before they left Philadelphia, Congress gave Washington full authority to conduct the war. Previously he'd had to obtain their approval for all major actions, which meant that other generals could appeal to Congress to support their pet plans. Some did and, unfortunately, much of Washington's time was taken up countering these proposals.

Washington was very happy with his new authority. Artimis said that he'd seen a letter in which the general told his wife that for the first time since he'd taken command, he was free of the fetters that had limited him. He could now make a bold stroke that would change the course of the war.

"William, join a game of French Ruff?" Artimis asked one night. "Klaus, Joseph, and I need a fourth." They played every night they could. Stephen Ward was their usual fourth, but he was busy that night.

"I've no money." They usually played for ha'penny a point.

"Then we won't play for money, just the honour of knowing you've won."

My parents were adamantly opposed to any form of gambling. I never learned the details of the story, but my father said that as a young man, before he married my mother, he'd gambled away a considerable sum. He didn't want me making the same mistake and banned playing cards from our home. My mother was in full agreement. But with no money involved it seemed harmless to join them.

"You'll have to teach me the rules. I've never played."

"Have a seat and let me explain this game to you," Artimis said, a broad smile on his face. "The goal is to win at least three tricks out of five." He then reeled off a bewildering set of instructions about trumps and right bowers and left bowers. My confusion must have shown on my face because finally he said, "Let's just play and I'll explain as we go along. You can be my partner."

I spent the next two hours learning the game and by the end of that time even managed to win a hand.

"You'll have to join us again," Joseph said as the game broke up.

"I might just do that."

French Ruff seemed like a completely harmless diversion, and I wondered about my parents' strict rules against playing cards. Still I felt guilty as I lay on my pallet trying to fall asleep. It was the first thing I had done since leaving grandfather's house that I was certain they both would've disapproved of. Mother wouldn't have wanted me to join the rebels, but I thought that Father would've approved of that decision, and would've been proud of my being an orderly for General Washington.

I played French Ruff again two nights later. After mastering the rules, the game didn't seem that interesting a diversion, certainly not as engaging as it seemed to be the other orderlies. I'd heard them discussing the proper way to have played this or that hand the previous night, whilst I couldn't remember the details of play for more than a few minutes after a hand had been completed.

Washington kept up his correspondence with General Lee, imploring him to bring his soldiers, who by this time were in northern New Jersey, to Pennsylvania.

"The New Jersey militia wishes me to remain in Morristown," Lee claimed in a letter that reached Washington shortly after we arrived in Pennsylvania.

Washington's reply to this latest excuse was courtly, but insistent, "I have so frequently mentioned our situation and the necessity of your aid that it is painful to me to add a word on the subject. Let me once more request and entreat you to march immediately."

Lee didn't respond to this last letter. On 13th December, he left his soldiers, and taking only a small detachment as a guard, went to a tavern operated by a widow named White. He planned to spend the night there but was captured by a squadron of British dragoons.

"General Lee must have been looking for more comfortable quarters," Washington, ever the gentleman, said.

"I'm sure those comforts included the charms of the Widow White," Colonel Webb added under his breath.

Washington must have heard Colonel Webb because he looked at him sternly before continuing. "I shall write to General Sullivan asking him to join us with whatever remains of Lee's army."

Afterwards I asked Colonel Webb what he'd done to incur Washington's displeasure.

"As a young man, His Excellency copied out one hundred ten rules of civility and has endeavoured ever since to live by them," Webb explained as we walked back to our quarters. "One of those rules, which he too frequently has had occasion to quote to me, is, 'Speak not injurious words, neither in jest nor earnest; scoff at none although they give occasion.' I fear it's a lesson I've yet to learn."

For the first time, I appreciated the source of Washington's famous self-discipline.

Two weeks after arriving in Pennsylvania, Washington moved his headquarters ten miles north to McConkey's Ferry, the closest point where the river was easy to cross. Now that it was obvious that the British were not going to cross the river before it was covered with ice thick enough for them to march over, he ordered the militia companies that had been spread along the riverfront to take up positions near the ferry. We orderlies moved, too, to a less comfortable out-building. We still ate our meals together, and the ever dependable Stephen told the rest of us that he had seen a letter Washington had written to General Gates, who commanded some of our soldiers in New Jersey. He quoted Washington as saying, "If we can collect our forces speedily, I hope we may affect something of importance, or at least give our affairs such a turn as to make them assume a more promising aspect." None of us knew what this cryptic sentence meant.

"Washington's going to attack Trenton," Joseph said at breakfast the next morning. "It's the closest garrison and it only has fifteen hundred Hessians soldiers."

"Singer, you're a fool," was Stephen's retort. "General Washington doesn't have fifteen hundred soldiers fit for duty in this camp. The Hessians'd massacre us." The rest of us laughed.

We stopped laughing a few days later when Washington ordered all soldiers to have three days' rations available and to be ready to move on short notice, day or night. We orderlies agreed that there was no reason for Washington to retreat, and that this order could only mean that he was preparing to attack. It would be the thing of importance about which he'd written to General Gates.

A week after Lee's capture, General Sullivan brought two thou-sand soldiers to Pennsylvania, the remnants of the seven thousand men that Lee had commanded after the Battle of White Plains. The rest had either left when their enlistments were up or deserted. General Gates brought another six hundred. Fewer than half of these new additions were fit for duty. The rest were either sick or wounded. Meagre as their numbers were, they doubled Washington's force. But that increase was temporary. The enlistments of all of these men were up on 31st December. Washington had to attack and had to be vic-torious.

Ten days before Christmas, the men of Hunterdon County in northwest New Jersey rose up to defend their property against the Hessians, who were plundering their farms and raping their women. It took only a few days for defence of home and hearth to turn into active attacks, which, whilst they inflicted only a small number of casualties on the Hessians, caused them many problems. The Hessians could no longer travel in small groups. Colonel Rall had to send an escort of a hundred men to guard his dispatches to Princeton.

The Hunterdon County men weren't alone. The Pennsylvania Militia used small boats to cross the Delaware near Trenton and attack Rall's outposts. These attacks caused a few more casualties, but they forced the Hessians to be on constant alert and to post extra sentries. Rall's soldiers were soon exhausted by these extra duties.

Trenton wasn't the only point at which we attacked the British and Hessians. On 22nd December I saw a report from Colonel Reed. After providing details on the New Jersey militia's successful attacks on Burlington, Reed concluded that Washington could either give the militia strong reinforcement or make a separate attack. Reed recommended a separate attack on Trenton, then warned, "Our affairs are hastening fast to ruin if we do not retrieve them by some happy event. Delay now is equal to total defeat."

Washington took Reed's advice to heart. On 23rd December, he issued secret orders to collect all available boats as quickly as possible. This activity could not be kept secret, and by the end of that day, our whole army knew what was happening.

"When do you think we'll attack?" Klaus asked over breakfast on Christmas Eve.

"It'll be the day after tomorrow," Artimis replied. "It'll take all of today to collect the boats and I don't think our army would be happy if we attacked on Christmas Day. There's no reason to wait after that. I think we'll cross the river tomorrow night and attack the next morning."

Even Stephen, who had a retort for every opinion not his own, had to agree. I understood Artimis' logic, but still had my doubts. Our army had been retreating for four months. Would it be willing to turn and fight the Hessians? I fervently hoped so.

Christmas morning was cold, below freezing, and by noon the wind had shifted from westerly to northeast, a sure sign of a storm. Washington's Order of the Day told his soldiers to cook three days' rations and to ensure that their "arms, accoutrements, and ammunition are in best order."

At midafternoon Colonel Webb came to the room where we orderlies gathered when we were not working to tell us, "General Washington wishes all of you to meet him and his aides at the boat landing at nine o'clock this evening. We'll be crossing the river to attack the enemy. You are to act as messengers." Then he pulled Klaus and me aside. "You two are to stay close to His Excellency. He may need someone to translate German."

"I told you days ago. We're going to attack Trenton," Joseph said as soon as Colonel Webb left, a triumphant smile on his face.

"You were right," I said. Klaus and Artimis nodded in agreement.

As always, Stephen disagreed. "You're all wrong," he said. "I think General Washington is going to be a sly fox and attack Princeton." I didn't know whether Stephen meant that or was just trying to provoke an argument. I didn't find out because he was whisked off by Colonel Cary to deliver a message.

At dusk, we formed up for evening parade. Every soldier had his rifle or musket and was given as much ammunition as he could carry. The storm that had been brewing all afternoon broke and soon it was snowing.

We orderlies crossed the river with Washington at midnight, three hours behind schedule. We were rowed across in high-sided barges by the same regiment of Massachusetts fishermen who'd ferried the Marylanders from Brooklyn to New York when Washington retreated from Kings County. This trip was much less pleasant. Ice floes filled the river and the wind blew a steady spray of freezing water over us. We stood during the crossing, since the bottom of our boat was awash in several inches of water. My feet were soaked and cold enough to ache by the time we reached the New Jersey side, but my greatcoat and scarf kept the rest of my body warm.

I watched Washington during the twenty-minute crossing. He didn't speak to the thirty of us in the barge. His face looked serene. I could only imagine that he was thinking that he had done all that he could, and now his fate – and the fate of his army – were in God's hands. When we reached the New Jersey side, he thanked the oarsmen, then walked briskly to where a group of his officers, who'd crossed earlier, were gathered around a fire. He showed no sign that the cold and wet had affected him.

I stood next to Klaus on crossing. After ten minutes he began to shiver uncontrollably. I had to help him out of the boat and guide him to a fire. In the wind it did little good, so I hugged him in an attempt to warm him. After about five minutes his shivering began to subside and in another five minutes he was back in control of himself.

"Thank you, William. I'd have frozen to death if you hadn't done that," he said, a wan smile on his face.

"You're exaggerating. You just had a little chill."

But he wasn't exaggerating. Without help he would've died. Several men did that night. We found shelter behind some pine trees, close enough to Washington to hear his orders if we were needed.

Whilst hugging Klaus, I wondered what I'd do if Washington called for a messenger. I quickly decided that saving Klaus was more important than following orders. I pictured myself being clapped into irons for insubordination . . . in front of a court martial tribunal arguing the righteousness of what I had done . . . being found guilty and ordered shot . . . then Washington overturning the verdict and commending me for my virtue. Of course, this fantasy never happened. Washington had no need for a messenger during the ten minutes it took for Klaus to recover.

"Washington's plan isn't going to work," Klaus said as we waited for the remainder of the army to cross. "We'll never get to Trenton by dawn. The Hessians'll be ready for us." I thought his voice had a tone of despair, but it may simply have been the exhaustion caused by getting chilled. "The Germans say the Hessians are *teufel*, devils. We might win if we surprise them, but we're doomed if they know we're coming."

"Why don't you try to sleep?" I told him. "It'll be at least two hours more before we need to march. I'll wake you if we need to carry messages."

"Thank you again, William."

He was asleep in an instant. I sat there pondering what Klaus had said. Would it be prudent to turn back? How many of our soldiers would stay if we did? If the Hessians were ready for us, would I survive the battle? I thought about my brother and sister for the first time in weeks. If I died, would they ever learn what'd happened to me? And how were they faring? Was Robert still with the loyalist militia in Queens? How were Oma and Grootvader treating Charlotte?

These gloomy thoughts occupied me for an hour until Klaus woke. He seemed recovered. We talked for a few minutes then went to see if we could get anything hot to eat or drink. We found Joseph Singer boiling water for tea, which he offered to share with us.

"I'm eternally in your debt," I told him.

We sat there sipping tea and talking about nothing of great import whilst our army slowly crossed from Pennsylvania. A stranger might've assumed that we had not a care in the world.

Washington set out a piquet line to guard the army. No one was allowed through without the proper password, "Victory or Death." It was a grim choice, but it correctly summed up our prospects. It was impossible to keep a landing of this size a secret and, despite the sentries, many of the Hunterdon County men who'd been harassing the Hessians joined us.

The last of our army, including eighteen pieces of artillery, arrived at three o'clock, but it was another hour before we began marching. The storm had intensified and we were drenched by heavy rain and snow. I stamped my feet and swung my arms in a vain attempt to keep warm.

Our first challenge was to climb the two-hundred-foot embankment that rose from the riverside to the flat tableland that spread south towards Trenton. The road was steep and icy, and we proceeded at little more than a child's pace. Difficult as the climb was, it felt better than standing idle. The exertion warmed me and I opened my greatcoat to cool off as I climbed. I quickly closed it once I reached the top.

The next obstacle was three miles farther on, the hundred-foot deep ravine formed by Jacob's Creek. The whole army had to descend, cross the creek, then climb back up, an exhausting task. Fear of looking like a weakling to the other orderlies kept me moving. Despite Stephen Ward's harassment, they'd accepted me as one of them, even though I was the youngest by five years.

I stayed as close to Washington as I could as he rode up and down, encouraging our soldiers whilst they marched. He was mounted on a sorrel stallion named Nelson, one of the two horses he had with him. The other, Blue Skin, an impressive, almost white stallion, became skittish at the sound of gunfire.

On the descent to Jacob's Creek, I watched in horror as Nelson's front legs slipped and its body started collapsing, the type of fall that could maim or kill a rider. As always, Billy Lee was in close attendance. He was a superb horseman in his own right, but there was nothing he could do to help. My horror changed to amazement as I watched Washington shift his weight backwards to allow Nelson's hind legs to regain traction, then use his hands to pull its head up, so that it could regain its balance. I'd never seen an equivalent feat of horsemanship and strength.

After Jacob's Creek the land was more open, exposing us to the full force of the storm. Sleet and hail pelted us, and a few men dropped by the wayside from exhaustion. One or more of their comrades stayed with each of them, but I didn't stop, much as I wished I could. Nothing I'd experienced during the retreat through New Jersey could match the agony of this march. The road was now a gentle downhill slope, which normally would have provided a respite. But because of the ice, we had to struggle to keep from slipping and our artillerymen had to strain to keep their guns from careening into the infantry.

Washington's plan was for our column to march through woods to a half-mile-long open meadow north of Trenton, then past the first Hessian outpost, a cooper's shop a mile from the centre of the village. We emerged from the woods at about nine, but the snow was blowing so hard that we couldn't see the other end of the meadow. That meant that the Hessians in the cooper's shop couldn't see us.

Washington was at the head of the column with a company of Virginians commanded by his cousin, William Washington, immediately behind him. Washington liked having the Virginians nearby. They, along with Smallwood's Marylanders and Haslet's Delaware-men, were his army's elite.

"Captain Washington, we need to eliminate that Hessian outpost," General Washington said. "Can your men do it?"

"They can, Your Excellency."

At William Washington's command, the Virginians charged forward. When they reached the middle of the meadow, the Hessians saw them, fired one volley, which didn't hit any of our men, then quickly abandoned their post. The snow slackened for a moment allowing us to see the Hessians running towards the centre of Trenton, but they were too far away for our riflemen to hit. The Virginians stopped at mid-meadow, waiting for the rest of the column to catch up.

General Washington seemed perplexed by the Hessian's strange behaviour. A more normal response would have been for them to wait until our soldiers were much closer before firing, then stand their ground until it was obvious they could no longer hold their position. He stopped to confer with his senior officers. Klaus and I were standing about twenty yards away, too far to hear what was being said, but close enough for Washington to see us. He shouted for a messenger. I started to walk towards him, but Klaus put his hand on my shoulder.

"I'll go," he said.

Before I could respond, he started trotting towards Washington, who bent over Nelson's neck and instructed Klaus on his task. Klaus ran towards the Pennsylvania Militia to deliver Washington's message.

"Advance," Washington commanded after he'd sent Klaus on his way.

As we reached the middle of the meadow, we saw the Hessians arrayed in battle order at its edge. Our column stopped, and our officers ordered their men into a line for their attack. It was a complicated manoeuvre that took at least five minutes to accomplish, long enough for me to become chilled. I could hear Hessian sergeants threatening their men with flogging or worse if they broke formation or fired before ordered to.

The artillery pieces that we'd laboriously pulled along with us were rolled into position and the command to fire given. Miraculously, considering all the rain, sleet, and snow, seven of the eighteen guns fired. Their canister tore holes in the Hessians' line, but reserves moved up to fill the gaps. Hessian artillery responded and we suffered many casualties.

"Charge," Washington ordered.

Our army rushed forward, but since Washington did not join the charge, I stayed with him at mid-meadow. Hessian artillery fired again, causing more holes in our line. Some of the canister shot passed quite close to me. The Hessians let our soldiers run until they were within musket range before firing a tremendous volley. Our men fell as wheat before the scythe. This was all that flesh and blood could withstand. Our line trembled, then almost as one, our soldiers – even the Virginians, the pride of our army – turned and ran towards the woods from which we had emerged less than half an hour earlier. The dead and wounded were left on the field.

The Hessians followed our retreating soldiers to the slow beat of their kettledrums. They didn't seem to care whether they caught us or not.

Washington was still at mid-meadow. "Halt! Reform your line," he shouted as the first of our soldiers streamed past him. He was ignored. The rest of our army quickly followed. "Halt, damn you! Turn and face the enemy," he continued shouting, but to no avail.

With his army fleeing and the Hessians advancing, Washington had no choice but to turn his horse and join the retreat. I and the other members of his staff followed. He walked Nelson just fast enough to keep up with the last of our soldiers. I caught a quick glimpse of his face. It was a picture of despair, not unlike it had been only two months before when he witnessed the Hessians murdering our soldiers after they had surrendered at Fort Washington.

Just as the first of our men reached the end of the meadow, British soldiers emerged from the woods. We were caught in a vice between the Hessians to our rear and the British in front of us. Our soldiers quickly threw down their weapons and surrendered. Some, who were at the edges of the meadow, ran to the right or left, trying to escape. Being at the centre of the meadow, I didn't have this opportunity. I raised my hands in the air to show I was unarmed.

Washington made no attempt to escape, but stopped Nelson, dismounted, and silently held his sword, hilt-first, in front of him. A British captain took the horse's bridle and held it until General Leslie emerged from the woods to formally accept Washington's sword as a token of his surrender. Billy Lee, who'd been riding slightly behind Washington, also dismounted and followed his master into captivity.

British and Hessian soldiers came up and took our weapons. They were respectful of our officers, but they stripped the rest of us of everything of value. My pack was torn off my shoulders by a Hessian private who didn't waste time looking at its contents. Without a word he roughly searched my hands and neck for any jewellery, then pulled at my pockets for coins. Finding nothing he wanted, he moved on to the private standing next to me and repeated the process. I was left with nothing but the clothes on my back and a few crusts of bread in my pockets.

The surrender happened so fast that I'd had no time to think. But now, standing there, waiting to find out my fate, I had more time than I wanted to contemplate the future. I'd heard grisly tales of the suffering aboard British prison hulks, where men literally melted away from starvation and disease. I'd seen Hessian soldiers abuse and murder our soldiers after they'd surrendered. I felt myself shaking as these thoughts ran through my mind.

After about a quarter hour, the British took charge of our officers; the Hessians, our common soldiers. A Hessian captain divided us into groups of about a hundred. My group was marched off to an empty barn on the far side of the meadow. I was now a prisoner.

Even in my privileged position on General Washington's staff I didn't understand all that was happening during those hectic weeks between our arrival in Pennsylvania and our surrender at Trenton. Nobody, not even General Washington, could have. It was only many years after the war, when I had a chance to read histories of the events I'd lived through, that I understood why we'd walked so blindly into the trap the Hessians and British set for us. Let me retell the story of the Battle of Trenton and the end of the Great Rebellion, now with the benefit of this additional information.

The Hessians and British were able to trap us because they knew in advance when and where Washington planned to attack. Hans Knobel, a Hessian spy in our army, gave them this information. I'd met Knobel. He was an aide to Colonel Schneider, who commanded a regiment of German-speaking Pennsylvanians. He spoke English well and accompanied his colonel to the conferences Washington held with his regimental commanders.

I was shocked when I learned that he'd been a spy. He'd seemed dedicated to our cause. But he wouldn't have been a very good spy if I, a thirteen year-old boy, could've seen through his façade.

I've already related how Joseph Singer, one of my fellow orderlies, had deduced that Washington would attack Trenton days before the event. Knobel came to the same conclusion. To his credit, Knobel was patient enough to wait until he knew when the attack would occur. Washington's order to collect all available boats gave Knobel the last piece of information he needed. Using the same logic that Artimis Jones had, Knobel decided that the attack would be on the morning of the 26th of December.

As Knobel related in the memoir he wrote about his role in ending the rebellion, he waited until dusk on the 23rd of December, stole a boat, and crossed the Delaware. He'd been given the name of Andrew Benson, a loyalist in Hunterdon County, as a source of help if he needed it, and the location of Benson's farm. Since he wasn't familiar with the area, he wandered around until two in the morning before finding the farm. As he approached it, Benson's dogs howled an alert. Benson was wary because the Hunterdon County rebels had threatened to kill both him and his family. He almost shot Knobel as an intruder before Knobel could identify himself and explain his mission. Benson gave him a horse and directions to Trenton, then took another horse and set out for Princeton.

Knobel reached Trenton just after dawn on Christmas Eve and alerted Colonel Rall to Washington's plans. The attacks Rall's men had suffered from all directions made Knobel's report believable. What'd been independent action by the men of Hunterdon County and the Pennsylvania Militia looked to Rall like a carefully designed strategy to weaken him. He quickly sent a message to General Leslie in Princeton outlining a plan to defend Trenton. The Hessian regiment from Bordentown would reinforce his regiment and face our army directly. The Highland Scots regiment from Burlington would stay a few miles south of Trenton to block any support for us from that direction, and the two British regiments from Princeton would stay a few miles north and east of Trenton to circle behind us once we had passed.

Rall could only suggest his plan. Orders to move the other regiments had to come from General Grant in Brunswick, Commander of the British Army in New Jersey. Leslie relayed Rall's plan to Grant, who issued the necessary orders. Everything was put in place to trap our army.

Hunterdon County loyalists alerted the British and Hessians to our river crossing. Colonel Rall knew that our army was back in New Jersey three hours after the first of our soldiers had landed. He received a steady flow of reports about the slow progress we were making. He correctly guessed that we would not be in Trenton until well after sunrise, so he let his exhausted soldiers sleep until six o'clock. By this time the Hessians knew they had a few more hours and were able to have breakfast before assembling to confront us.

General Leslie also knew of our army's movements three hours after they started. Since his troops had to march twelve miles to Trenton, they didn't have the luxury of sleeping late. They were awoken at four in the morning and were marching towards Trenton an hour later. They arrived just in time to get into position to circle behind us once we had passed.

I have already related the details of the battle, short as it was. There's no need to repeat them.

Colonel Rall had been a soldier all his life and lacked the polished manners of most officers. He spoke nothing other than the coarse German dialect used by his soldiers. But he treated his men with sympathy and kindness, a rarity in any army, and they were devoted to him. Few officers would have let their men sleep later or have breakfast with an enemy army on its way.

After Washington handed his sword to the British captain, Rall joined the group of officers gathering in mid-meadow. Since he was junior to General Leslie and didn't speak any English, he was ignored. "*Scheisse bei scheiss,*" shit upon shit, I could hear him curse. It was his plan and his victory, yet he was being ignored. Histories of the Great Rebellion usually give Colonel Rall the credit he deserves, but he is nowhere to be seen in the picture most people remember, Thomas Gainsborough's famous painting, *Washington Surrendering to Leslie.* Gainsborough shows the winter sun breaking through the clouds to illuminate Leslie's face. It's a nice artistic touch, but the sun didn't shine on anyone that morning.

After the end of the rebellion, the British hailed General Howe as a hero and an exemplar of military wisdom. The Hessians were less kind. They claimed that the rebellion could have ended weeks, if not months, earlier if they had been given a free hand to pursue Washington. They faulted Howe for not destroying our army in New Jersey, for allowing what they considered no more than a peasant rebellion to proceed for as long as it did, and for leaving Colonel Rall in an exposed position at Trenton. The controversy rose to such a pitch that Howe felt compelled to answer the Hessian charges. He claimed that his strategy saved lives – British, Hessian, and rebel – by letting our army fade away. He said he would've been happy to wait until spring to destroy whatever remained of our army, but that Washington's ill-conceived attack had made waiting unnecessary. I'm sure historians will still be debating Howe's strategy a hundred years from now.

Americans, both loyalist and rebel, said little about the rebellion until the war against the French brought us firmly back into the British family. After that a flood of American memoirs appeared. It was only then that most people learned of the suffering and loss on both sides.

CHAPTER 8

The sides of the barn the Hessians had chosen as our prison had many gaps, allowing in enough light for us to see. After considerable pushing and shoving, we found places to rest. I sat against the wall of a stall that smelt of cow manure. It was comforting after the agony of the march and the horror of the battle. Inside the barn was no warmer than outside, but we were sheltered from the wind and, after a few minutes, I stopped shivering.

Three Hessian privates guarded us. They were warmly dressed in grey greatcoats, hats, and gloves and wore thick woollen scarves around their necks. Their boots gleamed, even in the mud of the barn floor. They were model soldiers, making me even more aware of how rag-tag our army had been.

"What will happen to us?" one of the other prisoners asked.

The Hessians showed no signs of comprehension. A few more questions established that they spoke no English.

"Anyone here speak German?" the prisoner finally asked.

"I do."

"Try to find out what's going to happen to us."

Rather than asking that question directly, I started by asking our guards their names.

"*Was sind Ihre Namen?*" Two of them pointed their muskets at me, but the oldest and fattest of the three smiled. He seemed happy to finally understand something that was being said.

"*Ich bin Dietrich*," he said pointing to himself. "*Er ist Thomas*," he continued, pointing to the tallest one, "*Und er ist Heinrich*," pointing to the third guard, who was short with brown eyes.

"*Vielen dank. Ich bin* William," I said to thank him and introduce myself. He started to put out his hand to shake mine, then pulled it back, realizing that he was supposed to be guarding, not befriending, me.

"*Was mit uns geschehen wird?*" I asked.

"*Ich weiß nicht.*" Dietrich shrugged his shoulders to signify that he didn't know what would happen to us. Several more questions received the same answer.

Noon came and went, but we received neither food nor water. I should've been hungry, but if I was, I hadn't noticed it in the turmoil. I hadn't even eaten the stale bread in my pocket. For water we sucked on icicles, which we broke from the barn rafters. Several of the prisoners had been wounded, but we could do nothing for them. The worst was a blond-haired man who had been shot in the belly and moaned piteously. He died in the early afternoon.

"Dietrich," I called, "a man has just died. Can we move his body out of the barn?"

There was a hurried conference, then a blunt response. "*Nein*, you will keep him there."

We moved his body to a corner and several prisoners kept watch to chase away the rats that were certain to be in the woodwork.

Our guards wouldn't let us out to relieve ourselves. With a hundred men in the barn and no latrine, the air soon became foul. The sleet and snow of the morning had turned into a light rain. It must have been about four p.m. because the winter sun was barely above the horizon. I returned to the stall where I'd claimed space. It was empty. The rest of the prisoners were congregated in the little bit of light at the centre of the barn, like children afraid of the dark. I sat head down against the wall in the growing darkness, thinking things couldn't get worse, when I heard a hoarse voice say, "What've we here? A pretty young lad who's going to be my fag."

I turned to see a big, stocky man, with at least three days' growth of heavy black beard on his face. He was clad in the ragged clothes that were the rebel army's uniform and his feet were bundled in rags. His breath reeked of rotten teeth.

"Come here, boy," he said, making a grab for my left shoulder. "Don't make me hurt you."

I scuttled away. He made another grab and this time caught me. I struggled to get out of his grasp and kicked at his legs, but to no avail.

"Leave the lad alone," a voice with a strong Scottish burr said.

"This is none of your affair."

"I said leave the lad alone." My protector appeared out the shadows. He was smaller than the man holding me, dressed in dirty buckskins, and wearing shoes rather than rags. My assailant let go of me and lunged at him, but my protector side-stepped easily and punched the big man in the face as he lurched past. My assailant turned quickly, but the Scotsman was ready and punched him in the gut. He followed with a kick to the groin. The big man fell in a heap. My protector kicked him several times in the head and ribs as he lay there groaning, after which he was silent. The fight occurred in what seemed like no more than fifteen seconds.

"Are ye harmed, laddie?"

"No, sir," I said, my whole body shaking from what I had just experienced. "Thank you for protecting me."

"What's your name?"

"William Watson, sir."

"Well, young Will," he said, sticking out his hand, "I'm Donald Mackenzie."

"My name is William, sir," I said, shaking his hand.

"Feisty, aren't you? Aye then, William, it is."

Donald studied the prostrate body on the floor for a moment before administering another kick.

"That lout will probably come after both of us when he wakes up. Sit by me. I was planning to depart these premises tonight anyway. Perhaps you should leave with me. Travelling alone is never a good idea, especially in the winter. And you speak German, which might come in handy if we run into Hessians."

He said this so casually that my jaw dropped. But his manner reassured me, and I followed him to the next stall. The other prisoners, who'd watched the fight, quickly moved out of our way.

"The Hessians'll starve us," he said matter-of-factly, as if it should've been obvious to me. "In three days we won't have the strength to escape. It's now or never."

I was too stunned to reply.

"What's wrong? Cat got your tongue?"

"But where will we go? The Hessians are all around. They'll shoot us."

"First they have to catch us. If I can escape from the Cherokee, I can certainly outwit a bunch of clumsy Hessians."

"You escaped from the Cherokee?"

"I did indeed, but it wasn't easy. I'll tell you about it sometime."

I was still pondering this turn of events when Donald said, "If you come with me, you'll have to follow my orders quickly and without question. Will you do that?"

"Yes," I said hesitantly, not knowing what I was promising.

"You're certain?"

"Yes, sir," I replied, in a louder, and I hoped, more confident, voice.

"Aye then. Get some sleep. We'll leave when it's dark." With that, he closed his eyes.

I sat there for a while as all sorts of visions floated through my head. I was standing against a wall in front of a Hessian firing squad as the officer-in-charge called, "Ready." I was climbing up the stairs to my grandparents' home above the ironmongery shop. I was in our kitchen in Graves End, watching my mother knead bread for baking. After a while I fell asleep.

The next thing I knew a hand was shaking my shoulder. "Wake up, William. Time to go." Slowly, as my eyes got used to the dim light, I made out the form of Donald Mackenzie standing above me. I stood up, adjusted my clothes, and followed him to the closed barn door. A half dozen other prisoners were gathered near it, also intent on escape.

"Let them go first," Donald said in a low voice. "They'll flush out whatever Hessian guards are still around."

Very slowly one of the prisoners eased the door open wide enough to squeeze through. Its hinges creaked with what seemed like the loudest sound in the world. I expected a Hessian guard to come running, but none appeared. The group of prisoners rushed through the door. I started to follow them, but Donald put his hand on my shoulder.

"Wait just a little while longer," he said.

I heard shouts of *halten sie,* then a musket shot.

We peered around the open barn door and, by the light of the full moon and a few stars, could see Hessian soldiers running towards the woods to our right. We could see none in the other direction. Donald waited for another half minute, then said, "Now, William," giving me a gentle push towards the woods on the left.

The rain had ceased and the temperature was still above freezing. I could see well enough to avoid walking into a tree, but with every branch dripping melting snow and ice, there was no way to stay dry. The ground was covered with slush and we were leaving a clear trail for the Hessians to follow. I wanted to go back to the barn but couldn't. The sodomizer was still there and I wouldn't have Donald to protect me.

After we had progressed a quarter mile into the woods, Donald found a large pine tree that provided some shelter.

"Stay here. I'll be back shortly," he said as he disappeared into the trees.

The position of the moon told me he'd been gone less than an hour, but it seemed like an eternity. The wind was calm, no leaves rustled or trees creaked. The weather had silenced the owls. The only sounds I could hear were my own breathing and the steady drip of water. The limbs of the tree I was under blocked my view. I was tempted to leave my den to explore but fearful that I'd miss Donald's return. I could only sit there as the hour-long minutes slowly passed.

I must have dozed off because the next thing I remember is Donald Mackenzie shaking me awake. This time he was holding two muskets and a large, bulging sack.

"We're in luck, William. Most of the Hessians are drunk from celebrating their victory. They won't miss the muskets and food I've collected for a while."

With that Donald pulled a bayonet and a ham from the sack. He carved a thick slice of meat and handed it and the bayonet to me. He retrieved another bayonet and carved an even thicker slice for himself. There was silence for the next few minutes whilst we filled our bellies. Besides the ham, we had roasted potatoes and hard tack for our supper. The sack also produced a canteen of water.

"Sorry there's no rum," he said with a laugh. "The Hessians emptied the hogshead."

"You'll have to do better next time," I replied.

He quickly turned serious. "The Hessians'll be out and about in the morning. We need to be far away from here by daybreak."

We finished eating and each took a musket. Donald handed me a cartridge box and a canteen from the sack. I stuck my bayonet in my belt and strapped on the rest of the equipment. Donald did the same and slung the no longer bulging sack over his shoulder. Except for the bayonets, we looked like impoverished hunters. They would've carried knives, which are shorter than bayonets. But if we were lucky no one would look closely enough to tell the difference. Our ragged clothes gave no indication that we'd been soldiers. I realized that if we were to survive, we needed to hide the fact that we'd been in the rebel army.

"We'll cover our tracks by going back the same way Washington came," Donald said.

We cautiously made our way through the woods until we reached the road our army had taken on its way to Trenton. The slush contained so many footprints that two more sets would make no difference, even if they were going the wrong way. We were wary, but didn't meet anyone, Hessians or escaped prisoners. No one else would have been wandering about that night. Once we found our army's tracks, following them was simple. Even when I couldn't see the path, the slush under foot told me that I was going the right way.

As we walked, I told Donald my life's story – how I'd been left an orphan, joined the rebels, and become an orderly for General Washington. Donald told me that he had been born on the Isle of Lewis in the Hebrides in 1745, the year that Bonnie Prince Charlie, the last of the Stuarts, raised the flag of rebellion. His father was a poor crofter, who, even though he knew the cause was doomed, joined the rebellion. He was taken prisoner at Culloden the next year, when the English defeated the Scots, but he escaped.

"My father told me that life in Scotland was never easy, but after the rebellion it became impossible for a Scotsman to feed his family. Somehow he scrounged up enough money to bring our family to Philadelphia when I was seven."

"So you were part of the Pennsylvania Militia."

"No. After a few years, my father made enough money to buy a wagon and took our family to North Carolina. First, we lived near the Moravians in Bethabara. Good people, the Moravians. They helped our family, even though we're Church of Scotland. Then we moved a little farther west and my father bought a farm in the Yadkin Valley from Squire Boone, my friend Daniel's father."

I'd never heard of Bethabara or the Moravians, but rather than ask about them, I wanted to know how Donald had ended up in the battle. "Which regiment were you with? There weren't any North Carolina Militia in our army."

He told me that when the colonies rebelled, he'd been in Virginia and had joined the company commanded by General Washington's cousin, William Washington. That's why he was close to the general when we surrendered. The Hessians didn't care which regiment you'd belonged to. Where you were standing on the battlefield at the time of the surrender determined which group of prisoners you ended up in. I was the only orderly close to Washington when he surrendered and thus the only orderly in the barn.

"Now we need to get away from the English and their Hessian servants," Donald said. "This rebellion is over and the damn English have won again. They'll grind us under their heels, just as they ground Scotland down."

"But how are we going to cross the river?"

"*But, but, but.* Have you no imagination, lad? We'll go back to the ferry and steal one of the boats the rebels left there. It shouldn't be difficult. We'll cross the river and make our way to Philadelphia. My father worked for a merchant named Angus McNeil when we lived there. They remained friends. He'll be easy to find if he still has his shop in Walnut Street. I'm sure he'll help me get back to North Carolina."

"To your father's farm?"

"No, I live south of there. I trade with the Cherokee for deerskin. I don't like farming. It ties a man too close to one place. I want to spend my time in the forest, not walking behind the arse end of a horse or an ox."

"I know what you mean," I said, even though I didn't. I knew nothing of life in the forest, or trading with Indians, or any of the other things that Donald was talking about. I knew that North Carolina was one of the southern colonies, but that's all I knew about it. My teacher Mr Anderson thought it more important to teach us the history and geography of Britain than that of the other colonies.

"You can come with me if you like. We'll have to work for a while in Philadelphia to earn enough money for the trip, but you don't look like a lad who is afraid of work."

I quickly said yes.

"You know I seem to be reliving my father's life. He was a soldier in a rebellion that failed. He was taken prisoner, but he escaped. He went to Philadelphia. He had to work for a while to make enough money to go to North Carolina. Here I am thirty years later doing the same thing."

"But he has a happy life in North Carolina."

"*But* again. Don't you know any other word? Yes, my father had a happy life in North Carolina for many years. He died four years ago, and my mother shortly afterwards. Like you, William, I'm alone."

After that we were both quiet for a long time.

Dawn found us on the Bear Tavern Road, less than two miles from where we'd crossed the Delaware scarcely thirty hours earlier.

"It's going to be too light for us to steal a boat," Donald announced. "We'd better hide until dark."

We found a collapsed shed and crawled in. Donald's sack provided more ham and hard tack. I was exhausted and soon fell asleep. When I awoke many hours later, the sun was low in the sky. It was nearly three p.m., about two hours before dark. Donald seemed not to need much sleep. He was awake and obviously had been busy. Instead of two sets of footprints in the slush, there were many. He'd walked back and forth enough times to make it look like our army had used the shed.

"I trust the young master has had a restful sleep," was his sarcastic greeting.

I didn't answer but left the shed to relieve myself.

"We'll leave as soon as it's dark and find a boat," Donald said when I returned. "You stand watch for a while. I'm going to get some sleep."

I hadn't looked carefully at Donald Mackenzie the day before, but now I studied him as he slept. He was medium height and wiry. He had fair skin and the tan of a man who spent most of his time outdoors. His hair was light, not quite blond, and I'd seen earlier that he had blue eyes. He wore stained buckskins, and his shoes were so worn that I couldn't tell much about them. He didn't snore.

Since I was supposed to keep watch, I stared out through a crack in the shed wall. Nothing was moving in the fading daylight. After a while my mind began to wander. I wasn't a very good sentry.

Donald Mackenzie had saved me from sodomy and starvation, and I was grateful, but should I follow him blindly? Life over my grandfather's ironmongery shop might not be pleasant, but it would be safer than going off into the wilderness with Donald. But if I left him now, I would have to make my way alone across New Jersey, which was swarming with brigands and British soldiers. Going with him as far as Philadelphia and making some money seemed like a good idea. I could decide later what to do.

Night had fallen and it was time to wake Donald up. I touched his shoulder, but before I could say anything, he stood up, fully alert. We ate the last of the food he'd stolen, left the shed, and followed our army's tracks to McConkey's Ferry.

The trip down the embankment that we'd so painfully climbed two nights before was equally challenging. I lost my footing and began to slide.

"Grab a tree branch," Donald yelled.

I did and was able to stop myself. Donald grabbed a branch on a nearby tree and we both stood there for a moment whilst I caught my breath.

"It's too slick for us to walk down. We'll have to slide on our arses. Dig your feet in to keep from going too fast."

With that he sat down and began to slowly slide down the slope. I did the same. In a few seconds, my pants were soaked and my rear end was freezing, but it was safer than trying to walk. It took no more than two minutes to get to the riverbank, by which time I was shaking with cold. Donald quickly ducked under a pine tree to grab handfuls of dry twigs and pine needles. Next, he found a birch tree and pulled off a large piece of bark. He rolled this into a ball and set it down. Then he tore open a paper cartridge, poured some gunpowder over the birch bark, and set it ablaze with a spark from his musket.

"Find wood, the driest you can," he ordered.

I rushed to this task, whilst Donald built the fire he'd started. When I returned with my first armful of wood, he had a roaring blaze going.

"We need to start a second fire so that we can dry both our fronts and backs at the same time. Bring more wood."

I quickly gathered a second armful of wood, by which time Donald had a second, smaller fire going. We spent several more minutes gathering wood for the two fires then stood between them to dry our clothes.

"Birch bark's a wonder for starting a fire," he said. "It'll burn even if it's wet. You just need something to get it started."

I said nothing, too cold to talk.

"Well, William, we've announced our presence to any Hessians who might be wandering these woods," Donald said after we'd both warmed up. "But it's better than freezing to death."

A few minutes later he took his musket and headed upstream, along the river bank. He soon reappeared.

"We're in luck again. The militia Washington left to guard the boats are gone and there don't seem to be any English or Hessians around. Let's borrow a boat and get ourselves to Pennsylvania."

I followed him along the riverbank to where the rebels had left their boats. We pulled a small rowboat onto the bank and turned it over to dump out the rainwater it had collected.

"I don't suppose you know how to row one of these?" Donald asked.

"I know how to row a boat. My brother and I used to row out into the harbour to fish."

"Well then, heave to, and get us across the river. I'll stand guard."

I positioned myself at the oars as he pushed the boat off the bank, then jumped in. A short distance from the shore the current took over and I couldn't keep the boat pointed in the right direction. Donald put down his musket, moved behind me and took over the oars. He got the boat back on course and twenty minutes later we were scrambling ashore in Pennsylvania. We pushed the boat back into the current. When he was sure that the boat would float downstream, Donald said, "We can't stay here, lad. We're strangers and we'll stand out too much. I don't want some damn loyalist reporting us to the English Army."

He headed for the road that ran alongside the river. I grabbed my musket and the rest of my gear and followed. He set a fast pace and at times I had to trot to keep up. We kept to the road as much as possible but circled around farms and hamlets. Dozens of dogs announced our presence. Since we didn't approach any of the houses they guarded, they soon lost interest, and no one came out to investigate. We must have covered ten miles before Donald relented. We rested under a large oak tree.

"Are ye all right, lad?"

"Yes, sir."

"Aye then, let's get moving."

He grabbed his musket and was off down the road. I jumped up and had to run for a few minutes to catch up with him.

"Give me a little more warning next time," I said, my breath coming in pants.

"You'll get no warning from anyone who wants to do you harm. You need to be prepared."

We approached a large grey stone farmhouse with a matching barn, a prosperous looking place, just as the sun was coming over the horizon. Instead of circling the buildings as we had been doing all night, Donald walked up the front path towards the house. Dogs howled and a large hound came out to greet us with a menacing growl. Instinctively, I dropped behind Donald.

"Hallo," he called loudly whilst we were still far from the house. The front door opened to reveal a grey-headed man with a full beard, dressed for work and wrapped in a blanket, pointing a rifle towards us.

"What'd you want?"

"My friend, my son, William, and I are travelling to Philadelphia and wonder if you could spare us a bite to eat in the name of Christian charity. We've no money, but we'll be happy to do some chores in exchange." He was taking a big risk. If the farmer was a loyalist, he might hold us prisoners until the British came.

A younger man appeared in the doorway behind the old man. He was similarly attired, and even from a distance, I could see that he was the old man's son.

"They're probably deserters from the rebel army," the son said. "Let's just chase them off. If the British find them here, we'll be in trouble."

"We were with the rebel army, but the rebel army is no more," Donald said calmly. "Washington surrendered to the English two days ago. We escaped and stole these muskets, but we need your help to go farther."

The farmer pondered this news for a moment, then said, "Come have breakfast and tell us your news. I'm Archibald Wainwright and this is my son Tobias." Donald introduced himself.

Mr Wainwright backed out of the doorway and beckoned us into the front room. The hound followed us in. A grey-haired woman was stoking the fire in the fireplace. It was a large room, but curiously empty of the furniture and other accoutrements that you would expect in a farmhouse.

"Leave your weapons by the door," Mr Wainwright said. Then, turning to the woman, he added, "Mrs Wainwright, these men will be joining us for breakfast. They say Washington has surrendered to the British."

"Thank God," she said. "I hope this means that the rebellion is over and that we can go back to leading a normal life instead of hiding everything." I noticed she had no words of welcome for us.

"I wouldn't take my belongings out of hiding yet," Donald said. "The Hessians'll be here soon and they'll be interested in only two things, women and plunder."

"You can wash at the rain barrel out back, then have a seat at the table," Mr Wainwright said pointing to the wood plank table along the far wall of the room.

I was bursting with questions as Donald and I walked out to the rain barrel. "Why did you tell him we'd escaped from the Hessians?"

"Later, William. Just stay quiet for now. I'll tell you if you should speak."

By the time we returned, there was a roaring fire in the fireplace and the table had been set with wooden trenchers. We took our places. Mrs Wainwright brought a large bowl of porridge, a plate of bread and cheese, a jug of water, and some wooden spoons, then joined us.

"Lord, make us truly grateful for thy bounty," Mr Wainwright prayed. "And bring thy blessing of peace unto this land."

We all said, "Amen."

After a few seconds of silence, he looked at us and said, "Fill your plates and tell us about Washington's surrender."

"Three nights ago," Donald began, "Washington's army crossed the Delaware to attack the Hessians."

"That's impossible," Tobias interrupted. "There was a nor'easter that night."

"Tobias, let Mr Mackenzie tell his story," Mr Wainwright scolded. "You can judge its truthfulness when he's finished." Tobias shrank back after this reprimand.

"Please continue, Mr Mackenzie."

"Tobias is right," Donald said. "There was a nor'easter that night, but we crossed the river anyway and marched to Trenton in the midst of the storm. We thought we could surprise the Hessians in the morning, but when we got there, they were ready for us. So were the English. They circled behind us and we were trapped. Washington surrendered and we were all taken prisoner. My son and I escaped. We're trying to get to Philadelphia."

"We've seen no soldiers since the rebels were here before Christmas," Mr Wainwright said. "Do you know where the British and Hessians are?"

"No, but I'm sure they'll cross the river soon and take Philadelphia. I hope that we can get to there before they do," Donald replied.

"Why are you heading to where the British will be?"

"We need help and that's where I have friends."

"You still have fifteen miles to walk, but you should reach Philadelphia by early afternoon. You'd best be on your way quickly. Eat your breakfast and Mrs Wainwright will give you some food for your dinner."

When we'd finished, Mrs Wainwright gave Donald and me some bread and jerky wrapped in a square of cloth. She seemed none too happy about this, but her husband had instructed her to do so. We thanked her and Mr Wainwright, collected our muskets, and headed towards the road. The hound that'd seemed so threatening when we approached the farm was friendly now and followed us for several hundred yards. As we walked, I noticed Donald glancing back at the farmhouse until it was out of sight. I asked him why he was doing that.

"I thought we could trust the Wainwrights," he answered, "but you must always be careful. If Mr Wainwright was going to alert the English, he would've sent Tobias to the nearest garrison as soon as we left. I wanted to be sure that no one was rushing away from the farm to report on us."

We walked about half a mile farther as I pondered what being careful meant.

"If we have to be careful, why'd you tell Wainwright that we had escaped from the Hessians?"

"It was a chance I had to take. When Tobias said that he was worried about the British, I guessed they were like most of the farmers around here and didn't want any trouble from either the English or the rebels. Loyalists would have welcomed us, then held us captive until they could turn us over to the nearest English garrison."

"You told them I was your son."

"It was easier than explaining who you were. Did I offend you?"

"No, I don't care."

Secretly, I was pleased. I'd loved my father, but he was dead, and Donald MacKenzie seemed like an ideal second father to me.

It was a clear, cold day and we were on a good road. The miles slipped by easily. Even though I had no idea what fate awaited me, I felt safer than I had since re-joining the rebel army.

CHAPTER 9

We reached a hamlet of a dozen buildings about two miles from Philadelphia in the early afternoon and sat next to a public well eating our bread and jerky.

"Right then, let's find Angus McNeil," Donald said when we'd finished. He picked up his musket and we started walking towards the centre of Philadelphia. We were the only ones on the road, which passed through a long stretch of trees. Perhaps it was because the afternoon was sunny and pleasant, or because our bellies were full, or because we were so close to our destination, but we were no longer wary. We paid little attention ten minutes later to the man, dressed in the rags that were the uniform of the rebel army, leaning against a tree to our left. He must have circled around us because a hundred yards down the road he and an equally unkempt companion confronted us.

"Your money or your lives," the first one said, pointing a pistol at us. He was about Donald's size. The second one, who was smaller in stature, stood holding his pistol, looking perplexed. We had our muskets, but were carrying them at our sides, and for safety's sake they weren't cocked. The thieves could've shot one or both of us before we had time to fire.

"My friend, that's a line from storybooks," Donald said. "I've got no money and I don't think you're man enough to take my life." My heart was pounding, but he seemed amazingly calm.

Donald's reply confused the first thief. His pistol was cocked, but he didn't fire. Donald charged and hit him across the ribs with the barrel of his musket.

The second thief grabbed me and held his pistol to my head. "Don't move or I'll shoot," he said. I stood as still as I could in his grip as the sour taste of bile filled my mouth. We could see that Donald had overcome the first thief and was beating him senseless. The second thief slowly pulled me back to put some distance between Donald and us.

The melee ended after no more than a minute with the first thief lying unconscious on the ground, his pistol now secure in Donald's belt. "Let the lad go," he ordered the second thief.

"Only if you let me go."

"I'll not hurt you."

The thief released me, then turned and ran. I jumped to the side as quickly as I could. Donald charged after him and, using his musket as a club, hit him on the side of his head. The man fell, as senseless as his companion. His pistol discharged harmlessly as it hit the ground.

"Shall we continue on our way?" Donald said, dusting himself off after he'd caught his breath. He was bleeding slightly from a cut lip but didn't seem to notice.

I was still shaken and speechless. Donald had just fought two thieves who could've killed us, but he sounded like he'd completed some minor chore.

"I knew those two were amateurs when both of them stood in front of us. If they'd been more skilled, one of them would have confronted us whilst the other got behind us."

"Oh," was the only thing I could think of saying.

"And the one who grabbed you should've held you until he was a good distance from me."

"You think you killed him?"

"Nah, I'm sure his head was too hard."

Donald picked up the pistol on the ground and held it out to me, but I shook my head no. I didn't know how to use a pistol, and as shaken as I was, it didn't seem like a good time to learn.

"Take the gun, William," he ordered. "We can't leave it here for these two and I've no way to carry it."

Reluctantly, I took the pistol and stuck it in my belt, as I'd seen Donald do. It was unloaded and he didn't tell me to load it.

It took us another half hour to reach the centre of Philadelphia. I paid no attention to my surroundings, but intently studied each man we passed, trying to judge whether he could be another robber. We saw no British or Hessian soldiers, but news of Washington's surrender must have reached the city. The few men on the streets – there were no women – seemed intent on getting where they were going as quickly as possible. With pistols in our belts and muskets in our hands, we looked dangerous. We had to ask three men for directions to Walnut Street before one would stop long enough to answer our questions.

Angus McNeil's shop was at number 34. Its sign read Provisions and General Merchandise, but the shop's door was closed and its windows shuttered. Donald rapped on the door with the lion-headed brass knocker.

"Who goes there?" a voice called out.

"It's Donald Mackenzie, Robert's son. I've got a lad named William Watson with me."

The door opened slowly and we saw a short, bald, rotund man holding a musket, which was pointed down at the floor rather than towards us. He was bundled up in a greatcoat, hat, scarf, and gloves, even though he was inside.

"Good God, what happened to you?" Mr McNeil asked.

"We were accosted by two thieves about an hour ago. I imagine they're waking up about now with very sore heads," Donald replied.

"I trust you're not hurt."

"Only a few bruises and this cut lip."

"And the boy?"

"Probably scared out of a few years' growth, but other than that he's fine. Right, William?"

"Yes," I said.

Was this the way men were supposed to act, making light of danger once it had passed? My father had taught me that men didn't cry or complain, but that was over little things, like hitting your finger with a hammer. The Battle of Brooklyn was the only time I saw him in a truly dangerous situation. He'd acted as fearlessly as Donald had, but I never got the chance to hear how he would've talked about the battle afterwards. Major Gist, Sergeant Roidan, and the other Marylanders who survived didn't say much about the battle. They didn't complain, but neither did they joke about it. I still had much to learn about the ways of men, but there was no one to ask. My father was dead and I was afraid that if I asked Donald he'd think less of me.

"Come in, come in," Mr McNeil said. "We don't want to be standing here in the street inviting more trouble."

He quickly closed and bolted the door behind us. We were in his shop, but other than a high stool and a counter in the middle of the room, it was bare, just like the Wainwright's farmhouse that morning. There was no fire in the fireplace.

"So, you're Donald. The last time I saw you, you were only twelve years old. And how is your father? I haven't heard from him in years."

"He died four years ago."

"May God rest his soul. What brings you to Philadelphia in these evil times?"

Donald explained that we'd been taken prisoner after the rebel defeat but had escaped, then he asked for Mr McNeil's help. "We've no money. Can you give us work?"

Mr McNeil's face brightened as if he had just found the solution to a problem. He told us that Philadelphia had been under rebel martial law for the past three weeks and that all commerce, except for public houses, had stopped. When news of Washington's defeat reached the city two nights ago, the militia that had been keeping the peace disappeared as quickly as drops of water off a hot stove. Thieves and vandals, like the two we'd encountered, had been running wild ever since. He'd driven one of them off the previous night with his musket.

"I need the two of you as guards. Even though the shop is empty, I've got my furniture and belongings upstairs," he said, glancing at the staircase in the corner of the room. "And the vandals might decide to burn the place just to see the fire."

"What will you pay us?" Donald asked.

"I can feed you and give you a place to sleep, but I can't give you any wages," Mr McNeil replied. Then he looked at me. "William, could you fire that musket at a thief?"

I said I could. I didn't tell him that my duties in the rebel army never involved firing a musket. He was offering us food and shelter and I wasn't going to say anything that might make him change his mind.

"Mr McNeil, you've hired two guards," Donald said, before McNeil could say anything more.

"Good. I tell you it's been frightening to be here alone." McNeil sat on the stool by the counter, his body slumped as if he was resting after a hard day's work. "You'll sleep in the attic. There're two straw ticks on the floor and quilts to keep you warm."

Donald waited a minute before continuing.

"We need to set up a watch. Are any of your neighbours still here?"

"DuPre, the silversmith next door, has remained. The rest have left."

"Does he have a musket?"

"I believe he has a pistol."

"Good. Why don't you ask him to join us for a few minutes?"

McNeil left, then returned within five minutes with a tall, thin man so bundled up in a greatcoat, hat, and scarf that I could see little of his face. McNeil introduced us, then Donald quickly described his plan. Each of us, McNeil, DuPre, Donald, and I, would stand two-hour watches through the night. If there was any trouble, we were to bang on a kettle as an alarm. The other three would come running. Four guns should be enough to scare off anything short of a mob. We would guard as much of the neighbourhood as we could, even the vacant houses. DuPre agreed and said that he and his daughter, Sarah, would move into Mr McNeil's house for greater safety. They would join us for supper.

"Will there be work for us once you open your shop again?" Donald asked after DuPre left.

"Possibly," Mr McNeil answered. "I employed two men, a warehouseman and a clerk. Both left a month ago to join the rebel army. If they come back before I open my shop, I'm honour-bound to restore their employment, and there's not enough work for anyone else."

"Well, if they're still alive, they're probably sitting in a Hessian prison."

Mr McNeil didn't respond to Donald's comment but turned to me.

"William, can you reckon and write in a decent hand?"

"I can, sir."

He handed me a slate and a piece of chalk.

"Write five bushels Indian corn at one and six each, four hams at a half crown each, and two quarts of maple syrup at three shillings each then tell me the total."

"One pound, three shillings, six pence," I replied after a few seconds, silently thanking Mr Anderson for his never-ending arithmetic drills.

"You'll do," he said after studying the slate.

Since I had his approval, I felt bold enough to ask, "Why's there no fire in your fireplace?"

"Smoke might invite unwelcome visitors. But with the two of you to help guard this place, I think we can lay a fire in the stove. Why don't you do that? You'll find everything you need by the fireplace."

After I had a good fire going, Donald and I went to the attic to look at our new home. We deposited the bayonets and pistols we were carrying. The bayonet hadn't bothered me – it was only a knife with a long blade – but the pistol had been held to my head. I wanted to forget that if I could.

At dusk there was a rap on the door. DuPre and his daughter Sarah quickly entered. She, like her father, was bundled up against the cold. I paid little attention to her that first time I saw her – I was too worried about my duties as guard.

Over a supper of Indian cornbread and dried cod, Donald and I learned that both McNeil and DuPre were widowers. Mr McNeil's wife had died six years earlier. He lived by himself in three rooms above the shop, one of which the DuPres now occupied. He had two grown sons, neither of whom lived in Philadelphia. Angus Jr, who had his own family, was a merchant in Germantown, seven miles to the northwest. Mr McNeil went on at great length about the antics of Sally and John, his grandchildren. George, his other son, had been the first mate on a brig that traded up and down the coast. When the British blockade made trade too risky, he joined the Pennsylvania Militia. Mr McNeil was worried for his safety.

Mr DuPre's wife had died two years earlier. Sarah was his only surviving child. They lived in rooms behind his shop.

Donald took the first watch, which began when everyone headed to bed. I had the second, two hours later. This meant that Donald had another watch in the early morning, but he didn't seem to care.

Nothing happened that first night, but on the second night, whilst I was standing watch at Mr McNeil's front door, I heard sounds coming from the street. It was late and no one should've been out. I banged the kettle and Donald, McNeil, and DuPre were quickly at my side, their weapons at the ready. I told them that I'd heard sounds from the Mr DuPre's shop and home next door.

"Open the door, William," Donald said. "Let's see what's happening."

I opened the door and saw three men trying to force open the shutter on Mr DuPre's house with their knives. They were so intent on their task they didn't see us line up behind them.

"Drop your knives," Donald ordered.

The three turned around. When they saw that they were facing three muskets and a pistol, they quickly dropped their knives. The one in the middle had a pistol in his belt.

"Hand your pistol butt first to young William here," Donald told him. "And if you try anything untoward, I'll be happy to put a musket ball in your skull." Then he turned to me. "Give your musket to Mr McNeil and collect the pistol."

When I stepped forward to take the pistol, I could see that its owner was sweating. The man to his right seemed to be praying, whilst the one to his left was staring intently at Donald as if searching for a way to attack.

"You gentlemen are lucky," Donald said, once I had the pistol safely out of the reach of the intruders. "I could execute you on the spot. But I've decided to be lenient. Take off your shoes and pants, and run to whatever hole you call home."

"That ain't lenient, Gov'nor," the thief on the right whined in a pure Cockney accent. "I'll catch me death a'cold."

"Stop snivelling, Alf, you coward," the one in the centre said.

They took off their shoes and pants, then left as quickly as they could, given that they were shoeless. The last we saw of them were three naked arses disappearing in the light of the nearly full moon.

"I don't think we'll see those three again," Donald said after they were out of sight. "Mr McNeil, why don't you take the watch? William's done a night's work already."

We collected the pants and shoes, and discovered that one of the men had shit himself. We guessed it was Alf.

"Toss those in the outhouse pit," Donald told me. "The rest can go to the poorhouse."

Donald, McNeil, and DuPre praised me extravagantly. I didn't care much about what McNeil and DuPre said, but I was very happy to have Donald's praise. Finally, I'd done something to start paying him back for protecting me since the moment we met. I hadn't felt any fear whilst we were confronting the intruders, and realized that I hadn't been in danger with three armed men protecting me. Still, Donald had trusted me to take the pistol. That was something to be proud of.

The next morning Sarah added to the praise I had received. She smiled at me for the first time and I was entranced. She had long black hair that seemed to glimmer, fair skin, and blue eyes. I could feel my face turning red as I stammered, "It was nothing."

Since the shop was closed, there was little to do. Donald and I spent many hours talking to Mr McNeil. He was a cheerful man, but he wasn't hopeful for the future.

"When the damn English and their Hessian mercenaries come, they'll plunder the city. I've hidden my goods as best I can. I hope I've done a proper job of it."

"Won't the British try to restore the peace?" I asked.

"The generals'll want peace, but the common soldiers'll expect some spoils for their efforts. We can live through that, but it's what Parliament will do afterwards that worries me. The rebellion was about money, and what happens next will also be about money."

"I thought the rebels were fighting for their rights as free men," I said.

"Lad," he said, looking at me as if I were a young child, "whatever the politicians say, it's about money. The English spent a great deal of it fighting the French and Indians twenty years ago and they thought the colonies should've paid for that protection. That's why we had the taxes that angered so many." Mr McNeil paused for a moment to be sure I understood him. I nodded to show that I did.

"Now they've spent even more money fighting the rebels," he continued, "and you can be certain they'll want us to pay for that too. We'll have so many taxes that an honest man won't be able to survive."

"My father said that poor men always have to pay rents and taxes."

"Your father was right," Mr McNeil said, "but too many rents and taxes can rob a man of his livelihood. That's what happened in Scotland. After Bonnie Prince Charlie was defeated, the lairds cast their lot with the English and raised rents until a crofter could no longer feed his family. I wasn't a crofter, but life was so difficult for everyone in Scotland that I left and came to Philadelphia."

He paused for a moment and looked at me to make sure that I was paying attention. I sensed he was trying to tell me something important that he wasn't sure I would understand.

"But the English didn't stop with taxes. To be sure that Scotland would never again rebel, they made it a crime for a Scot to wear a tartan or carry arms. I don't know what they'll do here, but the English won't allow another rebellion, even if they have to hang half the men in the colonies."

The British Army arrived four days after Donald and me. They were delayed because General Leslie wanted to curry favour with his superiors. After Washington's surrender, instead of crossing the Delaware and capturing Philadelphia, as he could easily have done, Leslie sent messages to General Grant in Brunswick and General Howe in New York telling them about the Battle of Trenton and asking for instructions. This allowed General Howe to resume direct command and make a triumphal entry into Philadelphia on New Year's Day, 1777, at the head of the British regiments that captured the city. No Hessians were with him. Howe wanted this to be a British victory.

Mr McNeil's worst fears weren't realized. There was some petty thievery, but the army didn't loot the city. Perhaps General Howe realized that if he let his soldiers run wild, they would fan the flames of rebellion, as they had when the British and Hessians plundered New Jersey.

The day after the British Army arrived, two privates armed with muskets came down our street, obviously looking for easy plunder. Donald and I stood by the front door of Mr McNeil's shop, our muskets by our sides. That was enough to convince the privates to look elsewhere. We were lucky. Had the privates decided to fight, the result would've been disastrous. The sound of musket fire would've brought soldiers by the score. We would've been shot on the spot or hanged after a brief trial. It was not a happy thought, but I'd been hired as a guard and it would've been cowardly not to carry out my duties.

Most of the British soldiers left Philadelphia after only three days. At first we didn't know where they went. Rumours abounded, but after a week General Howe announced that he'd dispatched Lord Cornwallis and Generals Grant, Leslie, and Clinton, each with a regiment of British regulars, to capture Boston, Baltimore, Williamsburg, and Charleston. The British Army met no resistance. Within three months the British were back in control everywhere.

Life in Philadelphia quickly returned to its more normal pattern. As soon as everyone realized that it was again safe to be on the streets, shops opened and farmers resumed bringing produce to market. But the city was far from peaceful.

Loyalists, who'd abandoned the city when the rebels took control, returned to reclaim their houses and belongings. In most cases the transfer was peaceful, but there were a few confrontations. Once it became clear that the British Army would support the loyalists in reclaiming their property, the rebel supporters ceased any resistance. Some loyalists attempted to benefit from the situation by claiming more than was rightfully theirs. Most were unsuccessful as clergymen and other respected citizens, whose main interest was keeping the peace, stepped forward to testify as to ownership. But no doubt some fortunes were enhanced and others diminished when it was simply the word of a loyalist against the word of a rebel.

There were also personal scores to be settled. Dead bodies labelled "Rebel" began appearing on the street or floating in the river. General Howe moved quickly to put an end to this violence.

He issued a proclamation saying that it was the role of the army to punish perpetrators of the rebellion. Anyone taking personal vengeance would be breaking the law and would be subject to arrest. The proclamation had little effect until a week later when an army patrol arrested a loyalist they found beating a former rebel. The loyalist was sentenced to ten days bread-and-water, a very light punishment, but it, and a few similar penalties, were sufficient to stop what'd been a growing wave of violence. There was crime in Philadelphia, but it was of the ordinary variety.

News from the countryside was less sanguine. Without the British Army to keep the peace, battles between loyalists and former rebels continued for much longer and with much bloodier outcomes, ending only when there were no longer any scores to be settled. And, as Alexander Hamilton had predicted, some of the rebels who'd plundered British and Hessian supply trains weren't willing to give up the practice just because Washington had surrendered. They didn't limit their activities to the British. Isolated farms and even small villages were attacked. The British Army dealt harshly with these brigands whenever they caught them. Most were hanged without the formality of a trial.

"I'm opening the shop tomorrow," Mr McNeil told Donald and me on our second Sunday in his house. "Donald, you'll be my warehouseman, and William, you'll be my clerk. Your salaries will be two shillings a week plus room and board, but I won't have cash to pay you until I generate some custom. We should only need normal vigilance now that the English Army is patrolling the streets, so you can put away your muskets."

My days as a guard were over. I was happy that I hadn't had to fire my musket.

"Start by uncovering the goods I buried in the garden and basement," Mr McNeil told us.

"The ground is frozen, even in the basement," Donald said. "Can we take a pick to it?"

"No, that'll damage too much of my merchandise. Scrape away the earth as best you can with shovels."

We worked as carefully as we could and managed to recover most of Mr McNeil's inventory in saleable condition.

"You've done a good job," Mr McNeil said when we had finished. "There's some damage, but I guess that couldn't be avoided."

The shop opened, but Mr McNeil's biggest problem was lack of cash. The paper money that the rebels had printed was worthless, and no one seemed willing to spend gold, silver, or even copper coins. Mr McNeil was sure that there was more money around, but that people were hoarding it, uncertain about what the future might bring. I suspected that he, too, had a stash of coins hidden away, but I would've never been so bold as to ask.

The British Army spent freely, but paid with paper receipts that were supposed to be redeemable in the future for gold or silver coins. Merchants had no choice but to accept these and were soon trading them, but not at full value. There was much haggling over how much the paper receipts were worth. Their value changed daily, depending on the latest rumour about when the British might redeem them. Mr McNeil was masterful at obtaining receipts at a low cost and selling them at a higher price. He had me keep meticulous records of these transactions and I soon found that a quarter of his profits were from dealings in receipts. He was careful not to accumulate too many of them. He turned them into goods as quickly as possible.

Barter replaced cash for most of the shop's transactions. I'd watched my father barter some of our farm's produce for goods from the village shop in Graves End. These negotiations had been quick and friendly. This was not always so in Mr McNeil's shop. One day he had to deal with a truculent farmer who wanted to trade his maize for a ham.

"You thief, a bushel of maize is worth more than that scrawny hunk of meat you're calling a ham," the farmer said, glaring at Mr McNeil.

"I can't give it to you for anything less than two and a half bushels," Mr McNeil said calmly.

"You're worse than a Jew. I'll give you a bushel and a half. No more," the farmer said, pounding the shop's counter.

"Two and a half bushels, that's my price. You can always take your custom elsewhere," Mr McNeil replied. They finally settled on two bushels of maize for the ham.

"Why didn't you kick that lout out of the shop when he called you a thief and all those other names?" I asked Mr McNeil when the farmer had left.

"Why should I've done that?" he replied, a wry smile on his face. "It's so much more satisfying to get the better of him in the bargaining. The normal price for that ham is a bushel and two-thirds of maize, and I might've been willing to sell it for a bushel and a half if he'd treated me with courtesy. Because he lost his temper and reviled me, he paid more than he had to."

I was often alone in the shop with nothing to do. Mr McNeil didn't complain if I read at those times. He had a small library, which of course included a Bible, as well as religious works like *The Pilgrim's Progress*. But he also had a full set of Shakespeare's plays and two novels. He allowed me to read *Robinson Crusoe*, which I greatly enjoyed, but quickly grabbed *The History of Tom Jones, A Foundling* from my hands, saying that I was too young for that book.

Mr McNeil had two books in Latin, Ovid's *Metamorphoses* and Caesar's *The Gallic Wars*. I believed Mr Anderson's claim that knowledge of Latin was one of the hallmarks of an educated man. The Great Rebellion had ended my schooling before I learned enough Latin to be proficient, but I saw no reason why I couldn't educate myself. I'd studied Ovid in Mr Anderson's class, so I spent many hours working my way through Caesar, with occasional help from Mr McNeil. He was amused by my effort since he'd found learning Latin one of the more painful aspects of his own education.

Admiral Lord Howe, General Howe's older brother and the senior British officer in North America, placed the colonies under martial law, with himself as the military governor. Anyone who had taken part in the rebellion was subject to arrest, but few arrests were made. There wouldn't have been enough gaols to hold all the guilty. Still Donald and I stayed off the streets as much as possible and told no one that we'd been part of the rebel army.

Admiral Howe moved quickly to re-establish British control. In mid-January, he issued a proclamation abolishing all representative bodies, such as Pennsylvania's Colonial Congress. They had been taken over by the rebels and could not be expected to serve the wishes of the King and Parliament. Even town meetings were banned. But martial law was short lived. Admiral Howe handed over authority to the King's royal governors as soon as they could resume their positions. Magistrates and justices of the peace appointed by the royal governors made decisions at the local level. By early summer all thirteen colonies were ruled as they had been before the rebellion.

CHAPTER 10

W illiam, take that ham and a bottle of maple syrup," Mr Mc-
Neil told me the morning after we learned that the British
Army had resumed quartering soldiers in private homes, one of the
practices the rebels said had led to the rebellion. "We need to pay a
call on Captain McElroy."

"Who's he?"

"He commands the Fifth Company of the Highlanders. He'll be
the one to decide whether any soldiers are quartered in my house."

My face must have shown the concern I felt about meeting a British officer, because Mr McNeil quickly added, "Don't worry. No one
will suspect that a lad as young as you had been in the rebel army."

Captain McElroy had commandeered a fine brick house two
blocks up Walnut Street from Mr McNeil's shop. The Johnsons, the
family who owned the house, had supported the rebels. They were
now forced to live in its cellar. Mr McNeil bribed the sentry at the
front door with a shilling to gain us admission to the captain.

"And who might you be?" was Captain McElroy's less than friendly greeting when we were ushered into the room he used as an office.

"I'm Angus McNeil and this lad is William Watson, my clerk. I
have the shop at number 34. I've come to welcome you to Philadelphia,
as one Scot to another." With this, Mr McNeil signalled me to lay

117

the ham and syrup on the table in front of the captain. He placed a gold coin under the ham, careful to let Captain McElroy see what he was doing.

"That's quite kind of you," the captain said, eyeing the gifts. "And how may I be of service?"

"I ask nothing in return. I'm a poor widower living with my two employees. There's no woman in our house to cook our meals or provide the comforts of a well-kept Scottish home."

"I see," said the captain. "If I quartered my soldiers with you, they'd be poorly looked after."

"I'd do my best to make them comfortable, but I've not got a woman's hand for these matters."

"Good day to you, Mr McNeil, and thank you for your kindness."

"Your servant, Captain McElroy."

I don't know whether it was the bribe or Mr McNeil's argument that was persuasive, but no soldiers appeared at his door demanding sleeping space.

Mr McNeil was right about taxes. At the end of January, a proclamation announced that the customs duties on molasses and tea, the only ones that remained when the rebellion started, would be collected henceforth. In March, Parliament reinstituted the stamp tax it had tried to impose a decade earlier, and the customs duties on glass, paper, paint, and lead it had tried to impose five years before the rebellion. All of these taxes had been withdrawn when the colonists refused to buy British goods.

Nobody grumbled in public, but there were many private complaints. Even Mr McNeil, who had predicted these taxes, had a few choice words to say on the subject. Most of the complaints were against Parliament, but to my surprise, there were also those who blamed the rebels. They argued that the colonies had forced the Parliament to withdraw most of the taxes by refusing to buy British goods, and that if this tactic had been continued, the remaining taxes would have been withdrawn. By going to war the rebels lost the benefit of the embargo and invited even more taxes. Others scoffed at this argument, calling it misguided sophistry. The private complaints didn't grow into public demonstrations. Patrick Henry, Samuel Adams, and the other orators who'd fanned the flames of discontent into open rebellion were either in prison, waiting to be executed, or in hiding.

Taxes and duties could be paid with British Army paper receipts, and the British tax collectors often made change in actual coin. This added to the amount of cash available, and slowly commerce returned to normal. In May, Mr McNeil was able to pay Donald and me two weeks' wages. For the first time in my life, I had money in my pocket that I'd earned myself. Since I wasn't officially a soldier, I hadn't been paid by the rebel army. I was pondering how best to enjoy my bounty, when Donald warned, "Don't spend any more than you have to. We need to save our money for our trip to North Carolina."

I didn't need to spend much money. Mr McNeil had let Donald and me pick out clothes from his stock and charged us a minimal price, which he deducted from our wages. But I needed a razor and a strop. I'd turned fourteen in February and had begun to sprout a beard.

"You didn't need to buy a razor. Ashes could've licked that fuzz off your face," Donald said when he saw my purchases. Ashes was Mr McNeil's grey cat. I'd expected some teasing, but my face turned red anyway and I quickly retreated to our attic bedroom.

Using a razor is not an easily learned skill. The next morning my face was covered with a dozen small cuts. Donald looked at me and grinned but was mercifully silent.

Turning fourteen had another effect. The surges of lust that I had felt occasionally for the past year now became more frequent, especially when Sarah DuPre came into the shop to make purchases, as she did every few days. I was too shy to say anything more to her than was necessary to sell her whatever she'd come to buy. When I saw her in the street, I only said "hello" or "nice day." I marvelled at boys who could stand in a street and chat with every girl who passed.

Stories in the London newspapers that arrived at the end of August told us that on the 4th July 1777, one year after the rebels declared their Declaration of Independence, King George III had granted amnesty for all but ten rebels; five generals: Washington, Lee, Greene, Putnam, and Sullivan; and five politicians: John and Samuel Adams, John Hancock, Patrick Henry, and Thomas Jefferson. All had been captured, transported to England, and imprisoned in the Tower of London. They were put on trial for treason before the House of Lords.

Records of the debates in the House of Commons had been published since 1771, but in 1777, proceedings of the House of Lords were still secret. Some enterprising soul – we never found out who – wrote down every word of the rebels' trial, which he published as a pamphlet titled *The True Record of the Trial of the Ten Colonial Rebels*. Many printers republished the pamphlet and copies of it flooded London. It didn't take long for a copy to make its way to Philadelphia, where a local printer reprinted it. With so many copies in circulation from so many printers, the British could not stop the information. No one was punished, and from that day forth, it was legal to publish records of the debates in the House of Lords.

Mr McNeil bought a copy of the pamphlet about the rebel's trial, when he knew that it was safe to own one, and passed it on to me after he'd read it. The trial of the rebels had been short. There was no question that all were guilty. Each defendant was allowed a final statement before the Lords. None pleaded for leniency, but each, in his own fashion, reiterated the arguments the rebels had used to justify their rebellion. Thomas Jefferson's speech was the most eloquent.

"My Lords," Jefferson began, "in Philadelphia last year, the thirteen United States of America presented you with a declaration of independence and a bill of particulars recounting the injustices that the King had inflicted upon us. I will not recount those injustices, which have only grown in magnitude over the past year. I wish, however, to remind you of the statement we made before the recounting.

"We hold these truths to be self-evident . . . that all men are created equal . . . that they are endowed by their Creator with certain unalienable rights . . . that amongst these are life, liberty, and the pursuit of happiness . . . that to secure these rights, governments are instituted amongst men, deriving their just powers from the consent of the governed . . . that whenever any form of government become destructive of these ends, it is the right of the people to alter or to abolish it.

"My Lords, the King denied the unalienable rights of the citizens of the United States and for this we had the right, nay, the duty, to abolish his government over us. We pledged our lives, our fortunes, and our sacred honours to achieving that end. We failed to do so, and it is within your power to deprive me of my life and fortune. My honour will remain untarnished, for I have served my fellow citizens of the United States to the best of my ability."

Reading Jefferson's words, I questioned whether he had the right to claim that his honour was untarnished. He'd spent the last months of the Great Rebellion safely in Virginia. He hadn't taken part in any of the battles, nor experienced the hardships of the retreat across New Jersey or the agony of the march to Trenton. Yet rhetoric like his, which ignored the cost of rebelling against the King, had led to the suffering and death we experienced. Surely that was a blemish on his honour.

The rebels were hanged publically at Tyburn on 20th August 1777. The London newspapers, which reached us six weeks later, said that over ten thousand people watched and that there was great festivity. Whilst I knew that Washington's hanging was inevitable after his surrender, I still felt a great sadness when I read the news. He'd been kind and generous to me. I admired the courage he'd shown in leading the rebels and his fortitude in surrendering, once the cause was lost. A lesser man would've tried running away.

The news of Washington's hanging led me to wonder what had happened to Klaus Moritz, the other orderlies, and all the people I met during the four months I was with the rebel army. Many died, no doubt, either at the Battle of Trenton or afterwards in British or Hessian prisons. A chapter of my life had ended, but without my knowing many of its details.

I cannot leave the story of those tumultuous times without saying a few more words about Washington. He was an amazing man who commanded deference from all who came into contact with him. I didn't realize it whilst I was with the rebel army, but his soldiers accorded Washington an unparalleled level of respect. In their private conversations, soldiers usually refer to officers either by their last name or by a nickname. Rank is almost never used, unless it's part of the nickname. A Lieutenant too full of himself might be referred to as The General. But rebel soldiers always referred to Washington as General Washington or His Excellency.

Exemplary as he was, Washington had one major flaw, his acceptance of slavery at a time when others had clearly seen its evils. He, like so many other slaveholders, could treat individual Negroes with kindness, whilst taking full advantage of the system of slavery. Billy Lee, his faithful manservant, repaid Washington's kindness as fully as any man could. Lee stayed at Washington's side when he was shipped to England, imprisoned, tried, and hanged, even though he was a free man from the moment he stepped on England's soil. The newspapers reported that he wept as Washington was executed, but said nothing about what happened to him afterwards.

Slavery had been abolished in England in 1772, when Judge Mansfield freed a slave named Somerset. Whilst the Judge's decision was limited to this one slave, slaveholders knew that if Somerset was free, there could be no justification for enslaving any black man. As William Cowper's famous verse put it:

Slaves cannot breathe in England; if their lungs
Receive our air, that moment they are free.

Washington's will, which became public after he was hanged, would've freed Billy. The rest of Washington's hundreds of slaves wouldn't have been freed until his wife Martha died. But Washington's will was moot. His estate, Mount Vernon, one of the finest in the colonies, and his slaves, were forfeit to the Crown.

Donald, Mr McNeil, and the customers who came into the shop knew that Washington and the other rebels had been hanged. No one talked about it; it was too difficult a subject. Any outward show of support or sympathy for the rebels was dangerous. The British wouldn't hang you for that, but they might arrest you or punish you in other ways. Everyone knew that most of the people in Philadelphia had supported the rebels. Speaking openly in support of the British might offend these people, who were friends and neighbours.

Not speaking about politics became a way of life. In Graves End, before the rebellion, the latest statements from this, that, or the other politician seemed to have been the major topic of conversation in Mr Fletcher's tavern and on market day. If there was that much discussion in a hamlet like Graves End, how much more must there have been in Philadelphia? I wasn't astute enough to judge what people were thinking. I didn't know how many who'd supported the rebels still would be willing to fight again, and how many realized that the cause was truly lost and that they'd better make the best of it. Mr McNeil fit in the latter category. I wasn't sure what Donald thought, but I guessed that he, too, realized that any further rebellion was doomed.

Perhaps McNeil had been right when he told me that the rebellion had been about money. If it was about money, it became easier to weigh the profit and loss and decide that fighting again would cost far more than it was worth.

The King and Parliament didn't exact individual punishment, but they did impose a severe communal punishment on the colonies. Suppressing the rebellion had cost many millions of pounds and as Mr McNeil had predicted, Parliament tried to make the colonies pay the bill. It was ingenious in coming up with new ways to extract revenue. New taxes were placed on an increasing number of products until Parliament replaced the hodgepodge with a tax of two shillings per pound of value on all imported or exported goods. Smuggling was rampant and even Mr McNeil, who normally was completely upright in his business dealings, was willing to buy from the unnamed purveyors of goods who appeared at strange hours at the shop's door. These transactions were recorded in a separate ledger that Mr McNeil had me start and keep.

The amnesty allowed me to write to my grandparents to tell them that I was alive and well and to ask about my brother and sister. In the most respectful words I could find, I told them I wouldn't return to their house. My grandfather replied in Dutch, telling me that my sister Charlotte was still living with him and that my brother Richard was apprenticed to a shipping house. He called me an ungrateful child and ordered me to return immediately. I worried about Charlotte. Would Oma be able to shield her from Grootvader's harsh demands? I felt I was being selfish by staying away, but that feeling was not strong enough to make me return to New York. I didn't answer my grandfather's letter.

Now that we were free to travel, Donald started making plans to return to North Carolina. "You're sure you want to come with me, and not return to your grandparents?" Donald asked.

"I don't want to spend my life living over an ironmonger's shop."

"You wouldn't have to do that. You've learned a lot here with McNeil. You could become a clerk for any merchant. I'm sure Mr McNeil would give a good character."

"I'd rather go with you and see the mountains and the Indians who live behind them. I've never seen either."

"So be it. We'll need rifles. The muskets I stole from the Hessians won't be useful for hunting or for protecting ourselves against the Indians. And unless you want to walk five hundred miles, we'll need a horse and wagon. That'll be cheaper than two horses and saddles. And we'll need enough money to buy food along the way and pay the tolls across the rivers. We can't ford the Susquehannah or the Patomack. I reckon that ten pounds cash should be enough. We can probably get a pound more for each of the muskets."

"Ten pounds! Even if we save as much as we can, it'll be another two years before we have the money you say we need."

"Patience, William. Going down the Great Wagon Road will be hard enough. We need the proper outfit."

Donald was right, of course, but the idea of waiting two years before we could start our journey filled me with dismay.

"Have you seen the latest proclamation from the damn English?" Donald asked me one day in September, his voice quivering with anger.

"No, what does it say?"

"The English Army will now strictly enforce the Proclamation Line. No white man will be allowed to cross it."

"Proclamation Line, where's that?" I asked.

"Fifteen years ago, after the English beat the French, King George issued a proclamation limiting settlement to the watersheds of rivers flowing into the Atlantic Ocean. The limit of settlement was called the Proclamation Line."

"Why would they do that?"

"To keep the Indians happy, but now I think they want all of us east of the line so they can keep an eye on us."

"But you say that white men can't even cross the line."

"That's right, and it's madness. Don't the English know the value of the deerskin and beaver pelts that hunters and traders bring back from Indian lands? North Carolina can't survive without that income. And how do they decide who's a white man? Traders have been fathering Indian children for generations. There are so many half-breeds out there, nobody knows who's white and who's Indian anymore. Or is it like with niggers? One drop of nigger blood makes you a nigger. Does one drop of Indian blood make you an Indian?"

The British soon discovered these difficulties and rescinded the ban. It was replaced by a ruling that, unless he was living with his Indian family in an established Indian village, no white man could build a permanent residence west of the Proclamation Line. No mention was made of the few white women living with their Indian families.

The Proclamation Line had not been enforced prior to the Great Rebellion and illegal settlements, such as Boonesborough in Kentucky and Sycamore Shoals in Tennessee, sprang up like mushrooms after a rain. They were now to be destroyed. The army knew their location and squadrons of cavalry were dispatched to carry out the King's orders. Most of their inhabitants fled before the British arrived. The army gave those who remained twenty-four hours to gather up their possessions and leave, then burned their houses, barns, and other buildings, even their churches. Individual homes and farms, which the Indians were more than happy to identify, were burned with less ceremony. Soldiers weren't supposed to plunder the homes of the settlers, but as many have testified, they did.

CHAPTER 11

Mr McNeil's business prospered when he became a supplier to the British regiments stationed in Philadelphia. He paid us our back wages and served better food at our meals. I followed Donald's advice and tried to live as frugally as possible, but it would be a long time before I had my share of the ten pounds we'd need before we could leave.

"How much money have you saved?" Donald asked me one morning in late February.

"Two pounds, five shillings, four pence."

"That's enough. Take a pound, a few shillings, your musket, and the pistol we took from that thief. Mr McNeil gave us the morning off. We're going to the gunsmith's and ordering proper rifles."

I rushed up to the attic and collected my money, musket, and pistol, then followed Donald to the gunsmith's in Cherry Street. His shop was a well-lit room with three workbenches, each with a vice and a wide array of tools. A dozen rifles were mounted on pegs on the wall. Their stocks were made of curly maple with its lovely grain. Some were simple wood; others had inlays of silver. They had brass fittings for their butt plates and patch boxes. The iron of their locks and frizzens didn't have a spot of rust. The gunsmith, Horst Rosenfeld, got up from the nearest work bench. He was a sturdy-looking man in his forties, who wore a leather apron over a linen shirt and wool pants.

"Well, Donald, are you ready to place an order today, or have you just brought this young man along to admire my handiwork?"

"This is William Watson, Mr Rosenfeld, and we're ordering rifles today. We've saved our wages all winter. How much will you give us for these two muskets and two pistols?"

"I don't make or sell pistols," Rosenfeld said, "but let me look at the muskets." He took Donald's and examined it carefully, then scrutinized mine. "Hessian, I see. Care to tell me how you come to have them?"

"Let's just say they were spoils of war."

"No need to say more. Let's go out back and see how they fire."

With that he picked up a powder horn and cartridge box and led us through the shop to his long, narrow rear garden, which was enclosed with a brick wall. He placed a sheet of paper over a bale of straw that sat against the far wall. Then he backed away as far as he could, perhaps twenty yards. He loaded my musket, shouldered it, said "cover your ears," then fired. A flash of flame erupted from the musket barrel, followed by a plume of black smoke. The smell of burnt gunpowder filled the small garden. A hole appeared in the middle of the paper. He repeated the process with Donald's musket. More smoke filled the garden, and a second hole appeared in the paper.

"They're workable. I'll give you one pound credit towards a rifle for each of them."

"Done," Donald replied.

"Let's go back to the shop and fit your rifles. A good rifle is like a fine suit of clothes. It must be personally fitted to its owner," Rosenfeld said, as if he was teaching us a fundamental truth. Then he turned to me.

"How old are you William?"

"I just turned fifteen."

"So you may grow another inch or two."

"I hope so." I was embarrassed by my short stature.

Rosenfeld looked at the rifles in his shop for a moment before picking one with fine inlay work on its stock.

"Hold this one in firing position," Rosenfeld instructed. It fit my shoulder perfectly. I could sight down the barrel with no difficulty, and my cheek felt right as it pressed against the stock.

"Now, place the butt of the rifle on the floor between your legs. Hold it straight up and stand up straight yourself." The end of the rifle barrel reached to the tip of my nose.

"We'll make the barrel an inch shorter for you. The longer the barrel, the truer the aim, but the harder the rifle is to load. A rifle should reach no higher than your chin. Mr Mackenzie has already told me that you cannot afford any inlay or other embellishments, so I'll give you a simple stock. The price will be three pounds, the musket and one pound now, the remainder when you get your rifle."

I said yes and dug into my pocket for a pound, which I promptly handed to Mr Rosenfeld. One didn't haggle with a fine craftsman like him.

"I thank you for the custom," he said. "I've a backlog of orders right now, so your rifle should be ready in about two months. Will that be satisfactory?"

I nodded.

"Thank you, Mr Watson," Rosenfeld said with a chuckle. I'm sure he was teasing me a bit, but he was treating me as an adult, one of the first times that'd happened since I was part of Washington's army.

Rosenfeld picked out another rifle and went through the fitting procedure with Donald. I kept holding the rifle he had given me for fitting.

"Can we leave as soon as we get our rifles?" I asked Donald as we left the shop, not thinking about the other things that we would need to do to prepare for our journey.

"McNeil's been discussing a partnership with the Moravians in Salem. If it all works out, in a few months he'll have a wagonload of ironmongery for us to take to North Carolina."

"Mr McNeil is willing to trust us with a wagon and goods worth scores of pounds?"

"I asked him the same question. He said we'd many opportunities to steal from him over the past year, but neither of us has taken so much as a farthing."

"But you said we'd need money for food and to pay tolls on the way down. After I pay for my rifle, I'll only have a few shillings left."

"McNeil'll advance us two months' wages for the trip, so we'll have money for food, tolls, and lodging, but I hope that we can sleep outdoors most of the time. We should have some of McNeil's money left over when we get to North Carolina, enough to tide us over till we find work. We'll still need to buy horses, saddles, and supplies before we can start trading with the Cherokee. The Moravians may have work for us in Salem, or I can go to some of the people my father knew."

"Won't Mr McNeil want us to bring his money to him?"

"We don't have to worry about that. The Moravians have a community in Bethlehem, about fifty miles north of here. They send messengers back and forth all the time. One of them will bring McNeil his money."

"Can we find someone to buy these pistols?"

"Not now. They're not very good, but I wouldn't feel comfortable without some sort of gun. We'll sell them once we have our rifles."

I was in a daze as we walked back to Mr McNeil's shop. I ached to leave for North Carolina and the adventure the trip promised. But if you'd asked me that morning how soon we could leave for North Carolina, I would've guessed another year or two. Now Donald was saying it could be only a few months.

Mr Rosenfeld was good to his word, and in late April, almost two months to the day after we ordered our rifles, Donald and I got a message saying they were ready. We hurried to the gunsmith's shop to pick them up. When we got there, Mr Rosenfeld handed them to us without saying a word. I ran my hand over the well-oiled maple of the stock. It was as smooth as a baby's skin. The brass and iron fittings gleamed. When I held it to my shoulder, it fit as if it were part of my body.

"It's beautiful," I said after I had had a chance to admire my new rifle. Mr Rosenfeld didn't say anything, but his smile seemed to say, "Of course it's beautiful. Would I make an ugly rifle?"

We followed Rosenfeld to the back garden. He again set up a target on a bale of hay against the back wall, then instructed me on the use of my rifle. I backed off as far as I could and fired. The rifle kicked against my shoulder, but no harder than my musket had. My shot was almost in the target's centre. I was elated. True it was only twenty yards – a distance at which even a musket was accurate – but I had no doubt that with this beautiful weapon, I could hunt and defend myself as well as any man.

"You'll have to practice until you can load your rifle smoothly and quickly. And you'll have to keep it clean. A fouled rifle won't fire," Mr Rosenberg said.

"Mr McNeil gives us Sundays off. I can practice then."

"Ach, lad, you shouldn't be practicing with a rifle on the Lord's Day. Sunday was made for prayer and rest."

I didn't reply. Donald tested his rifle, then we followed Rosenfeld back to his shop. He provided Donald and me with powder horns, cartridge boxes, and the tools necessary to keep our rifles clean. We paid and thanked him.

"I've reached agreement with Straub in Salem," Mr McNeil told us when we returned. "Now that you're properly armed, I can send you to the forges in New Jersey to buy the ironmongery I'm to ship to him. I've bought a cart and two oxen for the enterprise. I want the two of you to leave next Tuesday."

"Can't you buy the ironware here in Philadelphia?" I asked.

"I can, but it's cheaper if you go to the forges and buy directly. With a whole wagon load to buy, it's worth the trip."

Despite Mr Rosenfeld's injunction, Donald and I set out early the next Sunday morning for the woods along the Schuylkill River northwest of Philadelphia to find a place where I could practice firing my rifle. After about an hour, we were far enough into the countryside for there to be no danger of a stray rifle ball hitting anything. Donald picked out a small tree for me to use as a target.

"Can you load your rifle, or do you want me to instruct you?" Donald asked.

"I can do it," I said as I started the procedure Rosenfeld had shown me. It took me more than a minute to load my rifle, and I felt clumsy as I struggled to get the ramrod into its barrel, but finally I was ready. Donald didn't criticize.

"Back off fifty paces and then aim for the point where this limb joins the trunk," he said.

I paced off the distance and fired at the tree. To my amazement the rifle ball hit exactly where I'd aimed and the tree limb went flying.

"Good shot, William. Now try the limb on the other side at a hundred paces."

That shot was less successful. I only managed to clip off some of the leaves from the bottom of the branch.

"The farther you're shooting, the higher you have to aim. The ball drops as it travels through the air. Try again."

This time my shot was high, and I clipped leaves off the top of the branch.

"It takes practice. You'll learn. Try hitting the tree trunk from a hundred fifty paces."

I backed off another fifty paces, but when I fired, I missed the tree completely. I fired another dozen shots and by the end could hit the tree where I wanted to at a hundred paces, but not at 150 paces. I'd heard that an expert rifleman can hit a target at 250 paces, but it takes a fine eye and years of practice. Still, hitting my target at a hundred paces was much better than I could do with my musket, which wasn't accurate even at fifty paces.

The next day, as we were preparing for our trip to New Jersey, a sad looking family came to Mr McNeil's shop. They were dressed in fraying woollens and looked grey and tired. Each carried a small bundle. A boy who looked to be about eight held his father's hand, whilst a young girl tried to hide in her mother's skirt. I was alone in the shop when they entered.

"Is Mr Angus McNeil available?" the man asked.

"Who shall I say is looking for him?"

"Tell him that it's Robbie McNeil, his cousin from the Isle of Lewis."

"Wait here. I'll fetch him."

I went to the rear garden where Mr McNeil was planting vegetables and told him that he had visitors. He looked quizzical and said he didn't know of a cousin named Robbie, but he cleaned his hands and clothes and returned to the shop with me.

"I'm Angus McNeil," he said as he entered the shop.

"I'm your cousin, Robbie. Your Uncle Neil was my grandfather.

I've a letter here from Mr McPherson, the Minister of St. Andrews Church in Stornoway, attesting to that fact and to my good character."

Mr McNeil looked at the letter, then studied Robbie and his family for a moment.

"Well, Robbie, you seem to be who you claim. I left Scotland before you were born, but I remember Uncle Neil. He used to pinch my cheek hard when I was a boy to see if I would cry."

"He did the same to me," Robbie said with a small laugh. "Cousin Angus, this is my wife, Isobel, my son, Douglas, and my daughter, Mary. We've just landed in Philadelphia. Our crossing took thirty-three days." Robbie and his son held out their hands to shake Mr McNeil's. His wife and daughter curtseyed.

"That's not bad. Sometimes it takes six weeks or longer," Mr McNeil said, shaking Robbie's hand.

"The crossing was harder than I expected. There were few paying passengers. Most were either prisoners or indentured servants. After a few days, the Captain didn't seem to make any distinction, other than the prisoners were kept in chains. We all got the same short rations."

"Sea captains are absolute tyrants, and you're completely at their mercy once you put to sea. But you're on dry land now. What brings you to Philadelphia?"

"Life in Scotland is too hard for a crofter. Half my crop goes to pay the rent to the English, then the tacksmen come and take more for the Laird, who's in exile in France. We're often hungry, even in good years. I hear there's still good farm land available in the colonies, and a man can own his land instead of renting from the English," Robbie said, looking at Mr McNeil for confirmation.

Both Donald and Mr McNeil had told me how hard life was in Scotland. I believed them, but I didn't really understand the suffering the Scots were enduring until I saw how worn Robbie and his family looked.

"Yes, there's still some good land, but things are not as easy as they were before the rebellion. The English have banned settlement west of the mountains, so the price of good land in the east has gone up," Mr McNeil said.

"I've only a few shillings left after the crossing. I hope I can find work here in Philadelphia."

"You're in luck. I'll be needing some help in a few weeks. William here, my clerk, and Donald, my warehouseman, will be leaving for North Carolina soon. And I think it's time I hired a housekeeper. I'm tired of cooking and cleaning for myself. Are you interested in the jobs?" Mr McNeil asked, looking at both Robbie and his wife.

Robbie looked at his wife and both smiled. "Yes, we are, Cousin Angus."

"You're my cousin, but I'll be your master. You'll address me as Mr McNeil."

"Yes, Mr McNeil. Which job are you offering me, clerk or ware-houseman?"

"Can you reckon and write in a fair hand?"

"I can."

I was amused to watch Mr McNeil give his cousin the same test he'd given me when Donald and I first arrived. Robbie passed without difficulty.

"You'll be my clerk. The salary is two shillings a week. Isobel's salary will be a shilling a week, plus room and board for your whole family. You can live in the attic. William and Donald are there now, but they'll soon be gone. Till then, you'll have more room and more privacy than you had aboard ship. You can eat in the kitchen." Mr McNeil said this all rather gruffly, as if he wanted to make sure that Robbie and Isobel understood that they were employees, not family.

"William, show Robbie and Isobel the way to the attic and to the kitchen," Mr McNeil said, then returned to the garden.

Robbie McNeil and his family were amongst the small number of free immigrants to come to the colonies in the years immediately after the Great Rebellion. Cheap or free land had been the biggest inducement for settlers, but the ban on settlement west of the Proclamation Line made the barrier to becoming a freeholder much higher. Whilst the number of free settlers declined, the number of slaves, indentured servants, and prisoners shipped to the colonies seemed to increase.

Parliament banned import of slaves in 1808, and slavery six years ago in 1837, but it has yet to ban the practice of indenture or the transportation of prisoners. Indentured servants are supposed to be treated as employees, but in many cases they are treated little better than Negro slaves were. Prisoners are treated worse. Slave owners had an investment in their slaves. Those who employ prisoners have no such investment.

Thousands of people still arrive on our shores each year in these states of bondage. Many free people in the colonies have conflicting emotions towards these wretches. They provide cheap labour, but they are the dregs of society. I have no such conflict. Both practices are abominations.

Donald and I left for New Jersey shortly after dawn on Tuesday morning. The oxen moved slower than I could walk, but Donald didn't prod them. With frequent stops, we travelled only fifteen miles a day.

We crossed the Delaware River to Trenton on the ferry on our third day. There'd been no fighting in the village, but it bore melancholy scars of the rebellion. Its residents had fled when first the rebel army, then the Hessians, had bivouacked there. Many houses were still abandoned, and some of those that were occupied were missing windows or fences. Stumps protruded from gardens and courtyards. The trees had been cut by soldiers for firewood without consideration of their value for fruit or shade. Small trees and bushes were reclaiming the nearby farmland.

From Trenton, we made our way slowly to Princeton, reversing the route we'd taken with the rebel army. A corpse with a sign that read "Brigand" hung from a gallows in the Princeton Town Green, across from Nassau Hall. It must have been hanging there for a while because the dead man's skin was dried and black, even though his features showed that he'd been white. Seeing him hanging there, we decided to spend the night at the Princeton Inn rather than camping outside of town.

"Is the road from here to the Andover Forge safe?" Donald asked the innkeeper.

"Should be. We've had a little trouble with highwaymen lately, but it isn't as bad as it was a year ago, after the rebellion. By now most of the brigands have been scared off. The fellow with the long neck out there was Sean O'Farrell, the leader of a small band of thieving Irishmen. The army captured him three months ago. The rest of his

gang's disappeared. Probably like their necks the way they are. Still
I'd keep my rifle handy and not tempt fate by being on the road after
dark."

Donald and I kept that advice in mind the next day as we continued our journey. In late afternoon, as we were passing through a
heavily wooded area, a man on a mule approached us. He had a pistol
in his belt and was carrying a musket.

"Point your rifle at him. I'll do the talking," Donald whispered to
me. "Stay where you are and tell us your business," he called out when
the man was fifty paces away.

"I'm an honest traveller with as much right to use this road as you
have. Tell your young friend to put down his rifle."

I heard the sound of a pistol shot.

"William, on your right side," Donald shouted.

I turned to see the man who had fired rushing out of the trees
towards us, wielding a hatchet. Without thinking I fired and the man
dropped. Blood came pouring out of his chest. I'd killed him. The man
in front of us turned his mule and rode away as quickly as he could.
Donald grabbed his rifle and fired but missed. I started shaking.

"Well done, William," Donald said, putting his hand around my
shoulder. "Take a deep breath. Shooting a man is never easy."

I felt myself collapse against him, and sat there for a few moments
before pulling away. I was embarrassed to be acting like a child.

"You've saved our lives. I don't think those two would've been content with just taking our wagon." He climbed down off the wagon
and reloaded his rifle.

It took a few minutes before I could get any words out. "What'll
we do with him?" I asked, pointing to the corpse on the ground. I was
still shaking and didn't think I could move without falling.

"Just leave him there. The wolves and buzzards will take care of
him."

"I can't do that. Even a thief deserves a proper burial."

Donald looked at me for a few seconds then shrugged his shoulders. "Right then, we'll bury him." He pulled a mattock and a shovel
from the back of the wagon and started towards the trees. I just sat
on the wagon. He tested a few spots under the trees with the mattock
before choosing one.

"This looks like a good spot. Come down, William. Some hard work'll take your mind off unpleasant things."

I climbed down and slowly reloaded my rifle.

"Have you ever killed anyone?" I asked Donald as we dug.

"Three men. One was a thief, like the one you just killed. One was a Cherokee attacking our camp, and the last one was a Hessian during the fighting at Brooklyn. You do what you have to."

The soil under the trees had never been tilled. It took the two of us nearly an hour to dig the thief's grave. After searching his pockets and finding nothing, we dragged his body to the hole we'd dug.

"Should we say a prayer?" I asked Donald as we rolled the thief into his grave.

"Nah. He's probably in hell already, so why bother?"

We continued on our way, keeping a wary eye for the other high-wayman. He never reappeared. Nightfall found us far from a town but near an inn called Wood's Tavern. We decided to spend the night there.

"Best not talk about our little incident to anyone," Donald said as we approached the inn. "Best not talk at all. I'll say that you're feel-ing a little sickly and you can go directly to bed. I'll bring you some supper." I was happy to follow his instructions.

I lay awake for many hours that night. I couldn't get the picture of the thief, blood pouring out of his chest, out of my mind. What was his name? Had Donald been right when he said that the thieves would have killed us? Why it had been so easy for me to pull the trigger on my rifle? Why hadn't I given it a second thought? The questions multiplied in my mind as I lay there, and I didn't have answers for any of them. When I finally fell asleep that night, I didn't dream.

Donald let me sleep later than usual that next morning. Visions of the thief came to me at odd times during the day. I tried to put them out of my mind, but couldn't. I wanted to say something to Donald, but couldn't find the words.

"You did the right thing killing that bastard yesterday," Donald said when we stopped to take a midafternoon break. "You need to remember that he would've killed us, if you hadn't." Donald's words were comforting, but they didn't banish the visions or make it easier for me to sleep that night.

We arrived at Andover Forge six days later. The last part of the trip was through a wasteland. All the trees had been cut to make charcoal for the forge, but the stumps and small limbs hadn't been cleared. A few bushes and young trees poked through the debris, but the land looked battered and scarred.

It took most of a day to purchase the bars, nails, pots, and other ironware Mr McNeil wanted and load them in the wagon. By the time we finished it was too late to start out again. We spent the night at an inn close to the forge. Whilst we were eating, we overheard the conversation at the bar.

"I heard that some travellers killed Patty Shaughnessy, one of Sean O'Farrell's gang," a man named Jock announced to the other drinkers.

"Well, if they did, good riddance to him. He was a bad piece of business. Always starting fights. Had to let him drink on credit just to keep the peace. Owes me nearly a pound," the innkeeper replied.

"Has anyone seen his body?" one of the drinkers asked.

"Not that I've heard," Jock replied.

"Then Shaughnessy may've just left. With O'Farrell hanged, the gang's got no leader."

There was a round of muttered agreement from the others at the bar. I was about to blurt out that I'd shot Shaughnessy, but a look from Donald silenced me. I now knew the thief's name and that he had been a troublemaker. That comforted me somewhat, but visions of Shaughnessy with blood pouring out of a hole in his chest still came to me unbidden several times a day. I slept better than that first night, but only because I was exhausted. It was many weeks before the visions disappeared and I could sleep peacefully through the night.

With a heavy load of ironware, the oxen were even slower than on our outward trip. It took us two and a half weeks to return to Philadelphia. We had no difficulty, other than an argument with the ferryman who wanted to charge us double to cross the Delaware. We finally agreed that we would pay the regular price and help him pull the ferry across. Mr McNeil was pleased with our purchases, and without unpacking the wagon, we quickly prepared for our trip to North Carolina. We didn't have time to sell the pistols, but that no longer bothered me.

A week after our return, we said goodbye to Mr McNeil and Walnut Street. We were finally on our way.

CHAPTER 12

The first part of our trip to North Carolina was over good road, through rich Amish farms and villages. Late afternoon of our fifth day of travel, we arrived at the village of Paradise, and made our way to its inn. The fields were full of young maize and tobacco plants, and the ridges in the distance were covered with a blue haze. Near the road I could see a young boy in a broad-brimmed hat driving some dairy cows back to the barn for evening milking. It wasn't the picture book version of heaven, but a lush, pleasant scene that was certainly a close second.

Inside the inn a very drunk young Amishman was waving around a mug of ale, splashing some of it on the floor, and singing German hymns at the top of his voice. The innkeeper, a Mr Emmons, told him to sit down and be quiet but was ignored. When he tried to lead the Amishman away, the young man shoved him aside. Mr Emmons went behind the bar and returned with a stout club, which he quickly applied to the side of the Amishman's head. He did this calmly, as if he were tapping a cork into a bottle, just another task to be completed. The Amishman fell like a pole-axed steer.

"Get Mr Kurtz and tell him to take his son Karsten home," the innkeeper told a serving girl who'd been watching from a corner of the room.

"The Amish don't usually act like this," Mr Emmons said as he turned to us. "They have strict rules about behaving well in public. But their young men get one chance to kick up their heels. They call it *rumspringa*. It means jumping around." He waved his hand a bit and I half expected him to start jumping up and down to show us what he meant, but he didn't.

"Within a year they have to make up their minds to be baptised or leave the community. Karsten's a good boy. He'll decide to be baptised, probably long before his year is up." He paused for a second and put on the genial face required of all innkeepers. "Now gentlemen, how may I be of service?"

Donald had told me that it was time for me to learn how to deal with innkeepers, so I responded.

"We need a bed for the night and hay for our oxen."

"Will you be eating here, too?"

I looked at Donald before nodding yes.

"Room, board, and stabling for your oxen will be one shilling, one penny. You can have small beer with your supper, but ale will be extra."

I would've liked a mug of ale, but knowing Donald's desire to spend as little as possible, we drank small beer that night. After we'd eaten, Donald sought out Mr Emmons.

"Is the road safe west of here?" he asked.

"Very safe, as long as you're in Amish country. The Amish won't fight or use guns, but they're always watchful. If they see a brigand, they'll tell one of their English neighbours, who'll make sure that the troublemaker disappears. The Amish want a peaceable life, and so do the rest of us."

Four more days brought us to Harris Ferry on the Susquehannah River. We crossed after an argument with the ferryman about our wagon being too heavy. We'd been travelling mostly west, but now the road turned southwest over a flat plain. We could see a low ridge line to the west, but only the horizon to the east. Both the land and road were poorer than in Amish country. We passed through long stretches of forest, which would've provided hiding places for any highwaymen who might be lurking about. We were wary but had no difficulty other than potholes.

There were few inns or ordinaries – farm houses that would provide meals and lodging for travellers – along the way. Such places are now known by their French name, *gîte*. It seems a bit pretentious, given what little they offer. Even though we had money to pay for accommodations, we slept under our wagon whenever the weather allowed. It was far better than sleeping on a bug-infested straw tick in some smelly room, with who knows how many snoring, wind-passing family members and other travellers for companions.

Donald appointed me cook, and I was soon able to turn out better meals than the salt pork and stale bread we got the few times we stayed at ordinaries. The slow-moving streams in the lowlands of Pennsylvania were full of catfish, bass, and bream, and the faster moving streams in the mountains of Maryland had trout. All were easy to catch and made delicious eating. Some nights we were able to bag a duck or a wild turkey for our supper.

I'd never cooked over a campfire before. My father had done all the cooking when he'd taken us on camping trips. But with a little instruction from Donald, I had no difficulty. I cooked fish in a large cast iron skillet set on the fire ring's stones. Greasing the skillet with a little lard kept the fish from sticking to the metal. Butter would have been better, but we had no way of keeping it cool in the summer's heat. Cooking meat was a more elaborate affair. Donald taught me to bleed and gut any birds we shot as soon as we killed them, as far from camp as possible to avoid attracting scavengers. When we slaughtered chickens back on our farm, we didn't have to worry about scavengers. We threw the guts to our dogs and cats. They never left anything.

Back at camp, I plucked the birds, pushed a stick through their bodies, then suspended the carcasses over the fire using forked branches to hold them above the flames. This way I could turn the meat to cook it evenly on all sides. Donald showed me how to catch the drippings on a curled piece of bark and baste the meat with them to keep it moist as it cooked.

I made Indian bread from a simple dough of ground maize, salt, and water. I baked it in a Dutch oven, which was part of the iron-mongery that we were transporting to North Carolina. My first few attempts created either a rock-hard, inedible lump, or a pasty mush that stuck in our mouths and throats. But I eventually learned how to pack the right amount of hot coals on top of and around the cast iron pot and bake it for the proper length of time.

"You'll make someone a wonderful wife," Donald told me after my first successful batch.

"Keep quiet, or I'll eat it all myself."

It was too early in the year for berries, but we had some dried apples and were able to pick ramps and dig wild onions to vary our diet.

It took us ten more days to reach Watkins Ferry, on the Virginia side of the Patomack River, with its inn, forge, and store. We didn't need the services of the blacksmith, but we stocked up on bacon, ground maize, and other supplies. Northbound travellers told us that the only difficulties they'd encountered were mud and potholes.

Mr Watkins, the innkeeper and ferry owner, was a genial host. He knew everyone in the inn except Donald and me. They were either local people or regular travellers along the road. After a few questions to determine who we were and why we were travelling south, he turned to me.

"Do you know that the only reason you're travelling this road is because a herd of buffalo decided to walk this way a few hundred years ago?" he asked.

I must have had a confused look on my face, because he quickly continued.

"Buffalo looking for better pasture made a nice wide path. The Indians followed it because it was an easy route from north to south. They called it the Warrior Path, but they used it for trade more often than for war. We've now made it wider, but it's still the same path the buffalo chose."

"I didn't know there were buffalo here. I thought they only lived out west across the Mississippi River."

"There're still some in the deep woods," Mr Watkins said. "They're good eating and easy to hunt. And their hides make good leather. Everyone, white man and Indian, is slaughtering them. I fear we'll kill them all before too many years."

"I've never seen an Indian. Are there any around here?" I asked. Seeing an Indian would be an adventure for me. We hadn't had any on our trip, unless you call staying at ordinaries an adventure.

"Not around here, but you may see a few down south around Fort Roanoke. Mostly they stay on their side of the Proclamation Line.

That keeps everybody happy."

"I hope to see some soon. Donald and I are planning to trade with the Cherokee."

"That's a risky business these days," Mr Watkins said, shaking his head.

Donald, who hadn't been very interested in my conversation with Mr Watkins, suddenly became very attentive. "Why's that?" he asked.

"Don't you know there was a war with the Cherokee two summers ago down in North Carolina?" Mr Watkins replied.

"No, I was in Virginia, then up north. When I left the Cherokee seemed happy."

"Well they went on the warpath in June 1776 . . . killed three dozen people in North Carolina alone, and a few more in Georgia and South Carolina . . . said they didn't do it, that it was loyalists dressed up as Indians . . . but nobody believes that."

"Three dozen people! What did North Carolina do?" Donald asked.

"They sent General Rutherford and fifteen hundred militiamen into Cherokee country. But they didn't catch too many of them. The Cherokee knew the militia was coming and ran away. You can't hide fifteen hundred men. Rutherford burned dozens of Cherokee villages on our side of the mountains, but he didn't go over into Tennessee and destroy their villages along the Holston River."

"Did the Cherokee make peace after that?" I asked.

"No, they probably would've that following spring, but by that time the rebellion was over and the British were trying to keep the Indians happy. They put Rutherford in gaol and gave the savages thousands of pounds worth of gifts," Mr Watkins said, a look of disgust on his face.

"Damn English," Donald muttered just loud enough for me to hear. "Is it safe to go into Cherokee country again?" he asked.

"I don't know," Mr Watkins replied, shrugging his shoulders. "You hear all kinds of stories. Some traders come back with nice loads of deerskin. Others just disappear. They could've settled down with a squaw or they could've been murdered. Nobody knows for sure."

Donald was silent for a few moments, then asked, "Do we have to worry about highwaymen?"

"The Wagon Road is pretty safe. The British patrol it regularly. But I'd keep my rifle loaded and my eyes peeled. You never know what you'll run into."

"That's good advice anytime," Donald said, as Mr Watkins went off to talk to his other guests.

"In Princeton they told us that the road to Andover Forge was safe, and look what happened there," Donald said, once Mr Watkins was out of earshot.

"What about the Cherokee?" I asked. "Will we be able to trade with them?"

"Don't know. We need to find out more about what they're doing, but first we have to get to North Carolina without being robbed or murdered."

Donald's words were far from comforting. I wasn't afraid. I was sure that he would protect me, but my dreams of adventure were falling apart. If we couldn't trade with the Cherokee, what would we do?

We were approaching 21st June, Midsummer's Day. The days were long and hot, and we travelled through a moving cloud of gnats. The slow rocking of the wagon as our oxen plodded on often put me to sleep. More than once I had to grab hold of the wagon bench to keep from falling off. Most times I was jolted awake when the wagon rolled over a stone or into a pothole, but one day the roar of a bear woke me.

We'd seen bears before, almost always only their rear ends as they disappeared into the woods.

"Bears are more afraid of you than you are of them," Donald explained. "The only time they're a problem is if you get between a mother and her cubs. If that happens, find a way to slowly back away from both Momma and the babies. Don't run. Momma bear can run faster than you can."

Momma bear was on our left, about twenty feet in front of our wagon. She hunched her shoulders and looked ready to charge. Her two cubs were on our right, up a pine tree. The oxen stopped when Momma bear roared. They pawed the ground nervously, uncertain about what to do. Donald had his rifle in hand, aimed at the Momma bear. The best thing would have been to back the wagon up, but that's difficult to do unless you are standing in front of the oxen, pushing on their yoke. For a long ten seconds, two humans and five animals were frozen in position as each tried to figure out what to do. Then Momma bear slowly walked in front of our wagon, keeping her snout pointed towards us. Bears have good eyesight, but an even better sense of smell. With a short bark, she ordered her cubs down out of the tree. They slowly climbed down. With a gentle cuff, she herded them into the woods and all three disappeared.

"I'm glad I didn't have to shoot her," Donald said as he placed his rifle behind the wagon's bench. "Her cubs would've starved to death unless the wolves got them first." We waited a few minutes for the oxen to calm down, then proceeded on our way.

Four days later we met a British cavalry patrol. I never thought I'd be happy to see British soldiers, but these were a welcome sight.

"What are your names and what is your reason for travelling this road?" the lieutenant leading the patrol said when he came up to our wagon.

"I'm Donald Mackenzie and this is William Watson. We're taking this load of ironmongery to Salem."

The lieutenant walked his horse to the back of our wagon and made a show of looking at our load. When he could no longer see the soldiers in his patrol, they began snickering. They stopped as soon as the lieutenant came back into sight.

"Everything seems to be in order, Mr Mackenzie. You may proceed."

"Thank you, Lieutenant. Is the road safe south of here?"

"Of course it's safe. My orders are to make it safe." With that he rode off, his men following a short distance behind.

"Pompous arse, if I ever saw one," Donald said when they were gone. "Still I'd rather have him here than not. I'm sure that he's chased away most of the brigands."

It took three weeks longer for us to reach Big Lick and Ingles Ferry across the New River. The British had built Fort Roanoke there to control the entrance to the Wilderness Road, which hunters and traders used to get to Kentucky and Tennessee. Its stockade enclosed two clapboard buildings, the fort's headquarters and officers' quarters; a score of log cabins, barracks for two companies of infantry and two squadrons of cavalry; a large stable; a stone arsenal; and a dozen miscellaneous buildings. Besides enforcing the rule against settlement west of the Proclamation Line, the fort's soldiers protected travellers against highwaymen and Indian attacks.

A sprawling village had already grown up around the fort, with a tavern for the soldiers, an inn and blacksmith for travellers, and small farms to feed all. Everything had a raw, new look about it, except Ingles Tavern, whose sign proudly proclaimed "Established in 1772." At six years, it was the oldest building in the in the area and four years older than the fort, which now provided most of its customers.

We'd been on the road for six weeks and had travelled every day. We and our oxen needed a rest. Mr Ingles told us we could camp in the field behind his inn. Donald went hunting, and whilst he didn't bag any deer, he did shoot a turkey on our first day at Fort Roanoke.

"What say we have a pint of ale this fine evening?" Donald asked as I was cleaning up after our supper on our third night. It was the first time that he'd suggested we drink ale rather than small beer or water. I said I didn't have to be asked twice and we headed for the tavern.

The inside of the tavern was smoky and too hot for comfort, but I wasn't going to complain. We found a table and Donald went up to the bar to get our drinks.

"You're sitting at my table," a large man clad in buckskins growled as he walked towards me.

I started to apologize and move when Donald returned. "Stay where you are, William. The table is ours," he said, setting down two pewter pints of ale.

"I said the table is mine," the large man said, reaching for the knife in his belt.

Donald grabbed the man's arm and twisted it behind his back. The big man grunted and tried to break loose, but Donald held him tightly and steered him towards, then through, the open door. I watched Donald release his hold, kick the big man in the arse, and send him sprawling.

Whilst this was happening, Mr Ingles came out from behind the bar. He had a club in his hand but it wasn't raised for use. "I don't want any fighting in here," he said, when Donald returned to our table.

Donald sat down and calmly took a sip of ale. "Tell that to the ill-mannered bastard I just kicked out of your tavern."

"You could've moved. They're plenty of other tables available."

"I don't like being bullied. It upsets my digestion." Some of the men in the room cheered when Donald said this.

Sensing the mood of his customers, Mr Ingles softened his tone. "Then I assume you'll enjoy your ale in peace and not cause any further disruption," he said before returning to the bar. We drank our ale, chatted with a few of the other customers, and returned to our wagon.

The next morning we were off again for the ten-day trip over the mountains to Salem. On the morning of our ninth day of travel, I saw a large tree-covered mound rising like a giant wart on the top of a mountain ahead of us.

"That's Jomeokee," Donald said, pointing to the strange-shaped mountain. "It's two hundred feet high and tells you that you're in North Carolina. The settlers call it Pilot Mountain. We should be in Salem tomorrow night."

Everything on the trip had been so new and different that I hadn't worried about what would happen when we got to Salem. But our trip was almost over and there was no putting off the question. "What are we going to do after we find Straub and give him everything?" I asked.

"Find work," was Donald's brusque answer.

I was taken aback by his tone of voice. "Where?"

"From the Moravians," he said, in a more normal tone. "There aren't that many of them and they always need hired hands to do the work they can't. Of course, they give you the hardest work, but they pay fairly and you eat well when you work for them."

"But what about trading with the Cherokee?"

"We need to find a merchant who'll stake us to a kit, horses, and trade goods, so we can head for one of their villages in the fall. But after what we heard at Watkins Ferry, I don't know if that'll be safe." The oxen had slowed down. Donald gave them a swish with the reins to remind them that they needed to keep plodding forward.

"We could farm. That's something I know how to do," I said.

"Told you a long time ago, I don't like farming. It ties a man too close to one place. I want to be in the forest, not walking behind the arse end of a horse or ox." I thought Donald was angry with me, one of the few times I felt that way. I let a few minutes pass, then asked, "How does it all work, I mean with the merchant?"

"It'd take us years to save enough money to buy the horses and the goods we need for trade," he explained. "I worked for Amos Cartwright before and maybe he'll stake us to what we need. He'll take two-thirds or three-quarters of the skins we bring back, but with any luck we'll still have a tidy sum after the trip. Then we can buy some land and build a cabin. We need some place to come home to. Who knows, in a few years, you may even find a girl who's willing to marry you?"

"What about you? I'll wager you could find a wife quicker than I could."

"I had a wife. She died," he said in a quiet tone.

This news shocked me. Donald had never talked about being married. I was silent for a few minutes as the oxen plodded on before I found the courage to ask, "What happened?"

"An epidemic of fever. We both caught it. I lived, she died," Donald said in a low, flat voice, as if he had to force each word out. "She needed me and I was too sick to help her." Having started his story, Donald seemed determined to finish it. "I can't forgive myself for that. Her name was Rachel. She was pregnant with our first child. I buried her behind our home. Then I went a little daft. I burned the cabin and left for Virginia. I was there when the rebellion started. I joined the Virginia Militia. You know the rest of my story."

I looked over at him, but he stared straight forward.

"I'm sorry about your wife," I said after another few minutes had passed. "You going to be happy in North Carolina?"

"I'll be happy. Trading with the Cherokee is what I know and I'm good at it. I need to be back in the mountains. I hope that it'll be safe to go this fall." Donald didn't sound convincing.

It took us only a few minutes after we arrived in Salem to find Mr Straub and to hand over the oxcart and its load of ironmongery.

"I'll take a complete inventory of the goods later," Mr Straub said, after he'd taken a quick look at the wagon's contents. "Please call me Brother Straub. I trust you had a good journey."

"We did indeed," Donald replied. "No thieves or Indians to worry about. The road is rough, but our oxen pulled through all the mud and potholes. You've got two good beasts there."

"I know about the road. I travelled it two years ago on a trip to Bethlehem."

After a few more pleasantries, Donald asked, "Brother Straub, William and I aren't returning to Pennsylvania. North Carolina was my home before the rebellion. This is where I want to live and, at least for now, so does William. We've got a few shillings, but we need jobs to make enough money to buy a place of our own." Donald said nothing about our plans to trade with the Cherokee.

"See Brother Alder at the sawmill. He may have some work for you," Straub said, pointing us towards a low building just visible along a stream to the west.

The sawmill was an elaborate affair. A waterwheel turned another large wheel inside the mill building. This wheel was connected to linkages that converted its circular motion into an up-and-down motion that drew two saw blades through large logs, cutting a long, inch-wide plank. Weights, which looked like a larger version of those on a clock, pushed the log towards the saw blades. Sundry other devices held everything in place and adjusted the saw blades and log to get the right-sized plank. Everything was covered in sawdust. The sawn planks were neatly stacked behind the mill.

"We're in luck," Donald said. "When Straub told us to go to the sawmill I thought it'd be a saw pit, with us pulling the saw. It's the hardest work I've ever done and for extras, you get to breathe sawdust all day."

"Good day, gentlemen. How may I be of service?" Brother Alder said as we approached.

"I'm Donald Mackenzie and this is William Watson. We're looking for work. Brother Straub said that you might have some."

"Ever worked in a sawmill before?"

"Not with machinery like this, sir, but we're both hard workers and fast learners. I hope you'll give us a chance."

"I'll hire you by the day. If I'm pleased with your work, we can talk about longer employment."

"Thank you, sir. I'm sure you won't be disappointed."

I had said nothing to this point, and Brother Alder turned to me.

"You do speak?" he asked.

"Yes, sir."

"And you've never worked in a sawmill."

"No, sir." For some reason I was embarrassed, even though Brother

Alder was not being unkind.

"You'll both start an hour after dawn tomorrow. I must attend morning prayers first."

"Thank you again. Is there some place we can spend the night? We've a little money so we can pay our own way," Donald said.

"You can stay at the inn. It's along the highway you came in on." With that, Brother Alder turned back to the work he had been doing before we came up.

"Not the friendliest man around," Donald commented as soon as we were out of earshot. "He'll probably be a difficult master to work for. But we need to start with him. Then we can see if other work is available."

We found the inn, and soon negotiated lodgings for the week. The food was plentiful and excellent, as Donald had said it would be.

We reported to work on time the next morning. Brother Alder was waiting for us, and soon had us carrying logs to the mill and stacking the sawn planks. He was a tall, lean man with a ring of grey hair around his bald pate. He had a dour look about him, but we soon learned that he tried not to smile because he was embarrassed by his lack of front teeth.

"It's a vanity that I should overcome, but I can't, no matter how hard I try," he told us after we got to know him better. He probably didn't know it, but it was a vanity he shared with General Washington.

Brother Alder was not as difficult a master as Donald had feared. He demanded precise work, but was willing to take the time to teach us the proper care of the mill machinery. We soon learned how to sharpen the saw blades and set their teeth at the proper angle, a job that needed to be done daily. We also learned how to adjust the mill settings to cut planks of different thicknesses. The work was hard, but no harder than farming or a dozen other occupations, and there were many times during the day, as the saws were slowly cutting their way through a large log, when we could rest.

After a week at the inn, we were able to find lodgings on a farm a little over a mile from Salem, rented by a family named McAllister. We had to walk two extra miles each day, but bed and board at the inn cost almost as much as Brother Alder paid us, so we wouldn't have been able to save any money if we continued lodging there. Mrs McAllister's meals were not as tasty or plentiful as the ones at the inn, but we didn't go hungry.

Brother Alder and the other Moravians often talked to us about the example that Christ had set for the world and their belief that everyone could be saved. Donald and I were invited to attend their church services, which were held throughout the week, not just on Sunday, but they made no effort to get us to join their church. I attended some of their shorter services because their hymn singing was beautiful. Donald attended only one. His Church of Scotland beliefs on predestination were at odds with the Moravian beliefs on salvation. It was a side of Donald that I hadn't seen before. I knew him to be a good man who acted in a Christian way, but I never thought he cared about religious doctrine.

"Next Saturday is the 13th August Festival," Brother Alder told us after we'd been working for him for three weeks. "You'll have the day off from work. You are welcome to join us at church, if you wish. The service will last all morning."

"Two days'll give us a chance to go to Salisbury," Donald said as soon as Brother Alder was gone. "Maybe we can find Amos Cartwright or some other merchant there who'll stake us for fur trading,"

"Won't any of the merchants in Salem stake us? By now they know we're dependable."

"Brother Ettwein, the *Vorsteher*, has the final say on all business transactions in Salem. He'd have to approve, and he's too cautious a man to stake fur traders."

CHAPTER 13

Donald arranged for us to borrow horses. We set off just after dawn on a hazy, hot day and were in Salisbury by noon. The only horse I'd ever ridden was our farm horse in Graves End. I wasn't ready for the bouncing I took as we covered forty miles in six hours. My legs, back, and neck were so sore I could hardly walk. Donald promised we'd take it slower on our way back.

"Let's find Amos Cartwright," Donald said as we walked our horses down Salisbury's main street. "His shop used to be in Freemason Street, just around the corner."

"Well, if it isn't Donald Mackenzie. I haven't seen you in dogs' years," Mr Cartwright said by way of greeting as we entered his shop.

"It's been three years," Donald replied. "You're looking prosperous, Amos."

"Well, now that things have settled down a bit, more settlers are coming into the county. Business is good. Who's your young friend?"

"This is William Watson. He and I want to start trading with the Cherokee this fall, and we're looking for a stake. Would the usual terms interest you?"

"Haven't you heard?" Mr Cartwright said, a look of disbelief on his face. "Going into Cherokee country is much riskier than it used to be. We had a war with the Cherokee two years ago."

"I heard about that, but the Moravians say that things are safe again."

"If safe means the Cherokee aren't coming over the Proclamation Line looking for white scalps, things are safe. But I'm not sure they're safe enough for two white men to ride into Cherokee country alone. You'll need to join a larger party. Daniel Boone is organizing one to leave in mid-November, after the Cherokee have done their summer hunting and had time to prepare the skins."

"Daniel Boone? I thought he was in Kentucky. I know he doesn't like travelling in large groups. I've hunted with him. He wants to be alone, or with one or two others at most."

"He was in Kentucky and started a settlement called Boonesborough, but it was west of the Proclamation Line and the British burned it. He's back in North Carolina, living on the Yadkin River. Surprised you haven't run into him."

"I've only been back a month," Donald explained. "And I've been busy working for the Moravians."

"Even Daniel Boone has to change with the times. The Cherokee stole his furs more than once, but now that might not be enough. They just might take his scalp too."

"Is Daniel in town?" Donald asked.

"No, he went back to see Rebecca and the children," Mr Cartwright replied, a grin crossing his face. "He doesn't stay away from her as long as he used to. A few years back he was away for more than two years, and when he got home Rebecca presented him with his new baby. She told him she thought he was dead."

"I heard that story," Donald said, also grinning. "They say he didn't mind."

Mr Cartwright shrugged as if to say, who am I to judge? Then he returned to business.

"I'm sure that Boone will take you on. If you vouch for William here, that'll probably be good enough."

He paused, looked at the ceiling for several moments, then said, "I'll lend you four horses, two for riding and two for packing, and give you a full kit and a stake of trade goods – axes, cloth, beads, everything the Cherokee like. I get three-quarters of the profits and my horses back. Deal?"

"That's pretty harsh, Amos," Donald said. There was no anger in his voice. I could tell that he and Cartwright were engaged in some friendly bargaining.

"Even if we bring out a full load of deerskin," Donald continued, "we won't be left with enough money to keep us through the winter and to buy horses for next year. You get three-quarters and we each keep a horse. Deal?"

"My wife will probably think I'm crazy, but I like you, Donald. It's a deal. You two be back here by 15th November. I'll arrange everything with Boone." With that they shook hands.

Business concluded, Mr Cartwright could now be a genial host.

"I know you're not going back to Salem tonight," he said, "so come have supper with me and my family. You can sleep in our barn."

"That's the best offer I've had in months," Donald replied.

"And you, young man," Mr Cartwright said, a stern look on his face, "the price of your supper will be the story of how you got hooked up with this reprobate. But you'll have to be on your guard. I've got two daughters, one or both of whom might take a fancy to you."

We had an enjoyable supper of roast lamb and yams. The rest of the Cartwright family consisted of Mrs Cartwright, thirteen year-old Jenny, ten-year old Samantha, and Billy, who was six. After we had eaten, Mr Cartwright looked at me.

"Now, young man, you must tell us your story."

I told the Cartwrights about Washington's surrender, meeting Donald, and escaping from the Hessians. Billy peppered me with questions about every part of my adventure. Jenny said very little but smiled at me often, which made me nervous. She had light brown hair, large blue eyes, and a round face. I thought her smile was glorious. It seemed to light up the room. I just kept talking, adding stories about our trip to North Carolina.

"I think we've kept you talking long enough, William," Mr Cartwright said, when I paused for breath after what seemed like hours. "Children, say goodnight to Mr Mackenzie and Mr Watson. It's past your bedtime."

Only then did I realize that it was dark outside. We said our goodnights, slept in the barn, and left after a hearty breakfast. I liked all of the Cartwrights, but it was Jenny who filled my thoughts as we rode slowly back to Salem. Had I made a fool of myself talking as much as I did? How could I see her again?

Donald and I worked at the saw mill for as long as we could before we had to be in Salisbury. We had no choice but to walk. We couldn't borrow horses. How would we return them? To outfit ourselves for the trip, we each brought a hatchet, a wooden canteen, a tin plate, cup, knife and fork, and a large cane basket to use as a pack. The basket was far too big for the few things I owned, but Donald assured me it would be useful in the future. I again asked him about the pistols we'd taken from the thieves outside Philadelphia. Mine was a burden I'd have liked to shed. Donald told me to keep the pistol and learn how to use it – something I'd yet to do – that we might need them when we went into Cherokee country.

We said our goodbyes to the McAllisters the night before we left. Mrs McAllister gave us a baked chicken, some beef jerky, two loaves of bread, and a dozen apples for the trip. She and Mr McAllister wished us luck and invited us to visit when we returned.

We set out for Salisbury at dawn and planned to take two full days for the trip.

"It'll be good to get back to the mountains," Donald said. "All you'll have to worry about is some Cherokee taking your scalp."

"Won't you be there to protect me?"

"Nah, I'll be too busy protecting my own scalp. You'll have to fend for yourself."

I hoped he was joking.

We arrived at Mr Cartwright's shop in Freemason Street late in the afternoon of our second day.

"Donald, William, I'm happy to see the both of you," he said. "Everything is arranged with Boone. You leave tomorrow. There'll be six in the party, the two of you, Boone, his younger brother Squire, Ben Cutbirth, and Al Neely."

"Only six?" Donald said with a frown. "I know Squire, Ben, and Al. They're good men, but we won't have much of a chance if the Cherokee decide to be disagreeable."

"Having a few more won't make any difference in that case, and the Cherokee might not have enough furs to trade if there are too many of you."

I thought back to Donald's telling me that merchants were only interested in their profits and didn't give you anything for risking your scalp.

"Come see what I've got for you," Mr Cartwright said to change the subject.

We went out back and Donald carefully examined each of the four horses then the camping gear and the array of trade goods we were to carry. There were bales of cloth, axe and hoe heads, steel knives, some cook pots, and an assortment of brass buttons and buckles.

"No whiskey?" Donald asked when he had completed his inspection.

"Boone says you'll pick that up along the way. I'll give you a pound. That should buy all the whiskey you can carry. Now don't go drinking up the profits," Mr Cartwright replied with a grin.

"You know me better than that, Amos. Besides, getting drunk in Cherokee country is the best way I know to lose your horses and everything else of value, maybe even your scalp. No muskets, powder, or lead?"

"We can't trade in guns or ammunition anymore," Mr Cartwright said, a resigned look replacing the grin on his face. "The army controls how many muskets and how much ammunition the Cherokee have. They get them for free, as long as they behave."

"Damn English," Donald said, spitting on the ground in disgust. "Muskets were our best trade goods. Last time I went trading, you could get twenty best quality deerskins from the Cherokee for a musket." But then he brightened up. "You've done well by us, Amos."

"Good, now make me a rich man by bringing back plenty of deerskin."

"I'll do my best, and I'll make sure that William here learns how to tell the quality of a deerskin. The Cherokee will try to give you shoddy ones and claim they're best quality."

"They may be heathen savages, but they're canny traders," Mr Cartwright said. Then he turned to me. "Sorry I can't invite you home for supper. Mrs Cartwright took the children to Charleston to buy clothes for the winter. She thinks the seamstresses here in Salisbury are no longer good enough for her. She wanted me to come along, but I told her Larson, the Swedish tailor down the road, makes as fine a suit as anyone this side of London."

He shrugged in the way that said my wife is a good woman, even if I'm not happy with everything she does. Having dismissed Mrs

Cartwright's behaviour, he finished with, "But I hope you'll be my guests at the tavern."

Mr Cartwright must have seen my face fall when I heard that I wasn't going to see Jenny.

"Shall I tell Jenny that you were sorry not to be able to see her?"

"Yes, I mean no," I stammered. I could feel the heat rising in my face.

"I think he really means yes, Amos," Donald said with a wry smile.

"Young man, am I going to have to worry about whether your intentions towards my daughter are honourable?"

By this time I was completely tongue-tied. Donald and Mr Cartwright both laughed.

"I think we better let William wash up before we go to the tavern," Mr. Cartwright said, seeing my discomfort. I thanked him and left as quickly as I could for the rain barrel, which was on the other side of the shop.

As we entered the tavern that night, Donald pointed to Daniel Boone, who was sitting at a table, surrounded by what seemed like half the men in Salisbury, telling a story about rescuing his daughter Jemima and two other girls who'd been kidnapped by a band of Shawnee.

Boone was about five foot eight and eleven stone, with a large head and black hair. With his full chest and broad shoulders, he looked like a very strong man, but he didn't seem threatening in any way. He smiled and his blue eyes twinkled as he talked. A jug of whiskey sat on the table, and several men drank from it without asking Boone's permission. I soon found out that if he had whiskey when he was in a storytelling mood, Boone always invited his listeners to help themselves. He was one of the most generous men I've ever met.

Boone saw us enter, acknowledged us with a nod, and continued his story. We waited until he finished.

"Donald MacKenzie, I thought you'd gone up north for good. Amos says you want to join my trading party and that you're bringing a boy along,"

"He's no longer a boy, Daniel. This is William Watson. You'd better call him William. He gets mighty testy if you call him anything else. We escaped from the Hessians almost two years ago and we've been travelling together since. He's dependable and he knows how to use a rifle. I'll vouch for that."

"Well, William Watson, welcome to our expedition," Boone said, looking me up and down. "We leave at dawn tomorrow."

With that Boone turned back to his audience and started another story. Donald, Mr Cartwright, and I went to another corner of the room to have our supper. I would have expected Donald and Boone to have a longer exchange about our upcoming expedition, but story-telling was one of Boone's favourite pastimes, and few things could divert him when he had an audience.

The evening of our first day out of Salisbury, we stopped at a large, prosperous looking farm. Its house and barn were stone, and its fences and gates were all well-tended. Enos Samuelson, its owner, greeted Boone, then quickly got down to business.

"You've come to buy my whiskey?"

"How many gallons can you sell us?"

"Indian whiskey or for you?"

"Indian whiskey."

"I've got twenty-five gallons. You can have them for five shillings each."

"And your good whiskey?"

"I've got ten gallons, but they'll cost you eight shillings each."

"I'll take ten gallons of Indian whiskey and two gallons of your good whiskey," Boone said, without trying to bargain on the price. Donald later told me that the price of whiskey was set by agreement amongst the farmers in the area. They didn't want to compete against each other and have to sell at too low a price. The other traders bought the rest of Mr Samuelson's stock. Donald bought two gallons of Indian whiskey, but only a small flask of good whiskey.

"Can we camp down by your stream?" Boone asked once the commerce was completed.

"Certainly," Samuelson replied, but didn't offer any further hospitality.

The fur traders set up their tents along the stream and spread their blankets. The site had been used for camping before and there was an ash-filled fire ring. We gathered some dry wood and soon had a cook fire going. Even though it was our first night out we didn't have any fresh food. Supper was a stew of ham and dried maize, the same thing we would eat each night we were on the road.

After supper, whilst the rest of the party was settling in for the night, I saw Mr Samuelson tending his still about a hundred yards upstream. The still was under a roof but not enclosed by walls. I walked over and asked him to tell me how he made whiskey. Asking any craftsman about his work is a sure way to get him talking, and it worked with Mr Samuelson, even if he hadn't been hospitable when the fur traders were buying his whiskey.

"Maize is hard to ferment. You need to get it started with a little drake's tail," he said with the air of a school teacher starting a long lecture.

"You mean you put duck feathers in the maize?" I knew this was wrong, but it was the response he wanted.

"No, drake's tail is sprouted maize," he said with a smile. "You wet some maize kernels and cover 'em with sawdust for a few days. They'll start growing. When the sprouts are about three inches long, you wash off the sawdust and dry the sprouted maize. When it's dry, you grind it up and put some of it in with the ground maize and water to make wort."

Mr Samuelson showed me a large wooden hogshead where a batch of wort was fermenting. It had the pleasant smell of rising bread dough, but it was covered with an evil-looking brown froth. He stirred the brew with a large wooden panel, which set the mixture bubbling. There was a faint hiss as the bubbles reached the surface and broke.

"The first secret to making whiskey is to put just the right amount of water in the wort. Put in too much and you get a weak brew and you'll have to use extra wood to distil it. Put too little water in and not all of the maize ferments. When the wort stops bubbling, it's all fermented. You scoop it out and put it in this still pot." Mr Samuelson was proud of his craft and I could see his chest puff out as he explained this.

The still pot was a large kettle made from copper sheets. Its cover had a long copper tube that connected to a smaller wooden barrel.

"You build a fire under the still pot and bring it to a boil. The whiskey boils off, but it cools in the copper pipe and in the barrel," he said, pointing to each piece of equipment as he mentioned it. "Then you draw off the whiskey. If it's for Indians, you just mix it with water. If it's for white men, you boil it again and run the steam over charred willow to give it a nice smooth taste."

"The second secret to making whiskey is to know how long to boil the still. If you boil it too little, you'll leave whiskey in the still pot. If you boil it too long, you'll get too much water into the whiskey. It'll be weak and have a bad taste. It's easy to make whiskey, but making good whiskey is an art."

With that pronouncement, Mr Samuelson's lesson was over. I thanked him and returned to the fur traders. Donald wasn't in camp when I returned, so I sat by the fire next to Al Neely, who was drinking some of the whiskey he'd bought.

"William, m'lad, would you like to try a bit of Mr Samuelson's best?" he said, holding out a tin cup about half full of what looked like water.

"Yes, I would."

"Now sip it slowly." That first sip burned all the way down to my stomach. I gasped for breath, but tried to keep smiling.

"Have a bit more."

The second sip went down more smoothly, but my stomach was still not sure that it liked whiskey. The third and fourth sips just felt warm as they slid down my throat. The other traders gathered round and encouraged me to drink more. The cup was empty, but not for long.

I don't remember anything else until the next morning, when I woke up feeling like someone was pounding the side of my head with a hammer. I had a dry mouth and felt ready to vomit. I stood up and almost fell over with dizziness. Donald handed me a canteen and I took a few sips of water. These reached my stomach but immediately made a return trip. I managed not to vomit on anything other than the ground. Everyone else was laughing and offering advice.

"Give him a strong cup of willow tea. His head must be pounding."

"What he needs is the hair of the dog."

"Just let him go back to sleep."

I don't know who said what.

"Go to the stream and wash your face, then come back and have some willow tea. We're leaving in an hour. You need to be ready,"

Donald said. He wasn't scolding me, but he did nothing to hide his displeasure.

I was ready when the expedition left but felt sick the whole day.

"So you've decided to live," Donald said when we made camp that night.

"I'll never drink any more whiskey for the rest of my life," I muttered.

"Don't make promises you won't keep. But next time, leave some in the jug."

"Did I drink a whole jugful?" My stomach felt queasy again at the thought.

"No, but you drank much more than you should have. Not that I need to tell you that."

For three days we moved slowly west along a rough road through rolling hill country, stopping frequently to buy more whiskey. It seemed like every farmer had a still. On our fourth night, we camped at Davidson's Fort, at the base of the mountains. We could see them looming over us in the distance. The fort was only a few miles from the Proclamation Line and Cherokee land. Samuel Davidson had built the fort before the Great Rebellion to protect the settlers in the area, but now it housed fifty British infantrymen, a squadron of cavalry, and a customs officer. Fur and deerskin gotten in trade with the Indians were taxed at the same rate as imported goods, two shillings per pound. Since fur traders rarely had cash, the customs officer took one pelt in ten, and always seemed to take the best pelts.

The route west from Davidson's Fort had been a Cherokee trail. But two years earlier, General Rutherford and his North Carolina Militia turned it into a road, which ran over Swannanoa Gap, across the French Broad River, to the headwaters of the Pigeon River. It was the easiest way to the Cherokee middle villages, many of which Rutherford's men had burned.

"It doesn't matter which way we go into Cherokee country," Donald said when I asked him whether it was safe to use the road. "They remember what Rutherford did and they'll steal our goods and take our scalps if they think they can get away with it."

We left Davidson's Fort early the next morning and followed Rutherford's road through a forest of huge chestnut trees. Most of the land west of the Fort was too steep for farming, though farmers sometimes grazed their cattle there. It took an hour and a half to reach Swannanoa Gap, where we crossed the Proclamation Line.

Twenty years ago I read Dante's Inferno and learned that the inscription on the gates of hell was, "Abandon all hope, ye who enter here." Had I known that when I made that first trip into Cherokee country, I would have put it on a sign at Swannanoa Gap. I felt we were leaving civilization and, despite being with Donald, Daniel Boone, and the other fur traders, I couldn't help feeling afraid. The valley on the other side of the gap was completely forest covered. Who could know how many Indians were hidden beneath those trees?

Actually, we were not leaving civilization, but moving from one civilization to another. The Cherokee farmed and hunted much the same way that white settlers east of the Proclamation Line did. Both lived in log cabins and wore clothes made of cloth woven on looms. The Cherokee couldn't read or write, but neither could many of the settlers. Traders like us had brought them many of the conveniences of our civilization. We even met a Cherokee who wore spectacles.

That night we camped along a stream that ran from the gap to the French Broad River. It was cool, with a hint of winter in the air. The nearly full moon and stars shone brightly. I was settling into my blanket to sleep when I heard a hooting sound. It wasn't an owl. It sounded like someone pretending to be an owl. Squire Boone, Daniel's younger brother, was lying next to me, but when he heard the hooting, he snapped into a sitting position and put his finger to his lips, signalling me to be silent.

"Be as quiet as you can, but get your rifle and make sure it's loaded," he whispered.

I reached for my rifle and stared around in the darkness. We heard another hoot.

"What is it?" I whispered.

"Might be Cherokee."

I peered into the night but couldn't see or hear anything. Suddenly, I heard a loud whoop and the sound of something crashing through the woods towards me. I was frightened but didn't fire my rifle. I couldn't see anything to shoot at. Then Daniel Boone and Ben Cutbirth came strolling out of the woods.

"I'll wager you thought that was an Indian attack," Boone said with a grin.

"I didn't know what it was," I replied.

"Well done, William," Cutbirth added. "Or perhaps I should call you Mr Watson. You didn't panic and fire your rifle at shadows." By this time Al Neely and Donald had joined us.

"I think we have the makings of a real fur trader here," Boone said.

"If he's a real fur trader, maybe we should get him a piece of Cherokee cunny," Al said. Once again I could feel the heat rising in my face, which I knew was turning red at his suggestion.

"Let the boy be," Donald said before I could think of a reply. "There'll be plenty of time for that when he's a bit older."

"Donald's right," Boone added. "And besides, Cherokee women choose who they'll make love to, and I don't think William here is quite what any of them would have in mind."

I didn't know what to think. One moment Boone was treating me like a man, the next, like a boy. I lay awake for a long time that night trying to figure out what he thought of me.

The next morning Boone explained that getting me drunk and the fake Indian attack were tests and that I'd passed the first by not complaining or lagging behind and the second by not panicking or being overcome by fear.

"Weren't you worried I'd shoot either you or Ben?" I asked.

"Nah. Squire was watching you. He'd have knocked your rifle away before you could fire. Ben and me was safe." He was laughing as if remembering the joke he and the others had played on me, but then he turned serious. "I need to trust the men I'm travelling with. If it had been a real Indian attack, you'd only get one shot from your rifle and one from your pistol, if you're carrying one. In the minute it would take you to reload, they'd be on you, and you'd have to fight with your tomahawk or your rifle butt. You need to make your shots count and you need to stay calm to do that."

At the time I didn't think too much about what Boone had said about an Indian attack, but as we rode along deeper into Cherokee country, it worried me. Other than fights with my brother or in the schoolyard at Graves End, I'd never fought hand-to-hand. I'd never used a rifle butt or a tomahawk as a weapon. If we were attacked by Indians and weren't able to drive them away with our rifles, I'd either be dead or taken prisoner. From what I'd heard of how Indians tortured their prisoners, death seemed like the better option. For the first time, my pistol was a comfort, not a burden. Donald, Boone, and the other fur traders were wary but light-hearted. They had all been on Indian land before. That's how they earned their living. I could only hope they'd protect me if we were attacked.

Travellers tell us that pagan cultures have elaborate ceremonies to mark a boy's entry into manhood. Christians don't have such a ceremony, but my first trip over the mountains to trade with the Indians was when I entered manhood. At the beginning of the trip, I was a boy, tolerated because I was with Donald Mackenzie. Before we got to the first Cherokee village, I was a man accepted by the fur traders. I knew that I still had much to learn about life and the ways of men, but that didn't take away from the pride I felt. Looking back, the tests that Boone and the fur traders set for me – getting me drunk and trying to scare me with a fake Indian attack – seem childishly easy. They seemed designed to build my confidence, not to challenge me. Whatever their goal, I felt proud to be a full member of Daniel Boone's fur trading expedition.

Had the Great Rebellion not occurred, and had I continued living on my family's farm in Graves End, my passage into manhood would have occurred later and been more difficult. Even though my brother Robert was sixteen and doing a man's work when we left Graves End, Father wouldn't treat him as a man. As a younger son it would have been even harder to convince Father that I was no longer a child. There's more than a little truth in the saying that a man is not fully a man until his father dies.

CHAPTER 14

I'd been in the mountains on the way from Pennsylvania to North Carolina, but that'd been in the height of summer, when the trees had all their leaves and wildflowers grew along the sides of the road. Now that winter was approaching, the trees were bare and the flowers long gone. The road followed valley bottoms, where we could see nothing but the mountains on either side. Occasionally, we climbed to a gap where our view expanded to ridge after ridge of mountains out to the horizon. Even in the middle of the day, clouds lay in the hollows between these ridges. In spring or summer this vista would have been inviting, with the mountains dappled in a dozen different shades of green and sunlight shining off the clouds. But in November everything was grey and cold. No wonder bears found cosy dens and slept through the winter.

We reached Nikwasi, the main Cherokee village on the east side of the mountains, in the late afternoon of our ninth day of travel. It consisted of about fifty huts surrounded by a stockade. British Army stockades are always precise rectangles, but Cherokee stockades are ovals that occasionally divert to avoid obstacles. Acres of harvested fields surrounded the village.

Cherokee legend tells of ghost warriors who protect Nikwasi from attack. The ghosts must have been off-duty in 1776, when Rutherford and his North Carolina Militia burned it. The Cherokee moved back after he'd left and rebuilt their village. Their new stockade was a little larger than the old one, whose charred stumps reminded all of Rutherford's attack.

All eyes were on us as we rode slowly to the centre of the village and Nikwasi's council house, a wooden structure whose roof was covered with earth, large enough to hold all the inhabitants of the town, male and female. We were ushered into the house and greeted by Arcowee, the village's white chief. Each Cherokee village had two chiefs, a white chief for peace and a red chief for war, part of the Cherokee's belief in balance. Peace balances war, women balance men, summer balances winter. Maintaining these balances leads to happiness, whilst disturbing them leads to strife.

Inside the council house was almost as dark as a moonless night. The only light came from a small fire burning in the centre of its single large room. The draft was so poor that smoke filled the room instead of escaping through the hole in the roof above the fireplace. My eyes stung and my nose was assailed by the accumulated stink of the building. Our Cherokee hosts seemed unbothered by the smoke or smell. Mercifully, the greeting ceremony was short. Arcowee's speech took only a few minutes, then he and Boone shared a pipe. Boone presented a few gifts to the chief and invited all to share the whiskey he'd brought. We trooped outside and a riotous party began. Squire guarded our horses and trade goods. If not, we'd have lost both.

We set up our camp a short distance outside the stockade and began trading the next morning. The prices for our goods were well-established, so the only haggling was over the quality of the deerskin we were offered in trade. The best quality deerskin is soft, uniformly light brown in colour, and completely covered with fur, but few skins met that standard. Most had blemishes or areas not covered with fur. Identifying these flaws was easy; the skill came in deciding how much to pay for the flawed skins. I listened whilst Boone, Donald, and the other fur traders haggled with the Cherokee through interpreters. On the second day, I thought I recognized a pattern in the trade and started haggling myself. Thankfully, my errors were in offering too little for the deerskins. This caused the Cherokee to turn to other traders, who soon began running out of goods to trade. I was able to make up for my slow start by trading more at the end of our stay, but I ended up with poorer quality hides.

The only other white man in Nikwasi seemed none too happy to see us. He stayed out of the council house whilst Arcowee welcomed us, and made himself scarce when we and the Cherokee started drinking. My bad experience with whiskey was still fresh in my mind, and I left the group gathered around the fire as soon as I could. I was wandering along a small stream just outside the stockade when I saw him slowly casting stones into the water.

"Hello. I'm William Watson. Who are you?"

"Isaac Grossmann."

"Are you a fur trader too?

"No, I'm just here to spend some time with the Cherokee and learn their ways. Now, if you'll excuse me, I have work to do."

He left before I could say anything else. His strange behaviour aroused my curiosity. He was thin, medium height, had dark eyes, and a full black beard. He wore a linen shirt, homespun woollen pants, and a Quaker style hat with a broad brim, which he didn't remove despite the warmth of the evening. His dress marked him as a city man but told me little else.

The next day, after we had concluded our trading, I sought him out. He was sitting in front of one of the huts, speaking a strange language to an old Cherokee man, who seemed bemused but tolerant. When Grossmann saw me, he muttered "You again," just loud enough for me to hear before getting up and leaving. The Cherokee smiled and pointed, first to the glass beads and brass buttons on the ground in front of him, then in the direction that Grossmann had gone. This made me even more curious. Why was Grossmann giving gifts to this old man?

The following day, I found Grossmann sitting in front of another hut, this time talking in his strange language to an old woman. Again there were beads and buttons on the ground. I waited until he was finished, then followed him as he walked along the stream.

"Why are you following me?" Grossmann asked as he turned to face me.

"I'm curious about what you're doing."

"It's none of your affair."

"I know, but I mean you no harm."

"I guess the only way to get rid of you is to tell you why I'm here,"

Grossmann said, shrugging his shoulders. "I come from Charleston and am a member of the Carolina Israelite Congregation."

"A Jew," I said in amazement.

"Yes, a Jew. You've probably never met one before."

"You're right. I haven't."

"Well, don't worry. We don't have horns and we don't eat Christian children."

He squatted down by the stream and started casting stones into it, as he had done on the first day I'd seen him. I squatted down beside him.

"I'm here," Grossman started, "because my rabbi read a book by James Adair who claims that the Indians are the descendants of the ten lost tribes of Israel. The rabbi told me to find out whether it's true. He said I would be the most famous Jew since *Rambam* if I found the children of the ten lost tribes, and that even if I didn't find them, the congregation would honour me for trying. He picked me because I'm the only man in his congregation who'd ever been in the mountains. So here I am speaking Hebrew to the Cherokee. They listen to me because I give them trinkets, but they don't understand a word I say." He paused for a moment and picked up a few more stones to throw into the stream.

"Indians being the descendants of the ten lost tribes of Israel . . . that's the most preposterous thing I've ever heard," I said.

"You're right, it's probably a *bubba meinseh*, an old woman's tale, but what if it was true?" Grossmann said, looking wistfully across the stream.

"Did Adair explain why he thought the Indians were the descendants of ancient Hebrews?"

"The rabbi said he had twenty-three arguments," Grossmann said, smiling at what must have been a quizzical look on my face. "Everything from belonging to tribes to being concerned about impure foods. But most heathen people belong to tribes, and all people worry about impure food. Cherokee men aren't circumcised and they don't cover their heads. Even if they are descendants of the ten lost tribes, they forgot what it means to be a Jew centuries ago. I'm on a fool's errand," he said as he stood up and left.

The rabbi in Charleston wasn't the only one intrigued by Adair's outlandish claim that the Indians were the descendants of the ancient Israelites. Over the years I've read of many expeditions to Indian tribes more remote than the Cherokee looking for proof. In sixty years no one has come up with any evidence that Adair was right, but that hasn't stopped the search.

By the end of the fifth day, we had as many deerskins as our horses could carry and almost nothing left to trade. Boone told us that we would leave the next morning to return to Salisbury. "Now comes the dangerous part," he added ominously. "We didn't have to worry about the Cherokee attacking us on the way to their village. They could've stolen our goods, but their neighbours would be angry at them for not giving them a chance to trade. Now that all we have is hides, they can steal them and sell them again to the next group of traders who come by."

Boone's warning frightened me. I could do nothing but trust that he, Donald, and the other fur traders would protect me. We made our way back to the Proclamation Line as quickly as we could. We kept our rifles and pistols primed and ready, and at night took turns guarding our camp.

On our second night, Ben Cutbirth woke us up in the early hours of the morning after hearing a hooting sound that he didn't think was an owl. We listened as hard as we could. The sound was not repeated. No one went back to sleep that night, and we broke camp as soon as there was enough light for us to make our way. We didn't see any Cherokee, but the road was full of the hoof prints of unshod horses. Were they from Cherokee peacefully hunting, or were they from a war party planning to steal our goods? Prudence demanded that we assume the worst.

We saw no Cherokee for six days, but as we approached Swannanoa Gap and the Proclamation Line, a half dozen fully-armed warriors rode towards us. When they saw the size of our party, they turned off at an angle rather than passing us. We became even more wary, looking back over our shoulders every few minutes and peering at the forest on either side of us for any sign that the Cherokee had gotten reinforcements and returned to attack. I breathed a sigh of relief four hours later when we reached Davidson's Fort without further incident. The advice Donald and I had gotten about not going into Cherokee country alone had been correct.

On our return from Nikwasi, Al Neely argued that we should cut across country and smuggle our furs into Salisbury. Boone wouldn't hear of it. He was often in legal trouble over careless business dealings, but he was an honest man who never cheated or lied. Donald and Squire Boone agreed with Daniel about paying the customs duty. Ben Cutbirth and I stayed silent. Outnumbered, Al grumbled, but had no choice other than to stay with the group. Riding off alone was too dangerous. We paid the tariff of one fur in ten at Davidson's Fort, got a customs receipt, and continued on to Salisbury.

Our expedition had been successful and Mr Cartwright was pleased with the deerskins we'd brought back. My share of the proceeds was ten deerskins, worth about three pounds, very good wages for three weeks' work, and I owned a horse, a grey gelding named Smoke. When I commented that it wasn't a very imaginative name, Mr Cartwright told me that Jenny had been only five years old when she had named the horse. I said nothing further and banished any thought of changing the horse's name from my mind.

"Mrs Cartwright has returned from Charleston. Will the two of you join us for supper? You can keep your horses in the barn and sleep in the loft tonight. I'm sure Jenny will want to hear all about your adventures, William," Mr Cartwright said when we finished reckoning the proceeds from the trip.

I was embarrassed but managed to say yes and thank you without stammering. At supper I again talked too much, but the Cartwrights, especially Billy, seemed interested in every detail. Jenny spoke a little more this time. She wanted to know how Cherokee families lived, but whilst she was asking, I had a feeling that this was not her real question.

"Were the Cherokee girls pretty?" she finally asked. She'd been looking at me most of the evening but now looked down demurely.

"Not particularly," I said. I'd thought them very pretty, but knew enough not to tell her that. It was a good answer because she looked up and smiled at me. I didn't have the courage to say, "Not as pretty as you." Mr and Mrs Cartwright would surely have disapproved had I done that.

The evening was too soon over.

CHAPTER 15

It was cold when I awakened the next morning. Winter was coming, but I'd been so engrossed in my trip to the Cherokee that I'd given no thought to preparing for it. I remembered the fable of the ant and the grasshopper. Had I been a grasshopper all summer? I had more money in my purse that I'd ever had before, but no work or place to live, and a horse to care for. Donald obviously shared my worries.

"Amos, William and I need to find someplace to live for the next few months. It's too late this year to build a cabin," he said over breakfast.

"Widow Findley takes in lodgers," Mr Cartwright told us after thinking for a moment. "She's got a barn for your horses and she'll probably let you work for part of your rent. She lives in the Charleston Road, about a quarter mile out of town, in a big white clapboard house that needs painting. Tell her I'll vouch for you."

We found Mrs Findley later that morning. She was an elderly woman, somewhat unsteady on her feet, with white hair and a face deeply furrowed by wrinkles. She was a bit deaf, and we had to speak louder than normal to be understood, but age had not dulled her wits. After pouring us cups of tea and setting out a loaf of bread and a pot of jam, she questioned us carefully. We talked for well over an hour, and by the time we finished, she knew our life stories. She must have been satisfied with what she heard because, after putting more hot water in the tea pot, she told us about herself.

"My husband, John, was a blacksmith. He had his shop in the barn. He was a good man, but he died of apoplexy two years ago. It's a struggle for an old woman like me to live on her own. My son lives in Charleston and my daughter lives in Fairfax County, Virginia. They're good children, but I wouldn't want to live with either of them. I've much more than the two mites the widow in the Bible had, and as long as I do, I want to be independent." She paused for a moment, as if deciding what to say next.

"You can board here for six pence a week each, if you chop all the firewood I need, keep the fireplaces clean, bring water from the well, and do any other jobs that are hard for me. You can use the barn for your horses, but you'll have to feed them and keep the barn clean. And I expect you to behave like gentlemen in this house."

It was a generous offer, which we quickly accepted.

"The bedroom is on the first floor, up the stairs."

Mrs Findley – her first name was Alma, but we never called her that – was a good cook and housekeeper. After a week she treated us more like family than lodgers, mending our clothes and offering advice.

December passed slowly. There was no work to be had in Salisbury and I didn't know when I could go on another fur trading expedition. Donald and I went hunting and I shot an old buck, the first deer I'd ever bagged.

"Not worth skinning this one," Donald said, after we had bled and gutted the dead deer. "He's had a hard time of it . . . hardly got any hair left."

Looking at the deer's skin, I had to agree.

"His meat ought to be worth something," I said.

"Aye, you ought to get a few shillings for it. I'll find a pole and we'll carry him back to town. Cut off his head. He'll be easier to carry without it."

I chopped off the deer's head whilst Donald trimmed a tree limb into a pole. We trussed the carcass to the pole, which we carried on our shoulders to Mr Burns, Salisbury's butcher. Even without head, guts, or blood, it felt like the deer weighed at least ten stone, more than I did. Mr Burns looked at the meat and said that it would only be good for sausage and jerky. I sold him the deer for four shillings, which supplemented my dwindling funds.

I spent as much time as I could at the Cartwrights and got to know Jenny much better. I was besotted with her. I thought her perfect in every way and she seemed to like me. Before I knew what was happening, the Cartwrights were treating me like a member of their family. They invited me to supper and to join their evening activities on most nights. The family often spent an hour or more singing English ballads. Jenny had a fine soprano voice, which blended well with Mr Cartwright's rich baritone. The rest of the family provided harmony for the two of them. They invited me to sing along, but I declined. I didn't know the words to most of the songs they sang, and my voice still hadn't decided whether it was a boy's or a man's.

I was melancholy that December. I remembered my family and how we'd celebrated *Sint Nicolaas Dag* and Christmas only three years earlier, but I couldn't talk to anyone about it. I didn't want Jenny to think me weak after telling her such heroic stories about escaping from the Hessians and trading with the Cherokee. Mrs Findley probably would have responded with a kind word or two, but I couldn't see shouting out my story to her. Donald had his own loss to think about. Men are not supposed to show such feelings. They're supposed to suck in their guts and soldier on.

I didn't expect the Cartwrights to celebrate Sint Nicolaas Dag – it's a Dutch holiday – but I hoped they would have a big Christmas dinner, like those we had in Graves End. They didn't. Like many other families then, they paid little notice to Christmas.

When I was growing up, Sint Nicolaas Dag, 6th December, when Dutch children and half-Dutch ones like me received their presents, was far more important than Christmas.

"If you're a good boy, Sint Nicolaas will bring you presents, but if you're bad, *Schwartzer Piet*, Black Peter, will steal your presents and you'll end up with nothing," my mother told me when I was a child.

Picture books showed Sint Nicolaas as an old man with a long white beard, who smoked a pipe. Schwartzer Piet was a black boy dressed in a Moorish costume with an evil look on his face.

"Sint Nicolaas and Schwartzer Piet aren't real. The gifts come from Mother and Father and nobody will steal them," my brother, Richard, told me when I was six. I cried when he told me that, but I knew it was true. A few years later, my parents stopped telling me that my gifts came from Sint Nicolaas, but they still told that story to my younger sister, Charlotte.

Poor old Sint Nicolaas! Since that infernal poem about the night before Christmas first appeared twenty years ago, he's been changed into Saint Nicholas and made into an Englishman. The poet didn't even keep Schwartzer Piet. At least his spirit lives on. I've heard some parents tell their children that if they're bad, all they'll get for Christmas is a lump of coal.

After New Year's Day, Boone sent word inviting Donald and me to join the fur trading expedition he would be leading in the spring, as soon as the maple sugaring was over and the roads were passable. We quickly accepted. Mrs Findley promised to keep our room for us. Mr Cartwright agreed to supply us with packhorses and trade goods for only half of the proceeds. This was less than he had taken before, but he was only lending two horses, not giving us two others, as he had on our first trip.

We left on the last Saturday in March. Spring comes earlier in North Carolina than in Graves End or Philadelphia. Bloodroot and spring beauties were blooming, and the dawn chorus of birds was as loud and rich as in summer.

Most of the skins we traded for were otter and beaver. The prices for these were not as well established as for deerskin, so the haggling was more intense. Again I started by offering too little and bought only a few skins for the first two days. As on my first trip, by the time I learned the proper amount to offer, most of the high quality skins had been traded. I bought a full load of lesser quality skins, which meant less profit for me than I might've had. I was serving an apprenticeship, but other than a few hints from Donald, I had to learn by trial and error. Still the trip was a success and after settling up with Mr Cartwright, I had enough money to see me through the summer.

The Cherokee had names in their language for the fur traders they saw regularly. On this trip they began calling me *Dalonige-ugithi*, which I learned meant Yellow Hair. It was a fitting name for me, since my hair was only beginning to turn brown. They called Donald *Asheeshuh-yonuh*, Walking Bear, and Boone was *Ayatena-ahali*, Wide Mouth, because he was always smiling or grinning. At the time I was amused at having a Cherokee name, but it was an important step towards being accepted by them.

Donald had a letter from his cousin, Alexander, waiting for him when we returned to Salisbury. It had been following him for a while, from Mr McNeil in Philadelphia to Mr Straub in Salem to Mr Cartwright.

"Alexander wants me to join him and the family in Montreal. He's a clerk for the Hudson's Bay Company and says that the opportunities for fur traders in the Canadian woods are endless," Donald told me after reading the letter.

"But trade with the Cherokee is good here in North Carolina," I replied.

"I know, but there are too many memories around here. I thought getting back into the mountains would be all that I needed, but every time I pass a cabin with a family, I think of Rachel. I need to get as far away from here as I can. You could come with me."

"I think I'll stay here," I said as a vision of Jenny popped into my head.

Donald left two days later. He had no affairs to settle, no belongings to dispose of, and he wasn't interested in long farewells. I was to tell people that he was gone. He planned to ride to Charleston, sell his horse, and travel by boat to Montreal. It would have been simpler to take a boat to New York or Boston and travel overland from there, but that would have meant crossing the Proclamation Line and spending several days riding through Iroquois country, which wasn't safe for a lone traveller.

"If you change your mind, look me up in Montreal," were Donald's parting words. We shook hands and he disappeared from my life. I'd lost my second father. How would I learn all the things I needed to know to be a backwoodsman? Without Donald, would Daniel Boone continue to invite me to join his fur trading expeditions? I'd chosen Jenny over Donald. I could only hope I'd made the right choice.

CHAPTER 16

A few days after Donald left, Mr Cartwright called me to the small room in the back of the shop that he used as his office. It had a varnished pinewood desk and chair, two chairs for guests, and shelves piled high with ledgers and other records of his business. I'd never been in this room before and had no idea of what to expect. He motioned me into a seat across the desk from him.

"Young man, I've teased you about your intentions towards my daughter, but now let me be serious. I assume you want to marry her," he said, looking off to the side.

Jenny was his oldest daughter and I was her first suitor. He seemed embarrassed by having to talk about her future.

"Yes, sir, if she'll have me," I said, looking down. I, too, was embarrassed.

"From what Mrs Cartwright tells me, you have nothing to worry about. It seems you are the only young man she thinks about. She's fourteen this summer, but I don't want her marrying until she's sixteen. If she changes her mind between now and then, it's your misfortune. Or you may change your mind."

"Oh no, sir. She's the only girl I'll ever love." I fervently believed this to be true.

"Easy words for you to say now, but we'll see what happens," Mr

Cartwright replied. "Now the question every father asks. How will you support her?" He must have judged the conversation was going well, because his tone became more confident.

"I'm learning to be a fur trader. I think I can earn enough to support her." I still could not look him in the face.

"You've been lucky so far. You've made two trips and been able to bring back a full load of furs each time. Ask Boone how often fur traders come back empty-handed." I had no reply for that sobering thought.

"It's not the traders who make money out of furs," Mr Cartwright continued. "It's merchants like me who get a larger share of the profits and don't risk our necks. I can teach you to become one of us. From what you've told me, you already know quite a bit about commerce from your time in Philadelphia."

"Mr McNeil was a good teacher."

"Think about what I've said, and when you're ready, come see me. I think you've got the brains to be a good businessman," he concluded, now confident and looking directly at me.

"Thank you, sir," I said. I stood and backed out of the room as quickly as I could.

I knew Mr Cartwright was right, that being a fur trader was too risky for a married man, even if Boone and most of his companions were married and had families. But I kept thinking of my grandfather's ironmongery shop in New York City and how I'd run off with the rebel army rather than face life there. Two trips into Cherokee land had given me a taste of adventure and I wanted more. When Daniel Boone sent a message a week later asking whether I wanted to join his deer hunting expedition to Kentucky, I quickly said yes.

"Young men have to sow their wild oats," Mr Cartwright said, shaking his head, when I told him that I was going to Kentucky with Boone. "My offer to teach you to be a merchant won't be good forever. My son, Billy, will be old enough to start learning the business in a few years. I won't be able to teach both of you at the same time and I'll not let you marry Jenny until I'm sure that you can support her and your family. Now, go tell her that you'll be leaving her again and come back safely." It was a kinder response than I deserved.

Jenny knew about her father's conversation with me about marrying her and how I had answered. She wasn't surprised when I told her that I wanted to go deer hunting in Kentucky with Daniel Boone.

"I'll count the days until you return," she said, pecking my cheek with a quick kiss. "Keep this to remember me by." She gave me the ribbon from her hair.

"I'll keep it close to my heart," I said. It was a line I'd read in a story, but I hoped she would think it was original. "I'll be back soon." I didn't have the courage to return her kiss. Had I any sense, I would've changed my mind and stayed in Salisbury, but I had heard so much about Kentucky from Boone that I ached to see it.

I left Salisbury in late May and rode to Boone's homestead. Despite his misgivings about the trip, Mr Cartwright lent me a packhorse and provided the supplies I would need for the next two months in exchange for half the proceeds. Boone, his wife, Rebecca, their five unmarried children, and six of Rebecca's orphaned cousins lived in a log cabin he'd built on the Yadkin River after the British had chased them out of Kentucky.

Boone referred to his wife as "my little girl," even though she was a formidable woman, buxom, and nearly as tall as him, with black hair, which was showing the first signs of silver. She looked worn and tired from decades of child-bearing and housework, but I still thought her beautiful. She was well-respected by all who knew her for her strength of character and homemaking skills. She was reputed to be as fearless as her husband and just as good with a rifle, though I never had occasion to see her demonstrate either trait.

There were many conflicting sides to Daniel Boone's character. He loved the solitude of the woods, and would have hunted and trapped alone if not for the danger involved. But he was also a devoted family man, happy to put up with the crowding created by having all of his and Rebecca's family close by. He disliked living close to any neighbours and, before the Great Rebellion, had moved several times when others settled close to him. But he led a party of settlers to Boonesborough and lived with them for two years until the British burnt the settlement. He had a profound respect for the natural world, and knew that he and settlers like him were destroying it, but he would also brag about the number of deer and bear he'd killed.

The Boones had their share of family tragedy. Their oldest son, James, had been tortured and murdered by a band of Indians. Another son, William, died shortly after birth. In 1777, they had to leave Kentucky with only the clothes on their backs and what little of their possessions they could carry. Yet Boone was one of the most cheerful men I've ever met. Good fortune was always over the next mountain, and if not there, over the mountain after that. His answer to the financial difficulties he always seemed to face was to head for the forest to hunt and trap. A good load of furs would solve his immediate problems; the future would take care of itself.

Boone's cabin was grander than most with two large rooms and a split log, puncheon floor. Boone had split logs and laid them flat side up as close together as possible. The gaps between the logs were filled with sand from the creek bed. Building and maintaining such a floor was more work than most settlers were willing to do, but the result was more attractive and far cleaner than the usual earth floor. Boone made that kind of effort for his family without a second thought.

Suzy, the Boones' oldest daughter, her husband, Will Hays, and their baby, Will Jr., also lived in the cabin. Suzy was a brazen woman. She was nursing and would drop the top of her dress and flaunt her breasts before picking up baby Will. Women's breasts fascinated me, as they do all young men. I'd occasionally caught a quick glimpse of one, usually when a woman was shifting a nursing baby. I'd not seen Jenny's. They were beginning to fill her blouse and I imagined them to be small, perfect spheres. Suzy's breasts were shaped like small pouches with nipples at their ends, and they slanted away from each other. They weren't the melons that I'd heard breasts referred to and I thought them odd-shaped. It made me uncomfortable, but I couldn't help staring. Suzy seemed to take a malicious amusement from my discomfort at seeing her. She was very different from her mother, who was in no way flirtatious.

I stayed with the Boones for two days before five of us started for Kentucky: Boone, his younger brother, Squire, Ben Cutbirth, Al Neely, and me. I knew everyone from our earlier trading expeditions to the Cherokee, and felt honoured that Boone would invite me to join his party. We followed a route that Boone had explored on his first trip to Kentucky in 1769, over the mountains to the Watauga River, then along a Cherokee path to the Cumberland Gap.

As we came through the gap, we met a squadron of British cavalry headed back to Virginia, the first people we'd seen since leaving Boone's homestead.

"Good day to you, Lieutenant Sullivan," Boone said.

"And to you, Mr Boone. Off hunting, I see," the officer answered. "I trust you'll pay the duty on your furs when you return."

"You know that I always do," Boone answered. "Any Indians on the warpath?"

"None that we saw."

"That's good news."

Boone and the lieutenant passed some pleasantries and then we headed west into Kentucky. We travelled only a short distance farther before coming to a road that headed north.

"This is the road I built in 1775," Boone said, stretching in his saddle.

"Where does it go?" I asked.

"To the settlement I started for Richard Henderson," he answered, getting off his horse. We all followed his lead and dismounted.

"Henderson insisted on calling it Boonesborough," Boone continued, looking towards the north, "but I've always been embarrassed by that. We'll not go that far. The British burned it two years ago and it would break my heart to see it in ashes. We'd better rest here for a while. The road is overgrown and hard travelling.

"It's sad. Deer hunters like us are the only ones who use my road any more. None of us are going to spend the time clearing away the greenbrier and fallen trees. In another two years, it'll be hard to tell that there was a road here."

It was one of the few times I heard Boone express regrets over anything.

We stayed on Boone's road for a day, then headed west, cross-country towards the Great Meadow, the best hunting in Kentucky. The meadow was not the open grassland I'd imagined. We rode through trees that were more widely spaced than in the dense forest of North Carolina, and past the canebrakes, thick reeds higher than a man on horseback, that grew in the wet areas. It was fertile land, which would have been easy to clear for farming had the British allowed settlement.

After another day's travel, we set up camp in a large cave in the side of a limestone cliff. A nearby spring supplied us with cool, delicious water, and a salt lick about a mile away attracted deer, bear, and other game. Boone had been to this idyllic spot on an earlier hunting trip.

"Once our Daniel has been to a place, he never forgets it," Ben Cutbirth told me. The unerring way in which Boone led us to our campsite bore testimony to this claim.

Anyone who spends time in the woods quickly learns to identify a deer's two-toed hoof print and the pellets that make up its droppings, but Boone could find deer by many other markings.

"See this broken twig and the way this grass is pressed down?" Boone asked me one day whilst we were hunting. "A deer came through here about an hour ago." I could see these signs when he showed them to me, but I rarely could pick them out for myself. The few times I did, I felt a great sense of achievement.

Whilst Boone was a superb tracker, he rarely hunted by following deer. Usually he found a deer trail near a salt lick or a stream and waited for the deer to come to him. The best times were early morning, just after dawn, or late afternoon, just before sunset. We made two trips a day to the salt lick near our camp and were usually rewarded with at least one kill.

Hunters want a deer to fall where it's shot, not stagger off into the brush, so they try to kill it with a single bullet either to its head or to its heart. A head shot doesn't leave a hole in the deer's hide, but it's riskier, since a deer's head is small compared with the rest of its body. Boone was an excellent marksman and usually aimed for a deer's head.

Finding and killing deer were only the first parts of our work. We bled and gutted the deer where we killed them. When we could, we also skinned them in the woods because it's easier to remove a deer's skin whilst its body is still warm. Also, it saved us the work of carrying deer back to camp.

When we couldn't skin the deer where we killed it, the hunter would sling the deer over his shoulders, and holding on to its legs, which were draped over his chest, carry it back to camp. Boone called this *hoppusing*. I've never heard anyone other than deer hunters use that word. Hoppusing was hard, dirty work. No matter how carefully the deer had been bled and gutted, the hunter would be covered with blood and guts by the time he got to camp. Even though the deer could've been trussed up to a pole and carried by two men, as Donald and I had done the previous December, Boone and the other hunters on this trip made it a point of honour to carry their own kills back to camp.

On that trip I tried hoppusing a deer I'd shot. I collapsed before I'd walked a dozen steps. I still only weighted about eight stone and couldn't carry ten stone of deer.

"Wait until you've put on a little more weight before you try that again," Boone said.

"Yes, sir," was the only thing I could think to say whilst I caught my breath. Boone picked up the deer and hoppused it back to our camp without breathing hard.

We shot so many deer that we didn't need most of them for meat. We took their tongues, livers, and an occasional haunch for food, but most, sometimes all, of the skinned carcass was left on the ground. Wolves and buzzards ate well when deer hunters were around.

Skinning a deer to preserve its pelt is an art. Boone instructed me as I watched him skin the first deer he'd shot after we'd set up camp.

"First, cut a circle around the deer's neck, close to the shoulders," he said. "Then cut down from the throat and along the breast to the hole you made to gut the deer. If the cut doesn't go all the way to the tail, extend the cut through the deer's arse hole."

The next step was to cut circles around the deer's four legs, just below its knees. Boone then cut along the inside of the deer's legs to connect these circles to the cut he'd already made through the deer's belly. His final cut was a circle around the deer's tail. He was now ready to peel the skin off the deer.

"William, grab the deerskin at the neck and peel it back," he said.

I grabbed the edge of the deerskin and pulled it back. The skin slowly peeled away from the deer's body. Boone shoved his fist into the widening gap to speed the work. In the few places where the bond between skin and body was too tough for us to break, Boone used his knife to separate them.

"You need to use your knife very carefully," Boone said, the first time he did this. "You don't want to cut the skin or leave any flesh on it."

We still needed to prepare the skin for transport back to North Carolina. We did this work back at camp. First, we scraped away all traces of meat and fat from the inside of the skin. If we'd done a good job of skinning the deer, this was a quick, easy task. Then, we scraped the rough hair off the outside of the skin and softened the skin by rubbing it over a rounded board until we could fold it easily. Only then was the skin ready for packing. It took hours of work to prepare each skin.

One day, as I was walking through the woods with Boone and Al Neely, they spotted a small plant with red berries and clusters of three large leaves and two small ones growing under an oak tree.

"I'll be damned," Boone exclaimed. "I didn't think there'd be any 'seng growing in here. It usually likes thicker woods."

He carefully dug up the plant, which had two roots growing together, shaped like a little man. Once he had extracted the roots, he pulled off the berries and placed them in the hole he'd made then covered them over.

"Need to make sure there's a crop of 'seng the next time we're here," Boone said.

"What's 'seng?" I asked.

"'Seng is ginseng," Neely told me. "The Orientals think it's powerful medicine, that it'll make them stronger lovers. Me, I don't need any help from a silly looking root. But 'seng is worth two, three shillings a pound once you've washed and dried it. Some trips we make more money from it than from deerskin."

I looked at Boone, not willing to trust what Neely had told me.

"Al's right. We ought to spend a few hours looking around for more ginseng."

We did that and soon collected almost five hundred roots. It was easier work than hoppusing and skinning deer. When we brought them back to camp, we carefully washed all the soil off the roots, then set them out to dry on a rack we built for that purpose.

"Don't we have to worry that a squirrel or some other critter will eat the 'seng?" I asked.

"Nah," Ben Cutbirth replied. "Seems like the Celestials are the only ones who'll eat 'seng, and they make tea out of it."

After a month we had a full load of deerskins and about twenty-five pounds of ginseng. We were ready to return home. We started back through the Great Meadow towards Boone's road. On our second day of travel, as we were approaching the mountains, we suddenly found ourselves surrounded by a dozen Cherokee, all pointing British army muskets at us. We had no choice but surrender. Even Boone, who was as skilled in detecting danger as any man, had no indication that we were riding into a trap.

"Ayatena-ahali, I think you and your friends should trade with us," the leader of the Cherokee said, eyeing our horses and rifles. "I will give you this blanket for your packhorse and furs."

"That is very generous of you," Boone replied. With a dozen muskets pointed at him, what else could he say?

"We should also trade guns. I will give you this musket the British gave me for your rifle." Again Boone complied. The other Indians made similar trades with the rest of us, then rode off. Al Neely tried to fire the musket he'd just been given, only to discover that it was unloaded. We'd been tricked.

"Well, boys, I guess we go home and hope our wives still love us," Boone said after the Cherokee were gone.

"Is that all you're going to say?" I asked. "Those bloody Cherokee bastards just took all our deerskins, our 'seng, our packhorses, and our rifles."

"But, William, the Cherokee didn't steal anything from you; they traded," Boone explained. He was smiling as if we'd just been victims of a harmless prank, but I couldn't understand why. "For a Cherokee, stealing is the worst of bad manners, but getting the better of someone in a trade is admirable. By giving us something in exchange for what they took, the Cherokee satisfied their rules." Squire, Al, and Ben, all of whom had been the victims of such trades in the past, nodded in agreement.

"At least we still have our horses, and British Army muskets to hunt with," Boone added. "It'd be a long walk home."

We made the rest of the trip home without difficulty. For a while my anger grew, but then I started worrying about what I was going to say to Mr Cartwright. He'd been right in his warning of the dangers fur traders face. I could only hope that he'd still allow me to court Jenny. And what would she think of me? Everything I'd told her had made me seem like a hero, but what kind of a hero allows his furs to be stolen by a band of Indians?

I stayed with the Boones on the Yadkin River for one night. Rebecca was happy to see Daniel, even if he had come home empty-handed.

CHAPTER 17

Facing Mr Cartwright and telling him that the Cherokee had stolen my rifle, packhorse, and deerskins, and that he had lost his investment was not pleasant. He again told me that if I wanted to marry Jenny, I'd have to show him that I could support her and a family. I had no choice but to say I understood and accept his offer to train me to run a shop. I was only sixteen, but it seemed that my adventuring days were over.

"This means we're betrothed," Jenny said, when I told her that I'd start working as her father's clerk.

"I guess it does," I said, kissing her full on the mouth, the first time that I'd done that. She didn't draw back.

Jenny knew that we'd have to wait almost two years before we could marry, but that didn't stop her talking about our wedding and the type of home we would make.

"My birthday is in June, so we'll have fine weather for our wedding," she said a few weeks later. "Would you like to have our wedding meal outdoors?"

"Sounds good, but what if it rained?" I replied.

"Oh, maybe we shouldn't do that"

"I want to have lots of babies," she told me another time. "I remember when Billy was a baby. He was so cuddly. I could hold him for hours."

"Babies are nice," I said. I thought that families had as many children as God provided and didn't expect us to be any different. It would be a while before I learned that there were ways to avoid having babies, or at least to try to avoid having them.

"I'd like to live here in Salisbury, but in our own home," she said yet another time.

"I want our own home, too, even if it's just a one-room cabin," I said, nodding my head in agreement.

"We'll have a nicer home than that."

"I hope so."

I was deeply troubled during those first few months after I agreed to Mr Cartwright's terms. I thought I loved Jenny and wanted her more than anything else, but I couldn't envision myself as a married man and the head of a family, like my father or Mr Cartwright. When I tried to do this, a voice inside my head laughed and said, *William, you're only a boy.*

By winter, the idea of being married to Jenny was no longer new. I saw her every day, ate dinner and supper with the Cartwrights, and went to church with them every Sunday. I wasn't fully part of their family yet, but they treated me as if I was. I still slept at Mrs Findley's and did chores for her. It wouldn't have been proper for me to sleep in the Cartwrights' house.

After her initial excitement, Jenny stopped asking me questions about our wedding and how we'd live, but we still talked for what must have been hours at a time. She told me about her friends and relatives. Her mother was a Harris and came from a large family in Wilmington. Jenny had met all of her relatives several times when her mother had taken her to visit. Her father's family was smaller, and lived in many different places. She hadn't met any of them.

I told her much more about my life.

"We'll name our first girl Jacoba after your mother and our first boy David after your father," Jenny said after I'd told her about my parents and how they'd died.

"I'd like that," I said. I felt tears welling up in my eyes and turned away, pretending to cough. Jenny was the first person I'd told that my mother had died of smallpox. Saying that we would name our first daughter Jacoba was the best response she could have given me.

I told her about my sister, brother, and grandparents, the only family I knew.

"Your grandfather sounds frightful, but I should like to meet your grandmother. Do you think we could go to New York City?"

"I don't know if my grandfather would let us see her," I said, telling her about the letter I'd written to him whilst I was in Philadelphia and about his reply. "I didn't go back to New York two years ago when he ordered me to. He'd probably throw me out of his house."

"Did your father have a large family?" she asked.

I told her that my great-grandfather had settled in Northampton, Massachusetts, in 1693, and that dozens of his descendants still live there. I said that my father left because he was the fourth son in his family and had no chance of inheriting his father's farm . . . that I'd never met any of those relatives . . . that my father hadn't talked much about them . . . and that I didn't think he'd corresponded with them.

"Other than looking around Northampton for someone named Watson," I said, "I wouldn't know how we'd find any of them."

"Then the Cartwrights and Harrises will have to be your family."

I told her about Sint Nicolaas Dag.

"We'll tell our children about him, and give them presents on 6th December," she said, when she heard the story.

"I'd like to do that," I said. I had a wonderful vision of two boys and a girl, Jenny's and my children, sitting around a dining table looking up at me whilst I told them about Sint Nicolaas and Schwartzer Piet, then all of them promising to be good. I realized that I could be the head of a family – our family – and I wanted that very much.

Kissing Jenny and holding her hand were acceptable, but I knew of no way to satisfy the lust that burned inside of me. I'd heard Mr Worthington, our pastor in Graves End, say in one of his sermons that onanism was unnatural and a great sin. The Bible said that Onan spilled his seed on the ground. I thought this was something that men did when no women were around, but I wasn't sure and didn't know what Onan had done. I wished I had someone I could talk to about it. By this time I knew some boys my age in Salisbury, but their response to my being betrothed to Jenny was a stream of lewd jokes and comments. I might've been able to talk to Donald, but he was a thousand miles away. So I suffered and hoped that I was successfully hiding the wet sheets that I sometimes found myself lying on in the morning.

Mr Cartwright's business was similar to Mr McNeil's in many ways. Both kept the same records, but Mr Cartwright did not have the additional complication of keeping track of the value of British Army receipts or of goods bought from smugglers. I had no difficulty learning to keep his business accounts. Mr McNeil had bartered for produce from farmers and goods from ship captains. Mr Cartwright bartered for produce and furs. He watched me as I made my first few trades with the hunters and trappers who brought pelts to the shop. After that he was happy to let me handle these transactions myself. Mr McNeil's lessons about remaining calm whilst conducting business served me well. I never lost my temper or responded to the threats and curses I sometimes received, and made better profits from those who reviled me than from those who stayed calm.

As in Mr McNeil's shop in Philadelphia, there were many times in Mr Cartwright's shop when I had nothing to do. I spent many of those hours reading the Mr Cartwright's library, then books I borrowed from his neighbours. They were a varied lot, everything from practical books like *The Compleat Angler* to *Pamela* and other novels. And I continued my Latin studies with a book of Cicero's rhetoric. Jenny knew how to read but had no interest in books. I tried talking to her several times about what I had read, but she quickly became bored. This didn't trouble me. I'd never met a girl or woman who was interested in books other than the Bible.

I worked for Mr Cartwright through 1780 and into early 1781. Jenny and I planned to be married on the 21st June, Midsummer's Day, the Sunday after her sixteenth birthday. My life seemed all arranged.

In mid-February, Josiah Terrill, whom I knew from the many times he'd brought furs to Mr Cartwright's shop, told me that he, Alan Swain, and Geoff Carlyle were planning an expedition to buy furs from the Cherokee. Instead of bringing them back to Salisbury, they planned to continue on and sell them to the Spanish in New Orleans.

"Isn't that illegal? Didn't Parliament pass a law a few years ago saying that furs could only be traded to British merchants?" I asked when he told me his plan.

"Yes, it's illegal, but you can get more for your furs there than in Salisbury and you don't have to pay the customs duty. The British Army is too busy watching the Cherokee and the other Indian tribes to worry about a few fur traders sneaking off to trade with the Spanish," he replied.

A dozen years earlier, before there were any of the rules that were imposed after the Great Rebellion, Ben Cutbirth and some of his friends were the first to make the trip from North Carolina to New Orleans. They were successful in hunting and trading, and had gotten a good price for their furs. But on the way home they lost everything to white thieves. Ben swore he'd never go back. Several other expeditions had been successful, but most fur traders thought the extra profit they could make by trading with the Spanish wasn't worth the risks involved.

"Why don't you join us? One last chance at freedom before you're tied down as a married man. We can travel to New Orleans and return in two months. You'll be back in plenty of time to marry sweet Jenny," Terrill told me.

"Didn't Ben Cutbirth take much longer than that?" I asked.

"Yes, but he tried to float down the Mississippi and ended up getting stuck on snags and the river banks. We'll go overland and avoid those problems. It'll be faster," Terrill assured me. The Devil couldn't have been more persuasive had he been bargaining for my soul.

Terrill was not a man you would pick out of a crowd. He was average height, and had brown hair and eyes, but so did many other men. He wore a short beard and had a scar across his brow, the result of falling out of a tree when he was a boy, he once told me. He had a good reputation amongst the other fur traders. They said he was dependable and unafraid, but a bit of a loner. If he had a family, he never mentioned them. He wasn't a storyteller and usually didn't say very much. Travelling with him would be less entertaining than travelling with Boone.

I'd been a clerk in Mr Cartwright's shop for a year and a half and was growing bored. Going to New Orleans would be an adventure. If I make this trip, I told myself as I mulled over the idea, I'll miss Jenny and that'll prove how much I love her . . . the proceeds from this trip will help us get started as a married couple . . . the trip will keep me from worrying about the future. Much as I believed with all my heart that I loved Jenny, I was scared of marriage.

Two days after Terrill invited me to join his expedition, I made up my mind to go. I'd agreed to work as a clerk in Mr Cartwright's shop, but I never promised to give up fur trading. I was a free man who could do whatever I chose, or so I told myself. I talked to Jenny first.

"I don't want you to go. What if something happens to you? You need to be here with me," she argued. She didn't stamp her feet, but I could feel the anger in her words.

"Nothing will happen to me. I'll be back in mid-May, a month before our wedding. And I'll make heaps of money. We'll be able to start our married life in style," I replied, stroking her shoulder.

"You truly want to do this?" the tone of her voice changed from angry to concerned. My touch seemed to have changed her mood.

"Yes," I said, continuing to caress her shoulder.

"Then go, but come back quickly," she said, shifting her body to fold more easily into mine.

Mr Cartwright was even less happy about my plans.

"William, you're being irresponsible," he said, his eyes drilling holes in me. "The trip's too dangerous. Have you told Jenny?"

"Yes, and she said that I could go," I replied, trying my best not to flinch under his gaze.

"Then there's nothing I could say that would stop you, but I'm not going to finance this trip," he said.

"I wasn't going to ask you for help. Terrill's already arranged for trade goods and pack horses." That destroyed his last hold on me and he quickly shifted tone.

"I want your solemn oath that this will be your last trading trip."

"You have it, sir." I was happy to give him this assurance and gave no thought as to whether I actually meant it.

The next three weeks were difficult. I continued working in Mr Cartwright's shop, but I wasn't invited to join the family for their evening activities. I saw Jenny every day, but we no longer talked as freely as we had. Even Mrs Findley weighed in with her disapproval. She said that she couldn't promise to hold my room for two months, and anyway, if I did manage to return, I'd soon be moving out.

At dusk, on the day before I was to leave with Terrill, I was closing up the shop as usual when Jenny came in. "Come with me, William," she said quietly, then led me in a roundabout way to Mrs Findley's barn. It was dark by the time we arrived.

"No one will see us here and Mrs Findley's too deaf to hear us," she said as we made our way up the ladder to the hayloft. We'd made use of the privacy of the loft before, and I assumed that Jenny'd led me there to tell me that she was no longer angry with me.

"William, do you love me?" she asked as we embraced.

"With all my heart," I answered her, holding her even more tightly.

"I'm afraid I'll never see you again," she said, slipping away from me.

"Nothing will happen to me. I'll be back in two months and a month after that we'll be married." I wondered why she had left my embrace.

I heard the sound of movement in the dark, then Jenny placed my hand on her bare breast. I was surprised but knew what to do next. After caressing and kissing both her breasts, I quickly got out of my clothes. Her dress took longer to undo. My breath came in pants as if I had been running. She cried out when I penetrated her, then clawed at my shoulders. After a few thrusts a spasm passed through my body as I felt the release of my seed. When I was spent, I started to collapse on her but caught myself and rolled off. I lay there for a few moments until my heart stopped pounding and my breath returned to normal.

"Jenny, are you alright?" I asked, not knowing whether I'd hurt her. I'd heard from other boys that lovemaking was painful for women, especially the first time. She didn't reply in words, but with a sound someplace between a sigh and a groan.

I lay there for a few moments more as the enormity of what I had done descended on me. Jenny and I were no longer virgins.

"What if I've gotten you with child?" I finally asked.

"Then I won't be the first bride to walk to the altar with a baby in her womb." She seemed unconcerned. We lay there for a few minutes longer.

"I have to leave. If I stay any longer, I'll be missed," she said.

We got dressed and made our way down to the ground. I kissed her one more time, then she was gone.

CHAPTER 18

We left at dawn the next day. No one came to see us off. There were only three of us. Alan Swain had fallen off his horse and broken his arm a week earlier. We rode to Davidson's Fort, then along Rutherford's Road to Nikwasi. Our trading with the Cherokee went well and in four days we had a full load of furs.

"We'll leave at sunup tomorrow," Terrill told Geoff Carlyle and me as we folded and stacked our furs so that they could be loaded on the packhorses for the trip.

"I'm not going to New Orleans," Carlyle announced. "The little extra we can get for our furs isn't worth being away for another month."

"This ain't like you, Geoff. You're leaving William and me high and dry."

"I'm sorry, Josiah. I've got a wife and kids to think about."

"You knew that when you agreed to go with us. You ain't got no right to back out now." Terrill said, spitting on the ground in disgust.

When Carlyle didn't respond, Terrill turned to me. "You going to New Orleans?" he asked.

"I said I would."

"Right then. We leave at dawn."

Terrill said nothing further to Carlyle. The next morning the two of us headed west over the mountains to French Lick. From there we followed a well-established trail the Choctaws and Chickasaws used for trade with the British in Natchez.

"If we meet anyone, tell 'em that we're going to Natchez to sell our furs," Terrill said, as we rode along. "It's in British territory, so we'd be legal. We'll circle around the trading post and then head cross-country to New Orleans."

About twenty miles north of Natchez, we encountered a short, thin man with a full beard riding up the trail towards us. He was leading a string of packhorses with no loads and looked harmless, but Terrill took his rifle out of its saddle holster anyway. The man didn't seem bothered.

"Where ya headed?" he asked.

"Natchez," Terrill replied.

"I wouldn't do that," he said. "They've got fever there. It spread from New Orleans, which I guess is where you're really headed. Take your furs and go back to wherever you came from."

"Can't go back with our tails between our legs," Terrill said.

"Then head for Texas. Maybe you can sell your furs in Nacogdoches."

"How would we get there?" I asked.

"Cross the river and head south until you're level with Natchez. You'll find a trail that heads west. Follow it for about a week. It'll take you to Nacogdoches. But if I were you, I'd head north." With that he spurred his horse and followed his own advice.

Terrill turned to me, "What about it, William? Do we head for Texas? A week there . . . a week back . . . you can still be in Salisbury in plenty of time for your wedding. Better than returning home and saying we failed."

"I suppose so, but no farther than Nacogdoches," I said, not convinced that I'd made the right decision.

The Mississippi was the largest river I'd ever seen. The spring melt had started. Logs and tree branches were floating downstream at an alarming speed.

"Our horses can swim across, but the current's too strong for them to be carrying a load," Terrill said, after looking at the river. "We'll have to build a raft."

Building the raft took a day and a half. That worried me. We were already falling behind Terrill's schedule. If I spent too many more extra days I'd miss my wedding. When I told Terrill this, he laughed and said that he'd get me to Salisbury in time.

When the raft was complete, we loaded it with our furs and other belongings, tied our horses to it, jumped on, and pushed off from the shore. As soon as we left the shore, the current started carrying us downstream. We paddled as hard as we could, and our horses churned away, but the farther we got from the riverbank, the stronger the current. Logs and a dead elk crashed into our raft, but miraculously it held together.

Unlike the battles I'd been in, when I didn't realize the danger until after it had passed, I felt this peril whilst we were crossing. I had a vision of being swept all the way down the river, past New Orleans, and into the sea. For what seemed like hours we fought the current. Finally, an eddy caught our raft and carried us to the far bank. We untied our horses, tied the raft to a large tree, and collapsed, exhausted, on the sand. We laid there for more than an hour before unloading our furs and setting up camp.

The next morning we headed south and, after four hours, found the trail west. The river had carried us at least five miles downstream. We followed the trail for six days through a swampy, empty land, the worst country I'd ever seen. The air was fetid and swarms of insects tormented us. We passed a deserted fort but, other than that, saw no signs that anyone, white or Indian, had ever lived there. I wasn't surprised. I could see no reason why anyone would want to live in that swamp.

Seven days after crossing the Mississippi, we reached a slow-flowing river. I later learned that it was the Sabine, the border of Texas. We took the opportunity to wash and shave. We were cleaner than we'd been for weeks. Shortly after crossing the river, we saw a squadron of a dozen Spanish cavalry.

"*Qué limpiar y blanco son. Deben ser ángeles*," the officer in charge of the troop said to the soldier riding next to him. I didn't understand what he had said, but there was no mistaking his ironic tone of voice. When we didn't respond, he switched to Latin.

"*Quam mundi albique. Sicut Angeli.*" I could understand this and the reason for his irony. We were clean, and compared to his swarthy soldiers, white, but no one would have mistaken us for angels.

"*Non angeli, sed Angli,*" I answered in Latin.

"So you are not angels, only English," he responded in English. "But what are two Englishmen doing riding through Spanish territory? Do you not know that our countries are at war?"

He was a picture book Spanish gentleman, with a moustache and short beard that came to a point beneath his chin, and the only Spanish soldier in full uniform. He sat very erect in his saddle and spoke with great formality.

"War? When did this happen?" I asked.

"I do not know. Word that we are at war with England arrived only three days ago."

"It hadn't arrived in North Carolina six weeks ago, when we left."

"That is your misfortune. I am afraid that you two will have to be my guests until I receive orders telling me what to do with you." Then, in a softer voice, he said, "Allow me to introduce myself. I am Captain Manuel Ortiz y Gonzalez, and I have the honour to command His Most Catholic Majesty Carlos III's forces at Nacogdoches, at the end of the civilized world." He couldn't bow whilst sitting on his horse, but he dipped his head as a courtesy. "And who might you gentlemen be?"

"I'm William Watson and this is Josiah Terrill. Couldn't we just pretend that this never happened and we'll ride back to British territory?"

"Since you speak Latin, you must be a cultured man. I lack many things in this wilderness, but the thing I miss most is good conversation. We will have many interesting discussions."

"Captain, I don't speak Latin and I sure ain't no cultured man. Couldn't I go?" Terrill said.

Captain Ortiz looked at Terrill with disdain. A gentleman wouldn't have made such a request.

"I am afraid not. If I let you go, you will return with a troop of British cavalry to rescue your friend. There would be a battle, which my worthless soldiers would no doubt lose. It is disgrace enough for me, a member of one of the noblest families in Castile, to be exiled to this place. I cannot risk adding the ignominy of defeat. No, you will be my guests until I receive orders. Now I am going to tell my corporal to relieve you of your rifles and any other weapons you are carrying."

On Ortiz's command the Spanish soldiers levelled their muskets at us. The corporal, whose name was José, dismounted and took our rifles, pistols, and hunting knives. Once we were disarmed, Ortiz turned his horse and started back the way he had come. One of his soldiers grabbed my horse's bridle and we rode off towards Nacogdoches. We arrived in the late afternoon of the next day. Ortiz returned our knives, but kept our guns, furs, and horses as spoils of war.

"You will dine with me tonight. José will show you where to stay and will bring you to my quarters in two hours," Captain Ortiz said as he dismounted.

José was drunk and at least a half-hour late when he showed up to escort us to Captain Ortiz's quarters, which were a three-room cabin built into the side of the log stockade that was Nacogdoches' Presidio. The room in which we had supper contained an oak table and six chairs but no other furniture. Sconces on the walls provided candle light. The meal was no better than what his soldiers ate and clumsily served by an Indian servant.

Ortiz was a small man, not even as tall as me, but he stood stiffly as if he were at attention, which made him appear taller. He had changed out of his uniform, washed and shaved, and was dressed in a black jacket, tight black trousers, and a frilly white shirt. The jacket and pants were shiny from too many washings, and the shirt was more grey than white, but he was obviously making an attempt to impress us.

Over supper that first night in Nacogdoches, Captain Ortiz told us the terms of our incarceration. "You will sleep in the gaol. It will not be locked and you are free to walk around the town. You will eat your meals with my soldiers. If you try to escape, I will hunt you down and bring you back in chains. That will be a much better fate than if the Indians catch you. If you go east, you will be in the land of the Karankawa. They are cannibals. They tie you to a stake and cut slices of flesh off your body, which they roast and eat in front of you. I understand they start with your balls."

Ortiz said all of this like an officer giving orders, sitting erect and looking directly at Terrill and me. But then he paused. I could see the look of horror on Terrill's face. My face must have looked the same, but Ortiz's had a broad smile. He'd gotten the response he wanted.

"North is Kiowa country," he continued. "Their specialty is slow roasting. The men start by tying you to a tree and burning the small parts of your body, your balls, nose, fingers, toes." For emphasis he pointed his knife at those parts of my body.

"When these are charred, they cut them off, then they burn your hands and feet. When the men are tired of this amusement, they turn you over to their women. Those hellions are slow and patient. They can keep you alive for a day and night, or even longer, whilst you suffer the torments of hell."

Ortiz crossed himself and murmured a short prayer before continuing, as if to exorcize the evil images he was evoking.

"You have no reason to go west, but if you did, you would meet the Comanche. They are not as skilled in torture as the Kiowa. You would probably only suffer for a day. No, my friends, you have no choice but to accept my hospitality."

We sat in silence after Captain Ortiz finished recounting what might befall us at the hands of the Indians. After a few minutes, he picked up his knife and fork and began eating the baked fish on the plate before him. Neither Terrill nor I joined him.

"I am sorry to have ruined your appetites," Ortiz said as we left at the end of the meal. "But there are unpleasant things in this world and it is better that we speak openly about them. You will dine with me again soon and we will talk of happier subjects."

The gaol was a stone building with iron bars across its glassless window openings. It also served as the armoury for the Spanish soldiers. It had four cells, each with a wooden bench for sitting and a straw tick for sleeping. Terrill took one; I took another. I was angry at him for trying to win his own freedom from Captain Ortiz, but he assured me that if he had, he would've returned with British soldiers to free me. This was probably true, since he would've had to explain my disappearance. But my anger at Terrill was nothing compared to my anguish over not being able to return for my wedding to Jenny. Would she still love me if I failed to show up on schedule? Would she wait for me? Had I left her with child?

The next day we began exploring Nacogdoches. Ortiz's command was supposed to be fifty soldiers, but he had only thirty. He was the only officer. Sergeants and corporals took charge of most activities. Except for two sodomites, who lived together, all the soldiers had Mexican or Indian "wives," with whom they lived in a variety of shacks and huts both inside and outside of the Presidio. Ortiz also had a Mexican "wife," but officially she was his housekeeper.

About two hundred people lived in and around Nacogdoches, pure-blooded Spaniards, Indian converts, runaway black slaves, and every mixture of the three. Everyone lived in log cabins – there wasn't a sawn board to be seen. Some had flowers planted in front, and a few even had scraggly fruit trees, but most were adorned with piles of trash. Pigs roamed freely through the village, rooting at anything that looked edible. It was a dispirited place.

The Texas countryside was covered with scrawny pine forest very different from the lush woods of North Carolina's mountains. This made the land easier to clear and most of the settlers farmed. They produced maize, squash, beans, and cantaloupe, and also raised some Spanish cattle, which didn't fare well in the woodlands. But the river had many fish, and even though they were poor hunters, the settlers and Ortiz's soldiers bagged enough game to supply the settlement with meat. Everyone ate well.

Whilst food was plentiful, everything else was in short supply. Nacogdoches was far from any other town and dependent on the mule train that arrived twice a year with ironmongery, cloth, and other items that could not be made locally. Not that anyone had money to buy any goods. Ortiz's soldiers were paid a pittance and about the only thing the settlers could sell was deerskin, which brought less of a price than in Salisbury. The idea that we could have profitably sold our furs in this forlorn place was laughable. What could I have been thinking when I agreed to follow Terrill here?

Most of the people in Nacogdoches spoke not a word of English. Ortiz was the only person who spoke it fluently. I had no choice but to learn Spanish, which I did as quickly as I could. In a month I could make my needs known and understand simple instructions. In three months I could converse with everyone, though it took a bit longer to understand some of the ribald jokes that the Mexican soldiers made or Captain Ortiz's philosophical ramblings.

A week after our first supper, Captain Ortiz again invited us to dine with him.

"So, my English friends, how are you enjoying your stay in Nacogdoches?" he asked after greeting us.

"Everything's fine," I answered, knowing that it was useless to complain. Terrill nodded in agreement but said nothing. The conversation over supper was about the weather and similar weighty topics. After supper Ortiz turned morose.

"I am sorry that I do not have a fine brandy to offer you," he said. "The only liquor in this god-forsaken place is *mescal*, which my soldiers brew from cactus, which they find in the desert west of here. I am sure the cook has a flask in the kitchen."

Terrill and I had already tasted mescal, courtesy of one of the Mexican soldiers. It was even harsher than the whiskey we sold to the Cherokee. We declined the offer. Ortiz rose from his chair and started pacing around the room.

"You may wonder why I, a member of one of the noblest families in Castile, have been exiled to this outpost at the far end of His Most Catholic Majesty's domain."

Truth be told it was not a question I'd considered, but Ortiz was about to answer it.

"Three years ago my military career seemed blessed. I had been appointed aide-de-camp to the Viceroy of Mexico, a position from which I could win the favour of the highest-ranking nobles in Mexico, and perhaps even be noticed in Madrid." He smiled at the memory of this happy time, but a frown quickly replaced the smile.

"Shortly after I arrived, the viceroy's worthless brother invited me to go drinking. I could not refuse and by the end of the evening we were both drunk. I said something, I do not remember what, to which he took offense. Do you realize the error I had committed?" Ortiz looked at Terrill and me for a response. We both nodded.

"Instead of challenging me," Ortiz continued, "as any true gentlemen would, he inveigled his brother to have me exiled. I am sure it is because that son-of-a-dog knew of my reputation as a swordsman. So here I stay, at least until a new viceroy is appointed, and perhaps to the end of my life. With Karankawa, Kiowa, and Comanche, that may come sooner than I expect." He sighed, sat down, and said nothing more.

Neither Terrill nor I said anything. The awkward silence seemed to go on for many minutes. Finally Ortiz said, "When we dined last time, I promised you happier conversation. I have broken that promise, but I will invite you to supper again soon and we will talk about pleasant things."

With that, he said goodnight and we returned to our cells. I couldn't help thinking how much simpler things were in North Carolina. If a man insulted you, you either punched him in the nose or, if you couldn't get away with hitting him, swallowed the insult. Either way, the incident was soon over.

A pattern had been established. Captain Ortiz would invite Terrill and me to supper every week or two when he was melancholy and tell us more of his troubles.

The next time we dined, he told us the history of Nacogdoches and his fears for its future. As he had the last time, he waited until we were finished eating, then rose and started pacing around the room before speaking. He seemed like a school teacher delivering a lecture to his class. At the time, I still felt that as his prisoner I had no choice but to listen to him and respond when he wanted me to. It would be several more months before I realized that I could speak freely within the bounds of courtesy.

"Nacogdoches is only six years old, but we Spanish have been in this part of Texas for sixty years. For the first forty years we were here to protect His Majesty's lands from attack by the French in Louisiana. But in 1762, France gave Louisiana to Spain to keep it from falling into English hands. When that happened, there was no longer a border to defend, and no reason to maintain soldiers so far from Ciudad de Mexico. After ten years, the King ordered the missions north of San Antonio abandoned," he said, a grimace twisting his face.

It seemed to me that he would have said more if we had been Spanish, but that he didn't want to criticize his King in front of foreigners. After a few moments, to allow us to absorb what he must have considered an important event, he resumed his story.

"Over the decades, many people had settled in Texas. They wanted to stay, but they left their homes, as the King had ordered. When they got to San Antonio, they appealed to the viceroy. Two years later they were given permission to return. But instead of returning to their old villages, they built Nacogdoches. Since they needed protection from the Indians, the viceroy established a Presidio here, which four years later became my place of exile." He paused for a moment and without sitting down took his cup off the table and sipped some of the burnt grain and chicory brew that passed for coffee in Nacogdoches. After frowning at its taste, he put the cup down and continued.

"Nacogdoches survives, but it does not prosper. I fear that one day the Comanche, or the Kiowa, or the Karankawa will drive us from this place. It is possible. A hundred years ago, the Pueblos drove us out of Santa Fe and all of Nuevo Mexico. It was thirteen years before we could return.

"The Indians now have only a few guns, most of which they stole from us, and they do not use them very well. But across the Mississippi, you English give many guns to the Indians. Some of those guns will make their way west as surely as the sun travels this way each day. How will my miserable soldiers fight Indians armed with British muskets?" With that he sat down, his lecture over. Terrill and I assured him that we liked the British Army arming Indians as little as he did.

Captain Ortiz's history of Nacogdoches left me wondering. The people who lived there didn't seem happy with their lot. Most complained about how hard their lives were and all yearned for simple luxuries. A cautious few did say that they liked being far from the demands of the King and nobility. Perhaps Nacogdoches' privations were a small price to pay for this freedom.

Sunday, 21st June, the day I was supposed to marry Jenny, arrived. I knew that by now she must hate me. I concentrated as hard as I could on my love for her and on being sorry for not being in Salisbury. I hoped that as I did this somehow she would sense what I was thinking. But as the old saying goes, "If wishes were horses, beggars would ride." I couldn't tell her of the remorse I felt, or hope that she'd think anything but the worst of me. I started to tell Terrill my feelings, but he cut me short saying that he wasn't happy with being in Nacogdoches either. That was the last time I mentioned Jenny or my feelings to him.

Each month Captain Ortiz took a dozen men and rode out on patrol for a week. In July, after we'd been prisoners for three months, Terrill and I began riding with him. I don't know whether he'd decided to treat us as volunteer soldiers or whether this was part of his effort to treat us as guests, but the patrols were a welcome diversion from the boredom of life in Nacogdoches.

Captain Ortiz usually patrolled westward, as far as the Trinity River, which was the border between the wooded area of Texas and the drier grasslands. When we reached the river, Ortiz would go through a ritual as fixed as the Catholic mass. He would look around as if evaluating the merits of the place. After a moment or two, he would say to his corporal, "I think we will set up camp here."

"*Sí, Capitán*," the corporal would reply.

The soldiers would set up camp. If there were at least four more hours of daylight left, the corporal would return with the following request. "The men wish to patrol farther to the west. I will stay with you to guard the camp."

"If the men wish to, they may do so," Ortiz would reply with great formality, "but warn them to be on watch for Comanche."

If it was too late in the day, this scene would occur first thing the next morning. After three or four hours, the men would return with great sacks full of the cactus from which they brewed mescal. Ortiz would pretend not to see these sacks. He knew his soldiers would mutiny if he didn't permit them to make their harsh whiskey. Lovemaking and getting drunk were the only entertainment they had.

When we rode with Ortiz, we carried Spanish muskets and pistols. At first we had to return these weapons at the end of the patrol, but by September Ortiz no longer seemed concerned about our keeping them between patrols. Having muskets allowed Terrill and me to hunt. Either the deer in Texas were less cautious, or I had finally learned how to sneak up on them. Soon I was killing them and other game that the Mexican soldiers had such difficulty bagging. It gave me something to trade for the various goods that Captain Ortiz could not or would not provide.

"We need to get out of here," Terrill announced one day in late November. "Ortiz could keep us as his 'guests' till hell freezes over."

210Lenny Bernstein

"You heard what he said about the Indians," I replied. "You want to chance being tortured or eaten?"

"He was just trying to scare us. We rode in here without seeing any signs of Indians."

"You have a plan?"

"I've been watching," Terrill said. "Most nights the soldier on sentry duty makes his rounds at about ten o'clock then goes to the guard shack and falls asleep. I say we wait till the next full moon. Once the guard is sleeping, it'll be easy to steal two horses and ride out of here."

"The next full moon is two weeks away."

"That'll give us time to collect some food and anything else we need."

I nodded my agreement. If we escaped now, I could be back in Salisbury less than a year after leaving. Jenny might still be waiting for me. If Mr Cartwright wasn't willing to let us marry, we could run away. For the first time since I'd been captured, I had hope.

The night of the next full moon was cloudless and mild. I'd been watching the Mexican soldiers on guard duty for the past two weeks. Terrill was right. They did go to sleep after their ten o'clock rounds. We waited until we could hear Carlos, who was on guard duty that night, snoring in the guard shack. We quickly loaded the supplies we'd gathered on the two horses we took from the corral, then as quietly as we could, walked them away from the village. After a half-mile, we mounted up and rode north into Kiowa country. We rode all night and by dawn were at least thirty miles from Nacogdoches.

"Let's get some sleep," Terrill said.

"You're not worried about Ortiz catching us?" I replied.

"Nah. He's probably just finding out that we're gone. He'll probably say good riddance, but even if he does decide to come after us, it'll take him hours to get his Mexicans moving."

We set up camp in a small grove alongside a stream, tied our horses loosely so that they could graze, and went to sleep.

I was awakened by a sharp poke in my ribs. A grinning Kiowa in war paint was standing over me. Two other Kiowa pulled me erect and tied me to a tree. My kicks and other efforts at escape only amused them. Terrill was a little more effective. He managed to kick one of the Indians in the knee, which earned him a blow on the head before he was tied to another tree.

There were a half dozen Kiowa in all. The ones who weren't busy tying up Terrill and me gathered wood and built a fire. Then they got into an argument, apparently over whether to torture Terrill or me first. There was much gesturing and pointing – first at him, then at me.

I was terrified. Captain Ortiz's description of Kiowa torture came back to me and I was sure that I would soon be feeling flames on all parts of my body. I tried to think of a way I could kill myself, but I was helpless. I wanted to pray, but the words eluded me. Finally, I just said, "Dear God, please help me."

One of the Kiowa picked up a burning branch and waved it in front of Terrill's face, then in front of mine. I wet my pants, which amused our captors greatly. The flames on the branch died down, and the Indian went back to the fire to relight it.

Then I heard hoof beats and Captain Ortiz's shouts. My prayer had been answered. The Kiowa ran for their weapons. Ortiz and a dozen Mexican soldiers were on them before they were ready to fight. I saw Ortiz decapitate one of the Kiowa with his sabre and José club another to death with the butt of his musket. The other four Kiowa jumped on their horses and fled. The Mexicans pursued them for a short distance, but their horses were too tired for an effective chase. They must have been riding as fast as they could from Nacogdoches.

"Thank God you're here," I said as Ortiz cut me down from the tree.

"Perhaps now you believe what I told you about the Indians," he replied.

"Yes, I believe you. I'll be happy to be stay as your guest."

"Then it won't be necessary to put you in chains?"

"No, I will go willingly."

"And you," Ortiz said, looking at Terrill.

"I won't try running again," Terrill replied meekly.

We rode slowly back to Nacogdoches, arriving at nightfall.

The summer sun in Nacogdoches had been hotter than anything I'd ever experienced. My pale skin had turned bright red, then peeled off. I'd found a broad brimmed Mexican sombrero to protect my face, and tried to stay in the shade as much as possible during the day. That did some good. The Mexican soldiers, whose skins were all deep shades of brown, laughed at my suffering.

Since the summer was so hot, I assumed that winter would be mild. It started that way, with only a little frost at night, which quickly disappeared once the sun came up. But one day in February, nearly a year after we had first arrived, the wind started blowing from the north and the temperature dropped rapidly. A sleet storm followed, coating everything with a thick layer of ice. Tree limbs cracked and broke like twigs. The ground was so slippery that walking even a few steps invited a painful fall. The inside of the gaol was as cold as the outside and I spent a miserable night huddled in a corner, covered with everything I could find, trying to keep warm. The storm was over the next day, and by the day after that, the ice was also gone.

Captain Ortiz invited Terrill and me to supper two days after the storm and was in his usual melancholy state.

"Are you familiar with the poet Ovid?" he asked me.

"Yes, I studied his poem *Metamorphoses* in school," I replied.

"Do you know that the Emperor Augustus exiled him to the shores of the Black Sea, where he suffered cold worse than we have just endured?"

"No, Mr Anderson, my teacher, never taught us that."

Then he started reciting some Latin verses. I could only catch the first few words. "*Saepe sonant moti glacie* . . . Do you know what that means?"

"No, sir. It isn't a line we learned." It was something about cold and wine, but it was too complicated for me to translate.

"It is Ovid, complaining about the cold," he said. "He speaks of men walking around with icicles hanging from their hair and their beards coated with frost. It was cold enough to freeze wine and mead, so that instead of drinking them, they ate them in frozen lumps."

"And do you know Ovid's fate?" he continued.

"No."

"He died in exile, as I fear I shall."

When he first took Terrill and me captive, Captain Ortiz said that he and I would have many interesting discussions. That never happened. He knew the Greek and Roman classics well, but my days in school and my own studies had taught me too little for me to discuss them with him. And I knew nothing of the many Spanish classics he had read and seemed to have memorized. He talked at such length about one of his books, the story of a comic knight named Don Quixote de la Mancha, that I asked to borrow it. It was heavily thumbed, showing that he had read it many times. By this time I could converse in Spanish without any difficulty, but I could read it only by carefully sounding out each word. It was a very slow process, especially with the ornate language Cervantes, the author of Don Quixote, used. After a few weeks I returned the book to Captain Ortiz and said that I was unable to read it. This news saddened him even more.

After the ice storm, Terrill found an Indian woman to live with and moved into her shack. "At least she'll keep me warm, which is more than I'd want you to do for me," he said as he left the gaol. Other than planning our escape, we hadn't spoken much during our first year of imprisonment and would speak even less during our remaining time. He seethed with anger at our captivity, frustrated that there was nothing he could do about it. I was unhappy but didn't share his anger. I understood that Captain Ortiz was just doing his duty and trying in whatever way he could to make our lives bearable.

Captain Ortiz said nothing about Terrill's move. I wasn't attracted to any of the women, though I will admit to occasionally using some of them as receptacles for my lust. There were several who would perform that service for a haunch of venison or a few rabbits.

I thought of Jenny often, but as the months passed, my remorse slowly changed to resignation. More than a year had passed and by now she must believe me dead. Whether she mourned me or not, she would have to go on living. The enormity of my mistake in going with Terrill was a constant presence in my thoughts.

CHAPTER 19

Nacogdoches had a church and a priest, an amiable bear of a man named Padre Esteban. He lived with a sharp-tongued Indian woman named Maria, but as with Captain Ortiz, officially she was his housekeeper. She publicly berated Esteban for what she saw as his shortcomings, not the least of which was his lack of chastity. But she fed him well and he had an enormous belly, which protruded under his brown Franciscan robe. Esteban and Maria had five children when I first arrived, and in the time I was in Nacogdoches, they produced two more. Maria always seemed to be either nursing a baby or pregnant with the next one. Esteban was a good, if over-indulgent, father, who tried to teach his children to read and write, a rare skill in Nacogdoches. I doubt that St Francis, the founder of Esteban's order, would have approved of the way he lived, but if this troubled Esteban, he never once mentioned it in our conversations.

Esteban tried, but not too hard, to convert Terrill and me. We had to attend Mass each Sunday morning and on the surprising number of Holy Days in between. He had a few bottles of wine for the Mass, which his superiors in San Antonio sent with the supply trains Nacogdoches received every six months. He guarded the wine zealously, promising all sorts of hell and damnation to anyone who used them for anything other than their sacred purpose. The threats worked, because whilst there were many jests, including some from Captain Ortiz, about stealing the wine to enjoy with supper, no one touched a drop, other than during Communion.

Whilst Esteban was a subject of derision around Nacogdoches, once he put on his stole to conduct the Mass a mystical transformation occurred. He was now the priest, interceding on behalf of his flock. He spoke the words of the Mass in a firm, even voice, not the soft, self-deprecating tones he used in casual conversation. Even the most profane of Ortiz's soldiers became respectful. I'd never seen a similar transformation in a Church of England service.

"When we Spanish first came to Texas, it was on a holy mission to bring the Indians to Christ," Esteban told me one day. "As the years passed, the viceroy spent less and less money on the church, and controlling the Indians became more important than converting them. Then the King ordered us to abandon all the missions north of San Antonio. We no longer had any way to convert the Indians." He looked at me, and I wondered whether I should respond. I didn't, so he continued. "Now I am simply a parish priest," he said without any hint of anger or frustration.

I remembered my promise to my father to stay out of the clutches of Catholic priests. I suppose I was in Padre Esteban's clutches, but they were no more confining than Captain Ortiz's imprisonment.

Captain Ortiz invited the few travellers who arrived in Nacogdoches to dine with him. The price of their supper was whatever information they could provide about happenings in Ciudad de Mexico and elsewhere in the Spanish empire. As his "guests," Terrill and I were also invited to attend.

The first traveller, Lieutenant Rodriguez, who commanded the mule train from San Antonio, arrived two months after we did. After questioning Rodriguez closely about the viceroy's latest actions, Ortiz moved on to the subject that interested me, the war between Spain and Britain.

"Tell me, Lieutenant, why are we at war with England?" Ortiz asked, idly playing with his table knife.

"Because the English caught a Frenchman trading illegally with the Indians in Kentucky," Rodriguez answered.

"What has this to do with Spain?" Ortiz sounded mystified.

"According to General Sanchez, who was in San Antonio just before I left, the French demanded that the British release the trader. When the British refused, France declared war, and since we are France's ally, the King felt obligated to join them."

Ortiz speared an apple from the bowl in the middle of the table with his knife and started peeling it before speaking again.

"I do not think this war has anything to do with the fur trader," he said, pausing again for emphasis. Then, when he was satisfied that he had everyone's attention, he started his history lesson.

"Twenty years ago the English defeated us and the French. The French lost Canada and their empire in India. Just before they were defeated, the French gave us their huge colony of Louisiana, which then included the whole Mississippi River valley. The land wasn't worth very much. Most of it hadn't been explored. Even now, I doubt that more than three thousand white people live there and most of them are in New Orleans.

"At the end of the war, the English took Florida and the eastern part of Louisiana from us. We kept New Orleans and all of Louisiana west of the Mississippi. So even though we were defeated, we did not suffer greatly. Still, it was a blot on the honours of both our King and the King of France. I am sure both want to remove those blots. The French may think they are strong enough to do it. I pray they are, because I know that we are not."

Lieutenant Rodriguez returned six months later with more news of the war.

"The war, which is being called Bonhomme's War after the French fur trader who is still in an English gaol, is being fought mostly at sea. The British have given their pirates papers calling them privateers and instructed them to attack French and Spanish ships wherever they find them," he told us over supper.

"But that is what they were doing before the war," Captain Ortiz said.

"Yes, but now it is legal for them to do it."

"I am sure that is very important," Ortiz said, looking around to ensure that we all appreciated his sarcasm. "And is our navy able to protect our treasure fleets from Peru and Mexico?" From the tone of his voice, I understood that he expected the answer to be no.

Lieutenant Rodriguez, who had been talking casually, now answered formally, "I do not know, sir."

He may have known that Spain was losing ships to the privateers and not wished to tell this to a superior officer, or he may honestly have not known. I later learned that British privateers had been able to capture a number of Spanish treasure ships, greatly enriching their crews and the British Crown, which took half the loot.

"But we have had a victory on land," Rodriguez continued. "Major Mendoza, the Commandante of New Orleans, took a company of soldiers and chased the English out of Natchez. It is now a Spanish fort."

"That was a good move," Ortiz said. "It will protect New Orleans from attack by land, but the British could still attack it from the sea."

"They could, but it would be dangerous for them to send their navy so far into waters that we control."

"You are right, Lieutenant," Ortiz said after a moment. He seemed chagrined that Rodriguez had thought of an obvious point he'd overlooked.

I listened to the discussion, amazed at the way the two of them were analysing the movement of armies and navies. They knew so much more than the group of orderlies with whom I had discussed such matters at Washington's headquarters, less than five years earlier.

There was no more news of the war for two years until a Major Sandoval came through on an inspection tour. Since he was senior to Captain Ortiz, Terrill and I were not invited to supper, but the next day Ortiz told us what he'd learned. In November 1783, the Royal Navy had caught a large French fleet by surprise off the coast of Brittany and almost totally destroyed it. Peace talks were underway.

"It seems that you will not be my guests for much longer," he said. Terrill and I did not respond, and Ortiz walked away looking more morose than usual.

My first thoughts after Captain Ortiz left were of Jenny. I knew that she must have long ago decided that I was dead. Had she married someone else? What would she think when I appeared after such a long absence? What would her father think? Did he know that I had deflowered her? Would he take vengeance on me for doing that, then abandoning his daughter? I wanted to escape from Nacogdoches, but the thought of returning to Salisbury filled me with foreboding.

The news that Bonhomme's War was over reached Nacogdoches in April 1785. A peace treaty had been signed on 4th December 1784. Terrill and I were now free. Captain Ortiz was gracious and gave us horses, muskets, and sufficient food to reach New Orleans. He also provided us with a letter of introduction to the Spanish commander there, explaining that we had been held as enemy aliens for the last four years, and asking that, in the name of Christian charity, we be given enough supplies to return to our homes in North Carolina. He and his patrol escorted us as far as the Sabine River, near where we had been captured. Ortiz had explained that we would be safe travelling alone, since neither the Karankawa nor the Kiowa entered the empty land between the Sabine and the Mississippi.

I felt a strange sadness over leaving, as if I was losing a long-held friend.

"*Vayan con Dios*, my English friends," Ortiz said as we parted. "May God protect you on your journey."

"Thank you for your hospitality," I replied. "You told us that we would be your guests, and we were treated that way."

"I am sorry that I had to detain you so long. Perhaps we will meet again."

"I hope so," I said.

Terrill and I headed across the river. Ortiz and his soldiers headed in the opposite direction.

When we were safely apart, Terrill turned to me and said, "Thank God we'll never see that bastard again. Four years of my life gone for nothing."

"He was only doing his duty."

"I don't care. I just want to be back in Salisbury. I hope someone remembers me."

I was not as anxious as Terrill was to return to Salisbury. My foreboding about having to face Jenny and her father had grown in the months since I first learned that the war was ending, and now could better be described as dread. I pictured the worst — Jenny hating me, and her father killing me because I'd abandoned her.

At the time, Bonhomme's War seemed like a minor episode in the long history of wars England fought against France and Spain, but historians tell us that it led to events that changed the world forever. Britain demanded large indemnities from France and Spain to pay for the cost of the war, and took all the French and Spanish colonies in the Caribbean except Saint-Domingue and Cuba as spoils of war. Spain also had to return Natchez to Britain. Spain was able to pay its indemnity with gold and silver from the Americas. The French, who had the double burden of the indemnity and rebuilding their fleet, had no choice but to raise their already high taxes. These higher taxes became intolerable in 1788, when the harvest was poor. By early 1789 there were bread riots in Paris and other cities across France. A few months later these riots grew into the French Revolution. Louis XVI, the last King of France, was executed two years later.

Terrill and I arrived in New Orleans, our original destination four years earlier, after ten days' travel. There was a ferry, but we didn't have money to pay the fare. We had to swim our horses across the river, but this was much less of a challenge than it had been on our way to Texas. The river was not in flood and we didn't have pack horses to worry about. Our horses were swept a short way downriver, but they kept churning steadily and we soon reached the eastern bank.

In those days New Orleans was home to about three thousand people, more than half of them black or mulatto. Captain Ortiz had been correct about its size. The town sat on a low bluff above the river and was enclosed on its three landward sides by earthen walls. These walls would protect against Indian attack or a slave rebellion, but the ditch or moat needed to turn them into a true fortification was missing. I saw a large number of cannon, but most were not mounted on carriages and looked old and rusty. The Spanish soldiers I saw looked no more impressive that Captain Ortiz's Mexicans. I doubt they would put up much of a fight if a real army attacked New Orleans.

Even though many of New Orleans' white inhabitants were French, and French was heard in the street as often as Spanish, the town felt

Spanish. Like Nacogdoches it was a sleepy place during most of the day but came alive at sundown, when its residents emerged to gossip and stroll in the plaza in front of the cathedral.

We presented ourselves and Captain Ortiz's letter to the Commandante of New Orleans. "Señor Terrill, Señor Watson, now that our countries are no longer at war, I can be a gracious host. Please join me for supper tonight and we can discuss the supplies you need," Major Mendoza said after reading the letter. He was a portly man of sixty, who, despite his uniform and the victory he had won at Natchez a few years earlier, looked very unmilitary.

When we arrived that evening, we found a table covered with a linen cloth and set with crystal and silver. We dined on roast beef and had wine during the meal and brandy afterwards. I didn't know whether Mendoza dined that way every night or whether he was using our visit as an excuse for a fancy meal, but I didn't care. It was the best supper I'd had in four years.

When we finished Mendoza promised he would give us the supplies we needed for our return to North Carolina. "Come back tomorrow. They'll be waiting for you," were his parting words.

Terrill and I were jubilant as we headed back to the camp we had set up just outside of the town walls. Major Mendoza's hospitality had not extended to inviting us to stay with him. When we returned the next day, a sergeant told us that he had no orders to provide us with supplies and that the major was too busy to see us. We received the same message on the next two days, then concluded that we wouldn't get anything, despite Mendoza's promise. The merchants in town would have been happy to sell us all that we needed, but we had no money and they were not going to extend credit to two shabbily dressed Englishmen who had no plans to return.

We were beginning to despair when we met Edward Sinclair, a British merchant trying to establish trade with the Spanish. He was tall, thin, and looked to be about fifty years old. He carried an ebony walking stick with a brass lion on its head. It seemed absurdly elegant compared with the rest of his clothes, which were scarcely better than ours. I didn't know whether the walking stick was the one luxurious item he owned or the last remnant of a prior fortune, but it drew attention.

"The Spanish are like that," he said, after we told him our tale of woe. "They consider hospitality one of the highest virtues. They will promise a guest anything, but once the guest has left, they reconsider their promise and nine times out of ten change their mind. I could tell you many stories about promises made to me over supper that were worthless by breakfast time. The best I can do is to lend you five Spanish dollars to buy what supplies you can."

"That's most generous. How will we pay you back?" I asked.

"You can do that the next time we meet."

We thanked him profusely. He lifted his walking stick in a mock salute and departed.

Five Spanish dollars was not enough for Terrill and me to buy all the food we needed for our trip to North Carolina, but it was summer and we thought that between wild berries and what meat we could hunt, we could feed ourselves. We rode along a well-travelled road to Natchez, then headed north towards French Lick, the reverse of the route we had taken on our way to Texas. We saw only one deer on the trail between Natchez and French Lick. Terrill and I shot at it, but we both missed. Had we taken the time to hunt properly, we probably could have bagged a deer or some turkey, but Terrill was in a hurry to get back to Salisbury. He said he would rather go hungry than waste time. I was in no such hurry, since by now I dreaded the thought of having to face either Jenny or her father, but I had no choice other than to keep up with Terrill. By the time we got to French Lick, we were carefully rationing what little food we had and I was hungry all the time.

In the late morning of our second day out of French Lick, as we rode along the trail to Nikwasi, we saw a dead deer. Flies buzzed around the carcass, but no scavengers had found it.

"Doesn't look like it's been dead for long," I said. "You suppose it'll be safe to eat?"

"If we cook it well," Terrill replied. "Sure would be nice to have a full belly again."

We quickly skinned the deer, built a fire, and cooked several large slabs of meat cut from the deer's hind quarters. We ate our fill, packed the rest of the cooked meat away to eat over the next few days, and were on our way. We made camp that night and had some more of the deer meat for supper. Hunger pains had kept me awake the past few nights, but I slept very well that night.

The next morning I felt almost too weak to stand and was having trouble seeing. Everything seemed blurred. My mouth was dry. I
wanted to drink, but was having a hard time swallowing. I felt like I
was being slowly strangled.

"You feel as shick as I do?" Terrill asked. He sounded drunk, even
though he'd had no whiskey.

"Yesh," I answered. "Better stay here. Can't get on my horsh." I,
too, sounded drunk.

I wanted to say that I thought the deer meat had been tainted, but
couldn't get the words out. Terrill didn't say anything more. He just
sat down, then slumped over. I sat down too, and a few minutes later,
either fell asleep or lost consciousness. The next thing I knew it was
late afternoon and four Cherokee were standing in our camp.

"This one's alive," one of the Cherokee said, pointing to me, "but
the other one's dead."

"I think I know this one. He looks like Yellow Hair, one of the
traders who used to come to Nikwasi. I haven't seen him in many
years," a second one said.

"I'm Yellow Hair," I managed to whisper.

"We'll take him with us. Leave the other one for the wolves and
the crows," their leader, a tall man with a jagged scar on this left
cheek, said.

The Cherokee took Terrill's horse and gear, and laid me over my
saddle. In that inglorious position I was led off. We rode slowly for
the rest of the day, but I couldn't tell you in what direction. That night
the Cherokee camped by a stream in the woods. They offered me
some of the dried meat they were having for their evening meal, but
I couldn't eat it. I managed to drink a few mouthfuls of water from
a gourd they put in front of me. Every movement was painful and
exhausting, even sitting up seemed to take more strength than I had.
I fell asleep sitting against a tree, and at dawn, when I was shaken
awake by one of the Cherokee, I was in the same place but slumped
over. They were ready to move on and I was again laid across my
saddle and led off.

CHAPTER 20

I was barely conscious when we arrived at midmorning at the village of Tuskeegee on the Tennessee side of the mountains. The Cherokee carried me into the village's council house and I listened whilst they discussed my fate. I knew a little Cherokee, but in my weakened condition, I couldn't follow the debate. The Cherokee are very formal in such situations. They remain impassive with their hands by their sides and depend on the eloquence of their words to convey their emotions. Raising one's voice or making gestures is considered bad manners.

Later I was told that my arrival had caused great consternation amongst the men of the village. They were worried that I'd die and that they would have to explain my death to the British. They berated Usti-waya, who'd led the band that saved me, saying that it would have been better to leave me to die on the trail. Finally, Ahawee, Usti-waya's sister, said that she would care for me. Two men carried me to her cabin, laid me on a bearskin, and left.

I lay there, aware that I had soiled myself, but unable to do anything about it. Ahawee gave her daughter Awinita, a young woman of sixteen, a long set of instructions. She left immediately on the errand her mother had given her. Ahawee then stripped off my clothes and washed me as if I were an infant. I was ashamed, but too weak to protest. Awinita returned a half hour later carrying a variety of herbs. She seemed unperturbed by the sight of me laying there, but I was embarrassed at being naked in front of two strange women. I felt much better when, a few moments later, Ahawee covered me with a blanket.

Ahawee gave her daughter another set of instructions and Awinita started boiling water and making a potion with the herbs she had brought. When the brew had been completed and cooled sufficiently, Awinita gave me a cupful to drink. I sat up as best I could, took one mouthful, and nearly spit it out, the taste was so vile. But she put the cup to my mouth and with gestures insisted that I drink its contents. I swallowed what I could and fell back onto the bearskin.

The herbs acted quickly. My heart started beating at an alarming rate and I felt like I was about to vomit. Ahawee knelt down, placed her ear to my chest and listened to my racing heart. I could see her smiling when she stood up. My bladder suddenly felt full. I needed to get outside to relieve myself, but when I tried to stand, I collapsed back onto the bearskin. Ahawee and Awinita lifted me to a standing position, wrapped the blanket around me, and helped me walk out of the cabin. After I had relieved myself, they led me back inside and helped me lie back down. I quickly fell asleep.

It was dark when I next awoke. I again tried to stand but was still unable to. My movements woke Awinita, who came to help me out of the cabin to relieve myself. She then gave me some water to drink and I soon fell back asleep.

I felt stronger the next morning and was able to stand without help. Ahawee had washed my clothes, so I was able to dress. My belongings were neatly stacked next to where I'd been sleeping and my horse was tethered outside the cabin. As Daniel Boone had taught me, the Cherokee may force very uneven trades on those in their power, but they do not steal. Since I was in no condition to trade with Usti-waya, he was honour-bound to let me keep my meagre possessions.

Ahawee insisted that I drink another cup of the herbal potion and I did so without complaint. It seemed to have helped. Then she gave me a cup of broth, the first food I'd had in two days. I drank it slowly, even though I should have been ravenously hungry, and my stomach felt full when I had consumed it.

"*Wa-do*," I said to thank her, then "*Dalonige-ugithi*," pointing to myself to tell her that my name was Yellow Hair.

Ahawee didn't answer immediately, but after some thought said in slow, carefully pronounced English, "You speak words of the *Tsalagi* and have a name."

Like most Cherokee, Ahawee had a powerful memory. She had heard many English words spoken by fur traders, missionaries, and British soldiers. She remembered all of them and eventually pieced together their meanings. Whilst she could speak some English, she was reluctant to do so. It took her much effort to put together a sentence, and she was too proud to speak anything other than her precise thoughts. But now that she knew that my Cherokee name meant Yellow Hair, that's what she called me. Awinita was even less willing to speak English. She knew some words – I never found out how many – but used them only sparingly.

With my few remaining words of Cherokee, some English, and many gestures, I explained to Ahawee that I'd been a fur trader and learned a few words of her language. I was able to tell her that I knew that her name meant "deer" and her daughter's name meant "fawn."

My speaking Cherokee and knowing the meaning of her name had an immediate effect on Awinita. She had shown no shyness whilst helping me the previous day and night, but now she was reluctant to look at me. When I thanked her, she merely nodded her head and looked away. Had a girl in Salisbury done this, I would've considered it a model of modesty. But as I soon learned, Cherokee don't look at the face of the person they are talking to and are uncomfortable if that person looks directly at them. My knowing Cherokee ways meant that Awinita had to act like a proper Cherokee maiden. Her mother then said something I couldn't translate. It caused her to blush, and a few moments later she left the cabin.

Awinita had long, perfectly straight black hair that fell almost to her waist and gleamed in the sunlight. The name Fawn fit her well. She was lithe and graceful with dark eyes and skin that was the soft brown colour of a young deer. I was smitten. I hadn't felt that way since I'd first seen Jenny. I suppose I should've been thinking of Jenny and how to return to Salisbury, but the sight of Awinita swept away all such thoughts.

Awinita resembled her mother, who was no longer lithe, but was still graceful in her movements. Ahawee's hair was beginning to turn grey, but it hadn't lost any of its lustre. Unlike many of the women in the village, she still had all of her teeth. She wore a single ear pendant in her right ear. Awinita wore no jewellery.

Their small log cabin, which wouldn't have looked out of place in any settlement in North Carolina, had a door high enough to enter without stooping. It contained no furniture. Bowls, baskets, and other utensils were stacked in corners and the floor was covered with woven mats for sitting. The bearskins on which we slept were spread over piles of maize stalks to keep them off the hard-packed earth floor.

I soon learned that Ahawee, who had a vast knowledge of herbs, was renowned as a medicine woman. People in her own and sur-rounding villages sought her help. She wasn't a physician in the way that we white men think of that profession. She didn't seek out the sick or ask for payment for her services. But many of the people she helped gave her gifts, which made it possible for her and Awinita to live on their own. Still, they were poor, and had few of the goods that the British Army and traders brought to the village.

When I'd regained some of my strength, I asked Ahawee what herbs she'd used to cure me. She told me their Cherokee names, which meant nothing to me. She even showed me some of the dried flowers that were the main ingredients of the potion, but I couldn't cipher out what plants they'd come from. Awinita could add nothing to what her mother had told me.

What disease I'd had and how I was cured remain a mystery to me to this day, but Ahawee believed that she knew the answer.

"You said you ate some deer meat before you became ill. Did you ask forgiveness from the deer spirit before eating his meat?" she asked me after I'd recovered. We were sitting in the warm summer sunlight outside of her hut. By then I'd learned enough Cherokee to converse with her. I didn't know what she was talking about and my face must have shown that.

"You and your friend who died must have greatly insulted the deer spirit for you to have become so ill," she said as solemnly as a preach-er describing Adam and Eve's fall from grace. "Usually the deer spirit only causes rheumatism, but it is a strong spirit that can cause many sicknesses." I must have still looked confused because she continued as if she were explaining the legend to a young child.

"Animal spirits cause sickness as a revenge for people hurting and killing them. Long ago, each of the animals held a council and agreed upon which disease they would cause. Every time you kill an animal, you must explain to its spirit that you only did so only because you and your family are hungry and need its meat, or that it will be cold in the winter and you need its skin to keep warm. If you do this, the dead animal's spirit will forgive you and you will not become ill. But you do not need to ask forgiveness when you kill a bear. When the bears held their council, they could not agree, so they do not cause any disease. People survive because the plants promised to help us. For each illness that animal spirits cause, there is a plant spirit that will cure it. You must listen to the plant spirits to know which one."

I thought she was spouting nonsense, but she'd cured me and I wasn't going to argue with her. I nodded my head slowly to indicate I had heard her.

During my stay with them, I heard many Cherokee discuss which animal spirit caused each illness. Smallpox was a perplexing problem for them. It was a new disease that didn't fit into their mythology. Some Cherokee argued that the bears, the most powerful of the animals, must have finally come to an agreement and were now causing this deadly sickness. But others said that if this was so, there should be a plant spirit to cure the disease. The Cherokee could find no herbs to cure smallpox, so the debate over what caused the disease remained unresolved. There was no smallpox in Tuskeegee whilst I was there, but many Cherokee bore the scars of the disease. It had last ravaged the tribe a few years earlier, part of the still raging pestilence that had taken my mother.

After a week of caring for me, Ahawee disappeared for four days. This left me alone with Awinita for long periods of time. In Salisbury this would have been considered scandalous, but the Cherokee seemed to think nothing of it. Ahawee and Awinita were members of the Blue Clan, one of the seven Cherokee clans. In Ahawee's absence, other members the Blue Clan were in and out of her cabin several times a day. Had I in any way harmed Awinita, the men in the clan would have been obligated to avenge her.

A Cherokee child becomes a member of his mother's clan, not his father's, and a boy's mother's oldest brother is responsible for educating him in the ways of men.

"We always know who a child's mother is, but we can't always be sure who the father is," Salali, one of Ahawee's elderly aunts, told me. She was laughing at the time, so I don't know whether she was jesting with me, but hers was the only explanation I ever received for this strange custom.

I felt very uncomfortable being alone with Awinita that first time. I wanted to talk to her and impress her if I could, but I was still very weak and knew little of the Cherokee language. She seemed to pay very little attention to me, and when she did speak, showed the deference a child shows an adult, even though I was only six years older than her. I was relieved when Ahawee returned. Three days later, Awinita disappeared, also for four days. These disappearances were repeated a month later.

After a few months, I learned that Ahawee and Awinita's disappearances were due to their monthly courses. The Cherokee believed that blood held great power, and that a bleeding woman was dangerous. During their monthly period, Cherokee women remained in a small hut at the village edge. They did none of their normal work and other women took care of them and their families. When they were no longer bleeding, they plunged themselves into a running stream seven times and put on clean clothing before returning to the village. Men who had been exposed to blood during warfare underwent a similar cleansing before returning to their homes, and anyone taking part in one of the Cherokee's many ceremonies also had to cleanse themselves. I'm ashamed to say that the Cherokee, who started their day by washing their bodies in the river, were cleaner than white people, none of whom would have considered a daily bath.

Much has changed now that almost all Cherokee are Christians. The clan system no longer has much sway over their lives. The different churches that have established themselves amongst the tribe have replaced it. Whilst some of these churches care for their Indian members as well as the clans did, others don't, and some Cherokee are now destitute.

Christian Cherokee are embarrassed to be reminded of what their ancestors, and, in some cases, they believed. Few will retell the legend of the animals deciding which diseases to inflict on mankind, but since we don't understand what causes many diseases, malign animal spirits are as good an explanation as any.

It took a month for me to regain enough strength to no longer be considered an invalid. I spent many hours sitting in the sun, absorbing energy from its rays and thinking about my life. I convinced myself that Jenny must have long ago given me up for dead and there was no reason to return to Salisbury. I could stay in Tuskeegee, close to Awinita, and avoid the unpleasantness that I knew awaited me at the Cartwrights.

I could say that I spent the month learning to speak Cherokee. Everyone, especially young Cherokee children, seemed eager to teach me new words. One day, a boy, who I judged to be about eight years old, approached me somewhat warily.

"I am Yellow Hair. What is your name?" I asked, hoping to put him at ease.

"I am Usti-tsula."

"Have you come to help this *Gilisi*, this Englishman, learn to speak Cherokee?

"Yes, I will teach you some words. This is *adikada*," he said, pointing to a gourd of water and trying to suppress a giggle. From my trading trips to Nikwasi, I knew that *adikada* meant urine, but I decided to let him have his little prank.

"*Adikada*," I said slowly, emphasizing each syllable.

"Good, and this is *soquiliu nyvsdiagida*," he said pointing to some deer meat hanging outside the cabin. That meant excrement, but I tried the words several times as he corrected my pronunciation.

"*Wa-do*," I said when he was satisfied that I knew the words. He walked off giggling.

To keep up the pretence, I scolded him when I saw him the next day. "Usti-tsula, you have made Awinita angry with me. She did not like the words that you taught me. She said that they are not words to be used in front of women, that the word for water is *ahma*, and the word for meat is *hawiya*." This caused him even greater merriment.

Had he been a little older he would have realized that Cherokee women are quite blunt in their speech and regularly use words that would make the average white woman blush.

By the end of the month, I could speak well enough to converse with the Cherokee on many topics. I was helped by their custom of speaking slowly and deliberately, carefully considering their words. But during my stay with them, I was never able to match the eloquence of normal Cherokee discourse.

Whilst I was the only white man living in Tuskeegee, there were many white visitors. The first of these arrived two weeks after I did, a cavalry patrol led by Lieutenant Sullivan. They came to check on the Cherokee and to distribute the gifts – or should I say the bribes – that the army used to keep the peace.

I'd met Lieutenant Sullivan briefly six years earlier on my hunting expedition with Daniel Boone in Kentucky. He gave no sign of remembering me, and I saw no need to remind him. I told him about Terrill and me being held prisoner in Texas, our return, falling ill, and Terrill's death.

"That's quite a story you've told me, Mr Watson," Sullivan said. "I don't know why I should believe you."

After all that I'd suffered, I had to work hard to contain the anger I felt at being thought a liar. But it would have done me no good to make an enemy of the lieutenant, so I responded as gently as I could manage.

"If I'm just telling you a story, why am I wearing Spanish clothes and why do I have a Spanish musket?"

"You've a point, but you've got to admit that your story sounds preposterous."

"I know, but that doesn't make it any less true."

"We'll be heading back to Fort Roanoke in two days. You're welcome to travel with us if you're strong enough," he said.

"Thank you for the offer, but I think I'll stay here for a while longer," I replied. I was besotted with Awinita, and couldn't conceive of leaving her presence.

"Want me to tell anyone you're here?"

I had to think about that question for a moment. I didn't want the Cartwrights to know that whilst I could've returned to Salisbury, I'd chosen not to. Daniel Boone was the only other person who might've been interested in my whereabouts, and I couldn't see bothering him with the information. Besides, he might pass it on to Amos Cartwright.

"No, there's no one who'd care about my whereabouts," I lied.

Lieutenant Sullivan looked at me for a moment but didn't say anything further. I thought he knew I was lying but wasn't going to say anything about it. I was now committed to maintaining the lie. In one way or another, every white visitor to Tuskeegee asked me the same question. My answer was always the same. Despite my efforts, word that I was living with the Cherokee got back to both Boone and Mr Cartwright. The truth will always out.

"Anything you want me to bring you the next time I come through here on patrol?"

"A book would be nice. I haven't had anything in English to read for four years."

"I'll bring you a Bible. The missionaries are always trying to give me one."

"Thank you."

Sullivan questioned Usti-waya through an interpreter about the location of Terrill's body but, after a long discussion, decided that he wouldn't be able to find the place, and gave up the idea of retrieving it. That saddened me. Terrill and I hadn't been friendly, but every man deserves a proper grave.

Much had changed in the four years since I'd been a fur trader. Then the army had only supplied the Cherokee with guns and ammunition, but now they gave them cloth, blankets, and iron tools as well, items that traders used to supply. And there were now too few deer or other animals to provide enough skins for the Cherokee to trade for all the items that had become necessities in their lives. Without gifts from the army, the Cherokee would have been impoverished. This suited the army's generals. They wanted the Cherokee to be dependent on them. It ensured that they would comply with British wishes. But it angered the fur traders and the merchants who had previously profited from the fur trade. Since the army supplied the Cherokee with necessities, the only things left for traders to sell were whiskey and trinkets. The fur trade was a small fraction of its former level. The South Carolinians had closed their trading post at Chota, the largest Indian village in Tennessee. Small bands of traders, none of whom I knew, visited Tuskeegee twice a year whilst I was living there.

Ahawee had had three other children, all of whom died of smallpox. She didn't talk about them. I only learned of their existence many months later from Awinita. By this time I understood why Ahawee was unwilling to talk about her dead children. The Cherokee were very superstitious. They believed that any contact with disease would taint the exposed person, the more powerful the disease, the worse the taint. We whites aren't much better. I kept my mother's death from smallpox a secret for three years.

Ahawee had divorced her husband some years earlier. She wasn't celibate and occasionally went off with one man or another, but she showed no interest in remarrying. Her erstwhile husband still lived in the village and was on good terms with her and Awinita. Divorce, which is so rare amongst white people, was commonplace amongst the Cherokee. A man or woman no longer happy with their marriage could be released from those bonds at any time. The Green Maize Ceremony was a popular time to do this because it was a new beginning. The woman kept their house, children, and her possessions. Her brothers and her clan supported her and her children. The man kept his property and returned to his clan. Both were free to marry again and neither was shunned by the rest of the village.

Adultery, as we whites know it, had no meaning to the Cherokee. Both men and women were free to choose their lovers, whether married or single. If a wife was unhappy about her husband taking a lover, she could divorce him. I heard that in some Cherokee villages, men moved their lovers into their wives' houses and were polygamous, like the Moslems. I didn't see this in Tuskeegee but heard many men jest about it. Most of them said it was hard enough living with one woman, and that they couldn't understand why any man would try living with two or more. I never heard what Cherokee women thought about such arrangements.

Christian Cherokee have adopted our attitudes towards divorce, and it is now as rare amongst them as it is amongst whites. Whilst many celebrate this change as a triumph of morality, I wonder. Cherokee women can no longer own property and they are subservient to their husbands. Since the clan system has fallen into disrepute, they no longer have the protection it provided. I do not believe, as some romantics write, that the Cherokee were in a state of noble grace before they were converted to Christianity, but they were a happy people, who shared what goods they had more equitably than they do today.

Because there was no man in their house, Ahawee and Awinita ate very little meat. Still, they ate well. They had part of the communal field outside the village and raised lush crops of maize, beans, squash, pumpkins, and sunflowers. The iron hoes traders brought them were much better than the stone mattocks the Cherokee formerly used, but weeding these crops still took much hard labour.

"Ahawee, let me help weed the maize," I said when I felt strong enough to do such work.

"No. That is women's work," she replied. "Selu, the first woman, provided maize for her family, and now all women must do the same. If a man grows maize, it will upset the balance of the world."

"But I am not a Cherokee man. How could I upset the balance?"

"Men provide meat for their families, like Kanati, the first man, did. Take your musket and hunt. That is a man's job."

I'd learned a little about the Cherokee's belief in the importance of balance on the fur trading expeditions I'd made, but I hadn't realized how important it was to them, and how much it guided their day-to-day lives. Men and women both provided food, but in different ways. That maintained balance. Men could help prepare the fields, plant the crop, and harvest it, but only women were supposed to tend the growing plants. Old women who no longer had the strength for this work guarded the fields, sitting on platforms and shooing away birds or animals that might try to steal the produce. There were men who broke these rules and farmed, and even a few who took on more female roles as sodomites dressed in women's clothing. They were the butt of jokes from both men and women, but they weren't persecuted as they would have been in white society. Even Ahawee, who lectured me on the proper roles for men and women, turned a blind eye to these infractions.

Women could go along on hunts, but only to cook meals or prepare skins. They didn't stalk or kill animals. And whilst women weren't supposed to be warriors, the Cherokee told more than one story of women who took up arms to defend the tribe. They were known as War Women and highly regarded. They were always virtuous and abided by all the other Cherokee rules for proper behaviour. I couldn't help wondering whether the War Women were real or just a myth.

I took my musket and went hunting, but was unsuccessful at first. Any game near the village had long ago been killed or scared away. I was too weak to ride my horse, so I walked, but I couldn't travel the many miles necessary to find deer or turkey. My illness also had affected my balance. I was clumsy, not quite falling, but making enough noise to scare away any animals.

After I returned empty-handed for the fourth straight day, the Cherokee men in the village started making jokes about my failure. One of them held a pair of deer antlers above his head and said that he was the only deer that I could shoot. Awinita giggled at this crude jest. I felt heartsick.

The long walks I took through the forest on my unsuccessful hunts rebuilt my strength. By the middle of the second week, I began to feel more confident. I could again ride my horse and when I dismounted I could walk silently though the trees. During the third week of my hunt, I shot a turkey, my first kill. I remembered Ahawee's warning about asking forgiveness from the spirits of the animals I killed. Not being Cherokee, I didn't know what to say. I stood over the dead bird for a few moments feeling foolish, then rejected the idea of seeking forgiveness. For the next few weeks, I worried about falling ill again. I didn't, and after about a month, I dismissed Ahawee's story as mere superstition.

I gutted the turkey and took it back to Ahawee. She praised me profusely whilst she plucked the bird. Awinita said nothing.

After my first kill, I had other successes and soon was providing as much meat for Ahawee and Awinita as a Cherokee man would have. Hunting was not as good as it had been in Texas and more than half the time I returned empty-handed. The few deer I shot provided me with skins to trade. I bartered most of them for items Ahawee or Awinita needed, but I sold some for cash. I liked having a few shillings in my purse, even though there was no way to spend them in Tuskeegee.

Ahawee fed me huge portions of meat whenever I brought home a kill, then traded the remaining meat for items she needed. Having gone so long eating little or no meat, she and Awinita no longer enjoyed it, and after a few meals returned to their diet of bread and vegetables.

Ahawee made bread the same way I'd learned to make it, but she used an earthenware pot instead of an iron Dutch oven. The dough went into the pot, which was then covered and heaped with white-hot ashes. But her bread contained much more than the ground maize, salt, and water I'd used. She added whatever berries, nuts, or seeds were available, sometimes so many that the bread resembled a Christmas pudding. Before eating it, we dipped the baked bread in oil pressed from hickory nuts, which made for an even tastier meal. Donald Mackenzie and I had eaten the bread I baked dry, or with a little fat from the meat or fish we'd roasted.

I went hunting regularly but did little else when I was in the village. The Cherokee men spent much of their time practicing for war, even if the British enforced peace with both white settlers and other tribes. I wasn't a Cherokee warrior and couldn't partake in these activities.

After a while I could sense that the Cherokee were looking at me differently. There were quiet conversations amongst the men of the Blue Clan, which ended abruptly when I approached. I knew they were discussing me, but I had no idea what they were saying. Then one day, whilst I was sitting outside Ahawee's cabin, enjoying the late afternoon sun, Usti-waya came up and sat down beside me.

"Greetings," I said in the formal manner of the Cherokee.

"Greetings to you, Yellow Hair."

"Has your hunt been successful?"

"A deer stopped in front of me and its spirit told me that I could kill it," he answered modestly.

"That is good."

I could sense that he had something important to say to me, but he sat there for a few minutes gathering his thoughts. Finally, he spoke again.

"You are a good man, Yellow Hair. The Blue Clan wishes to adopt you. You would no longer be a stranger in our village. You would belong here and could become a Cherokee warrior."

The Cherokee sometimes adopted white men, giving them the protection of clan membership. But if I became a member of the Blue Clan, Awinita would be my sister, and my feelings towards her were anything but sisterly, even if I'd done nothing yet to show them. I had to think carefully about my answer, as I didn't want to make an enemy of Usti-waya.

"I am unworthy of this honour," I said after a proper interval to show that I had heard and considered what he'd said. "I am not one of the *Aniyunwiya*. I am a *Gilisi*, an Englishman, who knows little of your ways. Let me learn them before seeking to become a member of the Blue Clan."

This explanation satisfied Usti-waya. He nodded and never again mentioned adopting me.

The Green Maize Ceremony, the biggest festival of the Cherokee year, was held on the night of a full moon in July or August, when the village medicine man decided that the crop was ready for harvest. No Cherokee would eat any of the new maize crop until this ceremony had been performed. It was the tribe's spiritual rebirth, in some ways reminiscent of Easter. The sins of the past year were forgiven, and all animosities were supposed to be forgotten.

Preparations for the ceremony began during the last week of July. Ahawee told me one morning that there was to be a feast that night. We gathered in the square in front of the council house and had a huge meal of deer, turkey, maize, and squash. After we had eaten, Yona-equa, Tuskeegee's peace chief, rose. In a few seconds, there was complete silence as we waited to hear what he would say. He looked slowly around at us, then at Waya-adisi, the village's medicine man. After what seemed like many minutes, Waya-adisi nodded.

"The Green Maize Ceremony will be held seven days from now," Yona-equa said in a solemn voice. "We must not anger the spirits, lest they shrivel the maize and chase the deer from the forest. No one should speak angry words or drink the white man's whiskey."

There was a murmur of assent from the Cherokee. Yona-equa sat down and remained seated for a few minutes before standing and walking towards his cabin. That was the signal for the rest of us to leave.

The next seven days were a flurry of activity. The men of the village extinguished the council house fire that had burned for the past year and disposed of its ashes. They spruced up the building, replacing worn seating mats and renewing the earth covering the roof. They also cleaned the village's common areas, removing the weeds and refuse that had accumulated over the past year. Cleaning was usually considered women's work, beneath the dignity of a Cherokee warrior, but the sacredness of the ceremony overcame these prejudices. My offers to help Usti-waya and the other men of the Blue Clan were politely refused. I was told that only Cherokee could prepare for the ceremony.

Each woman cleaned her family's cabin and made sure her family's clothes were in their best condition. As the ceremony approached, she extinguished the fire in her hearth, disposed of the ashes, and threw out any food left over from the previous year, except for seven ears of maize, which were to attract the new crop. This was a surprising act for people as frugal as the Cherokee, but the Green Maize Ceremony was a new beginning and everything had to be fresh.

Two days before the ceremony the village's leading warriors and most respected old women gathered on the square in front of the council house. No one disturbed them as they sat there fasting. During their fast, the young women prepared a powerful purgative from the roots of seven different herbs, which they served to the warriors. They believed this cleansed their bodies both physically and spiritually. The Cherokee believed that the number seven had magical powers and seven items or actions repeated seven times were an important part of many of their ceremonies.

The rest of the tribe fasted only from dawn till noon on the second day. As part of their purification ritual, some Cherokee scratched themselves with sharpened fish bones until they bled in the manner of medieval penitents. Since I was not a Cherokee, I did not have to fast but did so out of respect for my hosts.

At the end of the fast, Waya-adisi lit a new fire in the council house using wood from seven different kinds of trees. All who wished for forgiveness, and had made amends to those they had injured, came forward and were given pardon. Much like the Old Testament Hebrews, the Cherokee believed in an eye for an eye, a tooth for a tooth retribution. Without the pardon provided by the Green Maize Ceremony, feuds could've disturbed the village's peace for many years.

Next Waya-adisi called the women forward and gave each of them a burning ember from the fire. Ahawee took one and returned to her cabin to light a new fire in her hearth. When she was satisfied that the fire was burning properly, she rejoined the men and children in the town square. When all of the women had returned, the whole village began a solemn dance that continued for many hours whilst Waya-adisi prayed for a good year. When the spirits had been suitably beseeched, maize from the new crop was roasted and eaten. This began a feast in which all partook, even visitors like me. When all of the food had been consumed, the Cherokee went to the river to bathe as a final purification, then painted themselves white, symbolizing peace and prosperity. This cleansing seemed to release the restraints that normally controlled young Cherokee. Couples who would have discreetly disappeared at other times were quite brazen about walking off openly. My heart sank as I watched Awinita leave with a young brave named Tsula-gigage.

A week after the Green Maize Ceremony, Ahawee again left for the four days of her monthly period. During the first day she was gone, Awinita acted as she had during the other times her mother had left us alone. But as I was falling asleep that first night, she stood over my bearskin and then lay down beside me. I lay there rigidly, not knowing what to do. I lusted for her but worried that if I took her and she were to scream, Usti-waya and the other men of the Blue Clan would kill me. When I did not respond to her presence, she wriggled her body against me in a manner that left no doubt as to what she wanted. I willingly complied. She didn't simply lie there under me as the Mexican women in Nacogdoches had, but moved so actively that our lovemaking was quickly over.

"No different than an *Aniyunwiya*," she muttered, as I lay there spent. When she saw that I had heard her, she continued, "I told my friend Ugidatli that I had seen you naked on your first day in the village and that other than being white, you looked no different from any other man." With that she left the cabin to wash. When she returned she lay down on her bearskin as if nothing had happened.

I was both elated and saddened. I'd achieved what I'd desired from the first time I'd seen Awinita, but her reason for making love to me held out no hope for the future. And indeed, having satisfied her and her friend's curiosity, Awinita treated me with the same indifference she'd previously shown. I could find no way to make her more interested in me. After a few weeks, I started thinking it would be better for me to return to Salisbury.

Many in Salisbury had called Cherokee women wanton because of acts such as Awinita's. It is true that the Cherokee women were much freer to dispense their favours than white women, but they had more freedom in every sphere of life. I wondered what the women of Salisbury would've been like if they were allowed to divorce their husbands whenever they wished, to own property, and to speak out in public.

Awinita started questioning me about the way white people lived. "The fur traders must be very rich men from all the skins they get from the Cherokee," she said one day.

"No, the traders are poor men. They give most of the skins they get to the rich men who give them goods to trade. The traders keep only one skin in three or four."

"If they gave the skins to poor men, they would be highly respected."

"They don't give the skins to poor men. They give them to rich men."

"Why would they do that? You should give things to poor people, not to rich people."

I tried but couldn't explain commerce to Awinita. The Cherokee were skilled and avid traders, but they didn't use money, so she didn't understand the idea of accumulating money or goods. It was a frustrating conversation for both of us. She'd been taught that any Cherokee who had more than he needed was expected to give the excess to those in need. Not all Cherokee lived up to this ideal, just as not all Christians live by the teachings of the Gospels, but there was much less difference between rich and poor in pagan Tuskeegee than in Christian Salisbury.

"Do white women grow maize the way Cherokee women do?" Awinita asked.

"White people grow maize, but amongst them, farming is man's work."

"And women go hunting?" she asked incredulously.

"No, men hunt, but not all the time the way Cherokee men do."

"How do they find time to both farm and hunt?"

"White men use horses and oxen to help them in their farm work. It makes the work easier."

"How can a horse or an ox help with the weeding?"

"They can't, but the weeding would go quicker if you let me help."

"No, weeding is woman's work. You are a man and should only do men's work."

Over the winter we had many similar conversations and I began
to understand that the Cherokee looked at the world very differently
than we *Gilisi* did. If I were older at the time, I probably would've
pondered these differences, but being a lustful young man, I only
noted that Awinita seemed much friendlier to me than she'd been. I
would've tried to share her bearskin, but because of the cold, we were
sleeping in the sweat lodge with at least a dozen other Cherokee. My
lust would have to wait.

With the British Army, fur traders, missionaries, and sundry other white men visiting and living with them, the Cherokee knew
about reading and writing. A few even learned to read and write English, though most showed little interest in these skills. They called
books and even odd scraps of paper talking leaves, often in a deroga-
tory tone. Cherokee men and women had powerful memories and
could retell their legends and myths in exactly the same words their
parents and grandparents had used. They listened very carefully and
could repeat even the most complicated story after hearing it just
once.

Sequoyah was one of the few Cherokee who seemed intrigued by
writing. He was a small young man, shorter than me, who walked
with a limp. As a silversmith, he often sold his work to English traders, but he spoke no English. He was reputed to be the son of Na-
thaniel Gist, a fur trader and backwoodsman, and some of the fur
traders referred to him as George Gist. But I wonder whether that
was true. Sequoyah had pure Cherokee features and I never saw his
"father" during my stay in Tuskeegee. Still, an English father might
explain his fascination with the written word.

"Yellow Hair, every time I sell a piece of silver to one of the traders, he makes marks on his talking leaves. Why does he do this?" he
asked me one day during my first winter in Tuskeegee.

"He's keeping records of how much he paid you, so he can decide
how much to charge when he sells your work to other white men."

"Can not the traders remember this? They do not seem like stupid
men."

"They can remember, but if they write it down, they don't have to
remember. They only have to look in their book."

My answer seemed to satisfy him, but a few days later he returned.

"Yellow Hair, when the missionary tells a story, he looks at the talking leaves, not at the people. Why is this? Does he not know the story?"

"I'm sure he knows the story, but if he reads it, he will be certain to get it right."

Again he seemed satisfied, but the next day he returned.

"Yellow Hair, can you teach me how to read the talking leaves?"

"I can try. I've never taught anyone to read before."

We started Sequoyah's English lessons using the Bible Lieutenant Sullivan had brought me as a text book. It reminded me of how my mother had first taught me to read using our family Bible. For a few weeks, Sequoyah listened to everything I said and didn't question or complain. He learned to read a few words, but he seemed very troubled. One day, about a month after we started, he slammed the Bible closed and grabbed at his head as if he was in pain.

"Yellow Hair, I will never learn this. It makes no sense. This letter you call cee. Sometimes it sounds like the caw of a crow, other times it sounds like the hiss of a snake. How can a man know whether he should sound like a crow or a snake?"

"You must learn all of the words."

"There are too many. How did you learn all of them?"

"First, my mother taught me, then I learned more from a teacher named Mr Anderson."

"My mother does not know these words and there is no Mr Anderson here."

"Do you want to continue?"

"No."

With that he stormed off and we never again talked about his learning to read English.

Sequoyah later became famous when he created the written Cherokee language. Instead of converting Cherokee into English letters, as the missionaries tried to do, he created eighty-five characters, one for each syllable used in Cherokee words. Once a Cherokee had memorized these characters, an easy feat for a people with such powerful memories, he could read or write any Cherokee word. In a year, almost all Cherokee, both men and women, learned to do this. Soon the Cherokee were publishing books and a newspaper. Other Indian tribes looked on in amazement, but none were able to duplicate Sequoyah's feat.

The Cherokee were the fastest of the Indian tribes to adopt the white man's ways when they made sense to them. They quickly saw that muskets were better weapons than bows and arrows and that iron tools worked better than the stone ones they had used from time immemorial. Before Europeans came, the Cherokee lived in mud-dabbed, wattle huts. When they saw log cabins, and had the axes and hatchets to build them, they rapidly switched. Knowing this, it came as no surprise that the Cherokee adopted Sequoyah's system of writing as soon as they saw its benefits.

CHAPTER 21

We moved back to Ahawee's cabin when spring and warmer weather arrived. I helped prepare the communal field for planting, a task men were allowed to perform. With only hoes and mattocks, it was backbreaking work. When we'd turned the soil and removed the rocks that grew in every farmer's field each winter, it was time for planting. This task was only slightly less difficult.

The first time Ahawee disappeared for her monthly period, I was too exhausted to be lustful, but the next month, I waited until dark and sidled over to Awinita's bearskin. She welcomed me and responded to my presence as energetically as she had when we'd made love the previous year. But I was afraid to approach her once her mother returned. Ahawee might take offense and call down the wrath of the Blue Clan's men. Awinita had no such concerns. When I didn't come to her bearskin, she came to mine. Ahawee said nothing.

There were no secrets in Tuskeegee, and soon everyone knew of my affections for Awinita. Tsula-gigage, who'd been paying court to her, was not happy. Whenever he saw me, he threatened me by moving his hand towards the knife he wore in his belt. He was a trained Cherokee warrior, and I knew nothing about his way of fighting, but showing fear would have made me seem less of a man in Awinita's eyes. I felt that the whole village was watching Tsula-gigage and me, waiting to see what would happen. Finally, after two weeks, he confronted me.

"Yellow Hair, you must leave. You are no longer welcome in Tuskeegee," he said.

"Greetings, Tsula-gigage," I replied, trying to stay calm. "The Blue Clan seems happy with my presence."

"I am not happy with your presence. A guest should leave after a short time. You have been here for a year."

"If the Blue Clan asks me to leave, I will go."

Tsula-gigage uttered what sounded like a snarl, then turned on his heel and left. Without planning, I'd responded in the correct way. If he hurt me, he would be challenging the honour of the Blue Clan. They would avenge any injury done to me with an equal injury to Tsula-gigage, including killing him if he killed me. He was a member of the Sweet Potato Clan, but his clan would accept his punishment if it was no greater than the injury he'd inflicted on me. The Cherokee were very meticulous about such matters.

Later that day, Awinita came and stood by my side, showing that she'd chosen me over Tsula-gigage. Cherokee women are free to choose their partners, but Tsula-gigage didn't give up that easily. He continued making threatening gestures towards me whenever we met. I was still afraid he might try to kill me and didn't want to give him the opportunity by going into the woods alone. For the next few months, I hunted only when I could join one of the men of the Blue Clan.

Three months later Awinita didn't disappear as she normally did at her time of month. I'd gotten her with child. Neither she nor Ahawee said anything for another month. Finally, Ahawee came up to me as I was relaxing in the early June sunshine after an unsuccessful hunt.

"It is time for you and Awinita to be married," she said without any preamble.

"Will Awinita marry me?" I asked, smiling. It was the happiest moment I'd had since leaving Salisbury five years earlier.

"Yes, I would not tell you this unless she was willing to be your wife."

"I'm very happy. Tell me what I have to do."

"We have to talk to Waya-adisi, the medicine man."

The pagan Cherokee had no fixed marriage ceremony. No minister admonished the groom to love, comfort, and honour his bride, and to keep her in sickness and health. A couple was considered married when a man moved into a woman's cabin, and was considered divorced when either he moved out or she threw his belongings out. Since Awinita and I were already living in her mother's cabin, Ahawee wanted a ceremony to show that we were married. Sometimes the bride's brother exchanged clothes with the groom as a way of welcoming him to the family, but Awinita had no living brothers. It would be up to Waya-adisi to come up with an appropriate ritual.

We found Waya-adisi at the council house. He was an old man with a wrinkled face and a mouth that contained only three teeth, but his mind was still clear and his body erect. I had no doubt that he could've bested me in a contest of strength. Ahawee explained to him that she'd agreed to my marrying Awinita and wanted a ceremony to show the rest of the village that we were a couple. After a suitable period of staring at the council house fire, Waya-adisi announced that he would marry us at dawn on the morning after the next full moon, ten days hence. I was overjoyed and began building the cabin Awinita and I would live in once we were married.

Lieutenant Sullivan's patrol arrived in Tuskeegee four days later. "Building a home for yourself, Mr Watson," he said. "You know my orders. If you don't have a Cherokee family to go with it, I'll have to burn it down."

"Don't worry, Lieutenant, I've a baby on the way and soon will have a wife." I knew from our past conversations that Sullivan did not approve of Englishmen who "went native" and took Indian wives.

"You've made your bed," Sullivan said, spitting on the ground in disgust. "I hope you find it a comfortable one, because you'll be an outcast if you ever return to civilization." He walked off before I had a chance to reply.

I'd made an enemy, but I didn't think it mattered. It did. I later found out that Lieutenant Sullivan was the first to tell Mr Cartwright, Boone, and many others that I was alive and living with the Cherokee in Tuskeegee. He didn't acknowledge Awinita as my wife, simply referring to her as "a Cherokee bitch." My attempt at keeping my whereabouts a secret had failed. The Cartwrights knew that I could've returned to Salisbury, but chose not to.

At dawn on the morning of our wedding, Awinita, Ahawee, and her brother Usti-waya, a dozen other members of the Blue Clan, and I went to the council house. Waya-adisi took the roots of two different herbs from the medicine pouch he wore at his waist and laid them on the palm of his hand. One was tan, the other black, but they were so dried and shrivelled that I couldn't tell what plants they'd come from. He then turned east towards the rising sun and in a prayer asked whether Awinita and I would be happy and have a long life together. The roots came together, which was the positive answer he was looking for. Even in my happy state, I knew this was a simple conjurer's trick, and we were receiving Waya-adisi's approval, not a message from the spirits. But the Cherokee took the omen seriously and congratulated us. Waya-adisi then prayed for the success of our marriage and warned us that if either was unfaithful, we would go to the Cherokee equivalent of hell. If that warning were true, most of the men and women in Tuskeegee were doomed.

Usti-waya, the oldest family member present, made a long, eloquent speech welcoming me to his family. Ahawee had prepared a feast of venison, maize, and squash. Even though it was early in the day, everyone ate with gusto. Awinita's smile, as she listened to the jests from her friends, was radiant. It was the happiest moment of my life, and I no longer had to fear Tsula-gigage.

Awinita's and my happiness lasted only three weeks. We were outside the cabin I'd completed doing chores. She was preparing river cane to weave into a basket; I was mending my boots. Suddenly, she jumped up and without a word ran towards her mother's cabin. As she left I could see that the back of her skirt was stained with a circle of fresh blood. A few moments later, I saw Ahawee leading her towards the women's hut. I feared the worst and my fears were soon confirmed.

"Your child will not be born," Ahawee told me the next morning. She was stoic, as Cherokee are taught to be, but I wasn't and let out a wail of anguish. The Cherokee who saw me averted their eyes. No one offered words of comfort. After a few minutes, I took my musket and headed for the woods. I pretended to be hunting, but I walked without noticing anything around me.

Awinita returned after seven days. She'd immersed herself seven times in the river near the village and was now clean both physically and spiritually. I didn't know what to say to her, so I asked her only about trivial matters. She didn't want to talk. We both resumed our household duties, speaking only when necessary. When I approached her that night, she pushed me away.

I knew that babies sometimes died in the womb, but it wasn't a subject that was openly discussed or even alluded to. My knowledge of Cherokee was too limited to have asked Awinita questions about what had happened. Even if I could, I doubt she would've answered them. Such matters were women's business, not to be discussed with men.

Awinita slowly returned to normal, but she was never as carefree as she'd been when we'd first met. After three months she came to the bearskin I was sleeping on and our lovemaking resumed. I was cautious at first, treating her like a fragile piece of pottery, but this was the wrong thing to do.

"Have you gotten weak, that you move so slowly?" she asked.

"No, but I don't want to hurt you."

"You will not hurt me if you act like a man."

Winter returned and we again slept in the sweat lodge. But since we were married, no one seemed to care if we coupled. Other married couples did so and were ignored. In early January, Awinita again missed her time of the month. I was apprehensive but couldn't put my feelings into words. Awinita said nothing on the subject, so I'd no way of knowing whether she shared my concern. The time passed slowly until spring arrived. It was time to turn over the fields and plant the new crop. The hard work had one extra benefit. I was too tired to worry about Awinita.

The women of the village knew that Awinita was with child because she didn't spend time in their hut each month, but it wasn't until April that they said anything. She told me that the women of the tribe said that she was past the danger period and that if she took proper care, she would have a healthy baby. Then they showered her with advice.

"You must wash your hands and feet each morning," Salali, Awinita's great-aunt, told her.

"Don't eat raccoon; it will make your baby sick," Ugidatli, Awinita's friend added. "And eating squirrel will cause your baby to climb up instead of down during birth."

Other women told Awinita not to eat speckled trout, because it would give our baby a birthmark, and that wearing a hat would crease our baby's head. No one, other than me, would eat food Awinita prepared or walk directly in her footsteps. Had I been Cherokee, there would've been restrictions on me. I wouldn't have been allowed to play the Cherokee ballgame or join in the communal dances. Pregnant white women withdraw from society, but I'd never heard of any restrictions on fathers-to-be.

Once Awinita's pregnancy was visible to all, we began visiting Waya-adisi each month on the day of the new moon. We gave him a piece of white cloth and two white beads. He took these and led Awinita into the river. I remained on the bank whilst he prayed that our child would have a safe birth and a peaceful, prosperous life. When he finished this prayer, Awinita gave him two black beads. Holding everything in his hand, he asked what the baby's sex would be. Each month he assured her that she would have a son.

"Before visiting the medicine man each month, you must drink a potion of slippery elm, touch-me-not stems, speedwell roots, and pine cones," Ahawee told her daughter. This strange brew was supposed to ensure an easy labour, a quick birth, and a long and healthy life for the child.

Awinita's breasts and belly swelled as her pregnancy progressed. She was transformed from the lithe, fawn-like creature that I had fallen in love with into a woman who reminded me of the Madonna I'd seen in pictures in the Catholic Church in Nacogdoches. It left me with a feeling of awe, even though I knew that my child was not the result of an immaculate conception, that much more earthly means had been employed.

It was a golden summer. The rain was gentle and sufficient for the crops to flourish. Since Awinita was pregnant, we were not allowed to participate in that year's Green Maize Ceremony, but Ahawee brought us an ember from the council house fire to light our hearth for the new year. Shortly afterwards I felt our baby kick for the first time.

"It must be a boy," Awinita said with a smile. "A girl would not kick so hard."

The last weeks of Awinita's pregnancy passed slowly. I was enthralled with the idea of being a father. The dream I'd first had six years ago of having a family of my own returned even more strongly. My wife's blossoming body was proof that it would soon come true. Awinita, who had seen the work of motherhood all her life, was also happy, but less enthusiastic. As her swollen body made normal movement difficult, she made more than one comment about her problems being my fault. I couldn't tell her how proud I was to have caused her condition. Instead I said that her confinement would soon be over and we would be joyful parents.

Awinita's labour pains began early on the morning of 2nd October 1787. Her mother, Ahawee, took charge and led her to the women's hut. I wanted to be close to Awinita when she gave birth, but that was forbidden. When I tried to approach the hut, an old woman shooed me away. I could just barely hear Awinita cry out in pain. Ahawee's brother, Usti-waya, who had five children, told me not to worry, that the other women were taking good care of her.

Awinita's labour continued all that day and into the following night. Since I could do nothing to help, I went back to our cabin and slept for a few hours. I awoke in darkness and made my way as quietly as I could towards the women's hut. It was the only lit building, and it seemed like every woman in the village was milling about – far more than had been in attendance during the day. Awinita was no longer crying out in pain. All I could hear was a low buzz of voices. There was none of the laughter or the joyous sounds that accompany a successful birth. Something was wrong, but I couldn't tell what. Had the baby died? Had Awinita?

My presence set a dog to barking. The other dogs in the village quickly joined it. Salali came to investigate. "You must not be here," she scolded when she saw me. "Return at dawn." I tried to argue, but she was soon joined by a handful of other women. One of them cast a stone in my direction. They were in no mood to tolerate a male presence. I had no choice but to retreat and await daybreak.

At soon as there was any light in the sky, I walked to the women's hut. The way the village women acted the night before told me that something was wrong, but I couldn't figure out what. My mother-in-law Ahawee was standing outside the hut, talking to her aunt Salali. As soon as she saw me, she broke off her conversation and came to meet me.

"You have a son, Yellow-Hair," she told me in a flat, emotionless voice, her hands at her side, as Cherokee are taught to do when they have something important to say, "but my daughter, Awinita, is dead. She started bleeding after the baby emerged, and we could do nothing to stop the flow. Ugidatli has taken the boy and will nurse him." Ugidatli had given birth to a daughter two months earlier.

I stood there so shocked that I couldn't even cry out. The happy life I envisioned had been destroyed in an instant for reasons I couldn't comprehend. Awinita, my beautiful fawn-like wife, had been healthy and strong. She had carefully followed the advice the women of the village had given her on how to ensure a healthy baby and an easy birth. It seemed that God had punished us, but I didn't know why. Surely, He didn't consider our marriage a sin, even if it had been performed by a Cherokee medicine man instead of a Christian minister. My silence must have scared Ahawee.

"Yellow Hair, can you speak?" she said, shaking my arm as if to wake me up.

"I have no words."

"We must bury Awinita."

"I cannot do that."

My only thought at that moment was that I needed to leave, to be as far from Tuskeegee as I could. I didn't want to see anything that could remind me of Awinita . . . no Cherokee faces . . . no Cherokee cabins . . . no council house . . . nothing.

I saddled my horse and rode out of the village. I rode all day, stopping only to allow my horse to drink from a stream and me to relieve myself. At dusk I realized how foolish I was being. I had ridden west, away from both Cherokee and white settlements. I had no food and no plan. I hadn't even taken my musket. I spent a cold night and in the morning slowly rode back to Tuskeegee.

Ahawee had washed Awinita's body to prepare it for burial. We dug her grave outside the village and laid her directly in the earth. We built a small mound over her body, which we covered with stones to prevent animals from disturbing the grave. The Cherokee believed that the bodies of the dead should feed the plants, which would then feed animals and people. We buried Awinita's clothes with her because they were now considered unclean. No Cherokee woman would use them.

The pagan Cherokee observed seven days of mourning, during which time they were not to show any strong emotions, to be neither angry nor jovial, and not to eat or drink more than necessary to stave off hunger and thirst. Those were easy rules for me to follow. I returned to the cabin I had built for Awinita and ate some food without tasting it. Then I lay down on my bearskin and tried to think.

I knew that the Cherokee would not allow me to raise my son. That would be the responsibility of the Blue Clan. His great-uncle Usti-waya would give him his first bow and teach him how to hunt. Later he would teach him to be a Cherokee warrior. He would be more of a father to my son than I would be. But I was not Cherokee. This was not my way. I wanted to watch my son grow, to tell him stories and answer his questions, as my father had done for me.

As I lay on that bearskin, I convinced myself that had Awinita lived, I would have found a way to be part of my son's life, but with her dead, he needed a woman to nurse and care for him. These were not things a man – English or Cherokee – could do. In Salisbury, I could have hired a wet nurse, but in Tuskeegee, I had no choice but to turn him over to his family and clan.

I could no longer live in Tuskeegee with the memory of Awinita around me every moment. I would stay in Tuskeegee, at least until the end of the mourning period, then I could decide when to leave.

The next morning I found Ahawee just as she was returning from her morning wash in the river. "Greetings, Mother-in-Law," I said, uncertain as to how to start our conversation.

"Greetings, Son-in-Law."

"How is my son?"

"Ugidatli says he nurses well and will grow big and strong."

I paused for a moment, unsure as to how to continue.

"Will Ugidatli raise him?" I finally found the courage to ask.

"No, that is my task," Ahawee said looking at her feet. "I have already talked to Ugidatli. She will nurse him along with her own daughter, but I will do everything else. All my own children have died, but Awinita was kind enough to leave me a baby so that I can again be a mother."

"Can I see the boy?" I asked, not knowing what was proper under the circumstances.

"He is your son. It is your right to see him."

I went to Ugidatli's cabin. She was alone with the two infants.

"Can I see my son?" I asked.

"He is sleeping," she said, pointing to a tiny bundle swaddled in deerskin lying on a bearskin.

I picked him up, cradled him in my right arm, and stared at his red, wrinkled face. He seemed light as a feather. I cannot remember how long I stood there or what thoughts passed through my head. It was as if time had stopped. The spell was broken when Ugidatli tapped gently on my arm.

"I think you should put him down," she said. "I do not want him to wake up. It is too soon for me to feed him again."

Reluctantly, I put my son down on the bearskin. I didn't know what to say to Ugidatli. How does a man thank a woman for keeping his son alive? I left her cabin without even the normal courtesies and returned to the cabin Awinita and I had shared. I lay on my bearskin all day, hardly moving. At dusk I drank some water and ate a little stale bread.

Some time that night I changed my mind and decided to leave Tuskeegee as quickly as possible. The longer I stayed, the more painful leaving would be. Best cauterize the wound now rather than letting it fester. Ahawee would care for my son and give him a name. Usti-waya would teach him the ways of men. My presence could only make life more difficult for the boy. I would remind everyone that he was only half Cherokee.

The next morning I again sought out Ahawee. She was in front of her cabin weaving flax. "I must leave Tuskeegee," I said when she looked up.

"It is right. When a man's wife dies, he should return to his own people."

I'd expected Ahawee to try to dissuade me, but when she agreed with me there was nothing more to say. I went to the cabin, collected my belongings, the seven shillings I'd earned selling deerskins to the fur traders, and all the food that I had. I could think of no choice but to return to Salisbury to face whatever fate awaited me there.

CHAPTER 22

I spent ten days riding from Tuskeegee to Salisbury. I would've liked to have made the trip longer, for whilst I was in the forest I didn't have to face the Cartwrights, but I had little food. I shot a squirrel and picked some berries that had dried on the vine, but these did little to assuage my growing hunger.

I thought long and hard about what I'd say to Jenny and to her father. There were no good words. I came up with a brief history of my absence, but I didn't know how to begin my story. Much as I feared having to see Mr Cartwright, there was no way to avoid it. I decided to accept whatever punishment he meted out and resolved to make his shop my first stop.

I rode into Salisbury shortly after noon on a beautiful October day. I'd eaten nothing since the previous morning and could hear my stomach rumbling as I slowly walked my horse through the outskirts of town. I hadn't paid much attention to my surroundings since leaving Tuskeegee, but now I grew intensely aware of them. The bright blue sky had none of summer's haze. The leaves had turned colour and were falling. Other than a handful of new buildings, Salisbury looked unchanged.

I headed directly to Mr Cartwright's shop and house on Freemason Street, but I hesitated in front of the building before getting off my horse. I still hadn't decided what to say to him or to Jenny, if I was allowed to see her. My resolve, which had seemed so strong in the mountains, disappeared.

I was about to turn around and ride out of town when Geoff Carlyle saw me. He'd started with Terrill and me on our ill-fated fur-trading expedition, but wisely had turned back early. He rubbed his eyes and shook his head as if he didn't believe what he was seeing, then waved and headed in my direction. I waved back at him and pointed to the shop to show that I was going in. Fate had intervened. I had no choice but to dismount and enter the shop.

Mr Cartwright was arranging inventory and didn't see me enter. He turned when he heard the door close.

"William?" he asked in a shocked voice.

"Yes," I answered softly.

"So you've finally decided to return. Lieutenant Sullivan told me you were living with a Cherokee bitch." Mr Cartwright was red-faced and gripping the counter top as if trying to restrain himself.

"She was a fine woman." I could feel bile rising in my throat. "I'll not listen to you defaming her." That must have surprised him because he closed his mouth abruptly, cutting off whatever else he'd planned to say. Then I told him the story I'd so carefully rehearsed in my mind . . . about Terrill and me being imprisoned by the Spanish . . . our return and Terrill's death . . . how Ahawee had saved my life . . . and about Awinita and that she had died giving birth only two weeks earlier. I didn't mention my son. Finally, I asked, "Is Jenny here?"

"No, she lives in Charleston with her husband." He emphasized the last word. "You left her with a son. Adam Stahlworth's a saint to have taken her and David. You'd best leave now before I give you the thrashing you deserve. I don't want to see you again. And don't bother Jenny or the boy. You've caused them enough trouble."

"I'm sorry. It was stupid of me to leave," I said, backing towards the door. "I shan't bother you again."

"Good," was his final word as I left his shop.

The news that I had another son and that, despite my abandoning her, Jenny had kept her promise and named him David, after my father, left me shaking. I grabbed the hitching rail to keep from falling. An immense wave of sadness passed over me as I realized that I'd never see this son. I stood outside the shop for a few moments, not knowing what to do until I heard Mr Cartwright moving about. I thought he might have changed his mind and was coming to give me "the thrashing I deserved." I quickly mounted my horse and rode away.

Once I was well away from Mr Cartwright's shop, I stopped, sat under a tree, and pondered what to do next. Much as I wanted to go to Charleston to see David, I'd promised not to bother Jenny or him. I knew I had to keep that promise. I couldn't stay in Salisbury and face Amos Cartwright. I couldn't go back to the Cherokee and face the memory of Awinita. I had the clothes on my back, a horse, a musket, and a few extra pieces of clothing that I might barter, but only seven shillings and no job. I thought about returning to Philadelphia and asking help from Mr McNeil – I even thought about returning to New York and my grandparents, or travelling to Montreal to find Donald Mackenzie – but seven shillings wasn't going to carry me that far. Slowly, I realized that the only person who might help me was Daniel Boone. I hadn't seen him since our hunting trip to Kentucky almost eight years earlier and wondered if he would remember me. By this time it was late afternoon. Despite the cost, I decided to spend the night at Salisbury's inn. It would make little difference whether I had five or seven shillings and I needed a meal to fill my empty stomach.

Word of who I was and what I'd done must have sped around the town because I could feel other people, both workers and guests at the inn, staring at me as I ate my supper and drank a pint of ale. Nobody said anything to me, not even the normal courtesies one expects amongst strangers. I was being shunned. I left early the next morning for Boone's homestead on the Yadkin River. I hoped he still lived there.

Boone wasn't home when I arrived at his cabin. A young woman opened the door as I mounted the steps to cabin's porch. Boone's wife, Rebecca, stood behind her, a rifle pointed at my head.

"Mrs Boone, I'm William Watson, a friend of Daniel's. We've been fur trading and deer hunting together."

"Mr Watson," she said, lowering the rifle. "I'm so sorry. I didn't recognize you at first, but now I remember you. Please come in. Would you like some tea?" The young woman, who I later learned was the Boones' daughter Becky, went to put the kettle on, not waiting for my answer.

"That's would be nice," I said as I entered the cabin. "Is Daniel here?"

"No, he's in Kentucky deer hunting with his brother, Squire, and three other men," Rebecca answered. "He left a month ago. He should be back any day now. You're welcome to stay if you're willing to wait for him."

The cabin looked shabbier than when I'd last seen it. The puncheon floor, which had taken so much work to build, needed replacement. Its split logs were worn and the gaps between them were filled with bits of food and other rubbish. The caning in the chairs around the kitchen table also needed repair; there were holes in several of the seats.

"I'd be happy to do that for a few days. Of course, I'll help with the chores."

She'd aged visibly since I last saw her. Her hair was now mostly grey and she looked tired. A boy, who appeared to be about five years old, was playing on the cabin floor. I assumed he was a grandson until she said, "This is Nathan, our youngest. Nathan, say hello to Mr Watson."

Nathan and I exchanged a few words as you do when introduced to a child.

Boone returned four days later. He'd had a successful hunt and brought home a full load of deerskin. He acknowledged me, but his first thoughts were for his family. Unlike Rebecca, he seemed not to have changed since I last saw him. His hair was still black, his shoulders still powerful, and his blue eyes still twinkled as he talked. It was not until the next day that I had a chance to tell him what'd happened to me over the last six years. He already knew that I'd lived with the Cherokee, but he listened politely.

"Daniel, I've no money and no place to live. I need a job," I said as I finished.

"You ever heard of Leonard Henderson?" Boone asked.

"No, I don't recognize that name."

"He's a merchant who owns a string of trading posts in villages near the Proclamation Line, and he's looking for someone to run the one at Davidson's Fort. You interested?"

"Yes, most definitely."

"I got to know Leonard when I worked for his father, Richard. Now that Richard is dead, he runs the family enterprises from his office in Guilford Courthouse. He likes more comfort than you can have on the frontier, but don't be fooled by that. He's a hard-headed businessman, not a dreamer like his father. I'll give you a good character to show him, if you'd like."

"That would be most kind. I'll see him as soon as I can."

I rode to Guilford Courthouse and had no trouble finding Leonard Henderson's office. A clerk told me to wait whilst he enquired whether Mr Henderson was available. After a few minutes, I was ushered in to see him. He was a ruddy-faced man, about ten years older than me, with the beginnings of a paunch. He sat behind a large cherry-wood desk that had writing implements and several neat stacks of papers. When I entered he was busy writing and motioned me into a seat.

"Well, Mr Watson, how may I be of service?" he asked when he'd finished his task.

"Daniel Boone told me that you're looking for someone to run your trading post at Davidson's Fort. He gave me this good character to show you," I said, handing him the note Boone had given me.

"Daniel says you are a good man, but then he thinks that of everybody," Henderson said, after reading the note. "Tell me about yourself."

I spent the next few minutes telling him the story of my life. He smiled when I told him about my times working for Mr McNeil and Mr Cartwright. He asked me a few simple questions about keeping shop accounts, which I was able answer to his satisfaction.

"You've packed a great deal into, what is it, twenty-six years?"

"Twenty-four."

"I grew up sharing my father's dream of great enterprises over the mountains." There was a note of sadness in his voice. "He started the Transylvania Company and bought twenty million acres of land in Kentucky from the Cherokee. It was to be the fourteenth colony. Boonesborough would have been its first town. But the Crown has decreed that settlement is limited to east of the mountains. Even though I still own the land, my father's dreams won't be achieved.

"But there are business empires to be built here in North Carolina," he continued, no longer sad. "More people are settling near the Proclamation Line. They need merchants to serve them. I've had a trading post at Davidson's Fort for five years, but Horatio Thatcher, the man I hired to run it, wants to return home to Maryland. He's had the decency to stay on until I can replace him. I need a reliable man for the job. Are you such a man?" He stared directly at me as he said these last words as if he were issuing a challenge.

"I think I am, sir. I've had all the adventure I want for the rest of my life these past six years." I tried to sound confident.

Henderson had his clerk bring some pelts into the office and asked me how much each of them was worth. I told him how much I would have been willing to pay for them six years earlier. Luckily the price of furs hadn't changed over that time and I passed this final test with ease.

"You seem to know how to run a trading post," he said as his clerk removed the pelts. "You're hired, but if I'm not satisfied with your work, I'll discharge you."

"Thank you," I said. "I'm certain you'll be happy with my work."

Henderson then explained that I could live rent-free in a room behind the shop and would draw a small salary plus a tenth of any profits the trading post generated. I could take what food, clothing, and other items I needed from the shop at cost – the total would be deducted from my earnings. It was a fair arrangement. I didn't think I would have much cash, but all my needs would be taken care of.

I listened carefully and said, "Thank you, sir," when I thought he was finished.

"Good. We can leave in a week with the monthly pack train carrying goods for the post." We shook hands to seal the agreement. But Henderson was far from finished.

"William, I don't hold with white men taking Indian wives," he said, after the briefest of pauses. "You do that in Davidson's Fort and I'll fire you."

"I understand," I said. I felt I was betraying Awinita by not defending her and other Cherokee women, but I needed the job he was offering and kept silent.

We then spent the next hour discussing the details of the job I'd just been hired to do. Henderson actually had four different businesses at the trading post and kept separate accounts for each. His most profitable operation was providing trade goods and provision to fur traders in exchange for a majority of the pelts they obtained from the Indians. Most fur traders also sold their share of pelts to him, since they would have to travel to Salisbury to find another buyer. Henderson also made a good profit from providing supplies to the army at Davidson's Fort. In addition, the trading post was the village general store. Henderson considered this a separate business, one which then provided only a small profit. He was optimistic that this profit would increase as more people moved into the area.

Henderson's final business was the most complicated. He bought the ginseng that everyone – fur traders, farmers, villagers, and even soldiers – collected, as well as the whiskey and crafts local people produced for extra income. These items were sent back on the pack trains that brought goods for the shop and army. Most of this trade was actually as barter, since almost all of the people coming to the shop to sell their products wanted goods in exchange. But I still had to know the value of the products they were offering. Ginseng and whiskey were not a problem. Their prices both in cash and barter were well established, but how much was I to give for the pottery, baskets, and other craft that farmers would try to sell? And should I barter for used goods? Henderson said that I would have to use my judgment and reminded me that it was in my interest to make good trades, since a tenth of the profits would be mine.

Mr Henderson wanted complete records of all purchases and sales for each of these businesses. He would visit once a year to inspect these records and check the inventory. He would accompany me to Davidson's Fort so that we could agree on the trading post's finances before I assumed responsibility for them. Some of the sales, selling to the fort and staking fur traders, had to be on credit, but I was not to extend credit to any other customers.

After we'd gone through these details, Henderson turned grim. "William, I've been in business long enough to know all the tricks that can be played. You may think that since I'll be 150 miles away and checking only once a year, you can defraud me. I advise you not to try. I'm also a barrister, and if you cheat me, I'll see you in gaol. And don't cheat the army, unless you want to spend the rest of your life in a military prison."

"Sir, all of my previous employers have found me trustworthy. I'm sure you'll find the same." He nodded when I said this, either to agree or to indicate that he'd heard me.

I needed a rifle – my Spanish Army musket was too poor a weapon for the life I was embarking on. Mr Henderson advanced me two pounds against my future earnings, enough for me to buy a used weapon. It was two inches shorter than it should have been, failing to reach my nose by that distance, but it was still accurate at over a hundred paces. It was a fine piece, yet it brought none of the joy I felt when I bought my first rifle, which was handcrafted for me in Horst Rosenfeld's shop in Philadelphia. No gun has ever matched the smooth feel of its stock against my cheek. I had that rifle for little over a year before a thieving band of Cherokee stole it from me.

Mr Henderson invited me to stay at his house. His wife, Hortensia, greeted me warmly and did everything she could to make me comfortable. I slept on a bed with a feather tick for the first time in six years. To my surprise, I found it too soft to be comfortable. Was I no longer capable of enjoying life's little pleasures?

Henderson spent most of the following week supervising the assembly of the pack train to Davidson's Fort. There was little I could do to help and I was left with much time to ponder my melancholy situation. I had two sons, neither of whom I would ever see. I'd loved two women. One was dead and the other must surely hate me for abandoning her. I was in debt for the first time in my life. I had a job, but it was as a shopkeeper, a fate I'd tried hard to escape.

My only happy thought was that I could make a new start in Davidson's Fort. I'd be a hundred miles from Salisbury. No one would know me, and with luck, word of my abandoning Jenny wouldn't follow me. I'd also abandoned my Cherokee son, but I doubted that anyone in Davidson's Fort would care about that transgression. I resolved to make the best of my situation.

CHAPTER 23

When Leonard Henderson and I arrived in November 1787, Davidson's Fort housed a half company of infantry – fifty British soldiers – commanded by a lieutenant, a squadron of cavalry commanded by an ensign, and a customs officer to collect the duty on furs from Indian lands. That hadn't changed since I'd passed through nine years earlier on my first fur-trading expedition with Daniel Boone. But everything else in the village had grown. A hundred people now lived close to the fort, and another two hundred lived on farms in the area, nearly three times as many as when I'd last been there. Davidson's Fort now had Henderson's trading post, a sawmill, a gristmill, a blacksmith's shop, an Anglican church, and a Methodist chapel, as additions to the tavern, which previously had been its only amenity. But even though the settlement was seventeen years old, it had a raw look about it. Only one house was painted. There were no streets. Pathways, which were muddy in wet weather and dusty in dry weather, ran from one building to another. The pack train Mr Henderson sent to his store every month was the main way that goods got to and from the village.

Henderson spent two days at the trading post determining that all was in order, then returned to Guilford Courthouse. I spent the next week learning the post's operations from Horatio Thatcher, who'd been running it for the past five years. Thatcher spent words as if each one cost him a great sum of money. Most times he merely pointed as he showed me around.

The trading post contained three rooms. A large front room housed the shop. It had a counter in the middle, shelves for goods on the walls, and a fireplace for warmth and cooking. A second large room provided storage area. A third, much smaller room, was furnished with a bed, a small table, and a chest. This is where I was supposed to live, but I lived in the shop, including cooking and eating my meals there, and used the bedroom only for sleeping. Thatcher had done the same. If this bothered any of my customers, none ever mentioned it.

The trading post sold everything – food from local farms, coffee, tea, cloth, leather, ironmongery, and anything else that Mr Henderson decided to send on the pack train. He also sent any newspapers he was finished reading. These were the village's main source of news of the outside world.

A small building behind the trading post served as a combination stable and tool shed. There was land for a garden, but I didn't plant one. I could've saved a bit of money by doing that, but by the time spring came, I was used to taking my food from the shop's stock and saw no reason to change. I kept shop, cooked and cleaned for myself, and chopped enough wood to keep the trading post warm. These tasks kept me busy most hours from dawn to dusk. I didn't need the extra work of a garden.

Thatcher introduced me to the people in the village and those farmers who came into the shop during the week we spent together. He hadn't made any friends. Customers wished him well, but there was no warmth in their words. They eyed me warily as if wondering whether I would be an improvement.

A month after I arrived, Sergeant Tilson, the fort's quartermaster, came into the post. He waited until we were alone.

"Watson," he said, in a low voice, even though no one but me could have heard him, "you look like a man who'd be willing to make a few extra pounds."

"What do you have in mind?"

"What if I agreed to let you charge the army a quarter more than your goods are worth, and we split the overcharge?"

"It wouldn't take long for your lieutenant to discover that I was charging the army more than my other customers. We'd both end up as prisoners, if not worse."

He went away shaking his head. He couldn't have been a very bright man because he never returned to suggest a more subtle approach. I was almost certain that he'd made the same proposal to Thatcher, who I assumed was smart enough to reject it. Thatcher should have warned me, but given how little he was willing to say, I wasn't surprised that he hadn't.

My arrival caused a stir amongst the four families in the community with marriageable daughters. One after another they invited me to Sunday dinner. The invitations never said anything about the girls. They were only welcoming me to the town.

"Mr Watson," Mrs Abernathy said, two weeks after I arrived, "you must be tired of eating your own cooking."

"Yes, ma'am, I am."

"Why don't you come to dinner next Sunday after church?"

"It would be my pleasure."

When I arrived for dinner that Sunday, I was seated next to Chloe, a sallow-faced, quiet girl of seventeen.

"Tell us about your stay with the Cherokee, Mr Watson," Mrs Abernathy said after we had said grace and filled our plates with roast chicken. "I'm sure that Chloe would like to hear about that."

I told the Abernathies some well-known things about the Cherokee. It was not a subject I wanted to talk about. Chloe said nothing when I finished, and for a few minutes, we ate in silence.

"Chloe, why don't you tell Mr Watson about your needlework," Mr Abernathy said, trying to restart the conversation.

"I'm working on a tapestry," Chloe said but didn't elaborate.

"That's nice," I said.

Mr and Mrs Abernathy made a few more attempts to get a conversation started between us, but they failed. I wasn't invited to dinner at that house again for a long time.

The three widows in town also tried to spark my interest. I still wanted a family, but none of the women in Davidson's Fort measured up to either Awinita or Jenny. I couldn't see myself courting any of them. I hope I was polite in rejecting the offers that came my way.

After several months I was no longer considered a marriage prospect and life became much simpler.

I sold my horse the spring after I moved to Davidson's Fort. This tied me to the village, but I wasn't going anywhere. I felt relieved not to have the additional work and expense of keeping a horse I hardly had time to exercise properly.

I was satisfied to run the trading post and do as little else as possible. Some men in this condition become slovenly and ill-tempered, but I didn't. Whether it was the training I received from my Dutch mother or the demands of being a shopkeeper, I stayed clean and, I believe, cheerful.

Whilst my life was solitary, it wasn't unsocial. The trading post was always full of people. Even if they had nothing to buy or sell, they would congregate to read the newspapers tacked to the walls or to talk to their neighbours and me. In short order I earned a reputation for being friendlier than Thatcher had been. I bantered and gossiped with my customers. I soon knew everything that was happening for miles around. Whilst not a regular churchgoer, I showed my face at the Church of England services often enough to allay any suspicion that I was a nonbeliever. After a year I was a fully accepted member of the community whose opinion was sought on many topics. If anyone thought my living alone was unusual, they said nothing about it to me.

With the passage of time, the pain of losing Awinita and of being unable to see Jenny and my sons softened somewhat. I fell into a comfortable routine. Decembers were the only times I felt lonely. Sint Nicolaas Dag, on the 6th, always brought back memories of my family and my life in Graves End. Christmas was easier to face, since most years one family or another would invite me to Christmas dinner.

Once I had made enough money to repay Mr Henderson, I started going to the tavern once or twice a week. I had a pint of ale and often played French Ruff for an hour or two with some of the men in the village. We played for small stakes, ha'penny a point, and it was rare that I won or lost as much as a shilling. I remembered my parents' injunctions against gambling, but what I was doing seemed harmless.

The Charleston newspapers that arrived early in 1789 were full of news of King George III's madness. He'd always been considered an eccentric, talking to farmers and tradesmen as if they were his equals, and shouting "What, what?" at the end of his questions, but until then, no one had doubted his sanity. Now there were reports of him assaulting his footmen, shouting obscenities at those around him, and generally behaving without restraint.

"So the King has finally shown his true colours," Robert McDowell said. "Only a madman would continue to tax us without giving us a voice in Parliament. He's inviting another rebellion."

McDowell was a local farmer well known for having supported the rebel cause during the Great Rebellion, but his remark shocked those present. Speaking openly about another rebellion risked arrest for sedition and opened wounds that had scabbed over in the last decade. It was far better not to talk about such matters.

"I don't like taxes any more than you do, Robert," David Vance said after a few moments of silence, "but it's Parliament that taxes us, not the King. From all that I've heard, he's a good man, abstemious and devoted to his wife."

"Besides, if the King is declared mad, the Prince of Wales will become Regent," Arthur Johnson added. "And he's not abstemious, nor devoted to anything except his friends and chasing women. Do you want him ruling the country?"

When I was with the rebel army during the last four months of the rebellion, the King was the personification of evil. Congress had said so in its Declaration of Independence, when it held him responsible for all the injustices the rebels felt had been committed against the colonies. My opinion of the King turned positive six months after the rebel's defeat, when he granted amnesty to all but Washington and nine other leaders of the rebellion. That amnesty freed me to get on with my life. After that I didn't think about the King very often. For much of that time, either as a prisoner of the Spanish or whilst I was living with the Cherokee, I knew nothing of what was happening in England.

The King's condition remained a major topic of discussion for the next six months until news of his recovery arrived. I avoided giving my opinion when asked because, truth be told, I didn't know what to think. The Great Rebellion had cost the lives of both of my parents and the loss of our farm and most of our belongings. More than once it could have cost me my life. Whilst George III was not solely responsible for the Great Rebellion, there had never been any doubt in my mind that he could've done more to avoid it. Yet, as David Vance had pointed out, he was a decent man and a magnanimous one too, as he showed by punishing only the leaders of the rebellion. The more I pondered my feelings, the less sure I was of how I viewed the King. I was very happy when the his recovery allowed the topic to change.

In Spring 1788, about the time I sold my horse, the Slaters – Edward and Judy, they had no children – moved onto a small farm a mile from the village. They joined the Methodist chapel and were quickly accepted by the community. I saw Judy when she came into the trading post to sell her eggs and vegetables or to make small purchases. A large, plain woman, with a weather-beaten face and hands that were almost as calloused as a man's, she was no stranger to farm work. She had a brusque way of speaking, which did not invite more than the polite, superficial conversation a shopkeeper must engage in with his customers. I guessed her to be about thirty years old when I first met her.

Edward Slater died in June 1790 when a tree he was felling cracked and landed on him. Judy decided to stay on the farm. Edward had left a large store of firewood and a maize crop in the field, and she could continue growing vegetables and raising chickens, some of which she sold to the trading post. Shortly after Edward died, she started caning baskets and sewing for some of the women in the village. I suspect they gave her this work more out of charity than out of necessity. Whilst these activities ensured that Widow Slater would be able to survive through the winter, I didn't know what would happen to her in the spring. Strong as she was, she couldn't do the heavy work of cutting firewood or ploughing the field for the next summer's crop.

I wasn't surprised when she walked into the shop one day in February, eight months after her husband had died. She was a regular customer.

"Good morning, Widow Slater," I said. "How may I serve you?"

"I need a pound of salt."

"It'll take a moment to get it for you," I said as I headed back to the storeroom.

When I returned with the salt, she was looking at the flasks of honey stacked on one of the shelves.

"The honey is from Jesse Williams' hives," I said. "Finest quality. Only three shillings a flask, plus two shillings deposit for the flask itself."

"I haven't had honey or anything sweet since Edward died, but five shillings is more than I can spend today," she said, still looking at the flasks. Then she turned and looked directly at me. "Mr Watson, why don't you come to supper tomorrow night? Some of that honey'll go well with my Indian corn bread."

"It'd be my pleasure," I replied. I never turned down an invitation for a meal prepared by someone else. I'd learned to cook over a campfire twelve years earlier on the trip Donald Mackenzie and I took down the Great Wagon Road, but hadn't added to my culinary skills since then.

"Wait until after dark. I don't want every old biddy in the village clucking about who I invite to supper."

"I understand."

I didn't know what to expect, but the next night I waited until an hour after sunset, took a flask of honey, then carefully made my way to Judy's cabin. I rapped softly on the door. She opened it immediately. The sparsely furnished room looked as if it had been tidied up in preparation for my visit. A table with two chairs was set close to the fireplace, which contained the embers of a dying fire. Another table with neat stacks of kitchen implements sat against the far wall, and a double bed had been pushed against the wall opposite the fireplace. A candle lantern on the dining table provided the room's only light. Judy had taken similar care with herself. She'd tied back her brown hair with a bit of red ribbon, and was wearing a dress I'd seen her wear to church. Her cheeks were redder than usual. I didn't know whether she was blushing or had pinched her cheeks to give them some colour.

"I wasn't sure you'd come, William," she said as I handed her the flask of honey. "You must be hungry. Take your coat off, then sit and eat."

"Thank you. Where would you like me to sit?"

"By the fire. It's a cold night. A little warmth'll feel good." She stirred the embers and added two logs.

We had chicken stew with Indian cornbread and honey for dinner and talked about the weather, people in the village, and other such weighty topics. We exchanged more words that evening than we had in the three years I'd known her.

"It must be difficult living here by yourself," I said after we'd finished eating.

"Yes, but it's better than living with Edward," she replied, almost spitting out the words.

I was taken aback. I thought they'd been happy, or at least content, with each other. In public, they'd treated each other courteously and neither made demeaning remarks about the other, the way some husbands and wives do.

"He beat me because I couldn't have children," she continued, seeing what must have been a shocked look on my face. "And he was right. He proved it by having a bastard son with an indentured servant girl up in Virginia. That's why we moved. Once that whore completed her term of service, she started hounding him. I hoped there'd be less temptation here."

Her anger had subsided, but she looked immensely sad. "I miss him at night though. It's so cold now that it's winter."

I ended up in her bed that night and discovered that, under her brusque manner, she was a lusty woman. I left at midnight, wondering what would happen next.

A week later Judy came to the trading post and again invited me to supper. This time she commented on how she needed a small cast iron pot. And as before, I ended up in her bed.

Being with Judy increased the pangs of lust that I'd chosen to ignore since moving to Davidson's Fort. I worried about satisfying them by sneaking into her cabin. Sooner or later we'd be discovered, which would ruin both our reputations unless we married quickly. But I couldn't see asking her to marry me. I had none of the feelings towards her that I'd felt for Awinita or Jenny, the two women I'd loved.

I rarely thought about Judy when we were apart, but visions of the times I'd spent with Jenny and Awinita still came to me at odd moments during the day. Some of those visions were lustful – my memories of the one time I'd coupled with Jenny in Widow Findley's barn, and of Awinita standing naked in the doorway of our cabin, her body just barely visible in the moonlight. But most of my thoughts were of more ordinary things: Jenny singing ballads in her clear soprano voice, or Awinita grinding corn with smooth, seemingly effortless strokes. No such visions of Judy came to me.

Lust triumphed. We fell into a pattern. Every two to three weeks she would invite me to supper. I would wait until after dark to go to her cabin. I always brought a gift, something she'd either asked for or that I knew she wanted or needed. We always ended up in her bed. I realized that I was paying for her favours, just as certainly as if she was a whore, but somehow having supper with her, spending the whole evening in her cabin, and giving her a gift rather than cash allowed me to put that thought out of my mind.

After a few visits, Judy's brusque manner softened. She told me about growing up poor on a farm in Virginia . . . how Edward had wooed and won her . . . how she married him when she was seventeen . . . and how the first two years of their marriage had been the happiest time of her life. The last ten years had been anything but happy. Edward had not only beaten her, but had belittled her for not being able to bear children. He'd said that she wasn't a real woman. I think that pained her more than the beatings, and soured her on the male half of the human race. I told her about my adventures, taking care not to mention either Awinita or Jenny. She didn't ask about the women in my life.

We became friends after a fashion. When we met we talked about what had happened in our lives since our last visit and gossiped about people in the village. But neither Judy nor I said anything about our feelings for each other. It was a strange arrangement, but it seemed to serve both of our needs. After a year my concerns about being discovered subsided. I was certain that people in the village knew what we were doing, but because we were discreet, they could choose to ignore us and not say anything.

The first spring after Edward's death some of the men from her church helped Judy by ploughing her vegetable garden and chopping wood for her. They may not have realized that I was sharing Judy's bed – men are slower to discover such arrangements than women. But they continued doing this work for the next five years, long after our arrangement must have been common knowledge. I could've done some of that work, but not all of it whilst still keeping the shop open from early morning to sunset. Also, my doing farm work for Judy would have set tongues wagging, the last thing either of us wanted. Judy never asked for my help on the farm.

At the time I didn't question the conspiracy of silence that protected Judy and me – I was too happy to be able to continue seeing Judy and I silently thanked the men from the Methodist chapel. But over the years, I've often wondered why they continued to help her. Perhaps they were being true Christians, helping her without judging her. Or perhaps they would've been embarrassed to admit they'd helped her that first year when, as an unchaste woman, she didn't deserve their charity. Continuing to treat her as a bereft widow was easier than calling attention to the truth. Or perhaps each man wished that he could have been in my position – having a bedmate who would be happy with a small gift and made none of the other demands of a wife.

I saw Daniel Boone occasionally during my years at Davidson's Fort. He was more than fifty when I moved there, but the years seemed to have little effect on him. He spent less time hunting, trapping, and trading. These activities had become less profitable as the area became hunted out. He'd found work guiding survey parties through the mountains.

Speculators had bought up large stretches of land east of the Proclamation Line and needed to know which parts of them were suitable for farming. Boone's prodigious memory for places he'd been served him well. He could take the surveyors to hidden hollows that few white men knew. It was another example of the contradictions in Boone's life. He wanted to keep the land wild, but he made his living by showing speculators how to tame and exploit it. At least the work kept him ahead of the debt collectors who seemed always to hound him. And he had another reason for staying close to home. By now some of his children were married and his daughters and daughters-in-law were churning out grandchildren at a rapid rate.

"Don't tell Rebecca, but it's harder to stay away from my

grandchildren than it was to stay away from her and my own children," he confessed one day.

Davidson's Fort was remote, but my neighbours and I couldn't escape news of the revolution in France that started in 1789. It was a confusing time. We got almost all of our news from the Charleston newspapers that Mr Henderson sent along with his monthly pack train of goods for the trading post. This meant that it took three months or more for us to learn what was happening in France and events were proceeding much faster than that.

Most of the news was stories reprinted from London newspapers, with an occasional story from French sources. With the army looking over their shoulders, the Charleston publishers had to scrupulously support the King and Parliament. Every few months we would hear more from a traveller from the coast, but some of what they said was so lurid that most of us doubted its veracity.

At first I was cheered by the stories of the successful rebellion against Louis XVI. Even the Charleston newspapers portrayed the storming of the Bastille as a heroic act. I saw it as a French version of the battles at Lexington and Concord that started the Great Rebellion. But what came next was less sanguine. The newspapers said that France had descended into anarchy ... that the mob controlled Paris and was slaughtering thousands ... that peasants were rampaging across the French countryside, burning chateaus and murdering the noble families that lived in them

Some, like Robert McDowell, claimed the stories couldn't be true ... that they must be fabrications designed to destroy support for the French revolutionaries. I disagreed. The grievances that led to the French revolution were much more severe and long-standing than the grievances that led to the Great Rebellion, but even in our colonies, men extracted vengeance when they could. The Sons of Liberty, the mob that ruled the streets of New York City whilst the rebels were in control, terrorized all. They threatened to burn my father's farm in Graves End to ensure his support for the rebellion, and I'd watched them tar and feather a man for not being vocal enough in his support of the rebels. After the end of the rebellion, when the loyalists were back in power, they took their vengeance by murdering rebels.

Unlike the colonists during the Great Rebellion, who were only concerned about taking control of the colonies in which they lived, the French revolutionaries saw their rebellion as the beginning of a universal rejection of monarchies. But they argued over tactics and soon split into factions. One faction, known as the Girondins, led by a Jacques Brissot, wanted to immediately spread the revolution beyond France's borders, whilst the Jacobins, led by Maximilien de Robespierre, wanted to first defeat the revolution's enemies within France. The London newspapers reported their arguments in surprising detail, with long quotes from the debate in the National Assembly, the revolutionaries' Parliament.

At first the Jacobins had the upper hand. They controlled the Paris National Guard, the revolutionary militia commanded by Citizen du Motier, the name adopted by the Marquis de Lafayette. Du Motier seemed to strike the right balance between supporting the revolution's goals and maintaining peace and order. My sympathies were with the Jacobins. They seemed less likely to start wars with France's neighbours.

In October, 1789, a mob of angry women stormed Versailles and threatened to kill Louis XVI and the Royal Family. Du Motier rescued them and took the King and his family to Paris. Whilst not du Motier's prisoners, their movements were restricted, both to protect them from the mob and to ensure that they remained under the control of the Jacobins.

I was surprised that it was a mob of women who threatened the Royal Family. I could think of no similar role that women had played in the Great Rebellion. They helped in caring for the sick and wounded, and some accompanied our army as cooks and laundresses. As I've already related, there were whores around the Harlem Heights encampment. These were all normal roles for women. But they disappeared as Washington's army shrank and its survival became more precarious. No women crossed into Pennsylvania with us, and none joined us in that state.

An uneasy peace prevailed until June 1791, when the Royal Family attempted to escape to the Austrian Netherlands, where they would be under the protection of the Queen's brother, Emperor Leopold. That attempt failed and they were taken back to Paris, where they were now prisoners of the National Guard. But du Motier's days as the King's gaoler were limited.

In July, the Guard, under his command, fired on an unruly crowd demanding the King be executed. Dozens were killed and du Motier, who claimed that he'd ordered the Guard to fire over the heads of the rioters, was forced to resign. He was allowed to retire to the countryside.

Leopold, and his ally, King Fredrick Wilhelm of Prussia, reacted to Louis XVI's imprisonment by threatening to go to war with France if any member of the Royal Family was harmed, and if the other nations of Europe joined them. It was a weak threat, since most of the other nations of Europe had no interest in fighting the French, but it was all that the Girondins needed. Brissot called for a new crusade for universal freedom. In April 1792, France declared war against Austria. Prussia, Austria's ally, declared war against France. Britain was able to stay out of the fray for almost a year.

The French suffered early defeats, but in September 1792, the combination of their revolutionary fervour and mistakes by the Austrians and Prussians allowed General Dumouriez to prevail at the Battle of Valmy. This amazing reversal of fortune did much to strengthen the revolutionary cause at what must've been its weakest moment. One can only imagine what might've happened had Washington had a similar victory during those dark months at the end of 1776.

With the Austrians and Prussians no longer a threat, the mood of the National Assembly turned bloody. The King was executed in January 1793, and immediately afterwards France declared war on Britain.

The Jacobins were in control and moved against those they perceived to be their enemies within France. In June, they accused Brissot and twenty-eight other Girondins, who'd called for the establishment of a constitutional monarchy liked Britain's, of being a counter-revolutionaries and agents of foreign powers. The National Guard arrested them and preparations were made for their trial, which would've been certain to find them guilty and sentence them to death.

Dumouriez, Brissot's ally, marched a division of his best troops, supported by artillery, to Paris and demanded the release of the

Girondins. The National Guard had no choice but to comply. Once free, Brissot ordered Dumouriez to arrest the leaders of the Jacobin faction in the National Assembly. They were charged with betraying the ideals of the revolution for their own personal gain and executed. The Girondins punished their enemies – real and imagined – inside France. Tens of thousands were executed, so many that the end of 1793 and first half of 1794 became known as The Terror.

The invention of the guillotine, a horrific new device that could behead a man with a single stroke, made such large numbers of executions possible. The executioner pulled up the guillotine blade with a rope before the victim was placed in position. Once the victim was in place on the block, the executioner released the rope and the blade descended under its own weight. He no longer had to use brute force to hack away at the victim's neck with a sword or axe. One can only hope that the claim that the guillotine is a painless death is true. Unfortunately, none of its victims have returned to verify it.

The Girondin wave of bloodletting left Brissot and Dumouriez in firm control of France. The National Guard was abolished and its members drafted into the army. True to his beliefs, Brissot embarked a long war to abolish monarchies across Europe. I eventually became a soldier in that war, a story I will tell in due course. The army became the strongest force in France, and Dumouriez soon eclipsed Brissot as the country's leader.

The guillotine intrigued all of us in Davidson's Fort, especially some of the young boys. They managed to construct their own version of this device from scraps of lumber, some string, and an old knife. They paraded it around the village and threatened to behead Sally Robinson's rag doll. Sally, only five, clutched the doll to her chest and ran home screaming. The adults who witnessed this cruelty were greatly amused, and several minutes passed before any of us could stop laughing long enough to chastise the boys for their misbehaviour.

CHAPTER 24

Shortly after arriving in Davidson's Fort, I wrote to my grandfather. His was the only address I had for my family. I was still a boy working for Mr McNeil in Philadelphia when I'd last written, ten years earlier. Then, his response was to order me to return to his house. I had no desire to live under his roof and didn't reply. For most of the next decade, whilst I was a prisoner in Texas or living with the Cherokee, I couldn't write. Now that I was a man and had a good position, I wanted my brother, sister, and grandparents to know that I was alive and well.

I didn't expect a reply for six months, but when a year passed with no response, I assumed that my grandfather wanted nothing to do with his wayward grandson. Then a letter from my sister, Charlotte, arrived. She was now eighteen, had recently married an apothecary, and was living in New York. She told me that both our grandparents were dead and that our brother, Richard, was a successful merchant. Over the next few years, we exchanged a series of letters. I told her about my life and she told me about hers and Richard's. I also wrote to Richard, but he never responded.

I became increasingly curious about the sister and brother I hadn't seen for so many years. The trading post was a successful business and, despite my gifts to Judy and nights at the tavern, I was able to save twenty pounds. Finally, in early 1796, I wrote to Mr Henderson asking him for permission to leave for three months that summer to visit New York. He agreed and said he would send one of his clerks to run the trading post in my absence. I could depart in early June. I bought a horse for the trip, and my neighbours gathered at the trading post to wish me well on my journey.

"Bring me something nice from New York," Judy Slater whispered to me, as she left the shop.

"I will," I whispered back.

I rode east towards Salisbury, then north on the Great Wagon Road to Philadelphia. The journey took three weeks. The road was somewhat improved from what it'd been in 1778, when Donald Mackenzie and I travelled down it in an oxcart full of ironmongery, but there were still enough pot holes and muddy spots to make it a difficult journey. When I got to Philadelphia, I looked for Mr McNeil at the shop at 34 Market Street, but he was long gone. Mr DuPre, the silversmith whose daughter Sarah had so enchanted me all those years ago, told me that he'd moved away six years earlier and was living with his son in Germantown. Visiting him would have been only a short detour, but I was anxious to see Charlotte, so I headed directly to New York via the Post Road.

I hadn't been in a city since 1778 and wasn't prepared for the crowds, noise, smoke, and stink I encountered in both Philadelphia and New York. The Quakers, still Philadelphia's most prominent group, were a calming influence there. But nothing calmed New York. Everything seemed to move at double time. It was exciting, but exhausting. I wondered how people survived.

New York was much changed from the city I'd known as a boy. Many streets had been widened and straightened when the city was rebuilt after the fire that destroyed half of it during the Great Rebellion. It was also a bigger city now, extending more than three miles north from The Battery.

Charlotte and her husband, Phillip Abelson, lived in a pleasant two-story clapboard house in a new section at the north end of town. Phillip's shop took up much of the ground floor, and they lived in rooms on the first floor. They had two surviving children, seven-year-old David and five-year-old Jacoba, who'd been named after our parents. In her letters Charlotte told me that two boys had died as infants, but that she hoped to be able to have more sons for Phillip.

"I'm William, your brother-in-law," I announced as I entered. I recognized Phillip from Charlotte's description. He was about my height, had light brown hair, and wore a trim beard.

"I'm so happy to meet you," Phillip said. "I've read the letters you sent Charlotte. Welcome to our home." He came from behind the counter, his arms extended as if to embrace me. Men in the mountains didn't embrace each other and I must have looked uncomfortable at his approach because he stopped short and offered me his hand to shake.

"My pleasure," I replied. "Is Charlotte here?"

"Yes, let me get her. She's talked of nothing but your arrival for the past week," he said, almost bounding up the stairs at the side of the shop.

"Charlotte, your brother's here," I heard him say. A squeal of delight followed, and a few seconds later Charlotte appeared. I didn't recognize her. She'd been a blond, round-faced, six year-old girl when I'd last seen her. Now, twenty years later, she was a fully-grown woman. She favoured our mother with fair skin, blue eyes, and light brown hair, but it took me a while to appreciate the resemblance. She must not have recognized me either because she paused for a few seconds at the top of the stairs to look at me before descending.

"William, at long last," she said as she hugged me. I stood rigidly and didn't return the embrace. Having a sister again was all too new and I didn't know how to react.

"You must be tired from your journey," Charlotte said, releasing her grip. "Come upstairs and I'll show you where to put your belongings. You can wash at the rain barrel."

I saw Richard and his wife Amanda on my second evening in New York. He'd invited Charlotte, Phillip, and me to dinner – the meal was too grand to be called a supper. Charlotte had told me, first in her letters, then in person, that Richard was a wealthy man, both as a result of his business ventures and because he had married well, but I wasn't prepared for the ostentatious display that greeted us. He lived in a townhouse in an expensive neighbourhood in the centre of the city. When we arrived a Negro butler in fine livery opened the door and ushered us into a marble-floored entrance way. I never found out whether he was a slave or a servant. Richard appeared a few seconds later.

I had less trouble recognizing him than Charlotte, but I was shocked at what I saw. He was dressed in a finely tailored coat of plum-coloured worsted. Compared to his attire, Charlotte, Phillip, and I looked shabby. He had a huge belly, a double chin, and a florid complexion that made him look like he had a fever.

"So good of you to come to my humble abode," he said. "Amanda will join us in a moment." He'd affected the accent of the British nobility, which I suppose went with the rest of the life he'd created, but it annoyed me. Charlotte thanked him for inviting us. I was mute.

Seeing my discomfort, Richard continued, "You should have come with me to Queens County twenty years ago, instead of running off with the rebel army. I daresay you might be living like this instead of in a log cabin in the wilderness."

Amanda's arrival saved me from having to reply to what I took as an insult from Richard. A short, slim, attractive woman, she had reddish-brown hair, which was piled up at least a foot above her head and held in place by several jewelled pins. She was dressed in what I took to be the latest fashion, a green velvet dress with a full skirt and a lace frill around the neck, and was the perfect addition to the elegant setting.

"Amanda, my dear," Richard said. "This is my brother, William, somewhat the prodigal of the family. But now that he's returned, perhaps we can mend his ways." Amanda was much more gracious.

"I'm so glad to be able to meet you at last," she said. "Richard and Charlotte have told me so much about your adventures."

Richard's description of me as a prodigal smarted, but I answered Amanda politely. "Your servant, ma'am. I'm pleased to be here and to meet you."

At this point the butler reappeared and announced that dinner was served. We entered the dining room and sat at a table set with gleaming silver and crystal, fine china, and white linen. We had oysters, a white fish I couldn't identify, roast lamb, and trifle. I'd never experienced anything like it before and was unsure of which piece of cutlery to use. I followed Amanda's lead and hoped that I wasn't too gauche.

Richard dominated the conversation, telling us about his exploits and dropping names and titles so fast I couldn't keep track of them. It was Lord This and the Duke of That. Finally, over coffee, Amanda interrupted.

"Richard, don't you think we should hear something of William's life?"

"Yes, by all means. Tell us about your life, William."

It was as insincere an invitation as I'd ever heard, but I took it anyway. I spent a few minutes talking about Washington's defeat, being a prisoner of the Spanish in Texas, living with the Cherokee, and describing Davidson's Fort. I didn't mention the two sons that I'd fathered. One does not speak of children born out of wedlock in polite company or of fathering an Indian child in any company. Amanda asked a few questions that kept the conversation going for a short while longer, but when no one followed her lead, it faltered. Richard must have gotten tired of harassing me because his next line of attack was on Phillip.

"I read the other day that most of the medicines that you apothecaries sell are useless. Is that true?"

"Not all of our medicines work as well as I would hope, but they're the best we have," Phillip answered calmly. He obviously knew Richard well enough not to lose his temper. Richard continued along this line for a few minutes, then, mercifully, the evening was over.

"What does Graves End look like these days?" I asked Charlotte over supper a week later.

"I don't know. Phillip took me there shortly after we were married, but I haven't been back since. Our house and farm hadn't changed much, but the farm seemed much closer to the village than I remembered. I didn't recognize much in the village. Not surprising. I was only six when we left. A family named Burdock was living on our farm when I visited."

Charlotte's answer sharpened my curiosity and I decided to visit my boyhood home. I wanted to know how it had changed. Two days later I saddled my horse and headed for the ferry across the East River. Brooklyn, on the Kings County side of the river, had grown rapidly in the twenty years since I last saw it, and was now more of a town than village. Walking my horse off the ferry brought back a flood of memories . . . the chaos that reigned that day when my family tried to cross the river to escape the British Army . . . Richard and I arguing about whether to go to Queens County or return to our father who'd joined the rebel army just a few hours earlier . . .

Richard's leaving and my re-joining my father. It may have been the most eventful day of my life.

Even though it wasn't the quickest way to Graves End, I decided to retrace the route my family had taken after we'd abandoned our farm. I rode along the Port Road to the remnants of the rebel fortifications. The earthen wall the rebels had built for protection still stood, though rain and snow had turned it into a knee-high mound. The ditch in front of the wall was now a low depression, and there was no sign of the abatis that had been the first line of defence. The area in front of the fortifications the rebels had cleared to give them an open field of fire was now overgrown with bushes and young trees, but was still clearly different from the untouched forest beyond.

I spent only a few minutes looking at the fortifications. The memories of what happened to me there were too painful . . . my father joining the rebel army . . . his introducing me to his messmates . . . my marching away with the rebel army … then returning alone from the fight at the Old Stone House. I found myself shaking as I heard in my mind Major Gist saying, "William, your father was a very brave man. He was killed in our third attack."

I continued along the Port Road, through the forest that still covered the Heights of Guana, to the village of Flatbush. The forest looked as foreboding as ever, and I remembered the night we spent hiding from the British Army and how fearful I'd been.

As a boy I rarely visited Flatbush, so riding through it didn't bring back any memories. From the village it was an easy ride to our farm. When I got there, I introduced myself to Mrs Burdock, a short, pleasantly chubby, grey-haired woman of perhaps fifty, who was standing in the doorway when I rode up.

"My sister and her husband visited here about eight years ago," I said once introductions were complete.

"I remember them," she replied after a moment's hesitation. "Charlotte and Phillip, wasn't it?"

"Yes, that's right."

"Why don't you come in and have a cup of tea?"

"Thank you. Tea would be most welcome." I sat at the table in the centre of the kitchen. Some things hadn't changed. The dry sink was still against the far wall, and a ladder still led to the loft where my brother, sister, and I used to sleep. But the room seemed wrong. My mother's three Delftware plates no longer hung on the walls. They'd been replaced with framed silhouettes of what I took to be the Bur-docks' children. The table was maple, not oak, and my father's musket no longer rested on pegs over the fireplace.

"How long have you been living here?"

"Fifteen years. The place was derelict when we took it over."

"I can believe that. We left when the British Army came in 1776, so it would have been empty for five years. Does Lord Simpson still own this land?"

"I think so. We only see an agent. There seems to be a new one every year."

"That hasn't changed."

Mr Burdock came in from the fields and joined us. He was taller than his wife, with a broad bald strip down the centre of his scalp. He looked to be a powerful man with the strong shoulders and legs of a farmer.

"I hope you don't expect me to return the tools and muskets I found buried in the garden," he said, eying me warily.

"Of course not. We abandoned them. They're yours." I didn't tell him about the pewter and Delftware we'd thrown into the outhouse pit. I didn't have any intention of trying to recover them, but talking about things that had been buried in excrement for twenty years didn't seem like the best topic for a friendly conversation.

"Let me show you around the place."

The farm looked more familiar than the house. The only change was a new barn, but it was the same size and shape as ours had been.

"I had to replace the old one," he said when he saw me studying the structure. "It was destroyed by a windstorm five years ago. I built the new barn on the old foundation. Whoever built the old one did a good job."

"My father built it." I was gratified to hear his work praised so many years after his death.

After spending a pleasant hour with the Burdocks, I rode to Graves End. Charlotte was right. The farm did seem much closer to the village than I'd remembered, but that might have been because I was riding, not walking.

I arrived at noon and tied my horse to the rail in front of what used to be Fletcher's Tavern, but was now called The Kings Arms. I entered and was surprised to see Mr Fletcher, looking greyer and fatter, behind the bar. I decided not to identify myself.

"A pint of ale please," I said, climbing onto a bar stool.

Mr Fletcher looked at me quizzically as he drew the ale from a barrel.

"You look familiar. Have you been in my tavern before?" he asked.

"Yes, but not for twenty years," I said, trying hard to suppress a laugh. "I'm William Watson. My father David used to rent the farm the Burdocks now have."

"And how is your father?" Mr Fletcher asked, a look of recognition crossing his face.

"He was killed in the Battle of Brooklyn."

"May God rest his soul. And your mother?"

"She died of smallpox two weeks later."

"I'm sorry to hear that. She was a good woman."

"Yes, she was. But that was all a long time ago."

Mr Fletcher spent the next hour telling me what had happened in Graves End over the past twenty years. The Graves End Academy, where I had gone to school, no longer existed. It had closed when the British Army invaded and stayed closed through the remainder of the Great Rebellion. My teacher, Mr Anderson, was left without an income and moved away. Mr Fletcher didn't know what'd happened to him. Without a teacher, the school never reopened. Children from the village attended class in New Utrecht, two miles to the north.

Bert Van Wyk, my boyhood friend, was married and renting a farm near Charlottesville, Virginia. Mr Worthington was still the pastor at St. Luke's Church. I could've visited him, but decided against it. We would have only one topic to talk about – what had happened to the members of my family. I knew that Mr Fletcher would provide him with all of that news. When I was a boy, Fletcher had been the best source of gossip in the village. That clearly hadn't changed.

I felt sad as I rode away from Graves End. I'd always considered Graves End my home, but now so little of what'd made it my home remained. My house had changed, my school no longer existed, and my friend was gone.

Over supper that night, I told Charlotte and Phillip about my trip and started to talk about my father. The day had been filled with so many reminders of him that I felt bad about how few times I'd thought about him over the years. Charlotte listened politely. She told me she remembered curling up in his lap after supper, but other than that, she had few memories of him. We agreed that he'd been a good father and a good man, then had nothing more to say. That troubled me. I felt that I'd never honoured Father in the way I should've. But twenty years after his death, and not knowing where he was buried, what could I do? The foundation under Burdock's barn was destined to be his most permanent memorial.

Charlotte and Phillip's easy domesticity made me question the way I was living. I wanted a place I could call home, something more than a small room behind a trading post. Two weeks after visiting Graves End, I decided to ask Judy to marry me. She couldn't bear children, but perhaps we could adopt some and I could finally have the family I'd first dreamed about all those years earlier with Jenny. We could live in Judy's cabin, and whilst I couldn't be both a shopkeeper and a farmer, I'd be able to do enough on the farm for Judy to continue raising chickens and vegetables as she had for the past five years. The more I thought about it, the more I liked the idea.

For two guineas I bought a silver bracelet with garnets and amethysts as an engagement gift for Judy. Once I had it, I was anxious to get back. I left New York ten days earlier than I'd planned. I didn't tell Charlotte about my plans to ask Judy to marry me. I said that the city exhausted me and I wanted to return to the calmer way of life I was used to. She complained mildly that we had spent so little time together, but her protest seemed more for form than substance. We'd led very different lives and, after learning about each other, had little to talk about.

I was the centre of attention for a few days after I got back to Davidson's Fort. Everyone wanted to know what Philadelphia and New York were like. They peppered me with questions about how people dressed, what they ate, whether it was safe to walk the streets, and on and on. My painful experience at Richard's house turned out to be the most interesting story I had to tell. Most of my neighbours couldn't picture the finery I described and walked away shaking their heads.

"Did you bring me anything from New York?" Judy asked when we were finally alone after everyone else had left the shop on the day of my return.

"Yes, but it's a surprise."

"Bring it when you come to supper tomorrow night."

Judy greeted me warmly when I arrived the next night. Supper was maize and roast pork, and she'd set out what remained of a bottle of apple brandy I'd given her before leaving for New York.

"Tell me again about dinner at your brother's house," she said, after we'd started eating.

I told her the story again, starting with the Negro butler opening the door. She listened with the same hungry look I'd seen on children's faces when they stared at the maple syrup sweets in my shop after their parents had told them they couldn't have any.

"I'd like to live that way, instead of in a cabin with a dirt floor, eating from wooden trenchers," she said when I finished the story.

"Most people in New York don't live the way Richard and Amanda do."

"I know, but even to be in New York and see that finery would be better than being in Davidson's Fort."

I reached into my pocket and brought out the bracelet.

"Judy, will you marry me?" I asked, handing her the bracelet. I guess I should've gotten down on one knee and given a long, flowery speech, the way suitors in books do, but just asking was difficult enough. I'd never before asked a woman to marry me. Jenny had decided that we were betrothed when I started working for her father, and Ahawee, Awinita's mother, had told me that it was time to marry her daughter after they were certain that I'd gotten her with child.

Judy turned the bracelet over and over in her hand, watching the candlelight play off the gems.

"Why would you want to marry me?" she finally asked.

"Because I'm tired of living alone and I think you'll make a good wife," I said. I couldn't tell her I loved her. Such an obvious lie would stick in my throat.

"You know I can't give you children."

"It's not important." It was not the time to talk about adoption.

"I need to think about this. Come back tomorrow night."

For the first time, I left her cabin without having shared her bed, not the response I'd hoped for.

The next day was one of the longest in my life. I thought about what Judy's answer might be. I slowly realized that she'd been in control of our relationship. She'd invited me to supper and to share her bed when she wanted to. She usually told me what gift she wanted in exchange for her favours. If we married that would change. Even if Edward's beating and belittlement hadn't soured her on men and marriage, would she be willing to give up her freedom? The longer I thought about it, the unhappier I became about my prospects.

When the sun finally set, I made my way to Judy's cabin. She was waiting for me with a supper of pork stew on the table. Her voice and manner seemed no different from any of the hundred or more times I'd eaten a meal with her.

"If I marry you, I want us to live in New York," she said, after we'd finished eating.

"I can't do that. I can't quit my job."

"I'm tired of living on this farm and I won't marry you if it means spending the rest of my life in Davidson's Fort . . . seeing the same people all the time . . . people I'm beholden to for ploughing my fields, chopping my firewood, and giving me work these past six years."

I'd seen Judy in many moods – lusty, angry, thoughtful, amused – but until that moment, I'd never seen her anguished. She took a deep breath before continuing. "If I don't marry you, there's only one thing I can do . . . live with my cousin and her husband. They have a farm in the Shenandoah Valley, near Fredrick Town. I'd be a widow living on their charity. God as my witness, I don't want to do that."

"I've seen New York, and I couldn't live there with the stink, the noise, the rushing around," I replied. Much as I thought I wanted to marry Judy, moving to New York was too high a price to pay.

We were quiet for a long while after that. "What will you do?" I finally asked.

"I don't know, but I've got to do something," she replied.

Since I wasn't the route to her dream of living in New York, Judy said good night and showed me to the door. She kept the bracelet I'd bought for her, but I never saw her wear it. If she had, she would've set a host of tongues wagging. I saw her regularly in the village after that night, but we were always politely formal with each other, as if all our nights in bed had never happened.

I sold the horse that I had bought for my trip and fell back into the routine of shopkeeping and caring for myself that had been my life before I decided to ask Judy to marry me. I tried not to think about what married life with her would have been like, but for the next few months, the thoughts came unbidden. Some of my neighbours noticed my sadness and asked if I was ill. I told them that I must've picked up some minor ailment on my trip to New York, but I was sure that I'd soon recover. By the New Year's Day, Judy's rejection had become just another dull ache, like my losses of Awinita and Jenny. In March she left Davidson's Fort to live with her cousin.

Two months after Judy rejected my marriage proposal, Gertrude Sachs, one of the two other young widows in the village, approached me on the street. Gertrude was a big, buxom German woman with copper-coloured hair that she curled into ringlets. She had two small daughters, aged three and five. Her husband, Hans, had been a carpenter and built a house for the family at the edge of the village. He'd died a year earlier of blood poisoning after he'd cut his hand.

"You must be hungry for a home-cooked meal," she said, "now that Judy Slater isn't inviting you to supper anymore."

I was mortified. I'd long assumed that other people in the village were aware of my arrangement with Judy. But nobody had ever said anything about it to me, and I hadn't talked about it with anyone. I knew the same was true with Judy. She'd taken great care to keep our meetings discreet, if not actually secret. Now here was Widow Sachs discussing our arrangement quite brazenly.

"Oh, I do fine cooking for myself," I managed to reply.

"I'd be happy to cook for you and provide the company Judy did if you brought me something nice," she said, her voice dropping down to a whisper.

It was one thing to sneak into Judy's cabin, a mile from the village, knowing that she'd be alone. It was quite another thing to sneak into Gertrude's house, so close to the village, knowing that two small girls were also there.

"I think I'll stick to my own cooking for a while."

"Tell me if you change your mind." With that she walked off. I couldn't see her face, but I sensed that she was smiling.

Whilst I was no longer happy with my solitary life, I didn't do anything to change it. I could've courted Agnes Whipple, the other widow in town, or one of the marriageable young girls, but after so many years, I didn't know how to begin. It was easier to stay as I was.

I spent more time at the tavern than I had previously, and I got drunk several times, but the headache and queasy stomach that these incidents caused were enough to convince me not to drink more than I could hold. I played French Ruff more often. There wasn't a regular game at the tavern, but there were usually three other men interested in playing. I didn't have the same partner every night, but teamed up with whoever was available. I became proficient at the game and won more times than I lost, but I usually spent my winnings and more buying pints of ale or glasses of whiskey or apple brandy for the other players. None of this eased the loneliness I felt. I sometimes berated myself for not accepting Judy's terms. Mostly, I suffered in silence, accepting my solitary condition as punishment for going off with Terrill rather than staying in Salisbury and marrying Jenny.

I was no longer living frugally. I'd spent my savings on my trip to New York, and now I was spending what I earned on my nights at the tavern. A year after Judy rejected my marriage proposal I had less than a pound in savings.

Now that I was thirty-five, the flame of lust burned a little less intensely than it had earlier in my life. When it became more than I wanted to bear, I visited Betty, a Cherokee woman who lived in a cabin halfway between Davidson's Fort and the Proclamation Line. For two shillings she was quite happy to satisfy me. Whilst I'd paid Judy as surely as I paid Betty, the fact that I'd not given her cash and that we had supper and conversation, allowed me to think that it was something different. There was no such pretence with Betty, and after a few years, I became so ashamed about what I was doing that I stopped visiting her.

CHAPTER 25

About the time Judy Slater rejected my marriage proposal, a Frenchman named Jean-Baptiste Bouchard began travelling around the frontier settlements of North Carolina. He was a little taller than me, chunky, with almost no neck. His thick lips and swarthy complexion were enough to start rumours that he had Negro blood. Bouchard claimed to be an *émigré* who'd fled France to escape the vengeance of the revolutionaries. Many Frenchmen in North America told similar stories.

Bouchard said he'd been a timber merchant in France and that he hoped to establish a similar business in North Carolina. On his first visit to Davidson's Fort, he came into my shop, introduced himself, and asked if I knew of any timber for sale. Bouchard told a plausible story and he established his *bona fides* by buying and selling a few lots of timber. England and France had been at war since 1793, which made him an enemy alien, but having established his émigré credentials, he could travel freely.

Bouchard was actually an agent of the French revolutionaries sent to stir up another rebellion amongst us Americans, as we'd begun to be called. He quickly gathered a handful of followers who'd never accepted the failure of the Great Rebellion, but they were too few to be a source of annoyance to the British Army. To recruit more supporters, he held secret meetings where, in good revolutionary fashion, he styled himself *Citoyen* Bouchard and preached *liberté, égalité, et fraternité,* the credo of the French Revolution. I attended one of his meetings, which was held in Robert McDowell's barn, five miles east of Davidson's Fort.

Bouchard stopped me at the door. "Ah, William, *mon ami,* I'm so glad you've come. But before I allow you to enter you must swear that you will not speak of what you hear to anyone who is not here tonight."

"I'll keep your secrets," I replied.

"If you break your oath, my colleagues will break your legs," he said, glancing over at two burly young toughs, who smiled as if to say that they'd be happy to inflict the punishment.

There were about thirty men in the barn, most of whom I recognized as neighbours. Bouchard climbed onto the back of a wagon and began speaking. "In 1775, Americans – which is the proper name for you, the people of the British colonies in North America – rose up against the tyranny of King George III. Some of you took part in that rebellion. You failed, not because you lacked courage, but because at Trenton a Hessian spy betrayed you, and because you had no assistance in your fight.

"Eight years ago the people of France rose up against the tyranny of Louis XVI. We succeeded. In the spirit of fraternité, we offer support to all who seek liberté and égalité and refuse to accept the tyranny of kings. If you rebel again against King George III, you will not be alone. France will be with you."

The audience applauded when Bouchard finished and there were even a few calls of "hear, hear." Many of the men seemed willing to follow him, but I knew better. I'd been with Washington and his rebels when they'd been chased out of New York and across New Jersey. Trenton was Washington's last, desperate throw of the dice. Even if the spy Knobel hadn't alerted the Hessians and Washington had been able to surprise them, I doubt his attack would've succeeded. The Hessians were too disciplined. They would have rallied and almost certainly defeated the rebels. And had Washington managed to achieve a victory, it would've only delayed the inevitable. Untrained volunteers couldn't hope to prevail against the finest army in the world.

I was also sceptical of Bouchard's promise of French aid. How could France help a rebellion in North Carolina? The Charleston newspapers I read each month said that the nearest French soldiers were in their colony of Saint-Domingue, over a thousand miles away, and that they were unable to put down the slave rebellion that had been raging for more than five years. The rest of the French Army was fighting in Europe. Joining Bouchard would've added some excitement to my dreary life, but that was not enough to entice me.

Others were willing to believe Bouchard. He recruited several dozen adherents, who followed him until 1798, when the Irish rebelled. True to what Bouchard had told us, the French landed a thousand soldiers in the south of Ireland to support the Irish rebellion. The British Army soon captured those soldiers. The Royal Navy chased off a second, larger French force before it could land. The Irish were forced to surrender and were punished much more severely than the American rebels had been. Hundreds were hanged and thousands more transported to work on the sugar plantations in the Caribbean, which was as good as a death sentence. Few survived there for even a year. This lesson was not lost on Bouchard's supporters, most of whom quickly changed their minds.

Davidson's Fort now was home to nearly two hundred people, almost double the number who'd lived there when I'd arrived ten years earlier. Henderson's Trading Post was no longer the only shop. The village now had a bakery, a butchery, a cooper, and a combination saddle and cobbler's shop. The surrounding area had also grown, and was now home to about five hundred people, more than double the number in 1787.

Land prices had gone up as all of the good farmland was taken. Some farmers couldn't afford to buy and had to rent land, which was a source of grievance since there was good land to be had across the Proclamation Line. In 1800, one landless family, the Webbs, crossed the Proclamation Line and tried to establish a farm in Tennessee, near French Lick on the Cumberland River. They picked a spot far from the nearest British Army post or Cherokee village. James Webb and his three teenage sons were able to clear about ten acres, plant a crop, and start in a cabin before the army sent a cavalry squad to burn them out. They returned to Davidson's Fort defeated, swearing eternal hatred for the British Army. Their fate was a lesson to any who considered testing the army's will to enforce the ban on settlement west of the mountains.

Many Irish came to the American colonies after their failed rebellion, and a few settled near Davidson's Fort. Their hearts burned with hatred for the British. Landless farmers, like James Webb, were another group that had reason to hate British rule. And there are always a few young men willing to join any cause that promise them a good fight. Bouchard persisted and soon built a new following from amongst these groups. He even enticed some of his former supporters to re-join his clandestine group.

France had given its Louisiana colony, the vast watershed of the Mississippi River valley, and Nouvelle Orleans, its port, to Spain in 1762 for safekeeping as it was about to lose a seven-year-long war with England. That strategy was only partially successful. England took the eastern half of Louisiana as spoils of war, but left Spain with Nouvelle Orleans and the western half. The Spanish kept the name Louisiana, but renamed the city Nuevo Orleans. In 1800, a stronger France took back the part of Louisiana that had remained in Spanish hands. The Spanish were too weak to protest. If France could land an army in Louisiana, she would threaten Britain's North American colonies.

In April 1801, Bouchard came to the trading post and busied himself looking at the leather goods on display until we were alone. "William, mon ami," he said in a low, conspiratorial voice, "the time has come for you to join the fight for liberté. You know that Louisiana is once again French."

"Yes, I heard that," I replied.

"Did you also hear that the Revolutionary Council will soon send an army to Nouvelle Orleans?"

"No."

"It's true, but I trust you will keep the information confidential," Bouchard continued as if he had just revealed a great state secret.

"And if I don't, your young friends will break both my legs," I said in what I hoped was a jocular tone of voice. I hadn't forgotten his earlier threat.

Bouchard was taken aback. "Of course it would never come to that. You are an honourable man."

The conversation was silly. We both knew that the Royal Navy blockade of French ports would keep them from moving an army across the Atlantic, but Bouchard continued as if he were planning grand strategy.

"I'm recruiting a militia that will lead the rebellion against the British, once the French Army is close enough to help in the fight. You should join us. You could be an officer and have high rank once the rebellion is a success."

"Citoyen Bouchard, I've been in one rebellion and that was enough."

"There's a little time, mon ami, for you to change your mind, but don't wait too long. Those who do not join us will be our enemies." With that threat hanging in the air, he left.

England signed a peace treaty with France in March 1802, but Bouchard continued fomenting rebellion. When I asked him why, he shrugged and said that peace would not last. He was correct. War between England and France resumed in May 1803, but it was far away and I thought it would have no consequence on my life.

Bouchard approached me several more times, each time making the same threat, and each time I rebuffed him. I didn't think his rebellion would ever come to pass. But I started worrying after a conversation with Robert McDowell, who was one of Bouchard's most loyal adherents.

McDowell had no difficulty finding me. My habits were well-known. In the summer I closed the trading post at six o'clock and, if the weather was pleasant, spent an hour or so strolling around the village green. I enjoyed being outdoors after working in the shop all day. One evening in early June 1804, he joined me on my promenade.

"This is your last chance to join the fight for liberty," he told me as we walked along. "We've got a hundred men ready to rise up and attack the British. We've even got a six-pounder to smash the fort's walls."

I was surprised by his announcement and it took me a few moments to respond. "You must know how foolish that would be.

Attack the British Army and you're a dead man. They'll hunt you down even if it takes ten years."

"The French will help us. It won't be like 1776 when we fought alone. This time we can be free," McDowell said, as solemnly as if he were intoning words from the Gospel. His certainty amazed me.

"If you've got a hundred men, you don't need me."

"Men in the village respect you. If you join us, dozens more will."

I couldn't help but be flattered by this claim, but it didn't change my mind. I made one more attempt to make him see reality.

"You actually believe Bouchard's promises? The French couldn't even defeat the slaves in Saint-Domingue. The slaves won and have declared the Republic of Haiti."

"The niggers didn't defeat the French Army, the fever did. You know a white man can't live in that climate. The French won't have that problem here."

McDowell took my arm and stopped our stroll. "William, I have to warn you that some of the men in the militia don't hold you in as high regard as I do. They think you've oppressed them by denying them credit, whilst extending it to others. When we defeat the British, they might act like the French revolutionaries who took vengeance on those who'd oppressed them. Bouchard and I might not be able to control them."

Mr Henderson had told me not to extend credit to any of my customers. I broke his rule occasionally when I judged a family to be in need through no fault of their own. But I denied many requests for credit from those I judged to be lazy or not truly in need. I was sure that'd made me some enemies along the way, so I had to take McDowell's threat more seriously than I had taken Bouchard's.

I promised McDowell I would think about joining Bouchard's militia, but it didn't take me long to reject the idea. I had more difficulty deciding whether to tell Lieutenant Carter, who commanded the troops at the fort, about the conspiracy. I wasn't sure who was in Bouchard's militia, but many of them had to be my neighbours. I didn't want to see them punished. Their families would suffer. And I was afraid that if I went to the lieutenant and the British Army rounded up Bouchard's militia, some might escape and take vengeance on me. But if there was a rebellion, and Bouchard's men attacked the fort, the village would be caught up in the battle and probably destroyed. I could prevent that from happening by warning the army.

Despite all that McDowell had told me, I couldn't bring myself to believe that there would be another rebellion. In the end I did nothing. Events proved that to be a good choice. The French army that Bouchard had promised never landed in Nouvelle Orleans. News of the revolutionaries' continual triumphs in Europe convinced more men to join Bouchard's secret militia. Some of them showed their support for the French by growing moustaches and goatees, in the style favoured by revolutionary officers.

Dumouriez had been President of the Revolutionary Council since 1800. In September 1804, word arrived that, four months earlier, a referendum had given him that title for life. He was now King of France in all but name.

McDowell came into the shop during the late afternoon the day after I posted the Charleston papers with this news. Since it was after the harvest, a half dozen other men were sitting around relaxing and gossiping.

"Have you seen the latest news, Robert?" David Vance began.

"No, is there something important?"

"You may think so. Dumouriez's had himself elected president for life."

"What's wrong with that? If the French want to choose him to be their president, it's their right. We don't have any choice about who our King will be."

"Strange vote, though," Vance mused. "The papers say that three and a half million votes were for making him President for Life and only two thousand five hundred votes against. More than a thousand to one in favour. Think you could get a thousand to one vote in favour of anything?"

McDowell was silent for what seemed like a very long time, even though everyone in the shop was waiting for his reply. "I'll have to think about this," he finally said, then hurriedly left the shop.

"I guess he'll have to ask Bouchard what to think," Vance said after McDowell was gone. There was a round of laughter before the conversation moved on to other topics.

Over the next few months support for Bouchard's rebellion vanished. Stories of revolutionaries' brutality in killing those they considered their enemies, and their plundering Flanders and the other lands they'd conquered, which had been ignored earlier, were now resurrected and taken more seriously. A wave of revulsion for everything French swept through the colonies. Those of Bouchard's followers who had grown French-style moustaches and goatees shaved them off.

I thought Bouchard had managed to keep his plot secret, but the British Army had long known of his activities. Spies – I never found out who they were – kept close watch and identified most of the men who supported him. In March 1805, the British Army arrested him and more than a hundred of his followers and charged them with fomenting rebellion. They were tried by a military tribunal. Bouchard was hanged in July. Robert McDowell and four other men who had been most active in supporting him were sent to prison. The rest of the militiamen were given the opportunity to sign an oath of allegiance to King George III. Once they signed, they were let go with no more than a stern lecture from Colonel Ambrose, the senior officer on the tribunal. At first a few of the Irishmen who had supported Bouchard refused to sign. Colonel Ambrose told them that if they didn't sign, they would be transported to the sugar plantations. That changed their minds.

Bouchard had not been alone. The French had agents in every colony. They, too, were arrested and hanged, but most of their supporters were let go without punishment. Whilst it was true that the followers of Bouchard and the other French agents never took up arms against the King, there could be no doubt about their intentions. The army could have hanged every one of them.

I sometimes wonder why the army treated Bouchard's followers so mildly. The best guess I can make is that faced with an implacable enemy like the French, they didn't want to anger us Americans. Had the army hanged all of the men they could have, they would have planted the seeds for another rebellion, as they had done so many times in Ireland. Americans responded to this gentle behaviour with a surge of patriotism. King George III was held in higher regard than at any time since before the Great Rebellion.

France's threat to invade England led a few Americans to try to join the British Army. At first the army rejected these volunteers. The army would not allow Americans to serve in the colonies, fearing that they might rebel, and it wasn't interested in shipping a small number of volunteers across the Atlantic to fight in Europe. But in Spring 1805, as the numbers of volunteers grew, the army formed a regiment of riflemen they called The King's Own Virginians. Membership in the Virginians, as the regiment quickly became known, was open to any man who had not taken part in the attempted French rebellion.

The army said that the mission of the Virginians was to protect the southern colonies from the French in Louisiana. Being on garrison duty, defending the colonies against a possible, but unlikely, French attack didn't sound appealing. At first only a few of the men who had wanted to fight the French joined. But shortly after the regiment was formed, rumours started circulating that the Virginians' real mission was to take Louisiana from the French. That was a much more exciting prospect and brought many more to the colours.

One day in March 1804, a young Cherokee man entered the trading post and began examining the ironmongery. I had few Indian customers. Most Cherokee preferred to stay on their own land, but every few months one would enter the shop. The young man took small tools off the shelf and turned them over in his hands as if testing their weight. After hefting each tool a few times, he returned it to the shelf. He didn't seem interested in the goods and kept looking at me. But when I looked back, he quickly averted his eyes.

"Hello, may I be of service?" I asked after we'd assessed each other for a few minutes.

"They say you are my father," he said in an impassive voice, the way Cherokee speak when they have something important to say.

I was shocked. My eyes seemed to lose their focus and for a moment I couldn't see the young man in front of me. I thought constantly about Awinita, my beautiful Cherokee wife who God had taken from me, but I rarely remembered the son she had died giving birth to. I'd seen him only once when he was two days old, before he'd even been given a name.

I quickly recovered my senses, but I didn't know what to say. I had no reason to doubt what this young man had said – he seemed to be the right age. Part of me wanted to open my arms and embrace him, whilst another part wanted to reject him and the memory of the pain his birth had caused me. That part of me needed some proof that he was my son.

"Who says that I'm your father?"

"My grandmother, Ahawee, and Mr Warren, the minister." He stood upright, his hands at his side, as Cherokee men do when they speak formally.

When I heard the name Ahawee, I knew that he was my son. I didn't recognize the name of the minister – that was of no consequence.

"What does your mother say?" I asked. I knew that she was dead, but needed some more time to think about how I could explain my abandoning him.

"She cannot say anything. She died when I was born."

"What is your name?"

"My grandmother calls me Onacona, but Mr Warren calls me Elias."

"Which do you prefer?"

"Onacona."

"Yes, Onacona, I am your father. Come closer that I may get a better look at you."

He approached me cautiously, perhaps not knowing what to expect. Studying him more closely, I saw he had a mixture of English and Cherokee features. He was slim and a little taller than me, with hair as straight as a Cherokee's but not as black. At first glance his eyes looked Cherokee's, but when I looked closer, I saw that they were brown, not black. There seemed to be some of me in his face.

I knew that I was making Onacona uncomfortable by staring at him, but I was trying to glean whatever information I could out of his face. He took a step backward and looked down at the floor. My mind was racing. What could I tell my son? How could I explain my absence to him?

"Two years before you were born," I started, "a man named Terrill and I were travelling through Cherokee land on our way to North Carolina." Onacona raised his eyes but was careful not to look directly at me. I knew he was listening carefully.

"We became ill after eating some deer meat without asking the deer spirit's permission." That was the way Ahawee had explained my illness, and even if I didn't believe what she had told me, Onacona would.

"Your great-uncle Usti-waya and three other Cherokee warriors found us. Terrill was dead and I was only barely alive. The other warriors wanted to leave me to die, but Usti-waya told them to bring me to Tuskeegee. He saved my life. When we got to Tuskeegee, your grandmother nursed me back to health. I fell in love with your mother. She was the most beautiful woman I'd ever seen, and the day I found out that she would have you, our child, was the happiest day in my life." I looked at Onacona, hoping to see some reaction, but there was none. He face showed no sign of what he was thinking. He was Cherokee – I could expect no more.

"You already know she died giving birth to you. I was heartbroken." I could have said more, but I thought I would only embarrass him. "Ugidatli, your mother's friend, nursed you, and your grandmother said she would raise you. She told me that when a man's wife dies, he should return to his own people. It was the only thing I could do." There was a long pause. I tried not to stare at Onacona, but I know I did, still trying to figure out what he was thinking.

"Grandmother told me the same story," he said at last. "She said that you were a good man even if you weren't Cherokee. I had to see for myself what you looked like." Then he turned and started to walk out of the shop.

"Wait," I called. "Aren't you going to tell me anything about yourself?"

"No, you are my father, but I am not your son. You gave me to Grandmother when I was only three days old."

"Yes, I did that. How could I raise you without your mother's help? I knew nothing about being a father. I still don't."

Onacona said nothing more as he left the shop. I stood there transfixed. I had seen one of my two sons. He was a fine-looking young man, but he wanted nothing to do with me. His words, "I am not your son," weighed heavily on me. I knew I'd done nothing to deserve his respect or love. What else could I have done? I left him with women who knew how to raise a child and with a clan that would embrace him as one of their own.

I had no reason to think that anyone in Davidson's Fort knew that I had two sons and that I'd abandoned both of them. Had my neighbours known, I would have been censured for abandoning Jenny and David, but abandoning Onacona would have drawn a few snickers at most. Cherokee women were considered wanton, and if they were left with a child, that was the wages of their sin. No one would've believed that I had loved Awinita.

Onacona never could have lived in Davidson's Fort or anywhere but a Cherokee village. He would've been reviled and tormented as an outcast. Cruel as it may sound, leaving him with his grandmother was the best thing I could've done for him. Perhaps I should've returned to Tuskeegee to see him whilst he was growing up. I don't know whether it would've been better or worse for him to have a reminder of his absent father. I've pondered that question over the years, but never have been able to answer it.

During the years after Judy Slater rejected my marriage proposal, French Ruff became my passion. I played cards three or four nights a week. I still won more times than I lost, but these evenings ended up costing me money since I spent freely at the tavern. The games were friendly and the one bit of entertainment in my life.

In September 1804, Sergeant Ames joined the garrison at Davidson's Fort. He soon appeared at the tavern, and, unlike other British soldiers who kept their own company, he tried to befriend the men of the village. He was medium height, dark-haired, and had a scar on his right cheek. With his jovial manner, the tavern regulars soon accepted him. We were not surprised when, seeing that we lacked a fourth for our card game, he asked to join us.

"You've played this game before?" I asked.

"A few times," he answered. "I know the rules."

"It's a friendly game. We play for a ha'penny a point. Is that agreeable?"

"Certainly. I like a game better when there's something at stake."

"Well then, bring your pint and pull up a stool. You can be my partner."

I soon realized that Sergeant Ames knew more than he'd let on about French Ruff. He was a skilful player. We each won six pence that night, the sort of trivial sum I was used to winning or losing when I played. He joined our game twice more over the next few weeks, and he and his partner won both times, but not enough for any of us to feel that he controlled the game. Ames became one of the game's regulars when Zebulon Taft, who never quite mastered the game and lost much more often than he won, decided he could no longer afford to play. Ames soon suggested that we raise the stakes from a ha'penny a point to a penny, then tu'pence a point.

For the next three months, Ames won sometimes and lost others. Then he started winning consistently – not every time – but often enough that I had to dip into my meagre savings to continue playing. He continued to partner with whoever was available, and his partner for the night also benefited, but he frequently "went alone" on a hand. He won most these hands and was usually the big winner for the night. His luck, especially when he went alone, seemed uncanny. I wondered whether he was cheating, but I never had any evidence that he was.

By the end of May my card-playing losses to Sergeant Ames had exhausted my savings. To continue playing, I began withdrawing small sums, a shilling or two, from the trading post receipts. I was certain that I could repay them before September, when Mr Henderson came for his annual examination of the accounts and shop's inventory. All I needed was to regain the luck I'd had for so many years. It was the first time I'd ever cheated one of my employers, but this fact didn't enter my considerations. French Ruff had become an obsession. Each day I thought about the hands I'd played the night before, the mistakes I'd made, and how I'd do better the coming night.

In early August, a tall, lean man with a hawk-like face, wearing the uniform of a captain in the King's Own Virginian entered the trading post. I was busy with another customer. He stood silently, waiting for me to finish.

"I'm Andy Jackson," he said, when I turned to him.

I recognized that name. An article in the last Charleston newspaper I'd read related how Andrew Jackson had been a successful solicitor in South Carolina, but had given up his legal practice to buy one of the first of the captain's commissions in the Virginians that the army had advertised for sale earlier that year. He was now reported to be on a recruiting mission seeking skilled riflemen in the western settlements. I had no inkling as to why he'd come into the shop. I wouldn't qualify as a skilled rifleman.

"How may I help you, captain?"

"I'm told you speak both Cherokee and Spanish. We need men like you in The King's Own Virginians. I want you to join up," he said, as casually as if he were inviting me to the tavern for a pint of ale.

"Captain Jackson, since you know so much about me, you must know that I'm forty-one – too old to be a soldier."

"How old is too old? Samuel Smith joined last week, and he's nearly fifty. You're younger than that."

"I was a messenger for a Captain Samuel Smith in Smallwood's Maryland Regiment during the Great Rebellion. Is he the Samuel Smith who enlisted?"

"The same. He's only a private now, but we'll find a way to use his experience."

"I'll think about it."

"Don't think too long. The Virginians will muster at Fort Roanoke on the first of November. We're going to do great things. You'll want to be part of it." He didn't say what great things the Virginians were going to do, but I felt he was telling me that the rumours were true, that the Virginians' mission was to conquer Louisiana.

As the time for Mr Henderson's visit approached, I became more anxious about the money I had stolen from the shop. I'd tried to hide my theft by saying that goods valued at that amount had been damaged and were unsalable. My accounts showed some damaged goods each year, but their total value was usually less than two pounds. Before the first time I took the cash from the till, I'd shown one pound, five shillings for damaged goods. With my fraud, the accounts showed nearly four pounds, an amount that was increasing weekly.

I thought about trying to borrow money to replace the cash I'd taken from the shop. But if I went to any of the men I knew in the village and asked for a loan, they would've wanted to know why I needed it. I couldn't tell the truth – who'd lend to a man who would just gamble it away – and I couldn't think of a convincing lie. I even thought about selling some of my belongings, but the only thing I had that was worth more than a few shillings was my rifle. Trying to sell it would have raised even more questions than trying to borrow. I put these thoughts out of my mind and with a growing sense of dread awaited Mr Henderson's appearance.

I continued playing French Ruff in the vain hope that I would have a winning streak that would allow me to repay at least some of the cash I'd taken. In my effort to win, I played less skilfully than usual and lost even more money. My thefts became larger and more frequent.

My last theft was on the 1st September. I won that night – the first time in more than two weeks – but my winnings were too little to repay more than a pittance of what I'd stolen. I decided to keep them in hope of obtaining still more the next night.

Mr Henderson arrived for his annual inspection of the trading post the next day. "William, why were there so many damaged goods this year?" he asked after examining the accounts for only two hours. "The total is more than twice normal."

"I don't know, Mr Henderson. It seems to have just happened that way." I was trying to keep up a brave front, but Henderson had uncovered my crime. My heart fell.

"I'm curious about this item," he said, pointing to a line in the ledger. "You list damaged nails. How does one damage nails?"

"They were too rusty to be usable."

"Didn't you see that when you bought them?" He was now looking straight at me. I tried to return his gaze but ended up looking away. He knew something was amiss, but I felt I had to try to keep up my lie.

"I must've been careless and overlooked that."

"You've always been cautious in the past. Tell me what really happened."

"I was careless in making the purchase," I said with far more bravado than I felt. "Take the loss out of my pay if you must."

Henderson questioned me on several more items, growing more sceptical of my answers by the moment.

Finally, I said, "Mr Henderson, I've taken three pounds, ten shillings from the accounts." I stared down at the floor, unable to look him in the face. I remembered the threat, or the promise, he made when he hired me – to see me in gaol if I tried to cheat him.

Mr Henderson was silent for a long time before finally asking, "Why? Why did you do this, William? Your salary and share of the profits should have been sufficient."

I told him how Judy had rejected me ... how, despite my parents' injunctions when I was a boy, I'd begun gambling ... and how I'd lost both my savings and the money I took from the shop to Sergeant Ames. Henderson listened impassively, then went back to studying the ledger. I stood there, not knowing what was coming next.

"Was it only three pounds, ten shillings?" he asked as he closed the ledger.

"God as my witness," I said, raising my right hand. "That's all I took."

"By all rights, I should swear out a warrant and have you arrested for theft," he said, more in sorrow than in anger.

"I know that."

"But you've been a loyal employee for the past eighteen years. You deserve some consideration. You say you have no money."

"Only a few shillings." I had three shillings from my latest theft and one shilling, seven pence from my winnings the night before.

"Do you have anything of value?"

"Just my rifle and some extra clothing."

"Bring them here. Let's see what they're worth."

I complied and piled my belongings in front of Henderson. He set my rifle and a few of my clothes aside and told me to take the rest back to my room.

"Keep the money you have. I'll give you credit for two pounds for these," he said, pointing to the rifle and clothes. He was being generous. They'd never fetch that much if he tried to sell them.

"You'll have to leave my employ, but I don't want to disgrace you. You can decide what to tell people. I want you to stay on until I can replace you, but if you steal so much as a farthing more, I will swear out a warrant and have you arrested. Do you understand?"

I nodded.

"You'll probably have to remain until mid-October. Your salary and the profits from the shop for that time should be about another pound. I'll pay you half of that so you're not penniless and you can pay me the remaining pound you owe me when you have it. But I do expect to be paid."

I was mute. Mr Henderson was being kinder than I deserved. I finally managed to say, "Thank you, sir. I'll repay the pound with interest when I can." We talked a bit longer about the trading post, then he left, promising to be back as soon as possible with my replacement and warning me yet again not to take so much as a farthing from the accounts.

I kept the shop open for the rest of the day and bantered with my customers as usual. I must've been successful in hiding the problem I caused for myself because none of them said anything out of the ordinary. I swore to myself that I'd never gamble again, and that I wouldn't even go into the tavern during the six weeks longer that I expected to remain in Mr Henderson's employ.

I realized that I couldn't stay in Davidson's Fort. How could I possibly explain why I was no longer running the trading post? And I didn't have enough money to travel very far. I couldn't go back to Salisbury and face the disgrace of having left Jenny with a bastard son. I knew that her father still lived there and I couldn't expect him to have forgiven me. I couldn't ask Daniel Boone for help. He'd want to know why I'd given up the job he helped me get. I thought about asking my sister for a loan – I wouldn't consider asking my brother, after the demeaning way he treated me when I visited New York – but quickly put that idea out of my mind. Even if Charlotte were willing to help, it took nearly two months for a letter to travel to New York and an equal time for a reply to return. I needed money before that.

There seemed to be only one way out – join the Virginians. At first the idea appalled me. My experiences in the rebel army during the Great Rebellion had shown me war's horrors. I'd seen men with their guts blown open or their heads shattered. Yet what else could I do? Two days after Mr Henderson left, I started telling my customers about my decision.

"I'll be leaving soon. I've decided to join the Virginians," I told David Carpenter, who owned a farm about three miles north of the village.

"Why would you want to do a daft thing like that?" he said, a look of disbelief on his face.

"The King's Own Virginians are going to conquer Louisiana, and I want to be part of that enterprise," I told him, the answer I decided would be the best explanation I could give.

"Good luck to you. You've been a good friend and I'll miss you."

I had much on my mind during those weeks whilst I waited for Leonard Henderson to reappear with my replacement. I remembered how Sergeant Ames had first appeared in the tavern a year earlier . . . how he'd joined our card game . . . how he suggested that we raise the stakes . . . and how, after several months of winning and losing like the rest of us, he suddenly had an incredible streak of luck. At the time I thought that he might be cheating, but since I had no proof, I put the notion out of my mind. But thinking back over the events, it became clear to me that he must've been cheating. Nobody could've been that lucky for that long.

The revelation that I'd been cheated angered me. I thought of going to the fort and confronting Ames, but soon realized that without evidence, he would simply laugh at my accusation. There was nothing I could do.

Understanding that I'd been cheated had one benefit. Anytime that I thought about going to the tavern – and there were evenings on which I yearned for the small comfort that a pint of ale and a hand or two of French Ruff had provided – I quickly remembered that doing so could mean having to face Sergeant Ames. The thought of seeing Ames, and not being able to do anything about his having cheated me, was enough to keep me away from going. It conserved what little money I had and made it easier to resist the urge to gamble.

Leonard Henderson and John Ashe, my replacement, arrived on the 28th September.

"I'm going to join The Kings Own Virginians," I told Mr Henderson as quickly as I could get him aside for a private conversation. "I've been telling people that I want to be part of the conquest of Louisiana. I hope you'll join me in this fiction."

"I will if you haven't stolen any more from the shop."

"I swear to you I haven't."

He inspected the accounts but this time found no discrepancies. He left the next day.

John Ashe was about a dozen years older than me. His small, neatly trimmed beard was the thing I noticed first about him. A small beard was unusual in the mountains, where most men either went clean-shaven or wore long, full beards. It marked Ashe as a man who was fastidious in his personal habits and probably would be precise in his dealings with others. What I learned of him in the next two weeks confirmed this first impression.

Besides showing Ashe how to run the trading post, I introduced him to my customers. Most already knew that I was joining the Virginians. They were more interested in finding out about Ashe. They had little choice but to deal with the trading post and they needed to know whether they could trust him as they'd come to trust me. I must've gone through a similar inquisition when I first arrived. Truth be told, I didn't remember it.

"Young William here had an adventurous life before settling down in Davidson's Fort. What about you? Have you had your share of adventures?" Geoffrey Turner asked.

"You might say that. I was with General Charles Lee when he defeated the British at Charleston during the Great Rebellion," Ashe said, looking carefully at Turner to see how he would react.

Thirty years after the Great Rebellion, there was no risk of punishment for saying that you'd been with the rebels, but some who'd remained loyal to the King still showed their dislike of those who'd rebelled. Ashe was right to be a little wary.

"That was a famous victory for the rebels, but it did little good in the end," Turner replied. "And what did you do after Washington's defeat?"

"I did what everyone else not captured by the British or Hessians did," Ashe answered. "I took off my uniform, hid it away, and went back to as much of my old life as I could. Since then I've been a farmer, a fur trader, and a shopkeeper – whatever I needed to do to keep my family fed and clothed."

"And will your family be joining you?"

"No, I'm alone these days. My wife died three years ago and my children are all grown and flown the nest."

Ashe had similar conversations with many more of the trading post's customers and his answers to their questions used almost exactly the same words each time, like an actor who'd learned his lines. Towards the end of the first week he'd learned the prices of enough of the shop's goods to handle most of the sales. It was strange watching someone else do the job that I'd done for so long, but Ashe gave me no reason to criticise the way he dealt with the shop's customers. After a nod in my direction, they seemed happy to have him serve them.

TRANSCRIBER'S POSTSCRIPT

This portion of William Watson's story deals with a critical part of British North American history. The importance of the Great Rebellion is obvious, but how the British treated Americans after their failed rebellion is just as vital. They could have been as harsh as they were on the Highland Scots who rose in the Jacobite Rebellion of 1745. Instead they chose a gentler approach. Historians cite three reasons for this more moderate tack.

First is the sheer difficulty the British Army, even with the help of collaborators, would have faced trying to police the huge area of the colonies. The leaders of Parliament were rational men, who realized that harsh treatment would have led to either guerrilla warfare or another rebellion and a continuing drain on Britain's resources.

Second, American colonists could not threaten Britain the way the Highland Scots, who invaded England twice during the eighteenth century, could. The impracticality of Americans raising an army and building a fleet to invade Britain without being discovered and quashed would have been obvious to all on both sides of the Atlantic.

Third, while we now tend to think of Great Britain as an ancient nation, it took shape only in 1707 with the union of England and Wales with Scotland. At the time of the Great Rebellion, most British didn't think of themselves as British – they were English, Scots, or

Welsh at best, but more likely to identify themselves with some smaller locality. The English dominated this new nation. Since most, but far from all, of the colonists were of English origin, there was more affinity between the English and the colonists than between the English and Highland Scots. You are more likely to forgive someone who seems a lot like you than some wild, kilt-wearing creature who doesn't even speak the same language you do.

William Watson's adventures are not over. I hope you've enjoyed reading about the first part of his life enough to continue his saga in *The King's Own Virginians: Book Two of The Autobiography of William Watson.*

READ ON FOR AN EXCERPT FROM

The King's Own Virginians

BOOK TWO OF
THE AUTOBIOGRAPHY
OF WILLIAM WATSON

LENNY BERNSTEIN

KIMBERLY CREST BOOKS • ASHEVILLE, NC

CHAPTER 1

On Friday, 11th October 1805, I presented myself to the recruiting sergeant at Davidson's Fort. I took the King's shilling and a five-guinea enlistment bonus, swore to serve faithfully, and became a private in The King's Own Virginians, a regiment of riflemen. We were fencibles, obligated to serve in North America until the French were defeated — not regular Army recruits, who served for life and could be sent wherever they were needed . . . India, Australia, or some equally remote part of the world.

The following Monday, with five other recruits from Davidson's Fort, I began a thirteen-day journey to Fort Roanoke in Virginia. Since there was no direct road to the fort, we travelled east to Salisbury, then north on The Great Wagon Road. There hadn't been rifles or uniforms at Davidson's Fort to outfit us. I carried a British Army Brown Bess musket and wore my own clothes: a linen shirt, buckskin jacket and pants, and a broad-brimmed Quaker hat, which I put on only when it rained or I needed shade from the sun. The few extra clothes and other belongings I still owned fit easily into the wicker basket I carried on my back. Mr Henderson had taken most of my belongings to cover my debt to him.

Sergeant Pew, who commanded our little expedition, wore a uniform, the red coat of a British infantryman, not the green of a rifleman. Pew was not a martinet. He allowed us to walk and talk to each other rather than marching and maintaining silence. "You'll march enough once we get to Fort Roanoke," he said. I had no doubts about the truth of that statement.

Army regulations called for us to rest for fifteen minutes after each three miles of our journey. Since we weren't marching and carried far less than fully equipped soldiers, we stopped when convenient – usually by a stream. It was as gentle an introduction to army life as one could imagine, and did nothing to prepare me for the rigours I'd face once we got to Fort Roanoke.

We found quarters each night at a farmhouse or inn. Our hosts were not pleased to see us, since they had to accept the British Army's payment of four pence a head for our food, drink, and lodging, much less than they received from their civilian customers.

I should've been melancholy. Anyone looking at my situation would have said that I'd ruined my life. Instead I was cheerful. I'd committed a serious crime, but the punishment — banishment from Davidson's Fort — was almost a relief. Truth be told, it'd been a long time since I'd been happy in Davidson's Fort. Much had changed in my eighteen years there. Whilst Mr. Henderson still called his enterprise a trading post, it had become a general store. Decades of hunting and trapping had killed all the buffalo, elk, beaver, and otter on both sides of the mountains. Only a few deer remained and their skins were usually poor quality.

There was still some ginseng in the woods near Davidson's Fort, but diggers had to spend days to collect the four pounds of roots needed for one pound of dried 'seng. Everyone believed that there was much more 'seng on the other side of the Proclamation Line. But the few brave souls willing to cross into Cherokee land had no more success than the diggers who stayed east of the line.

Whilst hunters and ginseng diggers suffered, the farms around the village prospered. Britain needed to import more grain from America. The war with France had greatly reduced her trade with Europe. The price of grain rose, and farmers and their wives had more money to spend. They asked for, and I'd stocked, finer grades of woollen and linen cloth, ribbon with silver or gold trimming, and all manner of luxury items that previously wouldn't have been seen in the shop. In the early days, when the trading post still had fur traders and hunters amongst its customers, I'd enjoyed listening to their tales. There was no such pleasure listening to farm wives complain about their husbands and children.

Sergeant Pew had been in the army for thirty years. He was grey-haired and limped from a musket ball that had grazed his left hip during the Great Rebellion. "An inch to the right, and I'd have been a cripple," he told us more than once.

"Why'd you join the army?" I asked Pew over a supper of pork stew and cornbread on our first night on the road.

"'Twas simple. My family was starving and I poached a rabbit. The judge could've had me hanged, but he was lenient. He gave me the choice of being transported to America, as one of His Majesty's seven-year passengers, or enlisting in the army for life. I chose the army, and what's the first thing the army did? They transported me to America to fight in your Great Rebellion."

"What's a seven-year passenger?" I asked.

"A prisoner who's been sentenced to seven years' servitude, though few survive to the end of their terms."

Pew told us that whilst he'd not been at Trenton when the rebels surrendered to end the Great Rebellion, he'd been part of General Howe's triumphal march into Philadelphia a week later. I decided not to tell him about my service in the rebel army, though in all likelihood, he would've laughed at the coincidence.

"Why'd you stay in the army, once you got here?"

"I'm regular army, not a fencible like you lads. You'll be discharged after we beat the French. I'm in for the rest of my life or until some officer decides I'm too old and ships me off to Chelsea Hospital. I'd rather die from a French musket ball than face that fate. The Hospital is just a warehouse. They keep you there until you die."

We walked all day but had plenty of time to relax in the evenings. As men will do, we took the measure of each other. Gideon Long was easily the strongest of us, something he proved our third night on the road by quickly winning arm wrestling matches with the rest of us. He forced my arm down in less than ten seconds. Randolph Culpepper was the most argumentative — it didn't take long for the rest of us to start ignoring his acid comments. Manfred Zellenbach was the youngest and looked like he'd only started shaving a few months earlier. Since I was the oldest recruit, he started asking me questions about army life, even though I knew no more on the subject than he did. Morgan Trotter was an enigma — a tall, taciturn man who looked like he might have Indian blood. He would sit staring into the fire whilst the others of us bantered. Harry Judkins, the last member of our expedition, was a troubled man. He'd lost his wife in childbirth, an experience with which I was all too familiar. With her gone, seemed to have lost his will to live. I wondered how he'd survive.

"You six will probably end up as messmates," Pew told us. "You'll fight together, eat together, and sleep together. You'll be closer than brothers, so you'd better get to like each other."

I could easily see having Gideon Long as a brother, and Zellenbach and Trotter seemed sound, but the idea of having to be close to either Culpepper or Judkins was far from appealing. Not that I would have any choice in the matter.

"You Johnny Newcomes think you'll be rich, what with your five-guinea enlistment bonus and your pay of a shilling a day," Pew told us whilst we relaxed one evening during the second week of our journey. "The recruiting sergeant didn't tell you about stoppages, did he?"

"What stoppages?" Randolph Culpepper asked in a querulous tone of voice. He was a skinny twenty-year-old redhead from a farm near Davidson's Fort. I wasn't surprised that he'd asked the question that was on my mind and must have been on the minds of the other recruits. He'd been a rebellious boy and hadn't become any less contrary as he grew to manhood.

"You have to pay for your rifle, uniform, kit, and meals," Pew answered. "You'll be left with only a shilling a week, if you're lucky and don't have to pay for breaking a rifle or losing a knapsack. And you'll get your money only if your company commander and the paymaster are honest."

"Doesn't the army give you everything you need?" Culpepper asked.

"They don't give you enough rum to ease the pain, or a woman now and then, and a man needs both to survive."

"How do you live on so little money?" I asked.

"There are ways, but you'll have to discover them for yourself. Still it's better than when I first joined the army. We were paid only eight pence a day, and the stoppages could be more than that." Pew paused for a few moments whilst each of us pondered this news. "But cheer up, lads. Some of you will figure out how to enjoy army life. I have. And who knows, there may be a chance for a bit of plunder after we beat the French. A silver crucifix or a few gold coins can buy you more than one woman and more rum or gin than you can drink."

"You look like a fighter," Pew said to Gideon Long during a rest break the next day. "Think you can best me?"

Long's stature belied his name. Short and solidly built, he looked as if he could absorb the first blow and keep fighting.

"I ain't been in the army long, but I know better than to hit a sergeant," Long responded.

"I'll take off my coat with my sergeant's stripes, then I'll be just another soldier. Surely a strong young lad like you can get the better of a gimpy old man like me."

Long looked at the rest of us recruits. We smiled in anticipation of seeing a good fight. "No punishment if I beat you?"

"God as my witness, no punishment."

Long put his fists up in the classic boxer's pose. Pew took off his jacket and approached Long, his hands dangling loosely at his sides. Long took a swing, but Pew grabbed his arm and threw him to the ground. Then, in a motion too fast for me to follow, Pew pulled a knife and held it at Long's throat. The fight, such as it was, was over in less than fifteen seconds.

Pew put his knife back in the sheath he had hidden at the small of his back. He pulled Long up and began brushing the dust off him.

"How'd you do that?" Long said, more in amazement than anger.

"That's another thing you'll have to learn for yourself if you're going to survive," Pew replied. "I can't teach you."

"How'd you learn?" I asked.

"See this scar?" Pew said, pointing to his face. "Big bugger in my first company give it to me no more than two weeks after I joined the army. Said I was sitting in his place at the mess table. I caught him behind the barracks a few weeks later and cut him up so badly he had to be invalided out of the army. Was sentenced to three hundred lashes for that, but my colonel stopped the punishment after fifty. No one has ever challenged me again." He pulled off his shirt and showed us his back, which was covered with scars from the flogging.

Pew's story hadn't answered my question, but I couldn't ask it again. I felt ill thinking about some brute attacking me or being flogged for defending myself. No one said anything, so I think I was successful in not showing what I felt. I hadn't thought about these realities of army life when I decided to enlist.

Fort Roanoke had been a simple wooden stockade when I'd first seen it in 1778. Even in 1796 it had only one stone wall. Now it was a classic British fortress, a stone square with diamond-shaped bastions at each corner. There must have been forty gun ports, each with the nose of a twelve-pounder protruding. I wondered why the British Army needed to build such an imposing fortification at the edge of the North American wilderness. Even if the French managed to land an army at Nouvelle Orleans, as they threatened to do, they'd be over a thousand miles away.

The inside of the fort looked as if it was covered in canvas. It normally housed two companies of infantry, two squadrons of cavalry, and gunners for the cannon — fewer than five hundred men, who lived in barracks built into the fort's walls. They were still present, though some of them had been displaced to make room for The King's Own Virginians' officers. In addition, room had to be made for the thousand soldiers and non-commissioned officers who made up the regiment. Tents were packed tightly together, but even so, not all of the Virginians could be housed inside the fort's walls. Since our small party from Davidson's Fort was amongst the last to arrive, we had to find accommodations in the tent village that had sprung up in a field east of the fort.

"Thank God we're going to have cabins," Sergeant Pew said, looking at the construction underway beyond the tents. "It'd be damn cold in them tents once winter comes."

I hadn't thought about the coming winter, but I was rapidly learning that an old soldier like Pew always had an eye out for what few comforts army life provided.

Despite the crowd, Fort Roanoke was orderly. Tents stood in neat lines with narrow streets between them. Latrines had been dug and woe betided the man who didn't use one and cover over his droppings afterwards. Small logs or gravel covered the muddy spots.

I couldn't help but contrast this scene with the encampments I had lived in during my brief time with the rebel army. They had tents scattered hither and yon and, because so little care was taken to build proper latrines or streets, the look and smell of pigsties. I knew I would have to put aside what I learned in the rebel army, but until I saw Fort Roanoke, I didn't fully comprehend how different life in the British Army would be.

With Sergeant Pew and the other recruits from Davidson's Fort, I was assigned to Captain Meriwether Lewis's Fifth Company. After we signed the company roster, Pew marched us to the quartermasters. Our days of relaxed walking were over.

"Right, you Johnny Newcomes, hand me those muskets," the sergeant behind the counter said without greeting us or identifying himself.

"I signed for this musket at Davidson's Fort," Culpepper said. "I want a receipt to show that I returned it to the army."

"Well, well, well," the quartermaster sergeant said. "What've we here? A barracks room barrister? Give me any more of your lip and I'll have a receipt written on your back with a cat-o'-nine-tails."

We turned in our muskets without further complaint.

"This is a Baker rifle," the sergeant said, handing one to each of us. "You will be charged a stoppage of two pounds five shillings for it. Lose it or break it and you will be charged the same amount for a replacement. Now sign here to show that you've received your rifle."

My uniform and the rest of my kit brought the stoppage to four pounds, eight shillings, six pence. That left me with only eleven and six from my enlistment bonus, and the sergeant said he didn't know when it would be paid.

ACKNOWLEDGEMENTS

This book would never have come to be without the help of many people. My thanks to: Tommy Hays and Elizabeth Lutyens and the members of their classes in the Great Smokies Writing Program for teaching me how to write fiction; the members of the Appalachian Roundtable for their critiques of my drafts; Dave Wetmore for sharing his expertise on Revolutionary War era woodcraft and weaponry; Rob Swart for teaching me a bit of Dutch; and my son Neil for teaching me a bit of Latin. I am also indebted to all the historians I read to absorb the details of the first years of the American Revolution and of that era's Cherokee life and customs.

My thanks to my beta readers: Joe Burchfield, Michael Cornn, Marie Hefley, and Kathy Kyle for helping put this story in its final form, and to my production team: Nicole Ayers, copyeditor; Doug Gibson, layout designer; and Elizabeth Hunt, cover artist; for the expertise and effort they contributed to creating this book.

My special thanks to my wife Danny (Danielle), who encouraged me for the seven years it took to bring William Watson's story to life. Danny was the first to read every word of Watson's story. Her comments were invaluable.

ABOUT THE AUTHOR

Lenny Bernstein started writing fiction in 2008. The Autobiography of William Watson is his first project. It started as a single book but rapidly grew into a trilogy.

Lenny earned a PhD in chemical engineering from Purdue University in 1969, then pursued a forty-year industrial career that focused on environmental issues, most notably climate change. He was an author on the UN Intergovernmental Panel on Climate Change's Third and Fourth Assessment Reports, and was recognized as contributing to that organization's winning half the 2007 Nobel Peace Prize – Al Gore won the other half.

Lenny and his wife Danny (Danielle) have lived in Asheville, North Carolina, since 2001. They are avid hikers, who have hiked the full length of the Appalachian Trail, most of the high mountains east of the Mississippi, and trails in Australia, Canada, Europe, and New Zealand. Lenny is currently President of Carolina Mountain Club, the oldest and largest hiking and trail-maintaining club in Western North Carolina, and holds a variety of volunteer leadership positions in the Appalachian Trail Conservancy.

HOW THIS STORY CAME TO BE

I learned about the Revolutionary War in elementary school. I was taught that, while difficult, an American victory over the British was inevitable. It took a visit to Washington's Crossing State Park, Pennsylvania, in the early 1980s, to learn how desperate the Americans were at the end of 1776, and how close the revolution was to collapsing. This raised an obvious question: what if Americans had lost? I conceived of telling this story as the autobiography of an old man named William Watson, who, as a young boy, lived through the failed revolution and its aftermath.

My idea lay dormant for over two decades until I retired in 2008 and had time to develop William Watson's story. I enrolled in the Great Smokies Writing Program (GSWP) where I discovered that before I could interest readers in my story, I had to learn how to write fiction – a very different skill from writing the hundreds of technical reports I'd authored during my career. With the help of GSWP and my fellow authors in the Appalachian Roundtable, I learned enough to write this book, but I'm still learning.

Lenny Bernstein
April 2015

Kimberly Crest Books

COMING FROM KIMBERLY CREST BOOKS

Forests, Alligators, Battlefields: My Journey through the National Parks of the South

Danny Bernstein
April 2016

The King's Own Virginians: Book Two of The Autobiography of William Watson

Lenny Bernstein
Fall 2016